Fertile Soil

Stories of the California Dream

Mary Smathers

Illustrations by Jess van der Westhuizen

mks publishing

Illustrations by Jess van der Westhuizen

Book design by Jess van der Westhuizen
Cover design by Mary Smathers and Jess van der Westhuizen
Cover photo by Mary Smathers

Library of Congress Control Number: 2016914111 (paperback)

ISBN # 978-0-9978557-0-8 (e-book)
ISBN # 978-0-9978557-1-5 (paperback)

In memory of my parents, John and Katrina, who climbed into a 1961 Volkswagen Bug, with their baby and few belongings, and drove west to pursue their California dreams.

For Dave

and for Sarah and Dwight

In America, we get up in the morning and go to work and solve our problems.

—William Martin, *The Lost Constitution*

Stories

Fertile Soil

Stories of the California Dream

Valencia, Paz Student ID #743494

WILL DAD EVEN BE HOME when I get up there she wondered, staring at the cascade of cracked cement steps suspended from the apartment building like a concrete ribcage. Shaking her head, anticipating the worst, she hefted the backpack to both shoulders and began the climb. Paz Valencia ascended slowly, avoiding the rusting handrail, limping from the weight of heavy schoolbooks. She ignored the crippled tricycle and smashed beer cans in the weeds below and the multi-colored laundry flapping on the balcony railings as she passed each level. She reached the third floor landing, paused to catch her breath, and glanced through the breezeway to the back of the complex where Eddie parked his motorcycle. No bike. Paz borrowed the dirty Castrol motor oil box in front of her neighbor's apartment and stood on the reinforced cardboard to reach the ledge above her door. Her fingers scraped paint peelings and gritty cement sand. No key. She scowled. He knew I'd keep it this time so he didn't put it back in our spot. She pushed overgrown bangs out of her eyes and shook her head in disgust. No way in.

Paz slid her back down the wall to sit on the cold concrete What am I supposed to do now? He better come home before he goes to work so I can get some sleep tonight. She took the backpack out of the cardboard box and unzipped the largest pocket. Nothing to eat but an empty bag of Chili Doritos left over from lunch a few days ago. She poured the chip crumbs and neon orange chili dust right into her mouth. Her stomach rumbled. School lunch had been that awful doughy pizza smeared with what looked like ketchup. She hadn't eaten much. Paz pulled her oversized Army jacket tightly around her slight frame. At five in the afternoon, the fog crept through the valley from the distant ocean. Its heavy wet drizzle nourished the nearby lettuce field but chilled her. She steeled herself for a long night sitting on the freezing landing, leaning against the cinderblock. Opening up her school planner, Paz read through her homework, got out her math book and started in on the algebra problems.

Focused on the math, Paz barely noticed the increasing noise around her. As the workday ended, the apartment complex's lazy silence shifted to a humming. Mothers and kids argued, babies squealed and toddlers whined as everyone came home tired and hungry. Teenage boys cursed, lighting up king-sized Monte Carlos. Usually a fight or two broke out before haggard moms set kitchen tables with frozen pizzas, tacos or spaghetti with red sauce. Men came in thirsting for a beer and a quiet sofa for TV sports but found only crowded commotion. They lingered around their motorcycles, compared parts, mechanical problems and girlfriends. Girls in tight jeans and too small tops gathered, texting and whirling through photos on their phones, all while gossiping non-stop.

Paz absently noted dishes clanking and grease sizzling at the neighbors' below, while their TV screeched growling WWF wrestlers amid enthusiastic cheering. They always had it turned up so loud. She got hungrier as cooked chicken smells drifted up to the third floor. Spanish and English, with some Vietnamese thrown in, wafted through the projects. Since she had spent much of her childhood with her Mexican grandparents, Paz understood everything, except the Vietnamese. The guy in the apartment across the hall came home in his greasy jumpsuit with Jiffy Lube in red stitching on the pocket. He grunted as he unlocked his door but never looked at her or asked why she was sitting outside. Two kids from school stepped over her on the way to their third floor apartments. Without a word or glance, they opened their doors and disappeared inside.

Today, like every day, Paz tried to avoid the clamor, and potential complications, of apartment complex living. Shy, she stayed to herself. Didn't talk much. Did what she was supposed to. But she wasn't prissy or self-righteous. The other teenagers in the projects never harassed her. They mostly ignored her, and she was just fine with that. She shivered and looked down at her book. Find the x intercept of the graph of the equation 2x−4y=9.

Eddie, Paz's dad, worked at the commercial bakery on the edge of the neighborhood from 3:00 in the morning to 11:00 a.m. Exhausted after mixing vats of dough, scrubbing electric mixers and pushing trolleys filled with bread loaves to trucks in the cargo bay, Eddie rode his motorcycle home, had a few beers and fell asleep on the couch. Around 5:30 in the afternoon, after Paz got home from school, he usually woke up and headed over to one of the bars on the industrial strip near the bakery. At The Side Alley, Frank's Place or Los Perros Negros, he'd keep drinking beer, add in some tequila shots and often pick up one of the regulars. They'd head back to the apartment or to one of the cheap motels along the strip many working girls used for partying. Some just wanted free beer and tequila but some he had to pay. After hanging with the bar girls and old buddies from the neighborhood,

Eddie would get back on his bike and head home.

Recently, since Paz had started high school, Eddie seemed to be leaving earlier and staying out later, sometimes so late he had to go right over to the bakery to start his shift. And when he did get home, he passed out, drained from eight hours on his feet manning the industrial ovens or from the partying beforehand.

Eddie was a young dad, taking on the responsibility for Paz when he was just nineteen and her mother left him with a one-year-old baby. He didn't understand exactly why she had left. He didn't talk about it because it stung him. His whole body hurt when he thought of her. When Paz was about eight, she started asking Eddie harder questions and pushing him to answer. But he refused.

"I don't know, Paz. I don't know why she left. She didn't tell me nothin'. She just got up and left one night and never came back. I don't know where she went, where she is. Just forget about her. No mama leaves her kid. So you don't want her anyway."

But Eddie was not an unfeeling man. He knew Paz couldn't really forget her. He couldn't either. So he did what he could to raise a kid, and he closed within himself. Although a handsome charmer who generated bar girl gossip, he never let himself get involved. No one ever got close, got his heart, got his attention for more than a month. That was his rule. Sometimes the same girls were the only ones around and the restriction was pretty limiting. But mostly he stuck to his rule.

Eddie's mother helped out until she died of emphysema when Paz was ten. Paz was heartbroken and stopped talking for several months. She stayed with her grandpa while Eddie worked. He made sure that Eddie had a steady job at his friend's bakery and Paz got to school every day. But he couldn't do much else. By forty-six, Eddie's dad was old. He'd had to stop working because his back was so damaged from picking for more than thirty years. He couldn't go out to the lettuce or strawberry or zucchini fields anymore and keep up with the young guys. They started

4

out now at eighteen, not at twelve like he had, but they moved so quickly. Filled the truck so fast. The foremen wouldn't put up with his slow pace. He stayed out of the fields, at home with his granddaughter.

Then Abuelo got sick too. He had no energy, couldn't walk up stairs or even stand for very long. Paz was twelve when her grandfather died. She moved in with Eddie permanently, but they each couldn't have been more alone. Eddie thought the spraying in the fields and the heartache over losing his wife had killed his father. Bitter, he didn't talk much and made stricter rules for Paz as she went through junior high. No phone. No boys around. No short skirts. Her best friend, Cristina, could come over only once per weekend.

"No key, no phone," he insisted. "You just come right home and I'll let you in. I won't leave 'til you get here. And stay away from drugs. Those things'll kill you." He would make such pronouncements just before pushing arms through his gleaming black leather jacket with the worn elbows and jogging down the cement stairs to roar off on his bike. Paz, left to ponder the latest rules alone, turned on the TV and opened her schoolbooks. The TV's white noise, she wasn't really watching anything, made her feel a little less lonely while she distracted herself with science questions and Spanish verb conjugations. And math. Always the math—her favorite. There was a right and wrong answer and she liked that. She found it soothing.

Once she started high school, Eddie was terrified. He was secretly panicked Paz would suddenly grow taller, develop breasts and a sweet smile, get distracted by boys' attention. He pictured her finally discarding the baggy pants and white t-shirts entombed by the ever present khaki jacket for short skirts and sexy boots, tight jeans and cleavage-barring tops. He remembered her mom in high school. Their fights continued.

"Dad, why can't I have my own key?" she had asked him repeatedly since the beginning of ninth grade.

5

"You're only fourteen, a freshman. I know about those seniors. Who knows what you'd do with a key—open up my apartment to boys, those guys downstairs who smoke weed all the time. Everyone knows the party houses. I don't want you hangin' with kids who'll get you in trouble," he said.

Insulted and incredulous at his misguided view of her daily reality, she shook a small fist at him. "Look at me," she insisted, waiting for him to turn his dark eyes to hers. "Do I look like the party girl?" When he looked away again she stomped her foot to get his attention.

"Daaaad. I don't do drugs. I don't party. I know you think I'm gonna be like mom, like you were, or even worse. Don't you get it? I'm trying my hardest not to be anything like either of you. I want to graduate from high school like Abuelo told me. I need a key so I can do my homework."

Eddie raised an eyebrow at that but he didn't say anything for a while.

"Look Paz, I didn't graduate and your mom ran off. But you're a good kid. You can do it. You gotta finish high school. Your grandparents wanted that for you. You gotta come home right after school. I'll let you in." Then he'd turn, escape into his room and slam the door. Discussion over.

Paz begrudgingly admitted to herself that Eddie did at least have a job, an apartment—although she couldn't get into it—and a motorcycle. I'm not in the homeless shelter or one of those people begging by the freeway off ramp, she'd tell herself when she was so furious with him she wanted to break every dish in their flat. Her friend's mom was a meth addict. That was really bad. She had started to lose her teeth and had been bringing men to their apartment to sleep with for meth hits. They moved a lot. At least my dad doesn't do drugs, Paz reflected. She distracted herself by trying to do well in school, as her grandparents had insisted, and spending time with friends. Paz's social timidity limited her to hanging with a few girls from the Section 8 apartments she had known since elementary school.

Long after she'd finished her math problems, Eddie climbed the
stairs to her perch at 2:25 in the morning. He reeked of beer, was
unshaven and was missing his jacket.

"One of those girls stole my jacket, God damn it," he told Paz
as he kicked her to wake her up. "Get inside. What the hell you
doin' out here?" She jumped, startled awake by his berating.
Groggy, she rubbed her eyes, yawned. She twisted her stiff neck
slowly to look up at him.

"What, Dad? I've been here since I got home from school.
Where've you been? I need a key so I can get in." She pushed
down on the hard landing to get up, awkwardly with stiff limbs.
She tossed the motor oil box back in front of the neighbor's door
and crossed the threshold into her apartment, relieved to finally
be able to get warm and fill her stomach. She went right to the
kitchen. Eddie stumbled behind her and collapsed on the couch.
She opened the fridge. Not much in it but at least she found a
few items to make a little taco. She pulled out some cheese, cut
pieces off and put them on top of a tortilla in a pan on the stove.
She dribbled leftover rice on top of the cheese.

"Dad, don't you have to go to work?" she asked. "Get up, get in
the shower and get over there before Mr. Barraza notices you're
late."

Eddie groaned and went to his room. Paz heard him lock the
door. The shower water shushed on. She ate her rice taco. Then
she pulled out an extra blanket from the closet and climbed into
bed, fully clothed, and piled the blankets on top. I gotta get out of
here, she thought as she felt her brain getting soft and foggy with
exhaustion and warmth. I can't keep doin' this. I can't keep doin'
this. Barely keeping a job and telling me not to do drugs? That's
his idea of a good father? I don't think he's gonna change. He's
never gonna give me a key. I gotta get one. I can't keep doin' this....

The next day at school, Paz tried to make herself smaller and quieter than usual. She didn't feel like explaining to Cristina why she had dark, sunken eyes. Nor was she in the mood to conspire on ways to sneak into senior parties this coming weekend. She just wanted to sleep. But at the end of third period, Paz's Algebra teacher stopped her.

"Paz, can you stay for a minute?" Paz nodded. Her teacher continued. "I noticed you failed the last test and I haven't seen much homework come in from you over the past two weeks. What's going on?"

Paz liked this young teacher, who had style and creative ideas. She tried to make math class, which most kids hated, fun. Paz and Cristina looked forward to seeing her outfits and commented on her latest pair of cute shoes at lunch. But she did not want her in her life. The teacher was from somewhere far away, a different world filled with cheery friends, big, warm houses and two parents at home. Like on TV. She has no idea what life is like here, Paz thought.

"Nothing," she said.

"Paz, I know Algebra class and school are not your favorite places to be. But you always make a good effort and have decent grades. I've noticed a change lately. Is something going on that is stopping you from studying?"

"I'm fine," Paz said. She yanked the ever present jacket tighter around her shoulders, stuffed her left hand in the large pocket, threw her backpack over the right shoulder, turned her back and strode out the door.

Over the next three weeks, Paz slept in the building breezeway four full nights. She went to the Algebra teacher's study session to catch up on homework. The teacher stopped her again as the kids filed into the hallway.

"I'm glad you came to study hall," she said. "But you're still missing homework." Paz shrugged and sunk deep into her oversized jacket. Her hair hung over her cheekbones and into both eyes. She didn't look up.

8

"Do you like to dance?" the teacher asked. Paz hunched her shoulders and shook her head slightly.

"Well," the teacher continued, "I coach the dance club after school on Monday, Wednesday and Friday. We have a hip-hop guy doing some choreography. Even if you don't like to dance, we could really use some help with lights, music, programs for the show we are having later this year. Why don't you come to practice, help me and the girls out? And if there's nothing to do, you can do your homework."

This lady never knew when to quit, Paz thought. She's so goddamned cheerful. Why won't she just leave me alone? I just wanna get out of here.

"Aren't you friends with Cristina Morales?" the teacher asked. "Cristina joined last month and will be in the show. She's really good." Paz looked up at the sound of Cristina's name and examined the teacher's features clearly for the first time. She was young, sort of pretty but more than that. She looked a little like the one picture she had of her mom, hidden under the jeans in her bottom drawer, far from Eddie's eyes. The math teacher had mocha skin and thick black hair with curling waves of softness. Her long eyebrows arched thinly over dark eyes. Paz's breath caught. An involuntary shiver coursed through her, leaving her arms tingling and raising fine brown hairs.

"Okay, maybe, I'll come by," she surprised herself by blurting. "I have to ask my dad first if I can stay after school." Hurriedly, she pulled the classroom door and fled into the hallway.

Eddie was home when she got there but he had locked himself in the apartment. She could hear him singing and yelling with a woman. A female voice rose up over loud music. She banged her fist on the door and screamed for him to open it. When he didn't respond, she gave up and sat down, propping herself against the door. A half hour later, Paz fell into the living room as the door opened and a woman stumbled into her.

"Who the hell are you?" she asked.

9

"I live here. Ask him," Paz said as she walked into her room and slammed the door. Then she turned around and poked her head back out.

"Oh, and I'm going to stay after school three days a week to get help with my homework. Just wanted you to know," she yelled at her dad, who was sprawled on the couch. Miller High Life cans and a Montezuma tequila bottle sat on the coffee table. Cigarette butts overflowed off a small plate.

"Oh yeah?" he slurred. "Well, good, 'cause some teacher called this afternoon and said you need to turn in more homework and study for tests. Paz, damn it, you gotta do good in school or you'll have nothin'." Eddie lit another cigarette and stared toward Paz's door, not completely focusing on her face. She works fast, Paz thought, and was silently impressed.

"Dad, can I get a key, in case you aren't here by five-thirty or six when I get home?" she asked, trying this time with a pleading sweetness. Eddie just stared at the wall and dragged hard on his cigarette.

"You're too young," he said firmly. "I'll let you in. You got in today, didn't ya?" he mumbled.

And that was it. Her calmness and ability to absorb most neglect, which had deteriorated beyond benign, just screeched to a halt. Right then. No more. Later, when she let herself look back at this excruciating moment, she remembered that it felt like her entire body had been a blister on a spot rubbed raw, over and over, building up liquid, finally cracking open leaving a flap of skin, exposed epidermis and hot liquid all mixing together in a stinging mess. She was raw. Any loyalty, any defensive filial commitment to her father just oozed out like the blister water. All that remained was an open wound.

"Oh Eddie, are you fuckin' kiddin' me? I just sat outside that door for half an hour. You were so loaded with that ho that you didn't even hear me knocking and yellin'," she said. "You let some chick in you don't even know? But not me? Your own kid?"

She gulped to push down the growing lump in her throat. She refused to cry, to show him any weakness or caring.

"This is supposed to be our home." Her voice was icy but very soft now. "You're pathetic." Eddie looked up at that. He knew she was infuriated.

"Don't swear," he retorted. "And what's with the 'Eddie'?"

"I can't take it anymore. How can I live with you? This isn't really living here anyway, you know. I can't get in. There's no food. You're crazy and you're a drunk." She looked at him for a long time with a hard stare. He put out the cigarette and sat up a bit straighter. "I'll find a way out, somehow. And I'm not trash like you think my mom was. Get that out of your head. That was a long time ago. But I know you loved her too. You can't blame me for her shit. You gotta move on." She leaned in close to his face. "I can't deal with you anymore. You ain't shit for a father, not a provider or anything,"

Eddie's eyes got hard and cold. He sat straight up and for a moment Paz thought he would hit her. But he didn't. He just glared, his face turned dark and creases in his forehead appeared and deepened.

"You think you're better than everyone here, Paz? You ungrateful little.... I have a job. I stayed here so you could grow up with family. You'll see. It's not easy. Don't go gettin' pregnant and havin' your own kid. I do everything for the best for you. Don't you see that?"

"Forget it. I gotta do my homework," she snapped, whirling around and stomping into her room, swinging the door so hard the hinges vibrated. She turned the lock, then fell onto her bed, shaking. She hadn't said so much to him in months. There's no relationship here, she realized. We're just making each other miserable. Suddenly the truth was very clear. She felt like someone had slapped her. Like the breath had been knocked out of her from a soccer ball kicked hard to the stomach. She didn't cry but lay on her bed in stunned silence. She was completely alone.

Outside her door, Eddie shouted. Paz bent the pillow over her ears to mute the sound. It didn't work. She heard the click pop of him opening another beer can as he yelled. She had nothing more to say, no energy left for him. She was hungry but was not leaving the room. No way. She'd have to wait until he passed out to see if there was any food around. She had very little money so she'd need to scrounge through the apartment for some cash.

The next day, Paz stayed after school for dance practice. When she got home, the apartment was dark and locked. She decided she was not staying on the doorstep again and walked down the street to the doughnut shop. Sometimes the Vietnamese couple who ran it let her in even after they were closed. Paz knocked on the window and the owner came to the door. Just for a little while he told her in broken English. She nodded, no problem. She liked it there. It smelled warm and homey.

Some mornings she went in to get a pastry and coffee for breakfast. She'd pick out a different one each time. Paz enjoyed eating her doughnut quietly, sipping milk or coffee, as the tractor-trailer trucks rumbled by, gears groaning as they turned widely through the intersection on their way out of town. Bright red tomatoes wobbled, piled high in white trailers. Wisps of papery garlic skins whirled out of green boxes, and yellow crates of strawberries, zucchini or melons filled other trailer beds. She loved seeing food growing next to her neighborhood and watching the semis take it from the packing sheds out to distant destinations. Paz found it comforting that her hometown sent produce all over the country, even the world. It made her feel connected to something important. Sometimes, her mind wandered far enough to imagine jumping onto the back of one of the trucks and leaving town with the lettuce and onions.

When she finished most of her homework, Paz thanked the shop owner and walked home. The apartment was still locked so she sat on the steps to wait. When it was really dark and cold, Paz moved to the apartment entry, under the breezeway cover, and leaned against the door. Eddie never came home.

"Paz, can you stay after class, please?" the math teacher asked the next day. After the others had filed out, the teacher asked, "What's going on?" Her brown eyes were filled with concern. Paz shook her head, hidden behind her hair and coat.

"Look at me," the teacher directed. "Paz, what is it?" Paz raised her eyes, pushed back the wayward bangs and lost all resolve.

"I can't get in to my apartment a lot of nights. I don't know when my dad will be around. I sleep on the landing of my apartment building. I don't have anywhere else to go." The teacher gripped her shoulder, guided her to a desk and gently asked her to explain. Paz relented and finally told all the truth.

As she spoke, Paz felt like a divided person. She observed herself spilling out the details of her life to the teacher. But another part of her was thinking, this is it, this is going over the line, this is not anyone else's business. Why am I doing this? It frightened her at first. She knew the rules. You always stick with family over outside authorities. You don't tell people your problems. Families take care of their own. One burden lifted. But a new weight, an understanding of moving into a new reality, descended. Relief temporarily numbed the fear, but she knew she had violated the natural order of things in her small world. Nothing good ever came from that. But then fear just melted into detachment. Eddie gave me no choice, she rationalized, exhausted.

"You know, I have to report this. What your dad is doing isn't right. It's called neglect, Paz. He can't just leave you sleeping outside your door. I have to talk to the principal and we'll have to make a CPS report. I'm a mandated reporter. I have to..."

Paz's ears filled with a roar so loud that she couldn't hear who the teacher said she'd be talking to. She made a half-hearted attempt to alter the course of events but knew it wouldn't go anywhere.

"Please, please don't say anything. I'm fine. Don't worry about me. I gotta go now," she said and ran out. But she knew

13

the teacher had her own judgments and obligations and would ignore the request.

As she walked toward the apartment on the dirt path beside the busy road, cars whizzed past, garbage swirled in a mini cyclone ten yards ahead of her. She looked out across the lanes to the black dirt combed into straight rows for new planting. Paz heard a motorcycle come up behind her and she instinctively looked up to see if it was Eddie. The bike roared by, through the garbage cloud and on down the street. A knot started to grow in her stomach. She didn't know what to expect but she didn't see how the future could be good.

Eddie was home watching TV when she got there, empty beer cans strewn around. She was surprised to see him. He looked unkempt, worse than usual. She walked right past him into her room and didn't say a word. He grunted a hello and then started yelling at her about her manners. He left the apartment well before his work shift started.

Early one morning a few weeks later, while Paz was at school, a social worker showed up at the bakery. Mr. Barraza let her in to his office and called Eddie out of the warehouse. He shook his head at Eddie.

"I am disappointed in you," Mr. Barraza said. "Your dad would be embarrassed if he saw you hungover, unshaven. Looks like you never changed your clothes. There's some social worker lady here to see you. What did you do?"

Eddie shrugged. The social worker asked Eddie a lot of questions and told him she would be visiting him and his daughter.

"I would like to see the home for myself," she said.

"I gotta good job here. I gotta two bedroom apartment. What's the problem?" he grumbled.

"Well if you are never there...." she started, then stopped. "A fourteen-year-old cannot live on her own and run around town all night."

14

"Wait! What? What the hell? She doesn't run around. She's not like that. She's shy. She's....." Eddie stopped, suddenly realizing he didn't really know how she was at all. Maybe she did go out when he was at work. He didn't really know so he shut his mouth tight. The lady handed him her business card and gave him a disgusted look.

"How could she do this to me?" he asked Mr. Barraza after the social worker left. "I'm gonna kill that ungrateful little bitch," he said and then stopped himself. "You know I don't really mean that, right? I just can't believe this. How could she talk to anyone about our problems? We take care of our own shit." He stomped off.

As an old friend of his father's, Mr. Barraza felt some responsibility for Eddie and Paz. Eddie didn't seem to even realize that he had a good kid—how lucky he was that she wasn't pregnant or didn't do drugs. She even had decent grades and went to school regularly as far as he knew. He tracked Eddie down at the electric mixer he was cleaning. He pulled him behind pallets of flour sacks waiting for the forklift.

"Eddie, this is you. You gotta make it right. Get it together and take some responsibility. You look like shit. Not drinking so much would help. You have a decent job here. You should be able to provide for that kid and treat her right. Whatchya doing with your money? Where ya hanging out before work?"

Eddie glared. "Damn it. Leave me the fuck alone. What do you know about anything? Just 'cuz you were my dad's friend don't mean you can get into my business. Leave us alone. We're fine." He grabbed his jacket and keys, jumped on his bike and roared off. He didn't clock out. Mr. Barraza shook his head. So sad. What a waste. What would happen to the kid?

When Paz hauled herself up the stained concrete stairs that afternoon, there was a lady waiting at the door. She identified herself as a social worker from Child Protective Services and showed Paz her ID. Surprisingly, the door was unlocked but Eddie was nowhere to be found. The beer cans from the night before were gone. How can I let this stranger in my apartment, she asked herself, but she did. The social worker sat on the lumpy couch and asked a lot of questions. She asked to look in the fridge and in Paz's room. She asked if she had a key to the apartment and a phone. She asked what she did when she couldn't get in. The social worker did not reveal that she had already interviewed Eddie, but some of the questions led Paz to believe that she must have talked to him. She knew a lot. Paz decided not to lie, to answer everything truthfully.

"Where's your dad now?" the social worker asked.

"I don't know," Paz said. "Sometimes he hangs out with friends before work. He gets off at eleven, usually comes home to sleep for a while and sometimes meets his friends before his shift starts."

"Doesn't he start work at three a.m.?"

"Yeah."

"Wouldn't he be sleeping now or just getting up to eat?" the social worker pushed.

"Yeah, sometimes," Paz said.

The social worker said she would get more information, talk to the school and her dad and make a final report and recommendation. Paz shrugged. The lady gave her a business card and said to call if she had anything more to say. Paz let her out and locked the door. I gotta get out of here. Eddie's gonna be so mad. This time he really might hit me. She called Cristina to ask if she could come over. Cristina was still at dance practice but said she was sure it would be fine with her mom. Paz could go to her apartment and they'd meet there.

Cristina and Paz had been friends since kindergarten. While Paz blended in, Cristina was loud and bossy and self-assured. Small in stature, Paz was able to hide behind her taller, more fashion conscious friend. She kept Cristina from getting into too much trouble but could be convinced to go along for the adventure. Even through the junior high drama and girl fight years,

Paz and Cristina stuck together. They had come to rely on the consistency of the other—a comfort in the unpredictability of their environment.

Paz knew Cristina's mom liked her and felt she was a good influence. Cristina, who liked to go out with older boys, thought it was cool to finally be going to high school parties. Paz would tag along, but often she just didn't feel up to it and would convince Cristina to hang out at one of their apartments and watch TV. They'd paint their nails or color strands of their hair, make nachos and watch scary movies. Paz secretly preferred that to the parties with drunk seventeen-year-old boys trying to push them into dimly lit corners. It was a lot less stressful. Paz thought Cristina's apartment would be a safe place for one night. Then she'd have to figure out what next.

She searched her room and closet carefully, stuffing everything of value she could think of into her school backpack. She left all the textbooks but kept her notebooks and binder. She could borrow from the teacher or a friend at school. She put in clothes, a few pieces of jewelry and some makeup. The photo of her mom. She realized how little she had that was important. She went in to Eddie's room. She took a picture he kept of a very young Eddie holding her as a baby, her grandparents on either side. She found three twenties in his pants pocket and a debit card. She pocketed the cash and left the card. She locked the door behind her and walked out, down the noisy street and into the next complex of Section 8 apartments.

When she got to Cristina's door, she found Cristina's mom and her brother's girlfriend talking. The girlfriend's mother had kicked her out when she got pregnant as a junior in high school.

"How you gonna graduate after missing so much school with that bad morning sickness?" Cristina's mom was asking the girlfriend as Paz came in. The girlfriend was explaining that she could go to night school classes and probably finish high school on time. Paz perched at the kitchen counter awkwardly. A high-pitched newborn wail came from the bedroom. The girlfriend grabbed a bottle off the counter and went to feed the infant. Paz didn't know what to say to Cristina's mom. She collapsed inside the enormous jacket and looked at the floor.

"I need to talk to Cristina," Paz said. "It's kinda important."

"Here, have a Coke, while you wait. I just got called in to the hospital. Somebody went home sick mid shift. Gotta go cover." She went to the other bedroom to change into her orderly uniform. Paz knew in the mornings Cristina's mom worked at a diner down the street by the packing sheds. She served coffee and hot breakfast to the truckers before they drove out of town with their haul.

When Cristina got home, they went out front to talk. Cristina had to push Paz to get her to explain what was going on.

"It's bad," was all she said at first. Finally, she told her everything.

"Can I stay here with you? When Eddie gets home, he's going to be so drunk and so furious. I don't know what he'll do. Who knows when that social worker lady will come back. I can't stay there, Cristina."

"But there's no room here. I share with my mom. My brother, his girlfriend and the baby are in the other bedroom. You can sleep on the couch."

Paz didn't mind. She handed Cristina two of the twenties she had taken from Eddie's pocket.

"Give it to your mom," she said. "I can't ever go back, Cristina. Do you understand? Ever. I don't know what'll happen with the social worker or what Eddie will do. But I'm not going back. He won't give a shit. He'll be relieved. He can drink himself to death for all I care."

Cristina didn't think she really meant it but just nodded. She couldn't imagine where Paz would end up but she didn't say a word. She just hugged her friend, then went to talk to her mom and Paz sat down on the couch. By the time they came out of the bedroom, Paz had fallen asleep, slumped to one side of the worn sofa. Cristina's mom gave Cristina money for Pizza Hut and left for work. Later, in the dark, Paz woke up to the baby crying. She heard the mother and father arguing and the neighbor in the next apartment banging on the wall. She slept fitfully after that and woke whenever the baby cried. It seemed like it was pretty much all night. Paz ate leftover cold pizza in the morning dark, then headed for the doughnut shop at daylight, leaving a note for Cristina and her mom.

She spent the next few weeks in the same manner at Cristina's apartment, eating at the doughnut shop when she could. But she was running out of money. She wanted to give more to Cristina's mom who, mercifully, didn't ask for anything, including details. It was crowded and sometimes tense in the apartment with so many people, the tiny baby and Cristina's mom always running off to one job or another. Paz tried to get caught up in her classes, staying in at lunch and reading classroom copies of textbooks. The Algebra teacher watched her, asked how she was doing but didn't say anything else. Paz went to the after school dance program and did her schoolwork. At the teacher's request, she assembled a draft of the program for the show on the dance room computer and started to learn the sound equipment.

Then one day, Paz received an office summons. The social worker was waiting for her in the main office.

"Your dad has disappeared," the lady told her. "He hasn't been to work in ten days. His boss said he didn't say where he was going. Have you heard from him?"

Paz could answer truthfully that she hadn't. At first, it made her even sadder to admit this. But, at the same time, she was so mad at Eddie that her callused heart kept her aloof. He just took off, she thought. Wow—this is it. Now it really is just me. She felt a wave of loneliness, deeper than ever before, slide over her, and for just a moment she saw the determined face of her grandfa-

19

ther. He would not have let this happen. But that quickly passed through her mind. Concentrate, she scolded herself.

Through the principal's office window, her gaze stopped on the prom pictures on the bulletin board above the secretary's desk. Photos of laughing girls with pretty, flowing dresses and pink and white flowers on their wrists. Next to the prom pictures were notes with hearts dotting the i's written to the secretary, a favorite of the students. The social worker lady was saying something about talking to a judge and finding a foster home but Paz couldn't focus and get it all.

"I'm fine," she said.

The lady asked where she was staying. Paz did lie then. No hesitation. She said she had an aunt nearby who was letting her stay but didn't want to get in trouble. Couldn't she just stay with her aunt for a while?

"I thought there weren't any relatives around here," said the social worker.

"You must have missed this one. She's an aunt who didn't like my dad so we didn't see her much."

"Okay, Paz, for now stay there while I talk to my boss and we figure out what to do. Keep coming to school."

Are you kidding, lady? Paz thought. She knew kids who had dropped out and now loitered down the street at Sherman Park, smoking, desperate for action. She knew boys who delivered drugs from barren lots next to the projects. She knew a girl who got pregnant at fifteen and had to quit school. But this lady didn't get Paz at all. At least until the end of the school year, she was on the lunch program and could eat breakfast and lunch there if she had to. She liked being in a warm, dry place and seeing the people who used to be her friends. She liked the math teacher and being with the girls at after school dance. She liked learning about the sound system and creating music mixes on the computer. It all gave her some purpose. Even doing homework which she didn't really like. School gave Paz somewhere to go, some reason to get going each morning. A little rosiness in the gloom.

She worried that she was wearing out her welcome on Cristina's couch. She didn't have many belongings but tried to keep everything tidy so it was like she wasn't there. But five people and a baby in a small two-bedroom with one bathroom was cramped. She did not want to leave. Cristina's mom was kind, even though she was rarely there. Paz could always get in the door and had a warm place to sleep. She decided to talk to Cristina's mom about getting a job to pay for staying. She thought maybe she could help out at the diner on the weekends. Cristina's mom told her she appreciated the effort and yes, they could indeed use some more money, especially with the baby always needing diapers and formula.

"The diner doesn't need any help on the weekends. It's the weekday mornings they're busy," she said.

"Well, could I go in before school? Wouldn't even a few hours help out?"

Cristina's mom promised she'd ask her boss. It would be really early, like 4:00 a.m. until school started, she told her. That'd be fine. She needed money. It was very clear Eddie was not going to help her out financially. He had not reappeared or attempted to communicate. Paz had considered going to the bakery to ask Mr. Barraza what he knew but was afraid to draw attention to herself. She didn't want social services trying to move her in with some strangers, forcing her to leave school or the familiar neighborhood.

Cristina's mom took her aside a few days later and said her boss could use the help from 4:00 to 7:30 each morning, Tuesdays through Fridays. She would have to sweep, mop floors and wash dishes. She would not be able to bus tables or be a waitress. No tips. The boss would pay her five dollars an hour. She'd pay in cash each week and Paz could not talk to anyone about working there. Paz didn't know much about work yet, but she knew this was way under minimum wage and that she was too young to work legally. Just fine with her. She was grateful and told Cristina's mom so. She gave her a hug.

"Paz, you can call me by my name, Linda," she said. "I know you try to live here like a mouse, quiet and hidden. But it's okay. You can stay for a while. You're a good influence on Cristina, and I like that. Just make sure this job doesn't take away from school. You gotta get decent grades. You gotta pass all your classes. Have you heard from Eddie?" Paz shook her head and tried to keep her emotions below the surface. She missed her grandparents so much. But she pushed the memories deep, keeping them buried like the rest of her, beneath the enormous, omnipresent Army jacket, her hair hiding weary eyes.

The job was hard work and the hours early. She had to wake up at 3:15 in the morning to get there on time. Fortunately, it was close and she could walk. But it was dark and frigid. Her neighborhood was not a place a girl should be out at night. Some days Cristina's mom walked with her because she was working the same shift, but most times Paz had to walk alone.

The boss lady was tough, hardened by years of long hours on her feet. But she was fair and when Paz got seventy dollars at the end of her first Friday shift she was hopeful she wouldn't be cheated in the arrangement. She immediately gave it all to Linda. Each week after that, she gave her half of her earnings. She began to accumulate a little of her own money. Where do I keep it she wondered? Once her wad got too bulky, she ripped a hole in the liner of her Army jacket and stuffed the cash in. She sewed it shut with thread and needle she took from the secretary helping make costumes for the dance show.

Paz often had trouble staying awake in class. But at least she had somewhere to sleep and get most of her homework done each night. She and Cristina stayed after school with the dance group. She was not about to be up dancing in front of a crowd. She didn't even like dancing anyway. What she did like was listening when they selected music, then playing it just right

22

when they needed certain songs. She fiddled with the amplifiers and learned about the sound system from a senior boy who the teacher had recruited. He treated Paz like a little kid so she ignored him, except to learn the soundboard. She listened intently, watched how he manipulated the knobs and levers and then practiced on her own when he wasn't there. She felt like a DJ. If she could get good enough, she would convince the teacher to tell the senior boy he wasn't needed. She wanted to operate the sound equipment all by herself. Slowly, she was able to let her shoulders relax. Just a bit.

Anxious that the CPS lady would come back, she didn't let herself imagine sleeping on Cristina's couch endlessly. She silently hoped that her situation was so minor to CPS that her case would slip through the cracks of an overly taxed system. There were a lot more serious problems all around them in the projects. There were some little kids living below her dad's apartment who were taken away because their dad beat the mom and the kids. Maybe in homes like that a social worker should get involved. She knew they meant well but she was not about to go live with some crazy foster parents who just wanted the money and someone to do their bidding. She had heard stories.

After about three months, the social worker reappeared at school. Paz was called in to the office out of second period. Caught off guard, she thought maybe it had something to do with the technical aspects of the dance show and went when summoned. If she had realized it was the CPS lady, she would have run out of school and hid. The social worker apologized for not being in touch and mumbled something about having too many cases. She told Paz they could not find her father, nor any record of any aunt or relative in the area. Where was she living?

"I told you, with my aunt," she said coldly. The lady glared. Paz realized she better return to her fully controlled, listless manner or she was going to mess this up.

"Look, I'm fine. Can you close my case or something? I heard from my dad and he sends money to my aunt," she lied. "I'm doing good in school too. You can ask them here in the office, if you want." The lady's eyebrows went up.

"Really? I talked to Mr. Barraza at the bakery and he heard your dad moved away to Texas and has not been in touch with anyone."

"Yeah, well, Mr. Barraza doesn't know everything. My dad sends me money and we're fine now," she said.

"Look, Paz, I would like to close your case but I need to talk with your aunt and see your living situation. Then your aunt needs to get legal custody of you if you are going to stay there. What's the address? Can you give me her cell number?"

Paz panicked. "She lost her phone," she said. "If you give me a card, I'll have her call you. She works a lot."

The lady fumbled in her purse, then the bell rang, and the secretary with the prom pictures on her bulletin board poked her head in the office.

"Everything okay here?" she asked. "Paz really needs to go to her next class. She's working hard to stay on track and we need her in class." Paz gave her a grateful look, grabbed the card from the lady's outstretched hand, and hurried out.

At the end of dance practice, she dawdled, taking too long to clean up her homework and put the sound equipment back into its storage bins. Sensing something was off, the teacher approached. Paz didn't even wait for a question.

"The social worker lady came back today," she told her. "Can't you tell her that I'm fine so they'll leave me alone? I can't go to a foster home. I'm okay where I am. I want to stay, if they'll let me. I'm turning fifteen in a few weeks. Doesn't that count for something?"

She knew the teacher felt partly responsible for her predicament. Paz didn't really blame her but she had to use all resources available to survive. Encouraging a little guilt might be useful

with this teacher. Just like the main office secretaries, the teachers who really cared were aware of what was going on with students. Most had guessed she was staying at Cristina's apartment
and were silently relieved someone responsible had taken her in.

"Have you heard from your dad?" the teacher asked quietly.

Paz looked down at the floor and shook her head.

"Don't you need money?"

"I'm okay," she said. She could not tell her about the diner. She
didn't think there'd be gossip about that. Almost no one knew she
was working there because her shift was so early in the morning and it wasn't a student hangout. Some of the parents drove
trucks or worked in the packing sheds and came in for coffee.
But the owner didn't want a young-looking girl to be visible anyway. Paz scrubbed floors in the kitchen, so few people saw her.

"I'll see what I can do," the teacher promised.

Paz thanked her and slowly packed up. She didn't want to
leave before dark. Paranoid that the social worker would follow
her, Paz took the long route to the apartment, cutting across the
soccer field, out the back gate and through an alley behind another apartment building. Several guys were drinking and smoking at the end of the alley; she could see their shadowy faces
illuminated by the joints and cigarettes. Quickly, stealthily, like
a neighborhood cat, she slipped through a gap in the buildings to
avoid walking past them. When she got to Cristina's apartment,
she didn't say a word to anyone, went right to her corner of the
couch and got out her homework.

The teacher asked around. She heard that the secretaries and
counselors knew of her case but there was no one to take Paz.
She had no family who could adopt her or become a guardian. It
was inevitable she would end up in foster care, they said, sadly.
Everyone liked Paz. She was quiet, hard-working, and didn't get
in trouble. She never volunteered to speak in front of others or
take leadership roles, but she would do what was asked. Re-
served but determined. She appeared calm, but they all knew

she was carrying a lot of anxiety. Her teachers could see it in her curved shoulders, the way she hid in her big coat all winter or when her hair fell across her eyes and cheeks and she just let it sit there. The Algebra teacher drove to her renovated house in a town down the highway and tried to figure out a course of action. She started making calls.

A few days later, the kind main office secretary called Paz out of class and handed her an envelope. It was a letter from the social worker listing a hearing with a CPS official regarding foster care placement. Paz froze, her face got hot and flushed, as if she were embarrassed, and her heart started beating rapidly. She concentrated on the words on the page and told herself to get the fear under control. She grunted thanks and ran out. In the few minutes before the bell she went into the bathroom and locked herself in a stall, trying to catch her breath. I can't go live with some weird strangers far away, she thought. I can't leave this school, the kids I've known forever. She swallowed the panic. How could Eddie have done this to me? She was so mad at him she realized it was best he wasn't around anyway. She'd have to figure something out, and quick.

Over the next week, she was distracted by nightly dress rehearsals for the weekend dance show. She was consumed with managing all the sound equipment herself. After the practices, she did her homework until late, huddled on the couch in the dimly lit apartment with the sounds of Cristina's family around her. Late in the evening before the dance show's opening night, Paz was the only one awake when Linda came home from the hospital. Her hair was out of place and there were dark circles under her eyes. She got a Sprite out of the fridge and sat down next to Paz on the threadbare sofa.

"Paz, I want to talk to you." Fear rose up into Paz's stomach as she dreaded this might be the moment she would be asked to leave.

"I can give you forty-five dollars each week," Paz blurted. "And

I've been thinking maybe I could babysit sometimes if that would help out."

Linda smiled gently and patted her leg. "All that would be good. We can talk about it later," she said. "Right now I want you to know that your math teacher called me. She told me about the social worker and the letter and that no one has heard from Eddie. She said that CPS knows that you have no relatives around. She asked me to consider becoming your legal guardian so you could stay here with us and finish high school."

Paz sat up straight, swallowed hard. She was shocked. She did not even want to let herself hope. Linda said she had told the teacher she would think about it. That she already had a lot of responsibility. She explained that it was a long legal process. That they would come see the apartment, interview everyone, make an assessment. They would have to find Eddie to get his permission. Eddie had to sign off on giving anyone else guardianship. Paz listened in stunned silence. She nodded that she understood.

"I am telling you all this, Paz, because you're old enough to know what's going on in your life," Linda said. "I want you to know that I am seriously considering it. I can't really imagine taking on more right now, what with the girlfriend and baby here. That's been a lot. But you don't seem to add much to the craziness. And the extra money you give helps out. Babysitting might help too. But mostly, I feel how bad this is for you. I'll never forgive Eddie. We were in school together. I know your mom really got to him and tore him up, but I thought he had stepped up, raised you right. You're a good kid, Paz. You've always steered Cristina straight. We would be so upset if you had to go to a foster home. Cristina would never forgive me if she knew I could've stopped them taking you away and didn't do anything."

Paralyzed, Paz was afraid to breathe. She didn't know how to act. What do you say when you really want a person to do something so big but don't feel you can ask? She took a deep, imperceptible breath, keeping her body very still. She finally spoke.

27

"I don't know what to say. My teacher shouldn't have called you. It's none of her business. I can leave right after the show. After the weekend," she said.

"Where will you go?"

Paz shrugged.

"I'll figure it out. Thanks for all you've done for me the past few months. I really appreciate it." She let the air escape through her nose with a soft swoosh. "Cristina and her brother are really lucky to have you for a mom," she said.

Paz got up abruptly and crossed to the bathroom where she collapsed on the floor. All the uncertainty, apprehension, outrage with Eddie and the loneliness ballooned in her. She couldn't suppress the tears. She grabbed a towel and stuffed her face into it so she wouldn't make any sound. Her shoulders shook as she sobbed silently into the terrycloth. She lay on the bathroom floor until she could calm down. When she came out to return to her corner of the couch, Linda was gone. The lights were out. Drained, she collapsed on the sofa, and even though her homework wasn't finished, she fell asleep.

On closing night of the dance show, Linda came to watch. She brought the baby, since her son and his girlfriend were both at night school. After the performance in the cafeteria with the speckled linoleum floor, the pock-marked wooden stage and red velvet curtains worn purplish, Cristina's mom handed the baby to Paz. She wanted to take pictures of Cristina and the teacher and all the dancers. Paz had never held the baby and wasn't sure what to do, how to even maneuver with a baby. She awkwardly grasped her tight, afraid she would drop her.

The baby, who was named Lily but referred to as "the baby" by everyone, looked up at her and gurgled. Paz was startled. Suddenly, things came into very clear focus. She had never paid much attention to the baby and just saw her as a crying annoyance, about which she could say absolutely nothing. The baby had been ugly and red and wrinkled as an infant. But now, after four months, Lily had softened.

Her cheeks and limbs were chubby and mocha colored. Alert, her luminous eyes moved quickly, focusing on movements or people nearby. She smiled with a toothless, drooly mouth and engaged with people who looked at her. Paz noticed the tiny thick fringe of dark eyelashes framing her brown eyes. Fascinated, she watched the little warm, pink mouth move as the baby babbled and cooed. The baby's skin was powdery and soft. Paz had never felt anything so tender.

She sat down and got more settled on how to hold the baby comfortably, resting Lily's diapered bottom on her lap, the baby's back against her torso. She bounced her knees gently and held each tiny hand with three fingers. The baby's eyes scanned the big, noisy room and came back, with a turn of her head, to Paz's face. Laughter from the dancers and their families taking pictures, music blaring from the speakers, siblings running around the cafeteria with free cupcakes, all faded into the background. It got very quiet inside Paz's head as she focused on the baby's face. The numbness lightened. She leaned in to the baby's wispy hair, her lips on the sweet smelling scalp, and whispered,

"Lily, I'll keep an eye out for you. I won't let anyone leave you like what happened to me. You're gonna be just fine." The baby jabbered and saliva bubbles escaped as she gripped Paz's forefingers tightly. Paz rocked her toes, pushing her knees up and down steadily. And the two sat like that for some time, peacefully watching the commotion around them.

After the photos, Linda and Cristina and several dancer girls drifted over to Paz's perch at the cafeteria table.

"Now, it's your turn," said Cristina. "Come over to the sound system so my mom can take pictures of you too. You did awesome. You didn't mess up on the music! Paz laughed. Linda and the other girls laughed along with her.

"Yeah, you did great," they chimed in. "Not like that guy last

29

year, you remember?" one of them said.

"Yeah, there was some tech problem and we had to freeze in the middle of a dance while he fixed the music. It was kinda funny but I was so mad," the dancer said. "Yeah, you were much better at the music, Paz."

Always boisterous and enthusiastic, Cristina pulled her arm and dragged her toward the sound equipment. She well knew that Paz did not like pictures or any attention on herself. Paz had to quickly move baby Lily to the crook of her right arm and cradle her on her hip so they didn't both fall over. The natural ease of doing so surprised her. Cristina and the dancers in their feathery, sparkly costumes crowded around Paz at the sound mixer and giant speakers. She balanced the baby on her right hip and pretended to work the controls with her left hand. Everyone looked up at Linda and Paz gave a shy smile for the shot. The group froze for a quiet second. Click. And then, just as quickly, they disassembled, moved in different directions, shouted across the multi-purpose room to friends, and separated. Paz handed the baby back to Linda.

"I need to pack up the speakers and stuff," she muttered, leaning over to grab music equipment and packing crates.

"Paz?" Linda said. She looked up at her from bins of cables and the mixer board with a scrunched eyebrow, questioning.

"I'll do it," Linda said. "If it wasn't for you, your steadiness, I don't think Cristina would've stayed in this dance thing all year. I'm glad she stuck with it and finished something. I think that's your influence. And it's great you're here with them, not just by yourself, hiding in that jacket all the time. I think you two make each other better. I know you watch out for one another. But look, it won't be easy. I know you're only fifteen but you're gonna have to keep working, do some babysitting, keep some money coming in. But I can't put you on the street. Three years. I want you both to graduate. That's the deal. Get it?" She looked hard at Paz.

Paz nodded. Her dark eyes questioning in her impassive face.

"You two gotta finish high school. Both of you," Linda repeated. "No dropping out. No babies along the way. In three years from right now, I wanna be sitting at that graduation ceremony over at the auditorium and I wanna see both of you up on that stage. Got it?"

"Yeah," said Paz weakly, her voice barely audible. She cleared her throat. "Yes, I can do that. It would be amazing if I could stay with you. I'll do whatever I can to help out. I won't mess up. Thank you."

"All right then," Linda said. "Let's find out what this guardian thing involves. I'll see you back at the apartment." And she hefted the baby up on her right hip, slung her purse over her left shoulder and strode out of the school cafeteria.

Paz gripped the mixer board tightly to steady herself. She watched Linda carry the baby past noisy high schoolers. Her hair fell across her cheeks as she bent down to grab cables, circling them around her arm to prep for storage. She felt baby Lily's soft fingers caressing her own, heard Linda's pronouncement again, and relived Cristina gathering everyone for a post-show picture.

She didn't look up as a tear escaped, sliding down her cheek, while a hint of a smile formed on her lips. The ever present constriction across her collarbone relaxed, just slightly. It wouldn't be easy. Could they find Eddie? Would he give his permission? Three years was a long time. She had to get her grades up. Probably would have to go to summer school. But maybe, just maybe, she allowed herself, maybe I finally have somewhere I belong. She roughly brushed the tear away with her knuckles and cleared her throat. Tossing back her hair, she hoisted the heavy bin off the linoleum and carried it over to the backstage storage cabinet. Everything back in its place. Time to get going.

✧

The Great Stagnation

Dear Channel 6 Traffic Report—

In your Traffic Master series, I have seen you focus on highway patrol officers and traffic cops who manage the aftermath of accidents or direct exits at sporting events. Consider adding school traffic to your series, an overlooked, highly complex phenomenon that occurs twice daily in hundreds of thousands of schools all over America. I would like to nominate Connie, who has managed the traffic and parking lot at our school for over twenty five years, for your Traffic Master Spotlight.

Every morning Connie motions cars in and out of the school driveway from the road in an elegant orchestration of traffic management. The dance-like fluidity of her movements makes a difficult task appear simple. Armed with nothing more than a neon vest, whistle, ball cap, and white gloves, Connie effortlessly manages hundreds of cars through the parking lot via seven dif-

*ferent lanes, each in a hurry to get to school on time and move
on to the business of Silicon Valley. Connie deftly points which
lane to follow, uses her whole body to gesture for a group of cars
to pull forward, blows the whistle to move, move, move when
the light turns green, and calmly holds up one hand to indicate
a stop sign for another lane of cars. And all the while, she smiles
and waves, yes waves, to the children and parents as they come
to school. Year after year, parents chauffeur kids in and out of
that parking lot, amid construction, high school student drivers
and rushed commuters. Connie never mismanages the flow or
causes a long delay in the line. Any time someone else does the
traffic directing, the whistle does not match the green light or
the exit lanes back up and confusion ensues. Connie is not just a
manager of cars but a traffic artist. Bring your Channel 6 cam-
eras out to the morning rush and see a master at work.*

*—Anonymous nomination for Channel 6 Traffic Master
Spotlight series*

AFTER THE MORNING RUSH, Connie walked across campus to the
transportation office. She picked up a discarded water bottle and
candy wrapper along the way, smiling broadly and nodding to
every student and teacher she passed, disguising her anxiety. She
scanned the daily schedule to see if she was to drive buses, man
the curbside afternoon pickup, or assist with a field trip today.
She paused at the coffee machine, lifted a recyclable paper cup
from the side and pushed the button on Caffee Mocha, noticing
the clear hot water first, then the brown sludge of coffee and
chocolate shush into the cup. She slumped into the softest chair
in the staff break area and, for just five minutes, took her only
rest of the day.

After work, legs aching, Connie crossed the school parking
lot, her primary work space, climbed into her 2006 Camry with
115,000 miles on it and maneuvered through the increasing
traffic toward home. Turn signal clicking, she slowly swung off

bustling El Camino onto the private street bordered by tiny square patches of green outlined with red geraniums. A miniature landscape that looked like a giant had set up a play land with his toys. At the 5 MPH posted limit she wound through her neighbors' trailer homes to the fading yellow doublewide with the white trellis carport encased in lilac and honeysuckle vines. Connie loved when the green tentacles sprouted lavender and white each spring. It's like having a bouquet greet you home, she'd say to her neighbors. Once up the creaking steps into the trailer, exhaustion overtook her. She had to mask it for Dad and the kids while she made dinner.

She was not sleeping much most nights, busy caring for ninety-year-old Dad and listening to William, her son, argue with his wife through the thin walls. Dad was getting worse, often unsure where he was. He slept quietly for only short periods of time. Connie would drift off and just a few minutes later, it seemed, he'd call out or be up wandering in the tiny home. He was angrier every day. Connie knew it was the sickness taking hold of his brain but it made her sad to hear his increasing complaints. Witness his demise. He had been a proud technician for forty-eight years who could no longer program the microwave or make toast without blackening it. He lamented the changes in the valley, the family home for generations.

"All the rich people with their fancy cars clogging the roads," he grumbled. "So goddamned expensive now. And all the good jobs—gone. Americans build stuff. How do those people in Vietnam or China know how to do what we've been doing forever? What will happen to this country if everyone else is building and we don't anymore?" Lonely, he forgot that his wife had died of lung cancer years before—she'd been a lifelong smoker and just couldn't give it up in the '80s when everyone else did—and he'd call out for her.

"Shirley, where you at? You in that bathroom again? What's taking so goddamned long in there?" he'd ask the air.

Connie tried to coax him away from his delusions. "Dad, come on, your favorite show is on. Let's help the kids with their homework while I make dinner."

Connie massaged pepper, thyme and garlic into the turkey burger before forming it into a meatloaf. She sliced potatoes, layering them in a butter coated casserole dish and pouring in cream for au gratin. As she chopped vegetables for the iceburg lettuce salad, her mind wandered. How did it get this complicated? Dad's picking up our stress. He's getting worse. Why can't this family ever get ahead? How long am I going to have William and Melissa and the kids crammed in here with me and Dad?

Easy going, she was not a complainer. But that didn't mean she didn't have anxieties and frustrations swirling in her stomach. She'd had ulcers before and had to be careful what she ate. She just kept her worries to herself. Who was she going to tell anyway?

When William called two months back, saying the bank had finally kicked them out of their suburban house, what was she supposed to do? Of course she took them in. Her grandchildren on the street? She couldn't imagine it. Mother must be rolling over in her grave. Good thing Dad doesn't really understand why they're here. Connie's conservative nature propelled her to pay bills on time, no matter how low the bank account got or how much she had to scrimp. When Will admitted he was having trouble making his mortgage payments, she lamented she hadn't taught him better money management skills. The foreclosure process had dragged on for months, so Will and Melissa just stopped paying but stayed in the house. Connie was mortified. After eighteen months, bank officials finally appeared on Will's porch, sticking a neon orange sign on the front door, publicly giving him twenty-four hours to get out.

"Where else we going to go, Mom? It'll just be for a little while. 'Til we can get back on our feet." Connie doubled up with

Dad, put Will, Melissa and the toddler in her bedroom and con-
verted her TV alcove into a bedroom for the two older kids. The
kitchen and its tiny eating area were the only shared living space
for seven of them.

Connie enjoyed her job now, so going to work each morning
was a relief from the over-crowded trailer, Dad's incoherence
and her son's financial woes. But she was so tired. Would she
ever stop worrying about money? Would that bank account ever
have the six months of salary you're supposed to accumulate as
a buffer? Seemed like they never caught up. Were always behind.
When Dad had been more lucid, he'd complained regularly,

"This goddamned family seems to be stagnating. Not going
nowhere." It had been a long road to this point.

Will left early, at 5:00 each morning, fleeing the cramped
doublewide and his wife's wrath, for a job laying tile with the Del
Vecchia family. Years ago, when Connie, a young single mother, proudly attended his high school graduation, she had been
pleased he'd been hired at the respected company. They imported
fine stone from Italy, storing it in cavernous warehouses along
the freeway. As the local economy boomed and large high-end
homes with elegant flooring became fashionable, Del Vecchia
Stone and Tile flourished. Will earned a stable income. They even
let him do a little moonlighting for extra cash.

But Connie had always imagined William someday having
his own company, becoming a businessman. Making a better
living than she and her parents had. She pictured a nice house
in the suburbs with a big back yard for her son and his family.
But Will didn't have the same confidence. He felt he wasn't good
with computers. He didn't know how to run a business, manage
the finances. He just knew how to lay tile. Besides, how would he
ever compete with the Del Vecchia's?

Will met Melissa and got married a few years after graduation. Melissa wanted that house too and pushed Will to start
planning for it. When the Countrywide fliers showed up at their

apartment offering great deals and little paperwork to get in, Melissa jumped. Will wasn't so sure. He told Connie the expensive house didn't make sense in his gut but he gave in to Melissa's bullying and they bought a two-story with a wide lawn and a swing set. Perfect she said.

Melissa got a part-time job as a yard duty at the children's school. Then their third—the surprise baby—had mild cerebral palsy that required extra medical attention. It got harder and harder to make the mortgage payments as they went up in five-year balloon cycles. The medical bills worried him. He got benefits for himself but paid more than fourteen hundred dollars a month for family coverage they needed for his son's condition. And Melissa insisted on not changing jobs. "It would never work. I'd have to miss too much for all the doctor appointments," she told him. Will worked and worked through Del Vecchia's good and bad years but it all spiraled out of control. Now he was back at zero again, trying to rebuild a savings account, depending on his mother.

It was different in the neighborhood when Connie grew up. Their three-bedroom, off-white wood frame house over the fence from the railroad tracks cost her parents twenty-five thousand dollars. Dad started out as a janitor at a chip assembly plant several miles away. He walked to the factory. Liking his gumption, his bosses moved him up after a few years from sweeping to preparing clean rooms. Eventually, Dad got a job on the chip assembly line. He was so proud. When he had enough savings, he bought a Ford Ranch Wagon for the family, paying cash. Connie's mother never worked outside the house but cooked and cleaned and volunteered at the neighborhood library. She walked there three mornings a week to take books from the return slot, re-shelve them, answer phones and dust the card catalog cases. It was a simple, quiet life but one without huge debts or financial stresses. Connie grew up knowing what they could afford and what they couldn't. She was taught to never ask for more, be grateful for what you have, live within your means.

Connie ruined her mother's Connie-as-a-librarian dreams when she got pregnant at the end of high school. She refused to tell her parents who the father was—she did not want him around. He knew nothing about it. She would get a job, stay with Dad and Mother and care for the baby. Mother was horrified. How could her good girl, who got A's and B's on her report card, who could go to community college and study library science, get pregnant? What to do now? That seemed to be the only place Connie slipped up, Mother and Dad disappointedly said to each other. She's a good girl, such a good girl. And now a baby...well, what else are we going to do? She'll have to stay with us and start working. So she did.

After graduating in the class of '73, Connie had a hard time finding a job. Dad asked at the plant but the foreman told him they didn't hire girls. If she had some secretarial courses and could type fast, then maybe she could get a job in the offices. Connie's parents couldn't pay for secretarial courses and she needed to save for baby clothes, formula, Pampers and baby food. She had no idea how expensive having a baby was until she started shopping for one. Once she started to show, nobody wanted to hire a pregnant girl. Eventually, Connie got a janitorial position at one of the new fast-food places springing up, Jack-in-the-Box. The only job she could find.

Greasy, hot, fast-paced, Jack-in-the-Box opened a new world for her. The manager yelled at the girls at the register and the boys who cooked. There was little time to stop and rest or get fresh air. Slippery oil coated every surface. She never could get the smell out of her hair or uniform. Her work ethic apparent to the red-faced manager, he quickly promoted Connie to handling the register. Eventually she learned to cook on the sizzling grill plates. The employees changed frequently but Connie stayed. She needed the job and did not have time to look for another one, even if she wanted to.

Her favorite spot was at the drive-up. Connie could lean out the window, breathe in the cool air, schmooze with customers and shed some of the ever-present grime, which accumulated in the escaping tendrils below her hat, under her fingernails, and coated her skin. She loved seeing the kids behind the driver's open window. They were so excited about the drive-through. Little brown and blond heads bobbed up and down like jumping beans in the back seat in anticipation of munching burgers in the car. They'd watch the clown with wide eyes. Moms and Grandmas often weren't sure how to order at the drive-through by talking to the clown. The kids would squeal in delight or holler directions to the bewildered adults. Connie would motion over a shift colleague at the Coke station adjacent to the window and they would giggle into each other's shoulders at the hilarity of Jack stumping another hapless parent.

Even though she was quiet and could be shy at times, Connie was a friendly, people-oriented person. Fast food work wasn't really interacting with people beyond "Can I take your order?" Mother might have a librarian position in mind, but Connie dreamed of being an elementary school teacher.

She loved small children and imagined having her own classroom to prepare. Her own systems and lessons. She'd have an aquarium and a class pet, maybe a rat or a hamster. She'd take the kids out on walks to the park to observe the birds and trees and learn about nature. She imagined herself in front of the class, mousy brown hair, curling slightly, held back into a soft ponytail by a brassy clip. Small pearl earrings her only jewelry, she'd hold her crisp bloused shoulders back authoritatively, smooth her pale blue skirt with tidy, manicured, ungreasy fingernails, and give her nyloned legs and beige pumps a gentle stomp. She visualized twenty-four scrubbed, nine-year-old faces smiling up at her, primed for learning.

"Connie, these were supposed to be cheeseburgers, not plain

hamburgers," yelled her manager. "Pay attention." And she was out of her daydream.

Jack-in-the-Box didn't pay much despite many long, hot hours. The bills for a baby, and then a quickly growing toddler, always seemed to climb. Connie longed for her own place, not to be dependent on Mother and Dad. She needed more money. After the drive-through, she would collect Dad from the plant in the Ford Ranch Wagon. She would check in on Mother babysitting little William and then drive to her second job, waitressing at Old Lisboa.

Although the fanciest restaurant in Little Portugal was not as greasy as Jack-in-the-Box, it only paid a little better, especially when you started out as a hostess. But she felt lucky to even have the job. The Almeida family usually didn't take any non-Portuguese employees. She had caught them shorthanded when a bus boy and a waitress quit to get married in Las Vegas. Even with the two positions, Connie spent most of her paycheck each month. But always frugal, every other Friday, she took her check into United California Bank and made a deposit into her savings account, carefully recording the amount in her ledger. Sometimes it was only ten dollars, but she disciplined herself to never miss a deposit. Connie wanted her own home.

When little Will was two, a space heater caught fire in a back bedroom. Fortunately, Mother and Will were out at the park during the fire and no one was hurt. A neighbor saw the smoke and called the fire department. Miraculously, the house was saved but the damage was substantial and the repair bills were high. Connie had to contribute. Dad had a friend who needed help at his downtown liquor store on the weekends so Connie added cashiering to her schedule. Sometimes she wondered if she was spending enough time mothering Will. But really there were no extra hours for worrying. Just working, paying the bills and trying to save. No time for men or dating or anything like that.

By the time Will was seven, she had enough saved to put a

down payment on a small two bedroom mobile home in a trailer park down the street from her parents. Just room enough for herself and her son. Thrilled to finally be on her own with Will, Connie also was nervous about the additional expense. She perused the classifieds for other jobs which might pay more.

One August in the early '80s, she saw an ad in the San Jose Mercury News for a school custodian. Both she and Dad had started out as janitors. Connie had never quieted her elementary school teacher dream and she liked schools. She applied. The position was at an old private school that enrolled rich kids and was managed with efficiency. The custodians were all men. Promising she would still take weekend and night shifts, Connie convinced the liquor store owner and Mr. Almeida to call the school headmaster to recommend her. At first, the headmaster was hesitant to employ a female custodian, but he liked this woman's persistence. He remembered his mother's insistence on cleanliness and thought a female influence might be useful. He respected the Portuguese family patriarch of Old Lisboa who was on the planning commission and had voted to approve the school's building permit when they sought an expansion. The headmaster decided to hire Connie, assigning her to the late afternoon and evening shift.

After almost ten years, Connie was finally able to quit her job at Jack-in-the-Box. She pressed her new custodian's uniform each Sunday night, with eight-year-old Will piled on the kitchen table next to her, engrossed, listening for the hiss of steam. He begged for a turn and she taught him how to pull the fabric tight, flip the collar up, and slap the iron down with tender force to smooth every inch of the heavy cotton. No wrinkles allowed.

Mid-afternoons, Connie drove over to the school. She loved watching the parents parking their Cadillacs and Jaguars and gathering to meet the children. Mothers clucked at the latest school gossip in clusters, like a gaggle of geese strutting and preening, pecking and warbling in the parking lot habitat. Unkempt children, having lost headbands during the school day, shirts untucked, lunch pails clanking, swarmed out of the classrooms and ran toward the awaiting mothers. Shrieks and giggles, last-minute teacher reminders at the door, boasts and taunts, ringing bells and loudspeaker calls for a custodian or a spontaneous teacher meeting, and the cacophony of the school day's end swirled across the playground into the parking lot. Cars coughed back to life, impatient mothers honked, and the crossing guards, their orange stripes blazing in afternoon light, signaled and yelled to bring the chaos and noise to order.

Connie always paused at this moment. The after school rush gave most principals and teachers on bus and carpool duty anxiety headaches and clenched stomachs. But Connie was enthralled. She loved the energy, the noise, the mix of sounds, colors, adults and children and the roles they all assumed. To Connie, it was a dance. A show to be observed for anything out of place. Her eye was astute and somehow she saw it all, as if she were the Parking Lot Goddess looking down from the heavens. Any unusual cry, out of place car backing up too close to a student, or lost kindergartener disoriented in the rush caught her attention.

Occasionally, Connie intervened when something was amiss. A teacher didn't show up for bus duty, she would fill in. A father, foreign in the female world of after school pick-up, drove in the wrong end of the carpool lane and she would rush over and direct him to the proper entrance. A second grader dribbled papers, a sweater and art project pieces like breadcrumbs dotting the ground in a Hansel and Gretel performance, and Connie ran over, scooped up the littered treasures and organized them in the child's backpack. Connie was an invaluable carpool helper, even though it wasn't her assigned duty. The assistant headmaster noticed several of these rescues. He approached her as she mopped a classroom floor, swishing back and forth across the speckled linoleum.

"Connie, could you start your day at carpool pick-up? I talked to Mr. Rocha. He's fine with you getting to the custodian closet for your cart after the kids are gone. I could use your help out there at dismissal." She leaned the mop against a student desk and reached over to shake his hand, pumping it enthusiastically.

"I'd love to. Whatever I can do to help. I'll be there tomorrow. Thanks so much."

Eventually, Mr. Rocha, who oversaw the custodian crew and bus yard, moved her to daytimes when one guy went out on disability with a back injury. Now she could be at school during the day when the teachers and children were there. The schedule was a better match with Will's, as he was in his own classroom at their neighborhood public school. Connie continued to work Saturdays at the liquor store and two or three evenings a week for Mr. Almeida at the Old Lisboa. She had to make the payments on the mobile home, rebuild her savings and start a little account for Will's future. She was still living paycheck to paycheck. It always seemed they owed somebody, were always behind.

Price Club, then Costco, and eventually Walmart, came to the Bay Area and the liquor store could no longer compete. After two generations in business, the owner closed Cork and Bottle, perfectly located on the Main Street of town. A bead shop went in, lasted less than a year, and then a nail salon filled the liquor store void. Only aging Portuguese men went in to the Old Lisboa anymore. Mr. Almeida's son told Connie he could only use the patriarch's granddaughters and great granddaughters as waitresses.

Young businessmen now ate in the trendy and expensive places littering the valley. Indian curries and Chinese buffets competed with Mr. Almeida's fare. The tattered carpet and worn upholstery on the booths that once seemed luxurious no longer pulled in the new crowd running local government or managing businesses with offshore assembly plants. The old boys, who had wielded firm control over the city council, school districts, fire and police departments, had aged. Those remaining sat in Old

Lisboa's banquet room with the red velvet walls and played poker, telling stories of the days when they were in power.

Connie reflected that she'd been lucky to have all those jobs to get Will through to high school graduation. She adjusted her budget and was grateful the few times the school could offer raises. When Mother got sick, she was glad she only had one job so she could shuttle her to radiation treatments at the clinic and chemotherapy at the hospital.

Connie observed the changes in the valley and noted yet another boom. The rich kids' school continued to grow as the sons of foreign engineers and daughters of company executives enrolled. The cars in the parking lot became shinier, fancier, more European and expensive each year. And then the high school kids started driving them too. That really shocked her. How could you give a sixteen-year-old new driver a current model BMW to take to school? At Will's former elementary school near her trailer park, she noticed flotillas of Suburbans and Nissan Mini-Vans dropping kids off or lining up along the neighborhood street to wait for the school to disgorge the children. The cars weren't as expensive but they sure were big and omnipresent. What about the bus? What about the basic family car? What had happened to walking or riding bikes?

Cars just seemed to produce like rabbits, reflecting the growing economy and affluence of the area. You could tell if the Bay Area was in a boom or bust period by the traffic levels. Thick traffic jams even at 10:00 in the morning, it was boom time. Lighter, easier commutes, must be a downturn. Traffic was the Bay Area's economic thermometer. Connie saw it reflected in school parking lots too. But with every boom and bust, Connie plodded along with her old car and her trailer home. She didn't think she'd ever be able to afford a real house of her own. It was getting so expensive. Housing prices never seemed to stop going up. At least I have a job, and a place of my own, she'd console herself.

As the private school expanded, Connie's role broadened.

Gradually, she moved out of Custodial Services to the Transportation Department. She trained for a special license so she could drive the school vans and small buses for field trips, sporting events and pick-ups from the train station. She moved children from activity to activity and drove faculty to off-site meetings. The school grew so big and wealthy, it raised enough funds to buy and build another campus and split down the middle. She drove students and staff back and forth. She monitored parking lots and small alleyways on the cramped campus. She watched the carpool lanes for miscalculations and pattern violators. She guided cars out of the parking lot after football games and plays.

And then, one day after Connie had been at the school for almost ten years, Sam, who always did the morning traffic rush—the most complicated, dangerous and feared job in the Transportation Department—called in sick at 6:30 a.m. suffering from stomach flu. The department was a flutter and flurry with multiple field trips and afternoon sports runs that day.

"Connie," Mr. Rocha yelled out as the team was arriving for work at 7:00 a.m. She looked up, startled by his curt tone.

"Sam's out sick. Joe's got two runs to the other campus before the third grade field trip. I got a bus at the mechanic and, well..." and he stopped there, distracted with a blinking light on the phone and Stan waving at him through the window from the bus storage area.

"I need you to go out front and do the morning traffic. Just wave them in off the boulevard and wave them out from the exit. You'll do fine. Here, take the reflector vest and a whistle." Connie nodded in disbelief. Okay, wow... she thought. Now what? I have to go stand out there in the middle of the cars coming in and out from like five or six different directions. And keep them all moving...oh...okay, but I don't know....

"Yes, sir, no problem. Don't worry. I'll figure it out. You just work on the bus schedule. I got this." And she was off with her vest and whistle.

Connie walked quickly to the front of the school, past the playground and classroom wings, the front office and the main parking lot. She took two deep breaths, pushed her arms through the vest holes, swept the whistle cord over her head, and deepened her stride into the middle of the intersection. She planted herself at the center of the seven different lanes of entrances and exits. She looked all around and put up a hand to stop one line of cars and used the other to wave in an approaching group.

Oh, I gotta watch the traffic light, she realized, and keep count of how long 'til it turns. And this right turn lane goes more quickly so I gotta get them out fast. And that lane coming off the freeway, I gotta keep them moving into campus so they don't back up on the off ramp. Her mind buzzed. The juggling, spinning, whistling, gesturing, nodding took every ounce of her energy. She became completely focused as she engaged her entire being in traffic management. Someone honked and she jumped. A man shook his fist at her when she didn't get the lane started quickly enough for the stoplight. Others smiled as they drove past. Several shook their heads at her inexperience. Most didn't seem to notice Connie at all, staring through their windshields to the day ahead. As the number of cars thinned, one man opened his window and asked sharply,

"Where's Sam today?"

After forty minutes of directing traffic flow, Connie was sapped. She couldn't believe she still had a full day of work ahead. But the exhaustion was energizing, a bone weariness that did not deplete her. She had never experienced the sensation before. Her whole being had been anchored on that intersection pavement, moving hundreds of cars in minutes, almost without noticing. The responsibility and complexity of the task intoxicated her. She hustled back to the Transportation Office once it was clear all cars had moved on to their appropriate parking space, freeway or next destination.

"Can I do it again, tomorrow?" she asked Mr. Rocha. "I want to get it right and keep it moving smoothly. I can do better. But hey, there weren't any accidents." She smiled.

"Sure," he said. "Sam's gonna be out for a few days, it looks like. You liked it? Huh. Really? Most people are afraid to get out there in the middle of all that craziness."

That day, Connie re-lived the traffic directing. She went out to the football field when school was over to watch the cars leaving and the traffic lights changing. She tried to count the timing of it. The next day, she borrowed her son's favorite San Francisco Giants baseball cap so she didn't have to squint in the shiny brightness of early morning flash on cars. Will, about to graduate from high school, had just been hired by Del Vecchia Stone and Tile, and was narcissistically focused on his future and not much else, typical of most eighteen-year-olds. But when Connie told him why she needed the ball cap, he actually looked her directly in the eyes, startled.

"Mom, wait, what? You're standing in the middle of the road, cars driving all around you? Why the hell you want to do that? You're crazy. Doesn't sound safe to me. Be careful out there."

Connie was touched at his momentary concern but ignored him. "I'll be fine. Can I just borrow your hat?"

The following day she adjusted her position in the forks of the roadway. Each morning, she returned to the office and asked to be assigned the spot again. Her boss just nodded absent mindedly, and when Sam returned, greatly relieved someone else was taking morning traffic duty, he never asked for the position back.

Connie became the master of the parking lot. One weekend, she went out to a costume store and purchased puffy, oversized, bright white gloves that looked like cartoon character hands. The drivers will be able to see my directions better, she theorized. Another weekend, she asked a police officer neighbor where cops got their professional whistles. She needed to be really loud for those distracted drivers. A month later, a driver fiddling with the radio dial didn't look up in time to see her large white hand raised to indicate a STOP. Screeching to a halt right at her knees, the Acura stopped just before striking Connie and the SLK waiting at the light. Her heart raced, she gulped air quickly as the driver backed up, frantically waving sorry, opening his window to shout out more apologies.

"I need a neon green or orange vest," she told her boss. "I almost got hit this morning. These little reflector stripes are not enough." He bought her a collection of bright vests.

Connie was like an athlete who tones specific muscles to perfect one physical skill. She became a student of traffic patterns. She honed her observation skills during the daily routine of directing hundreds of cars as if through a dangerous, complex set of exercises. If the break fit within her day, she'd sneak by the busiest campus intersections and just watch. She made notes on problems and tried to remedy them immediately. After six months in the central position overseeing the morning commute, she realized the timing of the traffic signal at the school's entrance and exit aggravated a recurring backup. She went to her boss.

"I think the signal light is all wrong for our morning traffic pattern," she told Mr. Rocha. "Is there any way we can contact the city engineers or Cal Trans or whoever controls the lights to get a change? Just a little one in the timing?"

Mr. Rocha looked at her quizzically. What? Is this woman serious? But it was Connie, who everyone loved, and the morning commute and parking lot issues had been reduced to almost nothing since she'd moved out front. He couldn't complain, he told himself. "OK, I'll see what I can do," Mr. Rocha told her.

Indeed, the city traffic engineers paid attention and adjusted the timing Connie suggested. After they had altered the stoplight's sequence, the engineers watched the school commute and all intersections within a mile radius. They agreed. Traffic flow was smoother. They congratulated themselves for a job well done and went back to their offices and reports and meetings and traffic studies. While Connie continued as the morning traffic cop for the school lanes and parking lot, year after year, decade after decade.

"Dad, hey, guess what. You're never going to believe this," said Connie to her lethargic father and the grandkids over their meatloaf and creamy potatoes. Will and Melissa could be heard arguing in the bedroom next door. They had not appeared for dinner when she'd called them. Dad gazed at her absently, his eyes unfocused.

"I'm going to be on TV!! Can you believe that? Me?! On TV!" The kids looked up.

"What are you talking about, Grandma?" they asked in unison. Dad just looked blankly at her and tried to get his meatloaf pieces into his mouth without missing.

"Channel 6 is doing some report on people who work with cars and traffic. And they're coming out to the school and filming me at work. Kinda cool, huh kids?"

Her grandchildren bounced up, pushed aside the schoolwork and fired questions at her. Dad just stared ahead. But then he must have understood something.

"What ch'ya talking about? You're just a janitor. Who puts a janitor on TV? Quiet down, everyone. I gotta eat my dinner." He waved one hand, dismissively, and banged his fork on the table with the other.

"And they for hell certain don't put nobody who works at Jack-in-the-Box on TV," he said, ending the conversation. Connie hadn't worked at the fast food joint for thirty years. The children grabbed their notebooks and pushed their heads down into the homework problems. They knew when to avoid Great Gramps' grumpiness.

Connie hoped that she could get a full night's sleep before the TV crew came to film on Tuesday. It was a big deal; everyone at school was so excited. She loved the place like home and didn't want to disappoint the students or the faculty. Or her boss, Mr. Rocha, who was still there after all these years. I gotta get Dad to sleep this week, she thought. And Melissa and Will, I hope they can get their own apartment soon.

In reality, she didn't see how they were going to be moving out with the foreclosure now on their financial record. No new jobs or pay raise in sight. At Melissa's yard duty job, the school had just reduced her hours due to budget cuts. Connie had even heard them mention bankruptcy. Will was going to have to take on extra tiling. The latest round of Internet millionaires were buying houses again, finally, so maybe he could get some remodeling work. There had been quite a dry spell in remodels during the recent recession but the economy in the area was getting hot again. Connie did love seeing her grandchildren every day. They pay more attention to their homework when I'm helping, she observed. She'd put up with the family in her trailer as long as needed.

On Friday afternoon, after a long week, Connie drove home in the old Camry, picking up the two school-age grandkids from daycare at their elementary school. The kids were excited about watching the news that night and talked nonstop about upcoming field trips and weekend plans. They rushed in to the trailer and immediately looked for Dad.

"Great Gramps, Grandma's gonna be on TV tonight. You gotta stay awake for that. Can we take him outside, Grandma?" All three of them worked him into the wheelchair. The kids pushed him back and forth on the little driveway out front, giggling and chattering. Dad lifted his head slightly and sniffed the fresh air.

As the news got close, the kids, Connie and Dad set themselves up in front of the TV set with food on the coffee table. Melissa was in the back with the toddler, as usual. When Will came in from work he went in to the bedroom and the arguing started.

"When are we gonna get out of here, Will? This is too small. I can't take it anymore. Your grandfather is always yelling and bumping around at night and none of us sleep."

"Shhh everyone, here it is. Grandma's on TV," said Connie's grandson, and the trailer's living room and kitchen quieted while they watched the report. Will and Melissa never emerged.

The Channel 6 reporter introduced the Traffic Master Spotlight series and mentioned others who had been featured, like a Cal Trans engineer and a highway patrol motorcycle cop. They cut to a shot of Connie in her morning spot and the camera angled in on her face for a close up. Her serene concentration was evident. The wide-angle view showed the many lanes she had to manage and how the flow worked smoothly with her at the intersection. On screen, Connie's big white gloves waved while she whistled or wound her arm like a baseball pitcher. The cameraman clearly liked Connie waving at the students and parents, presenting different angles of her white-gloved salutes and instructions to hundreds of cars.

"Connie has directed school commuters and managed the parking lot traffic for twenty-four years. She has worked in the school's Transportation and Custodial departments for thirty-three years," the broadcaster reported into her oversized microphone standing on the football field with the school traffic visible behind her. She interviewed Mr. Rocha, scratchy voiced from decades of growling at kids, bus drivers and custodians, who confirmed Connie's record.

"There's never been an accident on Connie's watch. She's never been hit by a car. And since that first year she started with the morning rush, there've been almost no freeway ramp back ups. Connie's damn good. It's funny, you know. She likes it out there. I mean, look at it, would you want to be out there in the middle of that?" He gestured to the stream of cars.

The camera cut to Connie at her position again. His voice continued over the shot.

"Most people find that job too much, kinda stressful, you know. But not Connie. It's like she just fits in that place. We're damn lucky to have her."

The TV report had to bleep every time he said "damn" and the kids giggled. Connie just laughed and shook her head. That Mr. Rocha.

The reporter said how many cars went through the intersection and all the lights in each direction down the boulevard; it was a very busy place, even for a city regularly congested with traffic. The reporter interviewed parents and the school's headmaster.

"We rely on Connie for parking strategies and congestion planning. She has been here so long but has adapted as the school has grown. She is vital in helping us keep it safe and smooth in the transportation arena. We rely on her for so much." As he spoke, the program ran a scene of Connie giving traffic flow suggestions on architectural plans for a proposed campus expansion. One shot showed kids waving to Connie as she directed the afternoon carpool pick-up and another scene showed her chatting with students as she drove a school van. Clearly, the kids liked her.

The camera then followed a school assembly where Channel 6's most famous broadcaster showed up, surprising everyone, and presented Connie with a Traffic Master Spotlight Certificate of Recognition. The students, the faculty at the back, the custodians around the edges of the auditorium all stood up and gave Connie a standing ovation. The piece closed silently, with only the commute traffic and freeway noise in the background. The camera began with a close up shot, then pulled up slowly to an aerial view, and then higher to a wider and wider angle, of Connie and her whistle and ball cap, guiding the cars in and out of the school, in her fluid, dance-like fashion, waving the big white gloves as she worked. As the credits scrolled, Connie got smaller and smaller, shrinking as the shot encompassed the intersection, then the nearby freeway, then the entire neighborhood, rising so hundreds, then thousands of cars appeared like ants scurrying in all different directions.

As the commercial blared after the report, the kids hooted and clapped with enthusiasm. Connie's Dad leaned slightly toward her. He patted her knee and looked at her directly, with a clearness blazing through the filmy dullness that usually encased his eyes.

"Your mother would be proud," he said. "All those rich people in them fancy cars clogging up the roads...but you manage 'em, Connie. Yes, ma'am, you manage 'em. You've done good." And he patted her knee repeatedly.

"And don't you worry about those kids." He gestured to the back room where they could hear Will and Melissa arguing behind thin walls. "They might have to be here awhile, but they'll get through their problems. You gave that boy a good foundation. He's a worker. He'll figure something out." And he looked straight into her eyes and smiled.

Earthquake Weather

IT WAS ONE OF THOSE INDIAN SUMMER blue sky days where you pause as you walk your dog, or unlock your car door in the driveway, or carry the garbage bag at arm's length out to the cans behind the suburban fence, look up, take a step, and then stop again. There is not one cloud, one speck of white, one wisp of a feathery cirrus in sight. Just blue. An azure that is deep and light at the same time. It isn't royal, or feminine, like Carolina Blue, or faded, or that dark navy. It is pure. Sky blue mixed with a concentration of strong sapphire ocean to make it seem as if Sherwin-Williams invented it for you to roll on your ten-year-old son's walls. You suddenly realize why you paused and why your breath caught sharply at the sidewalk. Because it is nature at its most supreme. It is a perfect color. California blue sky.

In the afternoon, the heat presses down. The only breeze is not felt but visible up in the treetops, and widely longed for by the humans far below. There is a crystalline quality to that blue and heat combination—the absence of clouds and density of the air. The fields, which run up into rounded hills and over into ravines, are yellowish gold, just about to turn gray in their parched state. But a pale blond remains in the grasses, in contrast to the green of the sprawling oaks dotting the hillsides. It is an ancient landscape, baking to perfection in the early October heat wave. The stillness, heat and cyan sky. The golden ridges and aging oaks. The deer that drop elevations lower than usual seeking water. They were here when your grandfather was a boy exploring the creek beds, when the Mexican vaquero was herding his cattle, and when Ohlone Indian hunters were shooting elk with bows and arrows two hundred and fifty years ago. "Earthquake weather," the locals call it. And they nod at each other, knowingly, as they brush the back of a hand over a hot brow or sweaty upper lip. There is anticipation in such stillness and dry heat. A prospect of the unexpected.

It was the Ohlone landscape that the boys ventured into on their shortcut home that day. At the start, like most other days, they walked down the hill away from the elementary school, one ever so slightly ahead, as if to denote the status difference of second grader over first. Pockets laden with pointed rocks and stubby sticks carefully selected for digging at recess, they ambled, with stuffed backpacks, through the tract neighborhood. The two boys passed one four-bedroom-two-and-a-half-bath after another. Each house strikingly similar, with two-car garage facing the driveway and living room windows open to reveal faux wood paneling, designed to convey a country cozy ambiance.

These were true California boys. With mops of that blond hair streaked with brunette so people call it dirty, the boys were tanned from a summer filled with endless freedom. The older one had a smattering of freckles across his cheekbones.

The younger one's nose was sunburned reddish. All summer, they climbed trees, ran up to the creek trickling through the fields alongside their neighborhood, and constructed dams with water-worn rocks. One set of days they harvested grapes at a friend's house and tried to sell them to passersby, lemonade-stand style. Another pile of days they searched for sticks perfect for slingshots and spent hours fashioning the ideal weapon to shoot squirrels. The boys played non-stop hockey and kick-the-can with the bigger kids. They built rafts out of floatie mattresses and paddled around each others' swimming pools with PVC pipe oars. Now, they knew that the long summer was ending. Halloween rain and fall's crisp air were just a calendar page turn away.

And because they were good boys, they accepted that outdoor adventures were fading into a school year overstuffed with teachers, worksheets and rules. These California boys would grow up tall and lean, muscled and confident. They'd spend thousands of hours at organized soccer, baseball or football practices and decorate their shelves with trophies. They'd charm girls with orthodontia gleaming smiles, tufts of an uncontrollable cowlick poking up or hint of a dimple on one cheek. They'd drive their mothers' Honda Mini-Vans too fast and drink too much before the Winter Formal. But this day was before all that. An ordinary, six- and seven-year-old's school day on the cusp of fall. An Indian summer day tinted with nostalgia.

The boys arrived at the dry gully, the location of gushing runoff water in the rare heavy winters, and stopped.

"Let's take the shortcut," one of them said. No one really remembered who suggested it.

"Okay," said the other. "We have to climb the fence at the end to get into the yard."

"Yeah."

Agreed, they scrambled over the cement wall, jumped off the suburban pavement to the rocky drainage ditch below, and hiked up the steep terrain. It was hot and still and quiet. Not even a shallow breeze brushed through the uppermost branches of the broadest oak above them. A lone hawk circled lazily overhead, round and round without movement or single flap of his striped wings, gliding the thermals that pumped up from the sizzling air along the ridge. As they climbed, the gravel and loose dirt, grayed from months of no rain, spit out behind their boys' size seven Van's. It trickled down behind, like a wake made of dust, dirt and hay, betraying their detour off the expected route home. They lumbered up the ravine toward the distant fence line.

Suddenly, ahead a few feet, the dry grass twisted and bent. The rustling, whispery sound, like a wind, rode down the heat to the boys—but there was no breeze at all. The older one stopped first and the younger one almost bumped into his backpack.

"Shhhhhh," and he nodded up the hill. Both boys became completely still and watched the moving brush. The yellowed, fraying grass and gray weeds opened up and a coyote stepped out of thicker cover into a patch of rocky ground. His coat was coarse and silvery brown. His ears were raised in fierce, attentive points. His sinewy shoulders and back revealed muscles and ribs, lean and stretched for speed. His long, thin snout with a dark nose stuck out above the shrubs. A thick, bristled tail hung low, almost to the ground.

"The rocks," the older boy breathed, barely audible. The younger one nodded slightly, and slowly, very slowly, reached his right hand, the one hidden behind his friend's backpack, over to his pocket. The coyote took a step forward. The younger boy froze, small hand resting on the outside of his shorts. He could feel the pebbles beneath the khaki fabric. Both boys held their breath. The coyote took another step forward, then stopped again, nose pointed across to the next ridge. The younger boy made a decision. He decided to take a risk and reach his hand in for the closest rock his fingers could find. But at that moment, the coyote turned its head, faced down the hill, and looked directly at them with yellow eyes. Its ears still pricked forward, its mouth opened slightly, revealing an incisor.

Surprised, the younger boy moved his head ever so slightly left so he could get a full view. He stared right into those amber eyes. The hot air was suffocating. The hawk appeared to stop in its loops above. Endless blue blanketed the blistered landscape. Time froze. It was as if a camera shutter click had stopped the moment from passing, preserving it so it could be observed from afar. The younger boy felt as if he were the hawk watching the spectacle from high above. He was removed from the scene and yet so very deeply in it, all at the same moment. The boys and the coyote stared at each other. No one blinked.

The initial surprise of the wild dog's glare had delayed fear somewhat, causing it to tarry in its duty to clench stomachs, prickle necks and backs of arms and flush the boys' gentle, round faces with warm blood. But now it came in full force. It flooded into every capillary of their little boy bodies. The older one, in front, closest to the animal, had to physically tighten his stomach muscles to prevent a gasp from escaping. The younger one, pro-tected slightly by his friend, pushed his feet down into his shoes and the uneven terrain, curling his toes in an attempt to grip the earth to prevent him from falling forward into his friend, or backward into the open field. As the adrenaline swirled through them instinct resurfaced and their animal natures awakened.

Later, days after the sighting, protected by the schoolyard chain link at recess, the boys would claim that they were about to reach into their pockets and wildly begin throwing their collection of rocks and digging sticks at the coyote. It was clear that was going to happen next, they each said to the other. But that is not what occurred. At some point, amid the staring in the sweltering heat, the boys and the animal reached an understand-ing, a stalemate. After what seemed hours, but was indeed less than a minute, the coyote took a slight step forward, downward toward their position in the gully, deepening their fear. But then, unexpectedly, he turned and trotted, in the graceful lope of the four-legged, uphill toward the shaded cluster of oak trees with branches so old they grazed the ground.

"Let's get out of here," the younger one yelled and started running up the canyon toward the fence behind their neighborhood. The older one followed. They sprinted, backpacks bumping as they jumped across the dry streambed, and headed toward the safety of the familiar. They never looked back at the coyote's exit as he ambled up the opposite side of the ravine toward the oaks to the highest point of the hill where it sloped slightly to meet yet another rounded valley.

Once at the back of the fence that enclosed their neighborhood, they scrambled up, pushing worn shoes into the cracks, clinging to the top and tumbling over to safety. The older boy had to take several runs at the fence to make its height. The younger one scratched his leg as he rolled over the slats and departed with a scrape of fine redwood splinters. They ran through the neighbor's back yard where they had landed, around the pool, past the built-in barbecue and down the side yard, unlatching the gate by the garbage cans, and into the street. They tore down the sidewalk toward the older one's house and collapsed in the shade of their favorite climbing tree adjacent to his front yard. Sweaty and dirt-streaked, breathing hard, faces red with exertion and adrenaline, they gulped air as if it were tall glasses of ice water. No one spoke for some time.

"You can't tell anyone," said the older boy finally. "My mom will never let me walk home again." He gulped and hiccupped as he tried to catch his breath.

"My mom lets me 'cause I'm with you," observed the younger one softly. His breathing was beginning to slow but his heart thumped loudly in his chest and head. The soft flesh in the crease of his elbow fluttered, in and out.

"I gotta go." The flush-faced older boy stood up shakily, pushed off the side of the tree trunk with his fist, fled up the bricked steps and disappeared through his front door.

The younger boy waited for his body to calm. As he regained his breath, his mind re-lived the entire episode. At six, he already had the majority of the vocabulary he would use in his lifetime, but he instinctively knew that he would never have words for what had transpired. Staring into those wild, ochre eyes, he had heard the animal. They had communicated. Something indescribable had passed between them. A wordless, soundless electricity. A strength. And the coyote decided to leave the boys alone. I stared down a coyote, he thought. And his chapped lips stretched into a slight smile.

He picked up his backpack and walked slowly down the street to the variation of the house model he called home. He opened the door and stepped in, kicked off his shoes and dropped his belongings on the tile floor. Gray dust, stickers and rocky soil rolled out from his dirty socks. A voice from the kitchen called out.

"How was school, honey? What did you learn today?"

"Oh, nothing," he said casually, and paused to let his blood and heart finish calming. As he reached the kitchen, his mother turned to look at him. He added quickly,

"Well, there's this new computer thing we're gonna read chapter books on," already having learned that he had to give her a morsel or she would just keep at him.

"And how was walking home? It's hot out there, isn't it? You looked both ways at the corner, right?"

"Yeah, Mom. We looked both ways."

The Hero

"Good morning, Los Robles Elementary. How may I help you?" asked Mrs. Anita Garcia, principal's secretary, into the cracked cordless phone. "Oh, yes, Mrs. Lewis, how are....uh, huh. I know, I know. It's a tough situation. We'll check on that for you. Hold on a minute, please." Cradling the phone on her shoulder, she turned to the office clerk. "Lupita, can you pull up the attendance and check if Chardonnay Lewis is here? Mrs. Lewis is worried Dad didn't bring her to school again," she said.

At that moment, a sullen man, holding a baby and guiding a small boy, opened the front door of the typical California elementary school, single story with open air hallways. His eyes scanned over the green speckled linoleum and the mismatched visitors' chairs lining the glass wall, past the ladies' cramped work area behind the Formica counter, toward an open door with a wall sign reading Principal's Office. Mrs. Garcia and Lupita looked up from their desks littered with file folders, gray oversized computer monitors, worn keyboards, phones and walkie talkies, office supplies and personal photos.

Mrs. Garcia quickly pushed the hold button on the phone and said,

"*Buenos Días*, Mr. Sandoval. *Como está?* You really need to get Hector to school on time. He's been late twice...." She gestured at the little boy.

"Not good at all," Mr. Sandoval interrupted. "The goddamned government is gonna deport me. What am I supposed to do with my kids? Remember how they locked up *su madre* in that building—it's like a jail? Now they're after me. *La migra* came to the sheds last week, threatenin' everyone, throwin' those badges around and handin' out papers. They put me in jail for the weekend. I gotta go to some court next week."

Mrs. Garcia got up from her desk and moved to the counter to face the family. At the same time, Lupita said,

"Anita, Chardonnay isn't in class today. Mrs. Richardson said she wasn't here yesterday either and remember she missed two days last week."

"Thanks, Lupita. Hector, here's your pass," she said, handing the little boy a slip of paper. "Go straight to class, *mi amor*. I know you want to say hi to Mr. Rodriguez but he's on the phone right now, honey. Look for him when you're in the lunch line." Hector nodded and left the office, struggling with the heavy door.

"Mr. Sandoval, I'm so sorry to hear that, but Hector has to come to school. Is there someone else who can pick him up and get him here on time? Do you know Mrs. Ugalde's mother? I think she lives near you. She brings her grandkids to school. Excuse me a minute."

She leaned over to pick up the phone off her desk and spoke into it. "Mrs. Lewis, thanks for holding. Chardonnay isn't here. We'll call Mr. Lewis and remind him he needs to get her to school on time. Thanks for calling in. Yes, I know, hmmm, huh, uh...you can call us anytime. Bye, bye." She turned back to the clerk and said under her breath,

"Lupita, please call Mr. Lewis and tell him to get Chardonnay to school. Tell him we'll call the county and send the truancy officer over there if the absences continue."

Mrs. Garcia swung back around to face Mr. Sandoval and leaned slightly over the counter to focus on him.

"Now Mr. Sandoval, I am so sorry about your weekend. Have you heard from Mrs. Sandoval? We're so worried about her and really miss her. We could use her help organizing the Tamales and Turkey Night next month. Try Mrs. Ugalde's mother down the road from your place. She might be able to give Hector a ride." Before he could respond, a deep voice called out from the Principal's Office.

"Anita, can you come in here please?" Principal Rodriguez's voice asked. "I'm off the phone with the director. We've got to go through the schedule for the Tamale Feed and get the School Site Council packets together. I heard the moms gossiping on the sidewalk this morning—they want to know what day we're having Tamales and Turkey this year. Do you have the template for that grant application? I can't seem to find it in my files." He walked through his door into the main reception area and noticed the visitor.

"Oh, hello, Mr. Sandoval, how are you? The baby is just growing so quickly. She is so alert. *Muy preciosa*. And have you heard from Mrs. Sandoval? Is she okay? Is she still in that center?"

Before Mrs. Garcia could respond to his questions or protect her boss from the distraught parent, Mr. Sandoval was speaking.

"Oh *profesor*, can you help me? *La migra* came to the sheds. They might deport me. I have a hearing next week. I can't go back to San Pedro de Sula. It's crazy there with Mara Salvatrucha controlling the place. Honduras is worse than Mexico. And what about the kids? My wife is still in detention but they moved her to the big building down in LA. How'm I supposed to get down there to see her? At least her parents are in LA."

"Come on in, Mr. Sandoval," the principal said, gesturing for him to enter through the small swinging wooden door, pass by the secretaries' desks, and into his office. He turned back to his secretary.

"Hector got to class, right, Anita?" Then he put his hand lightly on Mr. Sandoval's shoulder and escorted him to a chair in front of his desk, saying, *"Con corage, señor.* Take a breath and let's see if we can come up with some ideas." All in fluid movement, as if choreographed, he turned slightly to his secretary and told her discreetly,

"Anita, please call Mrs. Reyes and ask her to come fifteen minutes later to the Site Council planning meeting. Thank you." Then turning, fully focused on the parent, he closed his office door while saying, "Now, Mr. Sandoval, tell me what happened. Remember you need to be strong for the children...."

The office ladies continued their work conversation.

"Anita, here's the Tamales and Turkey schedule from last year. We did have it on the Thursday—the last school day—just before the break. I have that grant form Mr. Rodriguez wanted too. Oh, and here's some principal's conference paperwork the district office sent over. Do you think he'll go this year?"

"Thanks, Lupita," said Mrs. Garcia. "Can you call Mrs. Reyes and just have her come a bit later? I have to get this monthly attendance report finished and in to the superintendent's secretary by 10:00. Get the Fog Days schedule copied so we can put it in this week's Friday Folders and on the website. Fog's starting. I hope he does go to the conference this year. It would be so nice if he could get to know that pretty new principal over at Fifth Avenue. They'd be perfect together. Both workaholics. But none of our other matchmaking has ever worked, has it?" The ladies laughed at their unsuccessful attempts to set up their boss and continued the morning's tasks.

Beyond the front doors of Los Robles Elementary School's main office stretched miles of fields of rich, dark soil plowed into rows so long and straight they looked like a giant had combed the earth. Sediment so black, so full of nutrients and promise that it had been labeled a Golden State treasure. Some thought the San Joaquin Valley's fertile dirt should be protected like an endangered frog or wetland bird. Farmers complained that federal government water policies were creating a drought. Rabid politicians prophesized a disaster, an environmental Armageddon. The deep, loamy topsoil inspired passion. It also nurtured a hefty percentage of the world's almonds and raisins, oranges and pistachios, kiwi and beef, milk and tomatoes, grapes, cotton and apricots, walnuts, pomegranates and olives. Seventy percent of the entire world's almonds came from the Central Valley and six thousand almond producers were headquartered along Highways 5 and 99, dissecting the agricultural trough.

Los Robles Elementary's principal, Salvador Rodriguez, knew the history, the emotions, the calamities and triumphs, the victories over nature's challenges. He knew the cycles. A native of Fresno County, he grew up between the parallel lines of tomato plants and the shade of orange groves. He had scampered up ladders to knock pomegranates to the ground and shake hairy green almonds off their branches, while his fathered lugged a burlap rucksack over his shoulder to collect the prize. A deeply religious man from a tiny, impoverished village high in central Mexico's mountains, Sal's father was grateful he had come to the Central Valley through the Bracero program. He never returned to Mexico, as the Braceros were expected to, eventually getting a green card through amnesty in the '80s. He resolved that his family would get every benefit from *el norte*.

"We didn't want to leave our home," he repeatedly lectured Sal and his five brothers. "But since we had no choice, then your mother and I and you boys have to take advantage of every opportunity in *los estados*. It is a tough place to live but it is a good place to work. Your mother and I may not have much of an education but work is something we know how to do," he told them. Sal's father assigned each of his six boys a biblical name and expected them to live up to the lofty expectations implied—Santiago, Salvador, Samuel, Gabriel, Jesus and Angel had no choice but to toil in the fields in June and July and complete their homework every weekday night.

And the boys excelled. They graduated from Fresno State or Fresno City Community College. They bought cars and houses. Only Angel, the baby, rebelling at the pressure of his name by fifteen, turned his mother's black hair gray as he zipped between Highway 99 traffic on a cousin's Harley, smoked marijuana, and was cited by the Fresno police for cruising. But he too, eventually, followed Salvador and his brothers into making their parents proud by settling into reliable work as a motorcycle mechanic.

Salvador, as the second oldest and quite a bit older than his four younger siblings, was greatly relieved when Angel finally grew out of his extended adolescence. By then, he was an assistant principal at a middle school and he just couldn't add Angel's misadventures into his busy days and nights. With so many boys and so much commotion for older parents, the four younger brothers looked to Sal as a second father. Even in his high school years, Sal had stood on the sidelines at *"los muchachos'"* soccer games, made sure they had proper football pads, since their father didn't understand American football, and hunched by their bedsides at night, listening, as they sought advice about girls. Most of the time, he managed to keep the four younger *muchachos* from driving his mother crazy. Sal was a father his whole life.

His big brother, Santiago, was strong and liked to talk tough so the gringo kids wouldn't beat him up after school. A few times he had to prove his fierceness with a fistfight in the abandoned irrigation ditch on the route home. But after he bloodied the nose of the almond farmer's son and bruised multiple ribs of the field foreman's many offspring, no one messed with him. And once he found success as a running back in high school football, Santiago Rodriguez was a name to respect. By the time he played for the nationally ranked Fresno State Bulldogs' football team in the mid '80s, the family's reputation was sealed. The entire Central Valley area around Fresno, from the small towns of Firebaugh and Hanford, east to Sanger and north to Madera, knew the football star, his five younger brothers and parents as hard working and accomplished.

A reader from his earliest years, Sal preferred school to football. Even though he was shy and skinny, he could find success in academics. He read and read. He joined the student government and watched out for his younger brothers. He found shelter in the long shadow of his football star older brother and was grateful for its shade and peace. Famous for being the hardest working Rodriguez and always in a teacherly role, Sal was *"el profesor"* from childhood on. Checking on his brother's homework, excelling in math, Spanish and English himself, being the family "bookworm," Sal naturally gravitated toward education. He was Fresno State's valedictorian and graduated right into their teaching program.

He hurried through requirements to get into his own classroom as quickly as possible. He never took time off, traveled, or dated the dark-haired girls with flirtatious eyes and reddened lips who tried to get his attention. He was a handsome catch for the Latinas who didn't want to end up as they stereotyped their immigrant mothers, behind a stove with an apron stretching over a pregnant belly. But he paid no attention. Head down, Sal prepared lessons for his sixth graders, circling grammar errors and writing out sample pre-algebra problems late each night.

His dedication stretched beyond his own classroom; he attended every school event and student performance. His whole life seemed to be focused on his job. When colleagues asked about marriage or becoming a father someday, Sal joked dismissively,

"These are my children. I have so many of them. Remember, I have five brothers, five sisters-in-law and so many nieces and nephews, I'm not sure how many there are."

Sal's first principal immediately noticed his calm care for students and their parents. The respect he garnered from his colleagues. His never-ending work ethic. His devotion to the school's neighborhood.

"Sal, you should become a principal," his boss told him. "Have you thought about that? We need bilingual, smart administrators in the schools here. You're from the community. You should go into the administrator training program," And so Sal returned to Fresno State. He got his Administrative Credential and a school district hired him as an assistant principal at a junior high two towns north on Highway 99. By thirty-four, Sal was an elementary principal back in Fresno. The position matched his calm, compassionate, academically focused personality. He just fit in the job, as if it had been tailor made for him like the homemade clothes his mother had sewed for all her boys. The principalship was his calling.

Mr. Sandoval, still visibly distraught, pleaded with Sal as he sat in the Los Robles Principal's Office clinging to the baby on his lap with one arm, nervously running his other hand through his hair.

"*Profesor*, what am I going to do? My great aunt Tía Gloria says she might be able to take the baby for awhile but she has no room for Hector. I have to show up at that ICE hearing next week or they're gonna arrest me. Even so, I think they'll put me in one of those centers after the hearing. I don't got much to show them. Can you write me a letter? Tell them that we're good parents and bring Hector to school? He's a good boy. He likes to read. You know...that boy is smart. He could be a teacher, like you, *profesor*."

Sal knew that the Sandovals and their relatives lived in pickers' shacks set close together between the drainage ditch and a frontage road. He'd been inside when doing home visits to get one of the Sandoval cousins to send their kids to school regularly. The shacks were small. Usually the children shared one bed or slept on the floor.

"Yes, Mr. Sandoval. I do know Hector is a good student," Sal said. "He was reading by the middle of kindergarten. He finds me on the playground and reads me his little stories at lunch recess. I'll write a letter about Hector's progress and how he needs to stay in school. I don't think it will help much though, you know. I think Mrs. Garcia already has some ideas about how to get Hector to school. Now you get on to work. Stay strong and see if Tía Gloria can take Hector for a week or so."

"I want Hector close to the baby, close to me and his cousins," Mr. Sandoval said. "And hopefully my wife will get back here soon. Her father in LA has a green card and is trying to get her out, or at least sent closer to Fresno. Kids need their mother."

"Yes, they do, Mr. Sandoval. They sure do." Sal gently rubbed the baby's soft check as he ushered them out of his cramped office to the reception area. Sal nodded to Anita. She grabbed her pile of papers and glided to join him in the office doorway. As they moved to the chairs on either side of the principal's desk, she began.

"Here's the grant form. I'm almost done with the monthly attendance report for you to look over. Here's your School Site Council material for the meeting and Mrs. Reyes is on her way over to prepare the packets and meet with you. Tamales and Turkey was on that last Thursday before December break last year so I put it on the calendar and we've got a flyer together for this week's Friday Folder and website Announcements section. Here's the Fog Day schedule—does it look okay to you? Mrs. Montenegro called to say the superintendent needs you to come a half-hour early for the principal's meeting. I tried to get her to tell me what was up, but I couldn't get her to talk. Sorry, I tried. Oh, and don't forget, the psychologist is coming today. Do you have that list from the IEP meetings ready for him? And the new

SRO, Officer Rogers, called. You know that gang fight over the weekend after the Bulldogs game? Well, they think it's continuing in the neighborhoods so we need to be aware at school and when the kids walk home. Do you want me to do a text alert to the parents? And do you want me to get the teachers out at the doors as school ends?" It was just 8:30 in the morning.

By the time Sal Rodriguez got home most nights, it was almost always after 9:00 p.m. He facilitated parent gatherings and clapped through student performances. He squirmed through dreary school board meetings and animatedly participated in principal meetings with his boss, the superintendent. Mr. Rodriguez was an honored guest at many neighborhood barbeques, holiday events and community meetings. The agenda of the Valley Water Board, the Joaquin Neighborhood Association and the Fresno State Outreach Initiative meetings often featured an "Education Update from Principal Rodriguez."

At least two afternoons a week, Sal walked over to the high school fields to monitor practices of the Fresno Area Sports League. He had established the organization by convincing almond and orange growers to donate coach stipends, balls and jerseys for low-income kids to play soccer, football, baseball, basketball and track. He wanted at least one sport going each season to keep as many children on teams as possible. Although Sal personally was a kid who had loved reading in the safety of the library, he knew that many children found success and friends through sports. All five of his brothers had. Setting up and overseeing the sports league really wasn't much different than his days making sure los muchachos were at practice with the right equipment and a motivated attitude.

At his school, Sal had organized the Los Robles Elementary's stay-at-home moms into a sort of old-fashioned sunshine club. "*Las Madres*" made food when parents got sick or lost work. They picked up kids on their stroller circuit through the neighborhood, as many parents left at six a.m., rumbling down the road in clunky old cars for picking jobs in the fields. Once a week, Sal met with *Las Madres* after the morning bell at 7:55 a.m. Gently, discreetly, he offered up suggestions of families in need or school projects to support. They advocated for their issues and he listened intently. They thought the projects were their idea and Sal got good information on what was going on in the neighborhood, his school community. They told everyone that *el director* listened to them, or *el profesor*, as they called him, still using his childhood nickname. Sal knew much of the neighborhood gossip before it left the school parking lot. It was a mutually beneficial relationship.

A week after he had been in the office with his dad and baby sister, Hector, disheveled, unlike his usual combed and starched appearance, pulled hard on the main office doorknob. Thousands of small child hands, sweaty pre-teen palms and callused fingers of laborer parents had worn it smooth and softly shiny. He wriggled through the heavy, institutional door, dried tears forming tiny salt crystals on his lashes. Silky brown cheeks streaked with tear residue and smeared dirt stains, he hiccupped as he tried to swallow the crying he'd been doing.

"Oh, Hector, honey, what's wrong?" Anita asked, as she peered over the Formica counter down at his ruffled head.

"Is Mr. Rodriguez, here?" he said. "Can I talk to Mr. Rodriguez, please?"

"He isn't here right now, sweetie. You just sit right there and he'll be back soon," she told him, pointing to the row of metal chairs with orangey brown upholstery lined along the office window-wall like sentries. Anita picked up the walkie talkie. We still use these old things, can you believe it, she mused when hearing it crackle. She radioed Mr. Rodriguez. He appeared five minutes later and found Hector slumped over in the chair.

"They took my dad. I don't know where he is. And my mom, when's she coming back?" he burbled through tears and gulps.

73

He hiccupped again.

"Where are you staying?" Sal asked. "Anita, who brought Hector to school?"

"I'm at Tía Gloria's with the baby. But they said they can't keep me. It's kinda crowded there. I sleep in the corner. I don't know where they're gonna send me. Maybe to my cousins' next door? When's my dad and mom coming back? I miss them. I don't have any clothes," he said. Sal sighed deeply but quietly.

"Okay, Hector, shhhh. Come on in now, it's going to be okay," Sal said, and had him sit in one of the chairs in front of his desk. He turned and leaned out the door, holding on to the frame.

"Anita, can you ask *Las Madres* to find another pair of pants and some shirts for Hector? And can you call Tía Gloria? Do we have her number? Maybe on the emergency card? We gotta find out where the Sandovals are." And he walked back in, pushed the door two-thirds of the way closed and sat down to comfort Hector.

"*Señoras*, I need your help," the principal told *Las Madres* at their informal meeting that week. "Both Mr. and Mrs. Sandoval have been arrested by la migra and are in two different detention centers. Their son Hector is a first grader here and there is a baby girl. The baby is with Gloria Paniagua, *el señor*'s great aunt. *Su esposo esta en Yuma.* He left early for the season, trying to get a sharecropping spot there. Tía Gloria doesn't have room or money for both kids so Hector is now next door with some older cousins. But they don't go to school or work. It's not a good place for a little boy. *Es muy peligroso allá.* Hector is a good boy who loves to read. He's a good student. He needs a safe place until his parents get back."

The ladies muttered among themselves, raised eyebrows and grimaced. This was a bad situation. They all knew it. Both parents in detention, and one in the big center in LA? Not good. They assured *el profesor* they would do what they could. They'd ask around for a safe place for little Hector to stay for a while. No other relatives here? Hmmmm, *muy duro*, they whispered. Two mothers said they would get some clothes to Gloria for the baby and the boy. Another said she would take over bags of rice and beans.

"And some formula for the baby. I'll send a can," said another. Sal expressed his appreciation and then moved on to their planned topic—the annual Tamales and Turkey feed and fiesta before the Christmas holiday break.

"Now, *señoras*, I know you all call this event *Las Posadas* out of habit. But, remember, we can't call it that—it's Tamales and Turkey. This is a public school. We have to honor everyone's culture and background. We have white kids and black kids here. We have Muslim and Hindu and Protestant kids here. *Las Posadas* is a Mexican tradition, *muy católico*. We'll do it the same as always and have the procession through the classrooms to see the students' work but let's just not call it *Las Posadas*. And no references to Mary and Joseph seeking shelter." He sounded a bit to them like he was pleading. They shook their heads at first but then slowly began nodding.

"*Ay, dios mío, éste país*," grumbled one of the mothers. "Maybe there wouldn't be so many problems here if we had a little bit of Jesus around," she said. "*Las Posadas* is harmless. It's about people who need a safe place seeking shelter and people doing what they can to help others."

"Yes, *señora*, you are right, of course," said Sal. "Let's keep the same sentiment and support all our children and families. But we are going to call it Tamales and Turkey. Okay?" And he looked directly at the group with his best teacher stare. Eventually, each of the ladies nodded in agreement.

That afternoon, in the brief quiet immediately following lunch, after recess disputes were settled, Anita tried to catch up on some paperwork in the school's main office.

"Mr. Rodriguez, do you want to go to that conference for principals this year?" Anita called out with her head toward the principal's office where Sal was eating a salad at his desk. "It's the Early Bird Discount deadline and the district wants to know if you're in. It's in San Diego."

"I hadn't thought about it. Do I have to decide today?" he asked while trying to keep his voice casual, almost bored sounding. His mind started working triple time. At conferences, far outside of his hometown and away from the claustrophobia of living in the tight knit community where he grew up, Sal Rodriguez occasionally relaxed the straight jacket he placed around his personal life and went out to bars to meet men.

Anita got up from her desk and moved to the doorjamb. With her expert principal's secretary awareness of what was going on in every space around her, she put her hand on the door sill, leaned in to his office slightly to look at him encouragingly, while maintaining her sense of the front door, the reception space, the loudspeaker to the classrooms, the pulse of the school.

"Oh, Mr. Rodriguez, you should go. San Diego in January will be lovely. I know you've skipped a bunch of these the last few years with the state budget freeze and district cuts. But I think the School Site Council would approve it if want you to go. We want our leader to be up on the latest things, after all," she said with a chuckle. Anita had joined the school's governing body when her granddaughter enrolled the year before. She was already its president. A few parents and teachers grumbled about the power Mrs. Garcia wielded through her job and volunteer position. But many valued the close working relationship she and her boss maintained and the efficiency it brought to the school's activities.

Sal's mind raced through his options. Yes, he had missed several conferences during the budget cuts and housing crisis years. It would be good to get back to the professional camaraderie and learning conferences engendered. Yes, there was more money available now. Yes, his superintendent was encouraging all the principals to go to a conference or two this year. And yes, he could get a little respite from his priest-like existence and venture out to a gay bar he liked in San Diego.

"If you go, do you want me to reserve a room at the conference hotel also? It's so convenient that way," she interrupted his thoughts.

"Oh, no. I mean, yes. I'll go. Sign me up for the conference. But no, if it's in San Diego, I'll have to stay with my cousins. My mother will be furious if I don't visit and they'll be offended if I stay in a hotel. You know," he said off-handedly and gave her that look of you-know-how-the-relatives-can-be. She smiled, nodded to him and turned to catch a parent opening the office door and the clerk returning from lunch.

"Very good, Mr. Rodriguez. I'll send all the paperwork in. Hello, Mrs. Anderson. What can we do for you?" and she was off to her next task.

Later, as she filled out the paperwork, she and the clerk gossiped.

"I hope that pretty new principal over at Fifth Avenue School is going to the conference," she thought out loud to her front office companion.

"Mr. Rodriguez," she called in to him, "you could take her out to dinner in San Diego. There are great restaurants in the Gas Lamp or Little Italy. She's just like you, I hear. Always working. Married to the job, they say. Just like you. You'd be perfect for each other. And she's very smart, and so pretty. She dresses nice. Have you talked to her after your principal meetings, Mr. Rodriguez?" She winked at the clerk. There was no response from the principal's office.

"I know the mothers are always trying to set him up," Anita said under her breath, "but this lady is more like him. Not someone's niece from LA or cousin from Texas." And they laughed at the memories of disastrous dinners Mr. Rodriguez had tolerated due to the best intentions of the parent community. Most of the ladies seemed to have given up and the invitations had lessened. No one seemed a fit for Sal. He works too hard, they would lament and shake their heads. But then they'd invite him to yet another community meeting or suggest a neighbor bring their problem to *el profesor*. He'll know what to do, they'd say. But then they didn't stop there either. And el profesor is not getting any younger. He needs a wife to take care of him. He'd be such a great father, they'd say. Look how he adores his nieces and nephews. Isn't he a *padrino* to like twelve kids, they'd gossip.

But no one said aloud what some silently might have entertained. Do you think he...? Could he be...? Men were marrying each other in San Francisco now. There were those sort of masculine teacher ladies at the high school who lived together and didn't try to hide it anymore. But, no, no, not Mr. Rodriguez, not *el profesor*. And the loudly unspoken question would quickly drift off into the great beyond like a wisp of smoke. Mr. Rodriguez being gay was just not a possibility.

Sal was not naïve. He was aware of likely speculation about his sexual preference. But long ago he had decided to live like an old-fashioned priest in a medieval village. One of the good priests, that is. It was a sacrifice he willingly made starting out and now, after years, his solitary life had become an unquestioned habit. He was a respected leader. A confessor to many, a watchdog and advocate for all, particularly the weak against the wealthier and stronger. He supported every aspect of the neighborhood and the town that he could conceive of. And he did it in an asexual, single, emotionally solitary way. For him, it was how he had to operate if he was going to do his job and stay in his hometown. Beloved by all, he was really quite alone, only closely connected to his large family.

Every Sunday, all his brothers, their wives and children gathered at his parents' home for a barbeque. Everyone was expected to attend. Unless they were out of town for work or had moved more than four hours away. Sal loved these afternoons. He could be himself, almost fully, laugh and wrestle with his brothers and nephews, gossip with his sisters-in-law and chat with his nieces. Sports, school, weddings and *quinceañeras*, water and agriculture were weekly topics. Uncle Sal was a favorite who advised on girlfriend issues, tutored on math homework and threw the football with the young boys. And he listened to his brothers as they struggled to raise their children and teenagers.

Most of the time, Sal had little energy to lament his celibate, lonely existence. He was exhausted when he got home to his tidy, elegant sanctuary. Often there was even a niece or nephew who was having trouble at home, or between semesters in college, sleeping on the couch for a few days or taking over an extra bedroom. To his brothers and their wives, Sal's quiet home was a safe place for an errant kid to stay until family tensions cooled off. Or for a young adult to learn some independence. Sal loved the company. He had always been a helper, an assistant parent in his family. He could no more say no to any of his brothers than he could imagine telling them his true identity. Being gay was just not an option in his world.

This fact added a quiet sadness to Sal's persona—one that only those highly skilled at reading eyes recognized. He hid it so well, telling himself year after year that he was like a priest. I have a community, my family, the neighbors and friends I grew up with to serve. And in that way, all the Los Robles Elementary moms and secretaries with the best of intentions were right. He was married to the job. He just didn't have a priest's ring to show for it.

When attending conferences in distant cities like San Francisco, LA or San Diego, he would go out awkwardly, always somewhat uncomfortable. As if it were another person who had taken over his body. And he engaged only in one night stands. He didn't want to allow himself the luxury of imagining a life companion, no matter how much he would like to have one. Once you let that guard down, he told himself, who knows what trouble might creep into your life. Sal fully understood why the priest had to make a solemn vow to God to be celibate and never marry. It was very difficult. A basic human need had to be compartmentalized, removed from daily existence.

But Sal was conflicted. Occasionally, at home late at night, when the house was empty, TV blue luminescence the only light, Sal allowed his mind to wander to the what ifs. There must be someone out there who I could love. Who I could have my own family with. A life partner for me. It would be so cool to be a dad. Maybe I could adopt. His mind drifted into the fantasy and he would imagine the brainy, serious little Hector doing homework at his kitchen table. But a gay man in a rural, traditional culture adopting? No way. And a single gay man? Never. Not happening. Coming out? No on that either.

But it's so much more accepted. Trendy even. All the characters on TV are gay now, he'd tell himself. Have some guts. Be yourself. You think you're a leader, Sal? But it's all a façade. They don't even know who you really are. And then reality would crash into the image of the modern TV sitcom life, shattering it completely as if it were the TV's glass itself breaking, sending dangerous shards everywhere. Oh my God, no. My family. Can't even think about telling them. Ever. Stay disciplined, he'd admonish himself, and he'd cut the gay couple or parenting images right out of his mind as if they were spoiled sections of an apple that had to be sliced clean with a knife.

The weeks before winter break turned cold and gray with tulle fog enclosing the school building in a fuzzy white bubble, as if it were a spaceship floating untethered. No streets or fields were visible through windshields. Walkers, blinded by the thick whiteness, searched for lights encircling the stop signs for markers. Cars poked in through the mists and dropped off students and deposited teachers. Where at one moment only a blur of grayish, gauzy vapor was visible, suddenly three moms, complete with strollers and little ones at their hands would appear. They looked as if they were gliding out of a cloud toward the school's entrance, past the flag drooping forlornly in the drizzle, into the welcoming, warm glow of office and classrooms.

School continued its inexorable march toward Christmas vacation. Anxious teachers crammed before semester's end. Parents planned holiday events. Giddy students anticipated parties and gifts. But regular school continued amid the fog and party planning. The *Las Madres* mothers found Hector some clothes and brought food staples to Tía Gloria. They called her every few days.

Then one day, mid-week, Hector didn't come to school. By the following Monday, his teacher and the mothers were worried. Anita got on the phone but couldn't reach Tía Gloria or any emergency numbers listed on his card, or find a Las Madres mother who knew his whereabouts. At Mr. Rodriguez's request, she went out to Tía Gloria's home with the county truancy officer. No one answered. The shacks looked quiet, almost deserted. They finally found a young man, maybe twenty, sprawled out on the back steps of one of the sheds. He appeared to have been sleeping off a long night of drinking Miller beer, as there were cans scattered on the ground. He swore at them as the truancy officer tried to wake him. He repeatedly shook his head at all the names they brought up. Anita reported back in detail and Sal himself, worried, called every neighbor or co-worker of Mr. Sandoval's he could think of. No one seemed to know anything, or if they did, they were not going to talk about the family. Sal told Anita not to forget about little Hector and keep calling all the numbers daily.

Las Posadas was Los Robles Elementary's second biggest celebration of the year, right after the *Cinco de Mayo* and sixth grade graduation combined event in the spring. Despite being renamed Tamales and Turkey more than ten years before, the new label was staunchly ignored by the school's oldest families. Parent volunteers decorated the cafeteria with *papel picado* squares of red, green and white tissue paper cut into elaborate patterns. Streamers looped over the squeaky-clean linoleum floor. The decorators covered the long industrial tables with attached benches with bright cloths of green and white, then dotted each one with Christmas red poinsettias with sparkly green foil covering the flower pot bases. A huge Douglas fir, sent over by a student's uncle who grew Christmas trees in the Santa Cruz Mountains, dressed up a drab corner by the stage and emergency exit door. First and second graders decorated the towering tree with twinkling white lights and paper ornaments. The cafeteria was ready for a celebration feast.

Scrubbed children, hair pulled tight in curled ponytails or slicked down with Gillette hair gel, excitedly dashed from warmly lit room to the dark chill outside and then back to another bright classroom. They wore pressed pants, frilly dresses and white tights, shiny patent leather shoes and small cowboy boots. Parents sporting cowboy hats and bolo ties, Mexican wedding shirts and starched blouses, black high heels, tinkling jewelry and red lipstick wandered from room to cafeteria and back. They tried to follow the children's enthusiastic journey but often stopped to greet a relative or neighbor. The kids grabbed the hand of an *abuelito* or a parent and pulled them into their homeroom where stations laden with creamy Mexican hot chocolate and *pan dulce* shared precious classroom space with bulletin boards and chart stands displaying student work.

"Look, *Abuelo*, here's the globe I made with paper maché. And have a cup of hot chocolate. We made it for you."

"Look Mom, my paper on frogs was the best. The teacher put it up on the board. Look at my drawings of the dissection we did."

"Papa, come see. We have a terrarium. Me and some of the other girls feed the turtle and mist the plants. We put in bugs for the frog to eat. But we don't have to water it much because it's a eco...eco...Hey, Manuela, what's it called when the terrarium makes its own rain?"

After the procession through the classrooms, families wound their way to the multi-purpose room for dinner. *Las Madres* members and the cafeteria ladies manned the buffet tables, carried out pitchers of *horchata* and juice and refilled platters with turkey, mashed potatoes and tamales. Mr. Rodriguez proudly presided, taking his own journey through each classroom, greeting the teacher and every parent he encountered. He knew the students' names, the fate of older siblings, who had been Los Robles students in most cases. He cooed over babies and bemoaned the Fresno Bulldogs' poor showing this past season with uncles and fathers. He nodded with respect to the grandparents and great grandparents. He discussed water politics with the sharecroppers and farmers.

Over time, Sal had convinced some of the wealthy almond and orange growers to send their grandchildren to the school—not moving their home bases to Clovis for "better schools," filled with a whiter, wealthier crowd. Although many of the landowners' offspring did go to high school in distant locations, quite a few enrolled in the elementary school due to the positive reputation Los Robles Elementary enjoyed. The growers knew Mr. Rodriguez recruited the best teachers, expecting them to perform and focus on each child's needs. They knew he provided his staff and families as many support services as he could accumulate. He created a respectful, symbiotic community and most everyone wanted to be a part of it, the pomegranate farmer with five thousand acres as much as the farmworker who picked his crop.

After families had consumed the final plate of tamale or turkey and mashed potatoes with gravy, children trooped up the worn wooden stairs to the stage. The kindergarteners sang Rudolph the Red Nosed Reindeer. The fifth graders did a *ballet folklorico* dance, complete with girls twirling in brightly colored swirling skirts and black suited boys as their escorts. The night ended with a surprise appearance by a Mariachi band. One of Mr. Rodriguez's sisters-in-law's brothers was a member. Parents danced *cumbia* style, toddlers swayed solo to their own rhythm and first graders grabbed grandparents and got them up dancing. All the while, the sixth graders stood in hunched clusters against the wall, faces lit by the greenish blue glow of cell phones, too cool to take part but completely enshrouded in the community's love. Their role remembered fondly, amusedly, by every adult present.

Sal was ushering students out of the cafeteria and saying goodbyes to parents, when Tía Gloria screeched into the parking lot in her old Ford Focus. She threw open the door and began yelling for Mr. Rodriguez. She ran frantically, searching for him, calling loudly.

"*Señora*, what's going on?" he asked, grabbing her arm and trying to calm her as he escorted her to a quieter area.

"It's Hector. They took him away! Can you believe that? A little boy? They deported Mr. Sandoval back to Honduras. It's all my fault, *profesor*! It's all my fault."

"Calm down, Gloria. What happened? Please tell me from the beginning." He motioned to the benches near the front door so he could continue to monitor the parking lot as families exited.

"Bye Mr. Rodriguez. Merry Christmas," students called as they left. He waved, distractedly.

One of the *Las Madres* walked over before Gloria could begin. "It was a good *Las Posadas, profesor. Gracías para su ayuda*," and she gave him a big smile. He nodded. "Yes it was, *señora*. You did a great job." Sal turned back to Tía Gloria.

"What happened to Hector?"

"I took the baby and Hector to see their dad at the detention center in Sacramento. We waited for hours. The baby was crying. It was so cold in there. When I finally got to the front of the line, I told them I had these little kids and they need to see their dad and I wanted to know when he was getting out. He needs to come home to take care of his kids. Well, they asked me all these questions, for identification and birth certificates. I don't have any of that. I just have these kids who need their parents. Then they started talking among themselves, in English, but I could understand. They said Enrique had a DUI on his record and they were sending him back to Honduras. But that his kids are American and so can stay.

"They finally let me talk to Enrique for about five minutes. He was thrilled to see the kids but he had to be strong for Hector. But he's suffering terribly. He said his wife who's in the center in LA is so worried about her babies that she's gotten very sick. And he reminded me that both kids were born here so they won't be deported. His wife crossed when she was pregnant with Hector but they hid it. That's not easy. They were lucky to make it.

"But then, oh, Mr. Rodriguez, it was the most awful thing ever, they took that boy and put him in that place. It's like a prison. Little, innocent Hector. He was happy to be with his dad. But I had a bad feeling. I tried to keep him with me but the guards insisted and said he should be with his dad. I kept arguing that it was no place for kids but they pushed me out of that room and then down the hallway and out into the road.

"And there I was. Just me and this baby. Sweet as can be, but not mine. Parents are in jail. Well, detention. But what am I to do? When I got home, I called the grandparents and told them everything. They asked me to keep baby Maria for a while longer and said they would keep trying to get the family out."

Tears rolled down her cheeks. Sal wished he had a handkerchief to hand her, like in the old movies. But he had nothing. He put his arm around her shoulders and told her he would look into it. See if he could talk to someone in immigration.

"But *profesor,* it gets worse. That was a few days ago. I knew everyone here was busy with *Las Posadas* so I didn't call the school, but I was frantic. So I spent all day on the phone with Mrs. Sandoval's parents in LA and trying to get back into that place. They finally gave me an appointment this morning. I went over there—this time I left the baby with my neighbor. I didn't want *la migra* taking any more children. They were gone. They said Enrique was deported and Hector was placed with

85

Child Protective Services to go into foster care. I said what are you talking about? He's six years old and needs to be with his family. They said the CPS people would find his family and that they always tried to keep families together. I stayed for hours trying to get someone to tell me where he is. Where'd they send a six-year-old boy? He must be terrified and so confused. And the parents, what about them? They must be frantic. Their little boy with some strangers? Who does this? What kind of government does that? What is wrong with these people?" And this time she collapsed into sobs.

The news stunned Sal. He stared into the dark. He patted Tia Gloria's shoulder. He had gotten to the point in his job, a position central to this impoverished neighborhood, where not much surprised him anymore. But deporting parents and then moving children to foster care without consulting relatives? He was so shocked he was speechless for a moment. And then he was just filled with a deep sadness. A blackness that seemed to pour into his body and take hold, like a blood transfusion. Oh, that poor boy, he thought. That poor, poor child. And he was overwhelmed with anger. He longed to scoop up Hector and comfort him, rub his spiky dark head and ask him to read from one of his first grade books. Tía Gloria's sobs pierced the quiet at the front of the now empty school.

Sal remembered his position, his responsibility, and tightened his arm around her shaking shoulders.

"Gloria, it's not your fault," he said. "You did the right thing by taking that boy to see his father."

"I don't know," she said. "I just wish I could rewind it all. That I'd never taken him there. That place is horrible. So ugly and cold. I'm so worried about the boy. What must he feel? With no parents or family around?" Gloria shook her head back and forth. She kept muttering, "I can't believe it," over and over.

"We gotta find him, *profesor*. We gotta find him. I don't know how I'll manage it. I'm moving away and I'm too old for this. But children have to be with family."

Sal got on his cell phone and called Gloria's husband, who fortunately was back from Yuma. Sal didn't want her driving home in this condition. She was distraught. While they waited for Gloria's husband to arrive, Sal called his immediate boss, the assistant superintendent, as well as the district psychologist, a counselor from the local community services agency, a social worker he knew at CPS, and a principal friend from another school. Did any of them have any advice? What did they recommend to help this family torn apart by ICE? Gloria gave him the number for Hector's grandparents in LA and he called them too. No one answered any of his calls.

Gloria's husband showed up after having walked almost two miles from the workers' shacks where they lived next to the frontage road. He looked miserable and just nodded at Sal. He helped load Gloria into the car and drove off without a word. Sal checked in with the night custodian to verify he would close and lock the buildings. The staff would be back tomorrow to clean up, but the kids were out for Winter Break. Thank goodness we won't have kids tomorrow, he thought. I can spend more time on Hector's case while everyone closes up for the holiday.

Sal walked to his Ford F150 with a heaviness that was alien to him. Despair. Is that what this is? He drove home extra slowly so he wouldn't cause an accident. He could barely focus on the traffic lights. He felt light headed, woozy. Once home, he got himself a Pacifico beer out of the fridge, grabbed a bag of chili cheese Doritos, the one junk food treat he allowed himself, turned on the TV to the NFL playoffs and collapsed on the sofa. He kicked off his shoes, undid his tie and the top button of his dress shirt and sank deep into the cushions. The blue and greens of the game swirled, casting a surreal glow in his dark living room. Whistles blew, commentators analyzed, players grunted from the screen but Sal heard none of it. He was alone. No errant nephews on the couch or nieces in the back bedroom this week.

For a moment, it was very quiet inside his head.

Helplessness was new to Sal. Despite a hardscrabble up-bringing he had never felt lost or without hope or without a plan. He had always felt so fortunate for all that he had. Understanding that he was gay and that he couldn't tell anyone in his family, that had been excruciating. Forcing himself to accept that maybe he would live a life alone; that was equally punishing. But even though he felt isolated by his secret, he still had never completely given up hope that he might live a more honest life one day. But this, this was a deep wound. This wrong twist of justice, denial of basic decency to an innocent child. It exhausted and baffled him. For the first time he could remember, he was at a loss. And then the silent clamor, the internal debate started.

This is crazy. Little Hector, that smart little boy who I've imagined as a stand-in for a son. We've got to get him out of there, back with family. But who's going to take him? Could I help out? Could I be like a second father, an uncle maybe, while the parents work out their immigration issues? Oh come on, Sal. Who are you kidding? I'll never be a father. I can't even dream about being openly gay. It would kill my parents. And adopting a son? A single, gay man? What were you dreaming, Sal? Things haven't changed that much. Not here. I can't believe they're deporting parents and putting their kids in foster care.

The anger was like a salve, lifting Sal from the lethargy of hopelessness. He was a man of action. That was what he knew how to do. He had to push aside his own turmoil and get moving. He picked up his well-worn cell phone and started making calls and sending texts. He got on his computer and sent emails. He reached out to every contact he could think of, including the area's Congressman who he knew from Fresno State days. No return texts. His email in box remained empty. The cursor just blinked at him from the computer screen. Not one response. The football game on TV came to an end.

He decided to call the children's grandparents one more time.

Hector's grandfather answered slowly, with a weak voice. Sal introduced himself.

"Hello, sir. My name is Sal Rodriguez. I'm the principal at Hector's school. Your daughter has been an active member in our parent club. Your son-in-law's great aunt Gloria Paniagua gave me your number. She told me about your son-in-law being deported and your grandson with CPS. I am so sorry. I've made calls to people I know who might be able to help." He summarized his contacts and the messages he'd left. He explained that he would rally resources for the family. Hector's grandfather was grateful but seemed overwhelmed by the tragedy that had lighted on his daughter, son-in-law and grandson.

"Mr. Rodriguez, thank you for your concern. My daughter and little Hector always spoke so highly of you. My daughter is not doing well. This has made her sick. They finally took her to a doctor but they put her in one of those mental wards, a clinic for crazy people. But she isn't crazy, she's just desperate to get her kids back. They think she'll hurt herself. They are giving her some strong medicine.

"It's possible they'll deport my daughter to Mexico, even though she's sick and I have a green card. But who knows? These cases stretch out forever. And now Enrique in San Pedro de Sula? Hector in a foster home? The family is in pieces all over. Do you know any good lawyers? I think we need one. We don't have much money but we need help."

Sal assured him he knew several immigration lawyers and he would have them call. He gave him names and phone numbers. He asked how they were holding up. The situation was so hard on all family members he lamented and sympathized.

"We're not so good. We're so worried," Hector's grandfather said. "My wife's pretty sick. Stress is not good for her diabetes. And next we have to figure out what to do with the baby, little Maria." He seemed relieved to have someone safe to talk to.

"She has nowhere to go and there is no way I'm gonna let that baby go to foster care. Whatever happens, she won't know her own parents and relatives by the time things get straightened out. She's a citizen. But a baby citizen with no parents. That's no good. Tía Gloria can't keep her. She's about to move to Yuma. And those cousins—that's no place for children. They just drink. The baby can't go there. But we can't keep her any longer. We already have other grandchildren here and my wife's health isn't good. She's got diabetes. She'll kill herself trying but I don't want her to add in a baby to this household. Mr. Rodriguez, do you have any ideas until we can get my daughter out? Who could help with the baby until we get things more settled?"

Sal froze at the question. He felt nauseated. His usually calm demeanor, the unchecked confidence that permeated his core in his principal role was suddenly rocked. Then cracked, as if an earthquake had struck him. There really was no choice here. He was who he was, that wasn't going to change. But his duty, his deep love for his community, his respect for what was right guided him now. He flashed on the San Diego conference he'd looked forward to next month and the bars, the distractions, the fun. But no, he decided right then. No more conferences. No more San Diegos or San Franciscos. He was needed right here, right now. He had the capacity to help these kids and this family and he had to stay loyal to his own. He would stay married to the job but he could do some good and bring some new children into his life.

As a professional, Sal hesitated to get too involved in students' personal lives. There was a fine line he worked hard to respect. To not step over inappropriately. But this situation was dire. His own family members could help make the plan palatable to the community and Hector's grandparents. Sal felt as if he were looking down on himself, as if a part of him were God pulling the puppet strings while the other half of him watched, detached, as if from the audience seats at the show. He made a decision. He cleared his throat,

"I think maybe my family can help you, sir. I can take baby Maria while you work on your daughter's case. I have lots of sisters-in-law who would love to care for her. I have nieces and nephews stay with me all the time who can help. Christmas vacation is starting so I can spend the next two weeks figuring out a schedule. And sir, once we get Hector out of foster care, he can come here also if he needs to. You can work on getting your daughter out of detention and I'll make sure the kids are cared for in the meantime. It could take a long time but you can focus on getting her home. Call my immigration lawyer friend. Don't you worry, sir. I have five brothers, five sisters-in-law and sixteen nieces and nephews. My family will be thrilled to have two more children to love. We'll take good care of them for as long as you need."

The grandfather expressed appreciation and said he'd talk to his wife. He'd call back soon. Sal glanced over to his desk and gazed at the framed picture of his family at a backyard barbeque, all twenty nine of them, his parents in the middle. He took a sip of beer and raised the bottle in a silent toast to the photograph. To family.

City Streets

ON THE LONG, SLOW DESCENT INTO LAX, you look out the thick-paned airplane window at the sprawl, the spreading vastness pressing out toward the Pacific ahead and creeping up the mountains over your right shoulder. At 10,000, then 5,000, then 2,500 feet, it looks as if a tsunami rolled in to litter the coastal plain, depositing a sludge of terra cotta-roofed houses, teal pools, pale strip malls, ribbony freeways, stuffed warehouses and cars, cars and more cars, as if they were broken shells and driftwood stumps. The magnitude of the expanse, coated with a layer of gauzy haze and sporting a burlap cloud blown out over Catalina Island by the Santa Ana winds, overwhelms you. You can almost see the creep, like a mold or those mosses that take over stepping stones, pushing up against the border mountains and oozing, without barrier, toward the desert heat.

The air isn't as bad as it used to be. When LA was famous for its smog rather than self-made celebrities, most visitors never knew there were mountains enclosing the area, creating a desirable, ocean-front bowl. Why's it called the LA Basin they'd ask, never seeing the snow topped mountains framing the place, peering over the five million strong, giving them a northern border. The city and its basin neighbors used to look as if they were continually coated with a brown fog. Now, after decades of pollution control and even at fifteen million souls, you don't see it so much. But when you live in it, you know it's there. Everyone's nursing a kind of perennial rasp. The LA croup.

From the airplane window, LA looks deceptively the same. The weather is always warm and sunny. It's all so predictable, so many tract homes and strip malls. And the traffic. It's everywhere. Omnipresent. It's a living presence pulsing within the sprawl, where freeways get a personal pronoun in front of their number—a distinction that betrays their importance in the daily life of the LA commuter. Despite that steady consistency of pleasant weather, in reality, "seventy-two and sunny" is the only thing you can count on here. But today, it's really hot.

When the heat pumps up higher, the Santa Ana winds blow out from the desert, dry but crackling with static electricity, the temperateness disappears. That's when you start to worry. Those winds are crazy-making they say. If, on that landing approach into LAX, you had Google Earth enabled eyes, you could drill down, down, down, past the vastness of the sprawl, closer, ever closer, past the skyscrapers, the repetitive tracts, past the Mexican markets, the cars and the 405, to Streetview—da da duh, still closer in, focus, change again, da da duh, until you'd really see a city block, the sidewalk glistening with heat.

Suddenly, into your Streetview would step Ava Callahan, swishing her way across the downtown plaza, in that rapid LA-SF-NYC-American-Business-City stride. An elongated, speedy, hard step of purpose. A forceful arm swing which conveys nothing less than I am importantly busy, have important things to attend to, and you don't, so you better get out of my way. If Streetview could peer into her subconscious, as Google probably has a secret team developing right at this moment, you would hear her wondering about that Santa Ana induced thermometer buster, hear her trying to think cooling thoughts as she stepped to avoid a scorching updraft, a mini-cyclone of dust and litter rising between the skyscrapers.

As she did every day, Ava strode past the homeless regulars in the plaza, seeking shade under a spindly tree, hunched over, twiddling meager belongings intensely or pleading with a scribbled cardboard sign—*Need a helping hand. Spare change? God bless.* Yet, this morning, Ava saw no sign, ignored no mumbled panhandle. Instead, she overheard an entire conversation.

"So, you won't believe it. Listen to this. This lady walks by my spot. I'm just waking up. And she has her dog on a leash, see. So the dog comes up to my bag and starts peeing. The lady turns the other way and just lets that dog pee all over my sleeping bag. She didn't try to stop him or move or anything. Just stood there and let that goddamned dog pee all over my bag. My sleeping bag is my home. Would she let that dog pee in some fancy friend's house? On the living room carpet? I don't think so. Can you believe it? I mean, what the fuck, man?"

Clutching the sleeping bag, the man leaned into the deep black granite laced with gold flecks at the skyscraper's base. A vibrant, magenta spray of bougainvillea looped down from a planter on the mezzanine bar deck, casting small shadows over his face. Coffee cups clinked on saucers as Angelenos breakfasted a floor above.

"No man, that sucks," his friend said "That is some bad shit. What kinda fancy lady lets her dog do that? People got no manners these days."

"No kidding. Now I gotta wash it again. I just did it two days ago. Costs me ten bucks to wash and dry it." The man with the soiled sleeping bag shook his head back and forth. He continued to twist his head from side to side as he pushed himself up to amble down the block, a black plastic trash bag stuffed with belongings in one arm and the sleeping bag haphazardly rolled into a bundle in the other.

Ava, her shiny high heels clicking and her crisp black suit with starched white blouse softly swishing, heard every word. She'd slowed temporarily to eavesdrop. Her long dark hair, tall, slender frame and confident posture, which she attributed to years of cross-country running, were an imposing presence as she crossed the plaza between the parking garage and her office building. She recognized many of the indigent since she had repeatedly walked Flower and Figueroa, Temple, Olive and the Financial District's numbered streets over her six years at Palisades Pacific Capital. Each new position giving her closer access to the office building. If she ever made partner, as the promotion she'd just been offered hinted, she wouldn't even have to touch the sidewalk. Then she would be able to park in the bowels of the building and ride the elevator to the 51st floor, never again passing any homeless on the gritty streets of downtown LA. That's what her colleagues aspired to. That's what the partners did, driving in from Beverly Hills in their Mercedes and Ferraris.

Ava shook her head, an unsuccessful attempt to dislodge the image of the dog peeing on the guy's bag. How sad that some-one would do that. What is wrong with people now? Where's the compassion? Everyone's too busy, I guess. Oh, whoa, it's the one whose been talking to me, she realized as he limped around the corner with his soiled belongings. For the past year, the sleeping bag guy had been making comments specific to her as she breezed by in her purposeful march. His typical post was slumped against the 1920s art deco Los Angeles County Library building with a paper coffee cup in his hand. Talkative, he usually was telling stories or complaining to his fellow sidewalk residents. Then he'd interrupt his stream with a comment to her.

"How's your day going?" "Lookin' good today." "Ooohh, got

the pearls on; goin' to court today?" "Perfect outfit. You got class, lady." "Nice shoes." "Oh, I am lovin' the red shoes." Whatever she was wearing, he always seemed to like her shoes. Then, about six months ago, he gave her a name.

"Hey, Heels, slow down. What'chya in a hurry for today? Big meetin'?" he'd say.

"Hey guys, check out Heels today. She must have a big to do comin' up. Look at the outfit. Don't blow it, Heels. We're countin' on ya!," and he'd give her an exaggerated thumbs up and a white toothed grin.

At first, uncomfortable at being singled out, Ava ignored the homeless man as best she could. She walked faster, lengthened her posture upward, turned her torso away from him. She researched other routes to the office. But she was often just getting to the garage in time to walk the quickest way to her building, up a block, through the plaza, across the street and over one. She didn't have time to walk farther to avoid some homeless guy. That's ridiculous. Just move quickly and get to work, she'd tell herself.

And then some days he was so funny she couldn't suppress a smile. Other mornings, he was so sweet that even Tough as Nails Ava, her nickname at the firm, couldn't escape the warmth he brought to her morning.

"Heels, you just made this beautiful LA day even prettier," he'd say. Or...

"Oh Heels, you are lookin' good tooooodaaaaay. So cool. So Uptown." Or...

"Oh folks, downtown LA weather report. It is sunny again because Heels is walkin' by." Or, her personal favorite, his little jingle:

"It's another beautiful, sunny day/ in dowwwwntowwwwwn Llllll Aaaaaaa/, 'cuz Heels is rolling through/on her prooooooo-feeeeesssssssional wheels." He would stretch out the phrases so it had a lilt to it, creating a tiny rap. Sometimes he would substitute "professional" with alternatives, "high class," "stylish," "high steppin." No one had ever composed poetry for her before.

The loquacious homeless man wasn't always communicative. Sometimes he was slumped over the decorative wall nearest the plaza, half in the bushes, unconscious. Some days he was missing entirely. Other times she would see him at the regular spot but he appeared depressed or drunk. No talking on those days. Ava started to look at him, surreptitiously, using her peripheral vision, turning her head slightly when he was asleep or comatose. She noticed that this guy, The Talker, she decided to name him, was pretty young. He's about my age, she was surprised to see. He was lanky, taller than many of his compatriots on the streets. He had a square jaw and thick eyebrows. He would even be handsome if he cleaned up, got a haircut and had a hot soapy shower and fresh clothes.

After a year of personal comments, she noticed his presence or absence every morning and wondered about The Talker's story. Why is such a young guy out here without a family helping him? Why can't he maintain a job? Is he mentally ill, an alcoholic, a drug addict? By the time she heard The Talker tell his buddy about a dog peeing on his sleeping bag, Ava had a relationship with him inside her head. As she locked her car and bounced up the garage stairs to the street above, she was almost always wondering, what will The Talker say today?

Staring out her floor-to-ceiling windowed office on the 51st floor, contemplating the recent promotion offer, Ava's thoughts wandered past buying and selling companies to the plan crystalizing in her mind. Six years here, plus the two years in investment banking. Eight years in finance is enough. I can't do it anymore, she told herself. Dad has controlled my life for too long. I'm too old to be afraid of him. I don't want to keep working with all these guys who don't care about anything but the size of their bonus, what car they drive or what pre-school their kids got accepted to. If I take the promotion, I'll be partner in two years and never get off this hamster wheel. I've got to do something meaningful. I've got some savings. Time to follow my dreams, not Dad's. Ava had to be her own cheerleader; no one else on the home team understood her perspective.

Even as a little girl, Ava had been unusual. At least her elegant mother and unflappable father thought so. She couldn't sit still. She showed signs of compulsion, overly scrubbing her hands raw and pink, closing every cupboard door she found ajar, straightening items on desktops and granite counters. Ava's mother, cool and shiny in her designer clothes, with a smooth, waxed skin that looked like a pastry chef had spatulaed her with a layer of tanned frosting, did not understand the disquiet. She wanted to send her to a psychiatrist for some calming meds.

"Put her in sports. She'll be fine," Dad said. The final word. So Ava ran and ran. She played soccer and basketball and field hockey and ran track. Any sport with running. Eventually, she ran the longest distances possible during cross country and track and field seasons. But even that didn't curtail her energy, her obsessions. All the years of Catholic school lectures, guilt and brainwashing affected Ava deeply. Somehow she had emerged with an attitude alien to her nouveau riche upbringing filled with sparkling homes and sculpted women, some even featured on TV.

"Dad, Mom, Orange County's got too much sun and too much money. I don't care about designer purses or blonde extensions. There are people struggling—they're just hidden from view. They talk about how we should help poor people at school and church. Don't you listen?" Ava would question her parents. Once in seventh grade, she began volunteering. She pushed hospital wheelchairs protecting the sick and elderly. She cleaned cages at the animal shelter. She stocked shelves for the church's weekly soup kitchen. By high school, she found a regular position at the Veteran's Assistance Center next door to her church, answering phones, copying, running errands.

She loved the sense of purpose it gave her, a place to channel her frenetic energy. Her mother distractedly dropped her off until she had a license. Her father nodded absently at her stories of disabled veterans and heroic doctors volunteering at the VA hospital. Blame it on the schools you sent me to, she'd repeat to her parents when they shook their heads at her idealistic notions. At least it's kept me out of trouble, she'd add when they squinted in further disbelief at the intensity of her patriotism and dedication to others. Then, at 17, she really got their attention.

"Dad, I want to go into the military too. I want to be an officer like Patrick. They need girls now. I think I have the grades to get in. My running should help."

But her father put his foot down. No more soldiers in this family. Yes, her older brother had attended West Point and commanded troops in Iraq and Afghanistan. Yes, Uncle Gerry was a Vietnam Vet and Grandpa had been in France at the end of WWII. But no girls. That is not appropriate. She mentioned the foreign service then. But he was adamant. No soldiers, no spies. You are good at math. You should go into business. Finance. There was no arguing. He didn't understand her at all. She had always been gutsy, as he expected, demanded even, but she was not rebellious enough to defy him.

So Ava followed the traditional route studying finance, eked out her college classmates for a coveted investment banking job and two years later moved to Palisades Pacific Capital. Her father's business drinking buddies from the Jonathan Club were partners there. Once she started working downtown, Dad was so proud. She basked in his sparse praise but squirmed when she heard him and his colleagues complaining about the homeless on the streets. What's wrong with these guys they'd say? Ava, now don't give any beggars money. That won't help. They'll just get drunk with it. Her smoothly skinned, perfectly coiffed mother avoided downtown completely, shopping online, at the Costa Mesa Mall or in Beverley Hills. Can't you get a parking spot in your building, honey? And her mother would sort of shudder with disgust at the thought of her daughter forced to walk down Fig or Olive. Places to be avoided at all costs.

Ava just sighed silently, ignored them and concentrated on work. Every December she sent a check to Families of the Deployed. That was the extent of a connection to her former passions. Driven, disciplined, obsessively focused on efficiency and company goals, she excelled in the male dominated finance industry. She kept moving up, receiving more responsibility, and now they'd offered a managing director position. Partner was not far off. But after eight years of working, maybe it was turning thirty, she was changing. She didn't see the point anymore. New obsessions had taken hold. Or maybe it was really a redrafting of former ones, coalescing with her increasing awareness of LA's chronic struggles. The heat off the streets was affecting her, she was sure her mother would say. Don't waste your time, her father would scold if he knew her questioning.

But Ava couldn't push a mental delete button to derail ruminations on a new target for her restlessness. With LA, she was in a tangled, passionate love affair with a hopeless end. It was her home. She had to try to make it better. The Catholic schools had ensured that. Ava shook her head in disbelief every time another millionaire built a Catholic Center with his name on it but nothing changed. Just another chandelier-enhanced venue for yet another party, another glittering awards event. More self-aggrandizement in Ava's view. She was pretty cynical about the Southern California Catholics.

For about a year, secretly, in her Hollywood Hills bungalow each night, Ava had been designing a downtown support center for veterans. The plan was hidden in her computer at first. She told no one. She remembered the heroes she'd had in high school working at the Veteran's Center. She admired her uncle and brother for their honorable service but was saddened by their difficulties upon returning home. Patrick had commanded troops in Iraq and now appeared to be a successful medevac helicopter pilot. But she had been startled awake by his nightmares on family vacations. Uncle Gerry returned from Vietnam an alcoholic in 1972 and had only just gotten himself sober ten years ago. He had Parkinson's, which his wife was convinced was due to Agent Orange sprays over his unit. The government had never agreed with that interpretation of Southeast Asian jungle events, so Gerry struggled with the aftermath on his own.

Ava was perplexed. How could society expect so much and then not respect and assist soldiers and officers afterward? And day after day, year after year, striding past the mostly male homeless on LA's streets she started to ask herself how many of these guys had been fighting in Iraq or Afghanistan recently? It's just not right, she mused. It's just not right. So she had set to work. Her audacious goal, her new obsession, was to end veterans' homelessness in downtown Los Angeles.

In the limited time away from launching financial deals at Palisades, Ava became a self-taught expert on veteran's issues. She poured over research, examined flourishing programs across the country and built financial models. With this new obsession taking hold, seeping into her veins and pushing out interest in private equity, she got ambitious. She started talking to real people. On weekends she visited organizations providing direct service. She interviewed men in shelters and families living in cars. She grilled social workers. She shadowed Veterans Administration doctors, many of whom were volunteers seeing cases in addition to residency responsibilities. Ava decided to start a center for veterans and establish a foundation to fund it. Dad was number one on the list of targeted donors but she figured she knew other wealthy families if he turned her down. She devised a plan on how to spin it to her father. She called Uncle Gerry and swore him to secrecy.

"Uncle Gerry, it's Ava. Can I talk to you privately? I have a new project I want your advice on. You can't tell my dad or anyone, okay? Can we meet for breakfast Saturday morning?"

Ava opened the door to Urth Café and spotted Uncle Gerry

immediately at the back table, head shaking slightly. He stood slowly, left arm vibrating, and gave her a hug. The shake was getting worse.

"Now tell me what this is all about, Ava," he said.

"First, how's the Parkinson's? Anything new?" she asked.

"I started acupuncture. Might as well try East and West medicine. Can't hurt at this point. Doesn't seem like what my doctor gives me does much good. I walk slower. Your aunt worries constantly. But I keep tellin' her I've had a good life. I'm over ten years sober—that's something. At least I don't think the alcohol will be what'll kill me. Damn Agent Orange's what's gonna do it most likely. Now what's on your mind? Why so secretive?" She explained the proposal. His eyes expanded wide in surprise.

"You know your dad won't like this, not one bit, right? Oh Ava, there's gonna be family fireworks, that's for sure."

Ava noted a mischievous twinkle in his eye. Uncle Gerry was going to be an advocate.

"You got savings, Ava? Your dad will not give you one penny, I bet. He's so proud of you and your brothers. He thinks you'll be a partner over there at Palisades. This will be a knife in him if you quit everything. You prepared for that?" Ava gulped that she was. She had savings to cover her for a year or two.

"I have other good contacts, Uncle Gerry. I can raise money. I can make deals with agencies. I have a plan but I am going to have to put it out there. Do you think he'll fight me on this?" Uncle Gerry said he loved her audacity to aim for her father's money and turf.

"You can try. But I don't think he'll go for it. But I'll support you no matter what. You're gonna lose some friends and family over this, but you got me and Auntie with you. Count on that. You're working on our issues now and we'll do anything to help. You know I don't have the resources your dad has but I sure am proud of you." He reached for her and gave her a shaky hug as

103

they stood up. Ava's chest warmed and her cheeks tingled with pleasure. I'm doing the right thing, she thought. Now just gotta figure out the timing for all this change, she mused as she escorted him out of the café to his car.

A week later, promotion offer still open and unresolved, Ava had to meet her boss for a client lunch at the restaurant in the plaza where many homeless congregated. LAPD chased most out before the lunch hour, but not all. She arrived at the restaurant's broad marble steps on time but her boss wasn't there. He had wanted to meet out front before joining the clients. She stood in the shade of the imported Italian olive trees spilling from giant terra cotta pots to wait. A text came in. *Running late.* After a few minutes standing, her foot started to throb. Cross-country races on rocky trails from fourth grade through college had left her with chronic plantar fasciitis and multiple knee injuries. She loved her heels and refused to give them up but she couldn't usually stand in them for too long. Ava moved to the bench in the plaza even though it was still extra hot from the Santa Ana winds.

She was lost in thought over the client's situation and the goals of the lunch meeting when The Talker appeared at the end of the bench. His hair was unkempt, his pants stained. He smelled like sweat. Ava turned slightly away from him, pretending not to see that anyone shared her seat. She looked down at the client notes on her phone. Of course, The Talker started right in.

"It is one gorgeous day, isn't it? Them cops busting our asses. It's getting pretty uppity downtown these days." Ava didn't respond. She acted like she didn't know he was talking to her.

"There've been people living on Skid Row for over a hundred years. There's history here. They can put in them Whole Foods and Starbucks but regular people gotta have a place to go."

Ava said nothing. Just faced out to her left, back toward him to make a clear statement that she was not interested in interacting. Despite her new interest, her upbringing was in full force and she deepened the posture. She turned her shoulders even more when a text vibrated her phone. Her foot was really throbbing so she didn't want to stand but she thought that she might have to. Where is he?

Be there soon. Just wait.

And then The Talker used his nickname for her.

"Oh, Heels, it's you. So nice to see you sitting and relaxing for a bit. You're always in a rush. You a lawyer? Oh come on, you can talk for a minute. Waiting to go in for a big lunch, right? Someone late? Well, you're just stuck talking to me." He chuckled at that. She turned her neck to glare at him but then quickly turned her back.

"OK, well I'll talk then. I know you hear me and you're not cold inside like so many of them that walk past here. You're a lawyer, right?"

"No, I'm in finance," she said reluctantly, softly. She moved her knees slightly toward the front of the bench.

"Oh, the big money. The real crooks! What do you do?" And he had a grin that showed white teeth that lit up his whole face. He has a great smile, she couldn't help observing. His brown eyes appeared clear.

"I work for a private equity company. We buy businesses; we get them money so they can grow. We have investors who put in money to help them improve and get bigger and then we sell them." She couldn't believe that she was explaining this to The Talker.

"But you're not a bank? Oh, you're a loan shark?! Ha, ha," he said excitedly.

Ava was taken aback. Offended. Her body tensed.

"Really, Heels, isn't that what it is if you think about it? How do you get those companies all that money? Who benefits in the end? Oh, no, no, no, I get it. You're like a real estate agent who's flipping houses? You just flip businesses. What's good about that for anyone but you, the real estate agent who makes the big bucks on the new, much higher price? A business flipper, that's what you are," The Talker said, definitively.

"Okay, hmmmm. I don't see it that way. But what about you?" She swung her knees to face forward, turned her head and looked in his eyes. There was a glinting fleck of hazel green in his left one. His eyes were almost two different colors. He definitely was not drunk. Just dirty, tired. Old for his age.

"I'm a veteran. U.S. Marine Corps. Semper Fi and all that. And look at me here. Problem is I'm also an alcoholic. Did my time, tours in Iraq and Afghanistan. Man, those crazy places ... some bad shit went down over there. You fancy-pants bankers in your skyscrapers have no idea the bad shit we all did in your name. With your tax money. But back here—kinda makes me miss the Marines. I could stay sober easier there with the discipline, the crazy stuff they made us do—exhausting. But then you get back here and there's too much thinking. Too much time. Can't keep my focus and stay in a job. Pay the rent. Gotta lot of demons in here, Heels." The Talker tapped his temple.

"Can't stay sober," he continued. "Can't get rid of the evil—you gotta compartmentalize it and I can't do that. I've tried. I'm swimmin' in the bad I did. I'm not a bad person but we did bad shit ... very bad shit." He looked at his shoes and shook his head. "Y'all lucky you don't know," he said softly, looking up, directly at her.

She was touched by his honesty. Wow, The Talker's a vet. It is so hard to come back. A text came in. *Just parked. Walking over.*

"I heard about what happened to your bag the other day," she said quietly. "I heard you telling your friend. I'm sorry. That's awful someone would just ignore you and leave the dog peeing like that."

"Don't you ignore me and all of us every day you walk in to work? How different are you than that lady? Really? Come on, Heels. Face facts."

"Can I contribute to you getting your bag clean?" She reached into her purse and pulled out three twenty-dollar bills. "Use this to wash your bag and your clothes again. And get a haircut. It will be easier to keep clean if your hair is shorter," she said with a future managing director inflection.

He looked at her. Hesitated. Then took the money and nodded. He mumbled thanks and looked down. Embarrassed. Ava realized he didn't want to beg. He was ashamed but also grateful. Slowly, she could see the humiliation envelop him and close him into a dark place. He hunched over and stopped talking. Ava looked away. She was sorry she had used a managerial tone with him. At that moment, Ava's boss walked up.

"Is this guy bothering you? Hey man, leave her alone. Go find another bench. In fact, why don't you just get yourself cleaned up and get a job. I have friends at the police department." He looked at Ava with concern.

"Everything's fine. Let's go in." She jumped up, wobbled briefly on the heels, grabbed his arm and bustled him up the steps to the gilt and glass front door, which gleamed in the midday sunshine.

"We need to talk before the clients come, remember," she said, taking charge, deflecting his attention from The Talker on the bench. "And you're late so our time is short." White roses in shiny blue ceramic pots lined the polished marble steps at the entrance. A rainbow of colors from the array of alcohol bottles on shelves facing a mirrored wall, fronted by a broad slate bar, were visible through the glass. As her boss opened the door, cool air-conditioned breeze pulled them into the bar and grill's sanctuary. The door swooshed closed. LA's grit was behind them.

Her boss began to relax as he called to the bartender.

"Belvedere and tonic with a twist." He turned to Ava, "Would you like a drink before they get here?" She shook her head and struggled to focus on the upcoming meeting. There was no going back. No question it was time. Time to change her focus to align with her passions. Time to do some good for downtown LA. Time to take action that might help The Talker. Time to face Dad.

That night, Ava called her father. She arranged to meet in his downtown flat at the top of the Ritz Carlton residences, where he stayed during the week to avoid the commute south to Orange County.

"So, what's this about? You were kind of mysterious on the phone," he asked, greeting her at the door with a formal cheek-brushing air kiss. "Great to see you, honey. You should come over when I'm here more often." His gravelly voice and luxuriant gray hair were most prominent, as he was uncharacteristically wearing casual clothes—khakis and a Links at Spanish Bay polo shirt. Usually his five thousand dollar tailored suits caught people's eye. He handed her a glass of wine and they sat on his leather couch facing the floor-to-ceiling windows exposing a view of the Hollywood sign and Beverly Hills.

"Dad, weren't you thinking about investing in some new ventures recently? Maybe even really starting to do some philanthropy, for a change?" She couldn't resist getting a little dig in. He was famous for making money, not for giving it away.

"Well, yes. So glad you are interested. I am thinking about joining the group who's going to buy the Dodgers. Wouldn't that be great to be part owner of the Dodgers? You know they've been having a lot of problems and we need to turn that around. A good group asked me to participate. A couple of guys from the club are involved. What do you think?"

"The Dodgers?" she asked. "You should do something worthwhile, meaningful with your money. You made it all in LA, you should help LA with it. I have a whole different proposal for you."

"The Dodgers is helping. Everyone in LA loves the Dodgers."

Although her parents had purposely chosen to raise their children in Orange County to avoid what they saw as the negatives of Beverly Hills affluence, her father was an LA boy to his core. A classic baby boomer raised in Torrance by a WWII veteran father who worked on the line assembling airplanes, Neal Callahan was a lifelong Dodgers fan. Owning the team would symbolize a life of accomplishment.

"Yeah, but really, what benefit do they provide besides expensive tickets, fights at the game, a few low-paying jobs and then the ball players? And that is like buying a horse for horse racing—they're all traded. There's no team loyalty really for the players anymore. It's all about money, Dad." This is it. Can't wait any longer. I've got to lay it out there or he's going to become a baseball team owner.

She had to present the whole plan to him. No ploys or deception. You had to play it straight with Neal Callahan or you would get skewered. She had learned that lesson early on and she and her brothers had adopted similar traits. It might have been a painful upbringing at times, but she attributed her success in the male dominated, no excuses financial industry to being raised in a culture that demanded excellence.

"I'm thinking about something really different, Dad. Listen. This could be a great legacy for the family." She hesitated, but only slightly. Then went for it at her energizer bunny pace.

"How about you take some of your extra money and start a foundation; you decide the amount, but it can't be too small. Serious foundation money. I'll run it. And the foundation focuses on veterans, including homeless ones, and provides a selection of the services they need to get back on their feet. Think about it—they have good values and discipline and work ethic in their background from military training."

Her dad sat quietly. He did not interrupt. He appeared to listen intently. She didn't stop or give him any opportunity to interject.

"But they got into problems along the way, mental health, alcoholism, debts, PTSD, family stuff. Some of them even have become homeless. Too many. So why not give them some counseling, small loans with a planned, realistic payback system? Support groups, and services like washing machines, showers and haircuts and access to clothes for job interviews. And then jobs...what if we eventually could provide some jobs like street sweeping or security guard work? These guys know the streets so let's get them to help clean it up themselves. And classes like how to manage your money, get bank accounts started, build emergency funds." Ava barely took a breath so she could get the pitch out quickly, before he stopped listening.

"And let's get other veterans to help the homeless ones. It could be good for everyone. Dad, you know Uncle Gerry has always struggled since Vietnam. I think he would love this idea. I'm sure he knows guys who were homeless at some point. And look at Patrick. Thank god he's doing great. But you know, it hasn't always been easy. Iraq was bad. He won't admit it to you. But Iraq was ugly." Her father did not move. His face impassive.

"I'm not thinking a shelter or food or housing. A lot of churches and other groups provide that—but all the wraparound services to support people finding a place to live or a steady job. We'd coordinate with the organizations that do exist and maybe help spawn new ones. There are too many homeless in this city, in this country. This is the richest place on earth—it's ridiculous we have so many homeless. And no one seems to care. There's no local or national will to work on the problem. It's just not right."

Ava paused. Finally taking a breath. Her father's face was closed, hard to read. She had to tell him about the promotion and that she wanted to make a change now. He wasn't going to like it. He dreamed of her being the first woman partner at Palisades Pacific.

"I don't want to complain or be the problem anymore, Dad. I've been working on a business plan and financials for a while. This isn't just some crazy idea. I have a plan. This could be great for the family too. I'm sure Patrick and Uncle Gerry would agree to be advisors and links to the veterans' networks and the VA." Her father raised his eyebrow at his son and brother being offered up to assist with her quest. He cleared his throat.

"So, Dad, I got offered a managing director position, unanimously agreed to by the partners. I think I could make partner in two years—that's basically what I was promised. I'm thrilled for the amazing opportunity. But you know what my boss said to me when he made the offer: 'You have to be prepared to be an asshole in this position'." She sighed.

"I'm tired of being on the wrong side. Some of our deals have shut down whole businesses, saddled companies with so much debt that the original had to close. I know my work has lost some people jobs. I'm not going to do it anymore. I'm not going to take the promotion. I'm going to quit." She stopped and looked straight in his Irish blue eyes. It was a challenging stare.

Neal Callahan cleared his throat, buying himself a little time for a response. His voice was stern. His eyes had grown dark, their usual confident sparkle dimmed. Deep creases appeared above his eyebrows.

"What? What are you talking about?" he demanded. "After six years there, you now decide maybe it's a little hard? Come on. You've had a stunning rise in your career. Ava Callahan is going places. Everyone says so. Some of the guys downtown are talking about you for the development group. Some even say you should run for city council in five years. Of course you're on the partner track. First women partner of Palisades Pacific Capital. That is no small deal. You can do your philanthropy thing on the side. That has nothing to do with your job. Take the promotion. Maybe I'll think about giving some to that Union Rescue Mission downtown. They've been around forever. They know what they're doing. But for God's sake, Ava, take the job. You give this up, it doesn't come around again. You know that."

And he sat back in the sofa a bit flagged from the shock. He pushed his right hand down into the soft leather and leaned in, as if exhausted from the effort, his disappointment apparent.

"You're not one of those who wear your privilege like a war wound on your sleeve, like some guilt inducing badge, are you? That's so ridiculous. I work damn hard for my money. And you and your brothers do too. No one just handed all this to us." He swept his arms toward the glamorous apartment and the sprawling view framed with snow capped mountains. His glare darkened to a scowl.

"You're throwing your life and career down the drain if you go work for the Salvation Army or United Way or whatever. Smart people don't go into those jobs." His face turned red. He was furious. The betrayal was shocking.

"Yes, you're right, Dad," Ava said, pains piercing her stomach. "The promotion is great. But I want to do direct service. I've never done it. Not sure how, but I can figure it out. I want to transfer my business and organizational and financial skills to do some good." She was firm. She held her head steady, refusing to shake in fear like she and her brothers usually did in confrontations with Dad. He was formidable and you did what he insisted. But I'm thirty now. I'm not a baby anymore. It's my life. I've got to grab it or he'll control it to his grave. A new mantra. Her father jumped in before she could go on.

"Ava, then, if you are restless, why don't you come work with your brother and me. Lots of hands-on operations. It is an exciting time. Downtown is hot right now. We're developing lofts, condos. They're talking about a pro football team and a stadium. Nathan and I could really use you right now. That's our family legacy, Ava. Don't kid yourself. We are developers. Pure and simple." He stood up, pacing before the window, then turning to face her with a fierce stare.

"Are you having some early mid-life crisis? Go get a boyfriend and get married finally. Maybe have a baby? Or make the family business your baby. We could use you because you know I won't be around forever. But don't throw away all your training, your whole profession because you feel bad for some homeless guy you saw walking to work."

Fortunately, Ava had mentally and emotionally prepared for his contempt. She snapped back, undaunted.

"Dad, you want to retire in a few years and play more golf. Fine. You've got Nathan to run the business. That's great. He's doing well and you don't need me. But let's seriously contribute positively to LA. Let's start a foundation and do this. Let's affect an intractable problem, not just make more housing for rich people. The Dodgers will be just fine without us. Patrick would support the idea. Even Nathan probably would if he knew it would help clean up the streets around the lofts he's developing near Skid Row," she added sarcastically. "But you should know, Dad, whatever you decide, I'm quitting. I'm sorry to disappoint you, but I'm not taking the promotion." She stood up to leave. Even this was a defiant moment. Her father always dictated when the conversation ended.

"I'll email you the details of my proposal. Please read it. I've been putting this together for a long time. I didn't just come up with it yesterday." Ava gave her father a quick kiss on the cheek as he rose to walk her to the door. He barely nodded a farewell, glaring at her with an icy silence. He refused to say goodbye.

As she rode down the elevator, she took deep cleansing breaths to clear her mind and calm her stomach. She had done it. Gone for it with her father who was the hardest obstacle to face. She had to follow through now, really quit and pursue the plan. He might not like the specifics but people in her family did what they said they'd do. No excuses, ever. Her brother Nathan had agreed to sign on early and run the real estate development firm when their father retired. Patrick had committed to military service and did all the years, all the moves and deployments. She had gone into investment banking and private equity as expected. But now, Ava would be a family rebel. They hadn't had one of those yet. Not sure how Dad would handle it.

She felt more resolute than ever. I can't brake now, she coached herself. She'd quit, see if she could convince her father to front the money, and if not, she'd approach other sources. She was well connected from both her upbringing and her work. She

FERTILE SOIL: STORIES OF THE CALIFORNIA DREAM

had significant savings to carry her through project development time. But she certainly was not getting married and having babies just now. So typical of him to pull out the traditional, sexist card when it served him and knew it would stab her.

A week later, Ava shocked her colleagues, friends and family by resigning from Palisades Pacific. She sent her business plan and financial models to her father, but also sent the planning documents to a slew of high wealth families focused on Los Angeles' history and growth. She decided to pressure Dad by simulating competition, putting her proposal out in the marketplace. An aggressive businessman, Neal Callahan paid attention to the strategy when he heard from his associates at the Jonathan Club that his daughter was soliciting donations to start a foundation focused on cleaning up downtown and helping veterans.

"Did you know anything about this, Neal?" they asked from their leather chairs as they twirled their tumblers of Macallan. Angry, but silently impressed, he realized how much she had learned from him and her years at Palisades Pacific.

"Oh, my goddamned do-gooder daughter," he growled back. "Just ignore her. She's got some crazy idea. Those goddamned Jesuit schools. I think that's what led her astray. I can't believe all the money I paid for her to throw away a great career at Palisades. She better come to her senses soon. I'm not bailing her out when she runs out of savings." And the Jonathan Club men nodded, shook their heads, flapped their wrists and sipped their scotch, commiserating over the headaches of wayward adult children.

Ava finished up at Palisades Pacific but started immediately implementing her plan, establishing a 501(c)3 to oversee the Downtown LA Veterans' and Homeless Support Center. She sought legal counsel, consulted with accountants and walked through buildings. She put out feelers to likely funders, met people for lunches, and drove up Mulholland to the homes of LA's entertainment and real estate industries' most successful.

Throughout her last week and a half of garage to office walks,

114

Ava saw The Talker a few mornings on the library steps. The times he was absent she worried. The Internet and office gossip was full of the latest LAPD efforts to clear the encampments in the streets of Downtown and Skid Row. They were cleaning up for neighborhood gentrification. For the new lofts everyone was excited about.

One morning, The Talker was at his hangout with a coffee in his hand and made one of his typical comments to her.

"Hey Heels, you're lookin' extra good today. You make this day even sunnier with those new shoes." She turned and winked at him and he just stared back at her, blankly. She wondered if he remembered their conversation on the bench.

"Ah, she's smiling today. Must be good things happenin'. Go get 'em, Heels!" She handed him a ten-dollar bill discreetly so the other guys wouldn't see. At the end of her last week at Palisades Pacific, The Talker was at his station. In the masculine manner of greeting, she gave him a slight heads up nod of acknowledgement as she walked past, more slowly now. He responded, rather softly, sadly,

"Go make the big money up there, Heels," and she was sure he remembered their talk in the plaza.

Once she finished her finance job, Ava's routes changed. She gave notice on her Hollywood Hills bungalow in the rose bush lined street inhabited with thirtysomethings planning to have babies. She rented a flat in downtown above the homeless-infested streets. Not going to waste time commuting anymore, she told herself. But even as she became a downtown resident, somehow her new routes never intersected with The Talker. The times she passed the library, his post was vacant.

Ava called her father to ask if he'd made a decision. She repeated her debate points for why the family fortune should serve LA's neediest.

"Dad, you have always been a business leader," she said. "Be a leader here. Your success can benefit others and live on for generations. Let's honor those in our family who have served. Let's find a job and a home for every single veteran in Los Angeles. You can get behind that goal, right?"

No, he told her, he would not start a foundation or give her money to ruin her career. He'd been quite clear all along what he expected his children to do with his resources.

"You're on your own, kid. I'm really disappointed you turned down the promotion and quit Palisades. Huge mistake, huge mistake... You know." he went on, "I'm embarrassed even. Please stop asking people I know for money for this cockamamie idea. It's ridiculous. What the heck are you going to do to help the lazy bastards on the streets? Really, Ava? Be realistic." She pushed the button on her phone and held it down to shut the whole thing off. No more calls or texts or emails tonight. How could he be so bullheaded, so unfeeling?

Despite his disapproval, she plowed ahead. She recognized, that maybe finally, at thirty, she had moved past her need for Daddy's acceptance at every juncture. She was finally her own woman. Frightening, but somehow freeing as well. She was mono-focused on this new obsession. But it isolated her. No one invited her to family events anymore. Her parents never called.

Ava continued to venture up Mulholland Drive, out to the canyons of Malibu and along the cliffs of Pacific Palisades, soliciting donations, event sponsors, and advisory board members. In her direct style, Ava made it clear to LA's elite that donating to the Veterans' and Homeless Support Center was a far superior cause to putting another Maserati in the garage or naming a building at their children's tony private school.

"Everyone complains about the homeless downtown. How you can't go to the parks anymore. How you can't walk without being panhandled. Don't you want to do something about it? Do you think it's right that a veteran who served his country honorably now lives on the streets? I don't and I know you don't either.

You can help us solve that problem with your contribution."
And she would provide her potential donors with statistics and
charts, pictures and testimonials. Many would nod vigorously
during her presentation, but then just offer her a limp handshake
or quick air kiss afterward.

"Dear, it's so nice you're doing this," she heard repeatedly.
"But we've already allocated all our giving this year. Good luck,
hon." She felt like she was ten again, being patted on the head by
the carpool mom after horseback riding shows or track meets.
But then, several surprised her by writing big checks. Most
donors told her they needed to remain anonymous due to her
father's vocal opposition to the project. One donor said he loved
downtown, had grown up in Koreatown and understood that a
different future had to be carved into the area.

"Things won't get better on hope or a prayer," he told her,
smiling. His accountant transferred five hundred thousand
dollars to the Veterans' Center account the next day. The Center's
account grew slowly but steadily. She put forming a foundation
to fully fund its activities on hold. One step at a time.

After months of searching for space on the border between
downtown and Skid Row where many homeless clustered, Ava
signed a lease for the bottom floor of an empty building across
from the plaza housing the trendy restaurant fronted by olive
trees and white roses. Wow, how things change, she thought as
she left the signing feeling optimistic. I haven't eaten there in
over ten months. And funny, I don't miss the place.

She set to work on the tenant improvements, putting in big
washers and dryers, bathrooms, two showers, a changing room,
a donated clothes closet, private and group counseling areas. She
made the space light and airy with calming mauves and grays
for the walls and carpets. And plants. Bright flowering dwarf
trees in pots, rock gardens with bonsai. Photographs of California scenery on the walls. She furnished with office style desks
and hardwood meeting tables. The place looked like a simple but

professional corporate office.

And she contracted, cajoled, and negotiated for services. Ava established AA meetings on Mondays and Fridays, scheduled a Veterans Administration representative on Wednesdays and a VA Hospital mental health specialist to offer counseling Tuesdays and Thursdays. Two banker friends agreed to send staff to present basic financial planning classes. Uncle Gerry and his wife solicited clothing donations to start a professional clothes closet. They were so proud, even if her parents were having a hard time, Uncle Gerry told her. She convinced the owner of Bunker Hill Barbers to send one of his guys over for four hours every other Monday to offer free haircuts. In return, she promised to try to put the word out that the Bunker Hill barbershop's front door was not a place to panhandle.

Ava hired an office manager, social worker, veterans' advocate and a community organizer. Her team coordinated with local soup kitchens, shelters and residence hotels. They managed the onsite services and recruited volunteers to answer phones, clean clothing donations, keep the center tidy and welcoming. The community organizer publicized the new Veteran's and Homeless Center on the city's streets and in the shelters. As the homeless and veterans dropped in once the center was open, the team offered volunteer and paid positions to some clients.

No boyfriend, not much family, dwindling supply of friends, Ava was pretty much on her own. Only Uncle Gerry seemed to think Ava was still sane. It was a lonely endeavor. But the new fascination consumed her. She stopped socializing. She had grown frustrated at the frivolity of gossip over destination weddings, luxury cars, and lavish home redecorating among her sorority sisters and childhood friends. It's so meaningless, she'd think as she'd roll her eyes at their conversations. Most of them thought Ava had become so self-righteous it was annoying to include her in brunches and happy hours. So obsessed, they complained. She won't talk about anything else besides those homeless people in downtown. It's depressing, they nodded to each other, munching on yet another kale cucumber salad. The invitations waned.

Ava decided she'd save her evenings and weekends for fund-raising visits. Cynical pragmatism guided her not to completely alienate her old friends. She didn't really want to hang out with any of those people anymore, but she didn't hesitate to pressure them, and their wealthy parents, into selecting her charity for their guilt money. She had to keep the network growing. Money was always an issue for the center. Ava had even started writing grants, which she thought were a waste of time because the dollars weren't usually what she needed and the restrictions were onerous. But she looked for funds in every pocketbook she could find. Propelled by a cause larger than herself, by an intensity and drive that she had only sampled before, Ava Callahan became a crusader.

Her father avoided her. She called repeatedly throughout the first year to ask him to reconsider his position. But he wouldn't answer, never returned her calls and didn't show up at family events when she was there. Ava was stung. Incensed. Finally, getting low on funds and concerned about making her payroll, she submerged her pride and dropped in without an appointment at his sleek, downtown high-rise office. He wasn't there but at his owner's box at the Dodgers' game. She drove up the 110 past Chinatown to Solano Canyon to Dodger Stadium, bought a ticket and talked her way past security to his suite. He was shocked but a bit impressed, it appeared, at her persistence. She told him about the center's opening, its progress and fundraising. She told him about the services offered and her long-term goals. She admitted the center was getting desperate for funds if it was to continue at its current level of service. He pretended not to listen.

"I'm watching the game, can't you see? Why don't you make an appointment and come to the office?" But she didn't stop and could see he actually was listening. Despite their estrangement, they knew each other well. They had maintained a close, tough-love-rimmed-with-mutual-respect relationship for over thirty years. Seeing him so distracted by the pomp of being a baseball team owner made her sad. What a waste, she thought. When she had finished forcing him to listen to her update, she leaned over and kissed him softly on the cheek.

"Dad, I hope you will reconsider my request. It still stands. I'm not giving up. You taught me that, you know, Daddy." She continued softly, discreetly amid the bustle of wealthy LA businessmen cheering on their team with raised beers and baby back ribs.

"You can start a family foundation and still be a Dodger's owner. Please come by the center and let me show you what we're doing." She put her business card in his hand, turned her back on the baseball diamond below and strode out.

Eighteen months after opening, the Downtown LA Veterans' and Homeless Support Center had recruited a group of regular clientele. They were slowly establishing themselves as part of a safety net for veterans and others without housing. AA groups were popular—free coffee and cookies at every session contributed to that. The VA representatives led sessions on housing options, managing medications, reapplying for honorable discharges so veterans' benefits could be distributed, and gaining access to PTSD treatment programs. A few, but growing, number of regulars came in for mental health services. It wasn't easy. Ava marveled at how much need there was. How much tragedy and pain on the streets. How much fear and distrust existed on both sides of her front door. She spent endless nights soliciting wealthy donors or filling out foundation and government paperwork. But clients improving, wealthy Angelenos contributing, and colleagues collaborating to resolve a never-ending list of problems energized her. She loved the work. It fit her obsessive personality, her laser focused approach to diagnosing and troubleshooting difficult issues. Ava's goal was to offer significant data on the center's effectiveness and impact on neighborhood alcoholism, joblessness, homelessness and improved financial security within three years. She loved devoting herself to what she considered making a positive contribution to her hometown.

One morning, Ava, working as the daily advocate for drop-ins, was meeting with a homeless veteran whose VA benefits had suddenly terminated. He didn't understand why. As they spoke she looked out the window and saw The Talker walk by. She quickly turned to the client and asked, "See that guy out there? Do you know him?"

"Yeah, Mouth. Yeah, I know him. I don't know him real good, but he's a good guy. They call him Mouth cuz he's got a big mouth. He talks a lot."

"Has he heard about this place, do you think? Why wouldn't he come in?"

"Yeah, he says he heard about it. The word is getting out on the street about this place. Everyone kinda wonders where it came from. Kinda out of the blue. I mean the churches are always around, Union Rescue, Mission Rescue, there's Chrysallis...the usual places but this one's different. Us vets get talkin'. It's kinda nice someone focused on us. I mean everyone can use a little support but it's cool someone gets our stuff, our issues. You know."

"What about Mouth? He's a vet too, right?"

"Yeah," the client said. "He heard about it but says he's not sure about comin' in. He thinks it's pretty cool. But he isn't sure, not sure who to trust. Says he might come in sometime and check it out. But might wait and see how it goes. Probably some crazy liberal, do-gooder feeling sorry for us and might not last. He says, the vets, whoever focused on them before? Everybody likes it when we win a war but you don't really win wars anymore so Americans don't really know what to do with us after they've used us up. That's the kind of thing Mouth says. He gets kinda cynical."

"Can you give him a message for me? " Ava asked him. "Tell him that Heels invited him to come in and check it out." She gulped as she said this, stumbling over the words. She shook her head, embarrassed at misspeaking, cleared her throat, trying to swallow away the surprising emotional lump in her throat.

The homeless vet looked at her with a skeptical raised eyebrow. "Huh?"

"He'll understand," Ava said, clearing her throat. Her voice unobstructed now she continued. "Just tell him, please. It's important. Just tell him, Heels says to come in some sunny day. Can you remember that?"

"Yeah sure," he said. "Heels says come in on some sunny day. Okay, whatever. I'll tell him. I'll get him to come in." She nodded, smiled, and they returned to his VA files.

Weeks later, Ava opened *The LA Times* on her laptop to read that the Dodgers' owners group had collapsed amid scandal and mismanagement. The wife in the couple among five parties cooperating to own the team was caught having an affair with a star first baseman. She had loaned him money, which he still owed, and now she wanted it back. Engrossed, Ava read that apparently this same woman had talked the owner's group into extending the first baseman a contract at a greatly increased rate when he became a free agent. The ballplayer had ditched her for the hot star of a new Reality TV drag racing show and the owner's wife was livid. The foolish couple had outed themselves via Twitter accusations and the Dodgers were again engrossed in a salacious Internet-enhanced scandal. Good Lord, this team is its own reality show, Ava thought. How ridiculous. And my dad is involved in this mess? It's embarrassing. And what about his money?

She called his office but no one answered. Not even his super-efficient secretary on the private line. She closed up her computer, told the office manager she'd be out for a bit and walked several blocks from the Veteran's Center to his building. She took the express elevator up to the 63rd floor. The secretary, who had known her since she was a little girl, just grimaced, raised an eyebrow and waved her in. Her brothers were already there.

Nathan, the downtown developer, nodded at her, coldly. Patrick, the retired Army Officer and Iraq War Veteran greeted her with a warm hug. Her father seemed touched to see her and gave her a polite kiss.

Dad told them that the Dodgers' ownership was a huge mess with multiple lawsuits now involved. Fortunately, and this part was not yet in the papers, an out of town tech billionaire had reached out to the group and was going to buy the team himself. No partners, no outside investors. They would be made whole. But all parties would probably lose some of their original investment in legal fees. Ava's father explained that he was relieved it appeared he'd be able to get his cash out but he was disenchanted with LA's elite, with group efforts. No more of that partnership stuff, he told them.

"It's gotta be family projects and investments. I can't trust anyone else. What a goddamned mess," he blustered. He sent them out and called in his secretary.

Ava met with her brothers in the foyer. They agreed to support Dad and not talk to any reporters or friends about the Dodgers' ownership collapse until it was resolved. It would quiet down. Thank goodness someone was buying out the group, they agreed.

"You've gotten some nice press, lately. It's great you are focusing on veterans." Patrick smiled at her.

"Yeah. Thanks. Why don't you come by so I can show you what we actually do? I'm sure you hear rumors among Mom and Dad's friends. But come see for yourselves." She pushed business cards into their hands and quickly strode toward the elevator door.

Less than ten days later, Ava saw her mother's name pop up on her iPhone. She never calls me. What's this about?

"Your father's in the hospital. Come over to UCLA Medical Center right away. They think he's had a stroke." Her mother was out of breath.

"What? Oh my God. Mom? Is he OK?"

"Just come to the hospital, please. Come now. He needs you,

Ava."

Ava raced to the parking garage and drove as quickly as possible over to Westwood. She navigated the maze of hospital wings and corridors to find her father pale and unresponsive in a metal bed in a private room. Her mother, looking uncharacteristically haggard, sat by his side holding his limp hand.

"Your brothers are on their way," she told Ava, and began to cry.

"He said he had a headache and went to bed early, then woke up saying it had gotten worse, went to get some Advil and collapsed on the bathroom floor. It was awful, Ava. I had to call 911. He got here in the ambulance." Her mother couldn't answer any more questions and just cried. Ava tracked down the doctor who explained her dad had suffered a major stroke. There were more tests to perform and there could be permanent damage.

Neal Callahan had always been the model of health and vigor. He personified strength. He worked long hours but always played golf and tennis hard too. He was fit and slim, didn't over indulge in junk food or alcohol. He was very disciplined. Sometimes that was painful to live with as a child but he certainly was a force that no one expected to diminish. Ava decided at that moment, waiting for her brothers, watching her mother cry helplessly, listening to the doctor give a less than positive prognosis, that right now, it was just about her dad. She had to help him get better. Neal's pale, shrunken form pushed aside her bitterness at his dismissal of her work, her altered obsessions. Today's priority and new preoccupation was Dad's recovery. That's what you do for family. Any internal argument reminding her that he'd abandoned her when she asked for help was squelched by the sight of him helpless in a white gown surrounded by beeping machines, needles and tubes puncturing his extremities.

Ava honored that promise to herself, and to her mother. She visited Dad daily, helping him to take small steps, eat soupy portions of hospital food, read magazines and newspapers for longer than a few minutes in one sitting.

At the time of Dad's stroke, the Veterans' Center had been operating for almost two years and she had strong staff members in place. They filled in as needed but she couldn't spend as much time fundraising. She worried constantly and worked to juggle both commitments, flashing through her cell phone and computer while Dad rested. She had to let two good staff members go when the dwindling budget couldn't support them. She developed an ulcer but ignored it most of the time. Her brothers showed up occasionally. Mom seemed to need to do even more shopping after the stroke. In his hospital room, most of the time, it was just Dad and Ava working on his stamina, moving limbs and practicing basics like walking, reading aloud, writing, making conversation. His doctor gave some advice on the ulcer and told her to rest. She ignored that too.

Dad was going to recover but he'd never be quite the same. His stature had shortened and he walked with a slight limp and curve over to the right side. His face muscles below his nose and ear on the right drooped, making talking a chore. The physical therapists said all these muscles could improve with exercises and discipline, but he would always have a droop on one side of his face. Formerly elegant, straight-backed, tanned and handsome, Neal Callahan would never command attention in quite the same way. Shrunken, pale face sinking down to flaccid jowls, the developer would no longer intimidate just by walking into a room. After a month, Ava's Dad was released to rehab on his own and she returned to a regular work schedule, still spending weekends in Orange County encouraging him to walk the trails behind the palatial family home.

One day, Neal Callahan showed up at the Veterans' Center door. Ava was shocked to see him but pleased. He explained he had made her mother drive over to see what she was up to. He was so bored at home. They wouldn't let him go back to work yet and he could only go to the driving range twice a week. Her mother had dropped him off and gone shopping over at the mall.

Of course, Ava muttered to herself. Typical. But delighted at Dad's interest, she beamed and gave him a big hug.

Ava took her father's arm and walked him slowly throughout the facility, explaining the services offered at each station, introducing him to the staff. He met several homeless clients and veterans along the way. He met the VA officer, now coming three days a week due to the demand, and a psychologist from the VA Hospital. He admired the clothes closet and counseling rooms, the cleanliness and professional air of the place. He was surprised to learn his brother Gerry was a clothes closet organizer and had been involved since the center's opening more than two years before.

As Ava and her father toured the facility, the front door swung wide and The Talker barreled in. She was so surprised and delighted to see him she dropped her father's arm and approached him quickly. Awkwardly, she hesitated, stopping herself from giving him a hug, and put out her hand.

"How are you? I have been hoping you'd come in. Are you ok?" He too was surprised, then flashed a skeptical grin and started talking while shaking her hand.

"Well, I'll be damned. Heels! It is you! They told me you worked here but I didn't believe it. I've come by a few times looking for you but you're never here. I figured that guy who told me to come over was drunk and confused. What the hell you doin' here? You really work here? You didn't give up that big money job at the top of them skyscrapers, did you? Now why would you go and do a fool thing like that?"

She was grinning broadly but could not get in a word. The Talker just kept on. She could feel her father staring, but also nodding in agreement at the question about leaving her old job.

"Now who is this guy? Oh, my. He's gotta be your father. You look just like him. And look at those shoes. Good Italian leather. Is that what that is, sir? I can tell you are Heels' father. She always has elegant shoes. I really admire a good pair of shoes.

Ever since losing mine in the mountains of Afghanistan shoes are kinda a mania of mine. You a veteran too, sir? Is that why Heels is here working at this place? 'Cause you're a veteran? Much appreciated. Your service, that is, Sir. I'm a vet too." He grabbed Neal's and shook it hard, almost pulling him over. He never stopped talking.

"Look, this center is doing some good things in downtown. You know, people get talking and I hear stuff. I got some friends that are doin' better, you know, tryin' not to drink. I got a couple friends got their VA benefits restored. A few I know are in residence hotels now, not out at night with me. Them AA groups here are pretty good. I might have to try one myself. I dunno though. Might be kinda extreme for me. I'm kinda an independent operator, you know what I mean?" The Talker finally took a breath. Ava cut in quickly, but tenderly.

"Yes, this is my father, Neal Callahan. No, he's not a veteran. He's recovering from a stroke. That's where I've been recently. With him. But my brother and uncle are veterans. Yes, that's one reason I'm here. I'm..." as she moved to introduce herself and shake his hand formally, she realized she had to ask his name, she couldn't call him The Talker. Just at that moment, he cut her off again as he noticed a friend at the desk nearby with the VA representative.

"Hey, Joe, what'chya doin' here? Good to see ya, man. They gonna help ya with those benefits for your kids you were tellin' me about? That's good, man. Look I used to see this lady going to work at my spot over on 5th and Grand. Kinda a small world on the streets, you know. She always made my day a little brighter." He looked at his feet, shuffled back and forth slightly, then raised his forehead a bit and peered out under floppy bangs. He pushed his hair back with a stained hand.

His friend looked up, gave him the nod of respectful recognition and said, "Mouth, you know, she don't just work here. She started the whole place. She raises the money and gets all these guys to come in to help us. If it wasn't for this lady, this center wouldn't be here. My kids wouldn't be gettin' them benefits I'm supposed to get."

The Talker turned abruptly, folded his arms in front of his chest, leaned back and to the right, forming his body into a curve of questioning. He took a long look at Ava. He didn't say anything at first, uncharacteristically quiet.

"Damn. You don't say. Well, I'll be damned," he said. "Good for you, Heels. You did some good shit. Throw down that corporate raider crap you used to do. Good for you, man. Well, well, Heels. You are making my day even sunnier, that is for sure." And he finally stopped talking and just stood and stared at her.

Ava couldn't suppress a laugh. She held out her hand.

"My name is Ava Callahan. I'm so pleased to really meet you. And this is my father, Neal. What's your name?" They shook hands again, different this time.

"Lance Corporal Oscar Villata," he said while shaking vigorously. "Very pleased to make your acquaintance, Miss Ava. Sir," he nodded at Ava's father. Looking over at Neal Callahan leaning against a desk he added, "You gotta be one proud father. I think you raised her right. Damn, don't you think? Yes sir. You sure did."

"Nice to meet you, Lance Corporal Villata," her father said with a slight head bow. He cleared his throat and took a step forward. "Ava, I have to go. I see your mother double parked out front." He walked slowly toward the glass door facing the street, a tilt to the right in his step. As he pushed the metal safety bar to open the door, he turned back to face Ava and The Talker. She noticed him strain to stretch his damaged height, as if he wanted to reach back to his former, imperial presence.

"Call me tonight, Ava. We have something we need to discuss." He cleared his throat again, bracing the door handle to stand as straight as possible. "Corporal Villata, I look forward to seeing you in here taking advantage of some of the center's services when I come back in for my next visit. I hear they have good cookies at the AA meetings. You ought to come by and check it out." He dipped his head to each, then turned to exit onto the hot sidewalk, bordering the bustling street and the freeway onramp jammed with cars aiming for the 110.

Suburban Epidemic

I'm only going once. I can't believe he talked me into this. That charm. Those goddamned straight white teeth in that gorgeous face. I fell for it—those eyes. Oh God, I hate hospitals. Even these clinics make me feel dizzy, sick to my stomach. Look at the damn chairs. They look so uncomfortable. Uggghh, I feel nauseous. Taupe carpet, really? Even the wall is light purple, good God. Is that supposed to make us feel calm? Like when you get on those Virgin flights with the purple glow. Everyone is still nervous, still knows planes are psycho tubes. Same here. Not one person looks happy about lavender décor. We all fucking have cancer. Soft lighting is just not going to change that. To be fair, being a hospital decorator would really suck. Oh God, why'd I say yes? I hate this shit. I'm the most unkumbayaish person I know. This is gonna be so depressing. I don't want to listen to other people's horror stories? I'm already in one. I don't even want to hear my own.

"AMY. COME ON IN. I am so glad you made it. Welcome to Thursday Support Group. This is Amy, everyone." Dr. Chaudhary gave her his dazzling white smile. She wanted to fall into those dark eyes luring her in, as if they were cauldrons of liquidy chocolate ganache, that stuff they put inside lava cake. Get a grip she told herself. She shook her head to loosen the inappropriate thoughts. Dr. Chaudhary was impossibly handsome. When she met the oncologist at her diagnosis visit, she felt as if his good looks were some sort of twisted hospital joke. Isn't this cruel to us hapless patients? Shouldn't a doctor just be round and comforting, with glasses and a floppy, oversized white coat and comfortable shoes?

Dr. Chaudhary, instead, looked like he had stepped off the pages of one of the good waiting room magazines, right out of a shimmering Longines or Dolce and Gabbana ad. His angular jaw, the smoothness of his forehead, his long cool fingers personified unaffected elegance. The doctor's uniform coat fit him splendidly and his expensive Berlutis revealed a fashion sense unexpected in a physician. Captivating. To make matters more complicated, Dr. Chaudhary was magnanimous. A cancer doctor filled with grace. He was the only reason she'd showed up for this group crap.

Calm and patient, he spoke with a delicate spicing of an Indian English lilt. Just a slight rounding trill peppered his vocabulary. Amy found it romantic in a nineteenth-century British novel sort of way. Combined with that rare ability to focus with such intensity that the recipient feels she is his only interest, his only patient, the doctor's speech and manner were irresistible. Handsome, charming, smart and charismatic. Where was this guy when I was in college? If I didn't have cancer, wasn't going to lose all my hair and curves, I'd be tempted to run off with him. He must have figured out I wouldn't go to a support group unless he was the facilitator. Those eyes are a waste. Made for love not poison. Amy tossed her head again to dislodge the thoughts. Didn't seem to be working very well.

Dr. Chaudhary gazed intently at a group member as he asked

her to talk about her experience. A young mother raising a five-year-old, having to hold down two jobs to pay for all the treatments. She was exhaustedly telling her story but then flashing a smile at Dr. Chaudhary between anecdotes. Oh my God, this guy is good Amy thought. He makes her feel the same way I do. She thinks she's the only one in his eyes. The other docs must see this guy as a player, probably hate the way their female patients come in drooling, looking over their shoulders for a Dr. Chaudhary sighting.

Amy folded her arms tightly around her torso and scowled. Dr. Chaudhary's prowess at focused patient care sucked her deeper into her anger. She was livid. Furious at cancer, at the doctor who told her she had it, at how he seemed to value all his patients, not just her. At her family for running on as if nothing had changed, at everyone at work for not being sick. At her life. At the unfairness of it all.

"Amy?...Amy?"

Her turn. He had publicly given her the option to tell her story now or next meeting. She didn't want to wait. If she was going to give this group therapy a serious effort then she better jump in, even if she really just felt like crawling under the plastic folding table in the corner. Tom had told her to try to curb her cynicism and give it a chance. Couldn't hurt, he'd said in that maddeningly practical way as she went out the door. Sent me off to sick people bonding time. Really? Thinks he knows so much from work. He's fucking clueless. Bet he wouldn't go to support group. Or maybe he'd be into it. Gotta attack this with every single tool available he'd say. Bullshit—talking to people I don't even know isn't going to make it disappear.

"Well, Dr. Chaudhary told me I have lung cancer," Amy said. "So that's why I'm here." Blunt. No candy coating. She sounded bitter and rude but she couldn't control it. She was mad. Didn't want to be there. All fourteen sad eyes squinted, glaring at her.

"Now see," she said. "I know what you're thinking. The extra big

133

problem with lung cancer, besides that it can kill you pretty damn quick, is that everyone thinks it's your fault. It's weird 'cause when people hear the type they blame you. You must have caused this cancer." She paused. There was, indeed, a guilty silence.

"See," she continued. "Aren't I right? Isn't that what you're thinking? Oh, she shouldn't have smoked. It's all her fault. But no. I exercise, eat healthy. I don't smoke. Never have. I did everything you're supposed to. And I got it anyway. Genetic? Maybe. Who knows? No known family history. It's so unfair," she sighed. "But I'm going to get through it. People survive cancer now these days, right?" She tossed her head and swung a hand, offhandedly, as if it were all a slight annoyance.

She stopped, suddenly realizing she didn't know anything about these people. Her blustering and headstrong charging forward without thinking wouldn't just get her into trouble here. She realized she'd probably offended someone who was suffering.

"That's it. I don't have anything else to say, Dr. Chaudhary," she said, more softly now, toning down the haughtiness. Amy looked directly into those molten pools. He nodded and rewarded her with a slight smile, at least showing some white against his silky brown skin. And then, a wink. Oh my God, this man is going to make me faint. But no wallowing in his focus allowed. He moved right on to someone else. How dare he ignore me. I'm the new kid in class. Amy folded her arms tightly and tossed her head.

She then zoned out as a dad who left his wife and kids to run off with a neighbor, but then it didn't work out, confessed he never returned to his family. He admitted he didn't want responsibility. Now he blamed himself and said maybe that's why he got sick. He felt guilty, like his kids only visit or call because he has cancer. Probably true, Amy thought.

The group went on. A young woman, twenty-five, who had to have a hysterectomy and would never have kids. Isn't it cruel that the doctors put her in a support group of parents who have cancer? Wow, she's been in this group a whole year? A masochist.

I wonder if she's punishing herself by staying with the Thursday Group. I'd insist on a new one.

Next, a stay-at-home mom. Oh, I've nothing in common with her Amy thought. I work full time. Never took more than four weeks off after having a baby, even after the twins. They were calling me from the office at labor and delivery. Remembering, she sat up taller in the hard chair, feeling important. The lady was describing how once her kids got older she wanted them to see their mom working and planned to get a job. But the kids guilted her into not leaving the house. She was resentful and then got sick before getting a job. Hmmmm. Who the heck is in charge at that house Amy wondered? The kids? Not good. And the husband is always gone traveling? Oh dear. What a mess.

Dr. Chaudhary ended the session by reminding everyone to attend their treatment appointments, take their meds, think healthy thoughts and consider the other classes the clinic offered. They had yoga and meditation that he particularly recommended. Amy reacted to that silently. Are you kidding? Me, meditate? Ha! I've got too much to do. He shook each person's hand on their way out.

"Amy. I am so glad you came. See you in two weeks. Keep coming back. It will help. You will see. Trust me."

Her heart melted a little more at that but she just nodded. Afraid she'd say something gooey sounding or unappreciative since she didn't really want to be there. In the parking lot, the stay-at-home mom approached her.

"I'm sorry about your diagnosis," the woman said. "No one here blames you for having lung cancer. We're all just sad that yet another good person, a hard-working woman trying to raise her kids and do her job, got cancer. It's hard on the whole family." And she got in her car and drove off.

Amy couldn't help but be touched by the woman's courtesy. The tension between stay-at-home and working moms was always lying right under the surface, like a greenish vein. Pulsing, visible, never resting, constantly circulating. She felt guilty for blaming the stay-at-home mom for her problems. It wasn't her fault she got cancer either.

Amy continued her suburban routine. She dropped the boys off at school each morning where they stayed in the daycare trailer in the afternoons. Like they had done for years. They complained furiously about it in August when school started—that they were too old. It was for little kids.

"But that's what we've always done, you're not too old," she retorted. "You can stay until Dad or me or Maddy pick you up." No one home alone," she told them. Homework had to be done right away. No TV or going online until it was done. There were rules.

Maddy had just earned her driver's license making commuting easier. Tom traveled so often it was a special occasion when he was around on the weekends. Then they would go skiing, watch the boys' soccer games or play a family basketball game to help Maddy practice. But other than that, it was a constant swirl of who was going where, who needed what permission form, what lunch bag, what equipment for a new sports season. And the ever-present transportation question. Who was going to get everyone to everywhere they needed to go? Tom needed a ride to the airport. Dylan to guitar lesson. Maddy to the basketball bus for the Saturday tournament. Jake to hikes at the county park junior ranger program. Both boys to the soccer tournament two hours away. Amy to work.

Amy managed a team of engineers and product designers. She had discovered that home and office worlds were strikingly similar to oversee. She had lists and schedules, roles and routines, deadlines, metrics, dashboards on performance. That way, whether at home or in business, she could navigate impossibly complex logistics with some semblance of success. The plate juggler, that's what I am, she mused sometimes on the commute home, the solo quiet space in her day. And then when the juggler

adds in that flaming torch and puts an apple in his mouth and
takes bites out of it. Yeah, that's it. The modern woman. Tossing
dishes, avoiding fire, snacking on the apple. Oh, and some of
those guys do it all on a unicycle too. That's really where cancer
came in to throw the whole rhythm off balance. Like the juggler
on the unicycle.

Now she had to add in doctor visits, weekly chemo appointments, recovery time. Cancer was one more thing to manage.
Oh, and that damn support group too. That took up a whole
evening every other week. Maddy's basketball games were often
on Thursday. She pushed aside the question of how she would
adjust the schedule when basketball started.

Tom added Taiwan to his travel routine and was gone a
third week out of the month. Just like that. He didn't discuss
it with her. Just told her the Biotech Industry Association had
chosen him to represent San Diego in Asia. It was an honor.
His innovative pharmaceutical company was moving forward,
getting recognition it deserved. What an opportunity. Yada
yada. He sounds mechanical, like he's reporting to the investors, not to me, his wife. Who has just been diagnosed with
cancer, by the way. What's going on with him? Paying attention
to other people's diseases but not mine? Hmmmmmph.

She was furious and relieved at the same time. Tom was
grumpy and depressed when home so maybe it was better he was
traveling. At least it was one less person she had to interact with
each day. They'd always been workaholics. That was how they
approached their lives. The positive of Taiwan was it gave Tom
further status in his field and a few more financial resources to
add to their mix. But it just made this new data point, the cancer,
more complicated. Maybe I should be more supportive. This is
good for his career. And it is stressful around here. Maybe I'd
travel more too if he got sick. No, don't think so. I'd be taking care
of him and organizing his appointments, like I do for everybody.
She shrugged off his indifference. Didn't have time to think about

it.

Maddy was a jewel, adding in carpooling the boys now that she had passed her driving test. Amy put a note in the car that Maddy had to drive her brothers for family reasons. She gave strict instructions on what to tell the officer if she ever got pulled over for having passengers in the first year of a probationary license.

"Just tell him your mom has cancer so you have to drive your brothers around. He won't hassle you then," she said curtly.

"Mahhhhm, don't joke about it," Dylan said. "It's not funny. You're gonna get better."

"Yeah, hon, I am. But might as well use this sickness for something," she said right back at him with a grin. He smiled sheepishly. Awkward in his gangly twelve-year-old boyishness, Dylan was still smaller and sweeter than his twin. Jake had the Watch Out Teenager Ahead warning signs all over him. She had to keep it light for them. They were just boys, still so young.

When the chemo made her feel tired and groggier than usual, Amy repeated to herself over and over, just keep swimming, just keep swimming. It was a family motto from Finding Nemo. She now had to use it frequently to maintain energy for the boys, for her staff, her teenage daughter, and occasionally, for her husband. He seemed to have checked out—Gone to Taiwan could be the sign on his closet—while her daughter had matured from sixteen to twenty-eight in her level of responsibility. "Don't worry about that, Mom. I'll take care of it," was the new Maddy catchphrase. She signed permission slips, dropped the boys at practices and selected birthday presents at Target. It flitted through Amy's mind to worry that Maddy was missing out on being a regular teenage girl. But then she was such a help she didn't have a moment to dwell on the fact. Plus, what would she do. Fire her? She admitted that she needed her, especially with Tom so absent.

The boys seemed to go about their days as usual until she started getting calls from Jake's teacher. He was failing several subjects. He wasn't turning in homework.

"But I saw him doing that sheet last night," she had to tell the teacher more than once.

"Jake, what the heck do you do with your homework? I know you do it." She was unsympathetic. "Is it swallowed by the backpack monster? You keep it for a souvenir of sixth grade? I don't get it. Where does it go? The teacher says you aren't handing it in. Why would you do all the work and not turn it in to get credit?" Jake was uncommunicative, shrugged and tried to escape. Despite her exhaustion, she started going through his backpack each night and again each morning. Maddy watched. Dylan retreated to his room.

"Jake, if you don't turn this around, I'm going to have to call your dad," she said after a month of teacher calls amid the chemo afternoons sitting with the tube dripping poison into her arm. Poison to kill poison? Really? Isn't this all going to seem barbaric some day?

"Why bother," Jake grumbled. "He's never here anyway. What's he gonna care?" And then Mrs. Whatshername, the teacher, was on the phone complaining about Jake again.

"Mrs. Anderson, I know he is a really smart boy. He just does not seem to be applying himself. Is there something going on that is distracting him? Could you get him a tutor or some way to help him get his work done?" I'm not telling this lady about being sick or Tom disappearing Amy thought as she adjusted her position in the chemo infusion recliner. None of her business. Jake's just going to have to learn how to cope, like we all do.

"A tutor? What about his parents, his big sister, his twin brother? Shouldn't we be able to help?" she retorted, without thinking first. She wanted to yank the clear tube and its needle gunstock right out of her arm and run screaming from the pastel-colored death chamber into the parking lot. Away from the euphemistically labeled Infusion Center, back to regular life.

"Well, yes, of course, Mrs. Anderson," the teacher continued. "But that does not seem to be working. Does it?" No compassion.

No nonsense.

Amy noted that the teacher was, indeed, absolutely right. So she took action, as any corporate manager would do. She called Tom and told him he better start getting home more. His boys needed him. She hinted that Jake was having some school troubles. He didn't ask for details. Maddy was already acting like a grownup and he had hardly been around for her high school years. The twins were becoming teenagers. She said nothing about needing his support during her cancer treatments, wanting her old companion back. She just felt empty. Sadly, she could hear his hollowness echo through the cellular network.

"I gotta be here, Aim. This is our time for the company. We're finally getting to what I've worked for all these years. We have new customers, our brand is being recognized in the industry. We're key in helping put San Diego on the map for Biotech. It's all coming together, don't you understand?" When she was silent, he just said, "All right, I'll see what I can do." And then he added hastily before she could hang up, "How are you feeling? You're doing okay, right? The treatment working?".

"Yeah, I'm fine, Tom. Just come home. The kids need you." And she pushed the button off quickly. He clearly was not going to be any help. She had to re-evaluate her home court. She did an internal review in her mind, as if she were utilizing her office's department evaluation processes. She had to change things.

A few nights later, Amy called Maddy in to her bedroom and asked her to pick up the twins after school each day. Maybe those complaints of theirs are legit. She had decided it was a mistake to keep them in that dreary trailer with the little kids at the back of the elementary school campus. They'd be in junior high soon.

"I know it's a lot to ask, but can you just do it until basketball practice starts? Then I'll get one of the neighbors to bring them home. And I'll leave early a couple of days or something. I'll figure out a schedule. But can you bring them home tomorrow and help them do their homework? Make them popcorn. Let them eat some cereal. Don't turn on the TV though, okay? No video games."

Maddy would of course do it but basketball started in three weeks. Amy asked her boss to drop down to four days a week. She arranged her chemo treatments on Fridays and picked the boys up right after school. If she had the energy, she tried to do something fun with them on those afternoons. Go on a bike ride around the neighborhood, watch a soccer game at the junior college or sample ice cream and pastries at their favorite down-town bakery. When her stamina was strong they walked along the lake. She even took old breadcrumbs to feed the ducks like when the kids were little. They rolled their eyes and groaned but then they did throw out snacks to the geese swimming around the algaed pond, laughing as the ducks squabbled for crumbs.

Tom came home from Taiwan and said he didn't have to return for a month. He changed his schedule to very early in the morning. He could beat the commute that way, he said, and then pick the boys up after school sometimes. They complained when he was late and they were sent back to the decrepit trailer to wait, but he got there eventually. When the calls came from the school, Amy sent them to Tom. They seemed to be less frequent but she wasn't completely sure. She waited for report cards to see the real results. Metrics.

And Amy got better. Her chemo finished, she regained some energy, extended her walks and gained color and weight back. When Dr. Chaudhary told her she was in remission and congrat-ulated her on her renewed health, she decided she was complete-ly in love with him. Oh, if I could just take this beautiful man and all his kindness home with me. Then she surprised herself by asking,

"Can I still come to Thursday Group?"

"Of course," he said with a raise of thick eyebrow. "Once in, you are never asked to leave. These are all stages of cancer and you can still help others and receive benefit yourself by participating in mutual support," he said in his rolling, formal English.

Amy couldn't believe it but she actually had started to tolerate the group. And not just because it was led by Dr. Chaudhary. Some of her colleague's situations were so drastic or sad that group time made her feel lucky. Other times she got a good idea from another participant. She had even started to mention Tom's long absences and emotional distance. She didn't want to reveal too much to strangers or in front of the charming doctor.

Amy was surprised when someone raised the possibility that Tom's disappearance might be due to fear and sadness over her illness and their changed status as a couple—his wife had a death sentence threatening her. It was a revelation that hadn't occurred to her. She just worked. He just worked. They ran and managed the kids and work—that's what they'd always done. And new challenges came up. They handled them. All business, no excuses. But the more some of her support group compatriots probed, the more she realized they might be right. She tried to talk to Tom but he just squeezed her and told her how happy he was that she was better.

"Let's go to Big Bear," he said. "Let's ski all our favorite runs like we used to. The kids are grown enough so we can just meet them for lunch. Won't that be great, Aim?" And he was off to plan a ski trip. Amy felt pretty strong and so they went. They took the kids out of school a day early since she was no longer working Fridays, and drove up Thursday afternoon to a rented cabin. They cooked bacon, eggs and home fry breakfasts, had snowball fights and skied until the lifts closed. They got hot chocolate and sat by the fire pit at the lodge. The kids met other teenagers. Jake entered a ski race on Sunday and got third place. She and Tom even made love. Well, not a lot of love in it actually, but at least some sex finally, she thought. It seemed to be a perfect weekend.

Amy felt reasonably well the rest of the school year and through the summer. She discussed with Tom the idea of returning to Friday work, but they agreed it was better for everyone if they stuck to the current schedule. Jake's grades were improving. The boys were moving to a big junior high in the fall. Maddy would be in that famously stressful junior year. Amy's boss was supportive as she got her work done, no matter how much she was in the office. She worked nights and Saturdays, checking in on her team, their progress, troubleshooting and guiding. They didn't really notice her schedule was different.

Tom still traveled but cut back a little, especially in summer when the kids had more flexibility. They all moved at a rapid pace. But at least, Amy felt, Tom was cordial and maybe made a little more effort to be present. Though they barely interacted. And they never talked about her sickness. The only reference he made was when he asked her about her Thursday sessions.

"Why you still going to that support group? I thought you didn't like the stuff. Isn't it kind of hippy dippy of you to still go when you're not sick anymore?"

She just shrugged and didn't answer. Didn't need to justify anything to him. He wasn't the one trying to get past cancer. Despite her frustrations with his compassion deficit, she tried to rally herself to be supportive of his activities. His company was doing well. They had trials going now on their latest new drug. Once fall school schedules started, they returned to a familiar rhythm.

Healthier and stronger than when she had started, Amy felt guilty at Thursday Group. Most of the others were still quite sick. She tried not to gloat or talk too much about positives but to listen, give advice, share when concerns did come up. They all seemed to welcome her energy, her bustling nature and unfettered opinions. The thoughts she had kept to herself at the beginning now spewed forth freely.

"Why don't you find a part time job for a few hours a week," she told the stay-at-home mom who wanted to return to work. Amy had heard around the Infusion Unit about a network of caregivers who supported cancer patients and those with other ailments. Some of the jobs required less physically demanding work, like reading to the bedridden. She referred the woman who began reading two mornings a week in another unit of the hospital. She was grateful to Amy, who just shushed her. "Go read," she said. She was an organizer, a manager. That's what she did.

She also didn't hold back with the man who'd left his family. The others seemed to sympathize in what felt to Amy like a wimpy manner. Enabling his bad behavior and guilt. Oh come on. This guy needs to fess up to what he's done and then beg forgiveness and put out some effort. Yeah, he has cancer but you gotta take responsibility and then try to move forward. Amy pulled him aside after one group session and told him exactly that. He was taken aback.

"But I'm sick. I don't have the energy for that."

"Oh, come on. Look at Lola over there. She's got a little kid she's caring for by herself, two jobs, and she's sick. You're better off than her. Stop feeling sorry for yourself. Get going and talk to them. Tell them you know you screwed up. You're making yourself sicker with this self-pity and constant guilt. You gotta take responsibility, but then move on."

Red faced, he looked at her with skepticism and anger. Who was she to lecture him? Dr. Chaudhary, returning to his office after the session, heard the grilling. He raised his eyebrow at Amy as he passed them in the foyer. But she was quite sure she saw a gleam in his soulful eyes and the hint of a grin. No white teeth but she was positive he was hiding a smile in there. She got all warm and squishy inside. She turned back to the abandoner and looked deep into his defiant eyes.

"Go own up. You won't get any healthier for sure if you don't." And she whirled off to return to her own life.

The word around town was that Amy Anderson had recovered from lung cancer. Wow, isn't that amazing. What good news, people said to each other. She's tough, that one. Was she a smoker when she was younger? Not surprised. Knew she could fight it off, they nodded. At work, only her boss and a few close colleagues even knew about her illness and they weren't surprised one bit. It had been a minor setback. A hiccup in a stunning career. Amy was still on top. Her team still performing despite new pressures in the industry.

"Mom, are you okay? What's that coughing?" Maddy called in to her mother's bedroom as they got ready for school on the last day before Spring Break. A nervous excitement filled the house. The twins were in a musical and had to have their costumes ready for the school day performance.

"Oh, I'm fine, honey. Seemed to have gotten a cough, a little cold." Amy dressed for work and bustled the kids through breakfast. Maddy ran upstairs.

"I forgot my keys. I'll be right there." She tiptoed into her mother's bedroom and looked around. Everything in order, neatly organized as always. A book of daily meditations on the bedside table. She moved into the bathroom. There she saw it. Bright red blood in the toilet, smeared on the sides of the bowl. The up flow flume had not had the force to wash it all away.

Maddy galloped down the stairs. "Mom, I'll take the boys to school today. It's on my way and then you don't have to rush." Her mother nodded and thanked her. Maddy hustled them into the car with her motherly tone. After she dropped them at school, she returned. Amy was surprised to see her back.

"Mom. I saw it. I know you're coughing up blood. Don't pretend. We gotta call your oncologist."

"Oh, Maddy. You're overreacting. I'm fine. There's no group next week but I can talk to him after the holiday. You better get on the road to school or you'll be late."

"No, Mom, this is serious. I'm calling if you don't. And I'm calling Dad. You have to have everything checked. I know you think you're cured or something miraculous. But you know, once you have cancer, you always have it. I've read online and learned about it in Biology. It doesn't just go away. It's always there lurking in your body."

Just waiting to pounce, to attack, like a stalker, Amy continued inside her head, caught up in Maddy's argument. The cancer's back, stealthily waiting for me. She felt a rush of blood to her checks and her gut filled with the sting of fear. A nausea of knowing. This again? Oh, God. No. She abruptly looked up from her iPad news and stared at her daughter. What had happened to her little girl who loved to joke and swim and climb trees with the boys? Now she was all business, attending practices while searching for college basketball placements. All while taking SATs, producing history papers and calculating problem sets. It was ridiculous. The kid was sixteen but had to operate like a thirty-year-old mid level manager. Amy's stomach pain sharpened.

"Please, Mom. Don't ignore me. Call Dr. Chaudhary. I'm going to school but if you haven't called by the time I get home, I'm calling Dad." She gave her a dry kiss on the cheek and swirled off, keys rattling. Amy stared after her, at the space left in her absence. She tried to focus but felt sucked in to her fate. Maddy was right.

The stalker had emerged and struck. She could feel his presence. The tightness in her chest, the burning when she swallowed. A clenching pain point in her abdomen. That one was fear she surmised. And a dull aching in her limbs. She had thought she'd had it licked. She had been telling herself it was the flu. But she knew better. The enemy had caught her with the castle gates flung open, the drawbridge down. She had not prepared for this moment. And that in itself frightened her more than anything. She was always ready. Always picturing the future and planning for every eventuality. I've been in denial. No room for that anymore she whispered to herself.

Amy returned to the Cancer Ward at the hospital for a new round of tests. She got a thorough checkup from Dr. Chaudhary but this setback did not allow her to enjoy seeing him. She skulked through the ward and grumbled about the hassle of the resurgence ruining her Spring Break plans. She was bad tempered with Tom when he returned from Asia. The tests showed the cancer had reappeared in her lungs but also in other parts of her body. Metastasized they called it. It was in her bones now. She felt like a science experiment in her daughter's biology class as the doctors drew blood samples, showed her charts and numbers, x-rays and scan reports. The doctors decided she needed to have surgery this time and more chemotherapy after, of course. They would now add radiation in too. She agreed, feeling like an automaton in her own life.

Tom went with her to the surgery prep appointment because he was in town. He held her hand but that was it. He was like an empty shell of the man she had married. He revived a bit around the children but not with her. He seemed as enervated as she was. Like he had his own cancer or another energy robbing illness. He spent all his time on the phone, on his computer, working on his company. It's really important. Gotta take this call. We're so close on this new Hepatitis C treatment, he'd repeat to Amy and the kids.

Amy's Thursday Group session started again after the spring break week off. She didn't want to show up. I went all those times when I was in remission, feeling guilty about it, and I participated anyway she congratulated herself, valiantly. Can't I just stay home now? Too bad I'm not in another group where the doctor doesn't know my charts. I can't lie or hide here. Dr. Chaudhary knows the reality.

Once there, she wanted to be silent, didn't want to talk about it. When the doctor looked in her direction, she squirmed on the hard plastic. She had to tell them so she gave in and elaborated on the specifics that only a cancer survivor group understands. The gruesome details only those in the know want to hear.

Some seemed relieved that she was sick again. And they

sympathized with Amy's plight. Someone else was in remission now and they delighted in that person's success. A short-timer who had breast cancer had quit the group because she was all better. Well, good for her, they mumbled and sighed. The man who had abandoned his family was in the hospital. Amy hoped he had listened to her last advice. Someone in the group thought he had reconciled a bit with his kids. It could be wishful thinking, Amy realized, but stopped short of blurting out loud. They didn't really know.

Even though they were a support group they didn't know everything. They weren't with each other through the searingness of it all. Through the heartaches. They just sat together in a sterile purple room twice a month and told stories. Who really knew the others' excruciating reality? She almost questioned them out loud. But she stopped her bitterness just in time. Her return to affliction was not their fault.

In the hospital after surgery, Dr. Chaudhary and the surgeon described scalpeling out layers of her lung. They showed test results on her bones. They recommended a chemo and radiation therapy. They said they wanted to try a new drug that showed some positive results in recent studies and was just approved for her type of cancer. She listened. She nodded. She could see the new reality. This lung cancer would kill her. And she wouldn't even get close to old age. The stalker would become a murderer.

"Can I make it until my sons graduate from eighth grade and my daughter graduates from high school?" she asked Dr. Chaudhary after all the appointments culminated in a treatment plan.

"That's in just over a year. Do you think I can make it? If I do everything you tell me? I'll work hard at the positives. I'll even go to that meditation thingy. I might not have been the best mother but my kids need me around as long as possible. And my husband, oh God...my husband. What's he going to do?" Her voice got very soft. Her tone distant. Amy tried to remember a time she and Tom had been intimate or even connected emotionally. It was so long ago she felt like he was a roommate, the kind that was a former best friend but you weren't sure you even liked anymore. She strained to conjure up a memory of past happiness but it was so unreachable, as if a thick fog had billowed in and completely obscured their shared life. What happened to us?

"I do not know Amy. It is possible," the doctor said. "We will do everything we can to treat you, make you comfortable, guide you toward that. Having a goal is very important. And meditation is great too. I am so glad you are willing to try it." He handed her a flyer with the course information, then rewarded her with a warm, sad smile, a glint of the gleaming whites, and a gentle squeeze on the shoulder. The dark eyes were concerned. How on earth does he do it? See people like me every day she wondered. Be consistently kind. Not get depressed or discouraged. He's like a saint. Where did this man come from? Thank God we have health coverage and good doctors.

"Thank you, Doctor. I'll do everything necessary," she assured him, gathering the forms and brochures into the hospital system folder. "I need to talk to my family now. Thanks for being on my team. I feel lucky to have you helping me fight this nastiness." She smiled at him, for the first time without a flirtatious thought or dreamy warmth anywhere in her body. I don't even have the energy to fantasize about this gorgeous man anymore. How sad is that?

Amy told Tom about the treatment plan and the revisions she was making to the family schedule. She did not reveal the severity of Dr. Chaudhary's inability to assure success and remission. Tom nodded, distractedly.

"Look, Amy. I know it's hard to have a setback but you'll kick this thing. I know it. You're so tough. The kids are grown up, thank goodness. I've got drug trials going in South America now, along with the Asian sites. We're so close to a revolutionary breakthrough. I can't slow down and help out more. Sorry. But we can change the quality of Hepatitis C patients' lives. I know we can. We're really moving toward that dream you and I used to talk about way back, before kids. Remember? It's so exciting. Why don't you cut back one more day at work? We can handle it financially." His phone rang. "Gotta take this call. You're gonna recover quick. I just know it." He left the room.

Amy just stared at the door behind him. What? The kids are grown up? Since when? They don't need parents now 'cause they're teenagers? Bullshit. Quality of life for Hep C patients? What about my quality of life? She felt more alone than ever. Her stitches burned as if coated with acid. She hobbled into the bathroom and threw up in the toilet.

After she recovered from surgery, Amy returned to work but cut back another day. On Thursdays and Fridays, she picked up the twins from school and took them to their practices and games. One time she overheard a boy ask Dylan, "Who's that skinny lady cheering so loudly for you?" Amy had not been to school sports, really ever. Just weekend activities for years. The boys' school friends and teammates didn't know her. It made her feel like she wanted to cry. Amy never cried.

With weekly chemo for two months followed by daily radiation for six weeks, Amy found she didn't have the vitality she was used to. But she kept up at work, attempted to create some normalcy for the children and tried to be understanding of her husband. She stopped berating him for absences or lack of attention to the kids. She just didn't have the fortitude for it anymore. Peace in the family is probably better for my health than constant frustration, constant doubting and harping. Wow, that meditation class must really be getting to me she marveled.

Tom reduced his travel some, saying he'd work from home one day a week. He told her he liked having her around the house on Thursdays and Fridays. They set up a home office with two desks facing each other. Trying politely to appear like colleagues or partners in sync. Like it had been long ago. He was still gone several weeks a month but having him sit across from her working at his computer or on the phone now and then was a revelation. She noticed a gray pallor to his skin. Creases in his forehead. Patches of shininess at his hairline. Who is this guy? Do we even know each other anymore? He looks so old. Who are we kidding? There is no relationship here. A melancholy settled in but she wasn't motivated to say or do anything about it. Why bother? He'll never change. His work is everything to him. I'm probably not going to get better.

The treatments came to an end. She was exhausted but also somehow able to keep up portions of her routine. She continued walking and was almost back to original distances and hilly routes. Amy could do her job, just barely. She had taken on an assistant at work, something she had steadfastly refused before. Her boss questioned her regularly about how she was managing but she didn't relent, change her schedule or slough off responsibilities.

Dr. Chaudhary had scheduled a six week break after the last radiation appointment. It was wonderful not to have to go over to the hospital. The kids had a few weeks of summer left so she tried to add in some of their favorite activities during her long weekends. She drove the boys to the batting cages and Maddy to the never-ending cycle of basketball camps and clinics. She and Maddy visited colleges within a two-hour driving distance and picked up brochures. She saved her walking energy on those days for the campus tours led by chipper backward-walking undergrads.

"Oh Mom, I might want to be a tour guide when I'm in college. They're so cool," Maddy cooed. Amy was thrilled to hear a youthful sentiment come out of her daughter's mouth.

Senior year and eighth grade began and the fall routine was out of the starting gate. Maddy spent all her time driving herself and the boys around or holed up in her room studying and applying for college. The twins were on the treadmill of school, sports practice, homework, another practice, sleep. Start again. Tom was on the road as usual but did spend more time in their study. She noticed he seemed happier somehow as the school routines began. They didn't talk much. Logistics only.

After the somber white coated lab technicians took thirteen vials of her blood and the chatty nurses ran her through the x-ray and scan machines, she had a follow up appointment with Dr. Chaudhary. The numbers were not good; all the chemo and radiation had had little impact. There was a new chemo drug to try. She would start again in a week. Nothing else could be done. Her organs and bones had more cancer, not less. She needed to prepare. When she asked how long, he shook his head. Maybe a few months, could be longer. Depended on how she reacted to the new drug.

Amy was angry at Dr. Chaudhary for fooling her all this time. He wasn't a saint after all. His handsomeness and charm were a deception. She hadn't recovered. She was going to die. Her children were young. Her parents were almost eighty and still alive. How could this be?

"I'm not even fifty," she shouted at him as she slammed his office door and stomped down the mauve hallway. Once in her car, fuming, she realized it was Thursday Group night. She texted all family members that she had to go into the office for a meeting and then was going to group. She'd be home late. They were used to fending for themselves. She bought a sandwich and iced tea at the cafeteria and went to the hospital's meditation garden to wait for group time.

The second she walked into the purple room, Dr. Chaudhary gave her a glance, a raised eyebrow, a forced smile. In front of the whole group, Amy apologized for her rude behavior in his office. She told them her prognosis and that she'd been in the meditation garden ever since she'd stormed out on Dr. Chaudhary. What would she say to her family?

"I don't know about my husband. I don't think he can handle it. He thinks I'm cured every time there is a bit of an improvement.

I'm afraid he'll completely leave. But my kids need at least one parent. They can't go from two to zero. Well, I guess neither of us have always been there one hundred percent. But zero? It's a big year for all of them." She stopped. Then, "I had hoped to make it to their graduations." And she choked up and swallowed back tears. Silence. Shuffling bodies. Creaks from the weakened cheap chairs. Amy Anderson was tough and they all knew it. If the monster was defeating her then this was not a good sign for any of them.

"I'm thinking about not saying anything for a while. Just letting them all have a bit more time believing it will go away." Silence. The old-fashioned analog wall clock's ticking droned. Tock, tock, tock. Dr. Chaudhary cleared his throat. Heads turned toward their leader, their hero and their villain. It came in a chorus.

"That's the worst idea yet," said the young single mother.

"You need to confront your husband. Make him face reality. The guy needs to step up, be a man, be a better dad, get someone else to run his company," said the abandoner, bonily thin, with clear tubes protruding from his nose, an oxygen tank at his side.

"Where's your husband been this whole time? He's checked out and there is no more luxury living in denial anymore. He's supposed to be supporting you. Not being a wuss," said the stay-at-home mom.

"You cannot be in denial either, Amy. You need to tell him the truth," chimed in Dr. Chaudhary quietly, forcefully. Amy allowed a tear to sit on her cheek longer than she'd intended. She brushed it away with a hard stroke.

"Wow. I'm sure glad he only has to face me and not all of you," she told them with a slight smile. Laughter. The tension relieved. Time for resettling in the hard seats.

"You're right, of course," she said. "Dr. Chaudhary knows I never wanted to join a group when this started. I didn't believe in therapy. I was not a willing participant at first. But it's nice to know you have someone behind you who understands the insanity of it all. I'm glad I've stuck it out with you, through illness, remission, treatments. This, now. Thanks guys. I'll tell him. And my kids too. Right away."

Uncharacteristically, Amy drove home exactly at the speed limit, on the freeway and the side streets. By chance, Tom had flown in that afternoon. Just say it and make plans, she told herself, always the manager. She checked in on each of the children, their homework, their days. Then she found Tom and pulled him into the sitting area in their master suite, with the fireplace lit. They hadn't sat there together in months, years maybe.

"Look, Tom. I know I haven't been the best wife or mother. I'm pretty good at my job but not always so great at the other two. I see that now and I'll do what I can to change things these next few months. Or weeks, whatever it is. I'm going to quit. I'll tell them tomorrow. I think I may not have the energy for long anyways." She told him Dr. Chaudhary's report on her test results, the new treatment, her timeline. She told him he had to change his work habits. Be home more because she would be gone soon. Kids, even teenagers, need a parent around. They can't go from two to none. They need at least one parent. Now it had to be him.

"We have to make plans," she said." We gotta help Maddy get through this awful college application thing. We gotta make sure the boys can adjust and finish strong in junior high. Jake's grades are not that great. Middle school completely sucks anyway, but then your mom dies? Oh, God. It's too awful." She forced herself to swallow back a throat-constricting sob. She had to be strong here. Tom started to cry.

"What, Aim? I thought you were getting better. The doctor must be wrong. I know you have a crush on that doctor but he's misdiagnosing you. We shouldn't have stayed with him just 'cause you fantasize about him. You've been feeling better. We had a really nice last few weeks of summer. Let's get another opinion. Some more tests."

"Tom. Stop. Get a grip. Dr. Chaudhary is brilliant and one of a whole team. He's not the only one that looks at my tests and blood. He had my surgeon come in and tell me they can't operate anymore. It's a great cancer center. They know what they're doing."

"I've researched a bit on the Internet," he said. "There are some alternative treatment centers in Mexico and Israel. Maybe you could try one of those. We can't give up. You're going to get better."

"What? Cancer centers in Israel? Are you kidding me? I'm not going anywhere else. Get out of the fucking denial you've been in for these past two and a half years. I'm dying, Tom. And you want to ship me off? So you don't have to deal with it in your face, is that it? And please. Do you really think I've been spending time at the hospital because I'm in love with my oncologist? No one ever, ever would want to visit an oncologist if they could avoid it. Believe me. You are deluded." He started to sob.

"You gotta step up. Be the adult here when I'm gone. You understand?" There was no time for his whimpers. "Shhh, shh, the kids will hear you. Tom. Tom."

She reached her hand across to his armchair and put it on his elbow. It was pathetically insufficient. She realized they hadn't touched in months. She slid out of her chair and put her arms around him. He moved over and she squeezed in next to him. She was so thin. Her arms encircled his back. His head sank into her shoulder. They sat like that until his sobs slowed down, side by side in the same armchair with the fire crackling in front of them.

"Amy, honey. I just can't lose you. I love you so much and have just been terrified of things changing. Of losing you." Tears poured out again. Amy was taken aback. Tom afraid? He still cared? Tom crying? She hadn't seen that since they were very young and a beloved uncle had died in a tragic motorcycle accident. Tom was not the emoting kind. He was practical and efficient. Driven and ambitious. Never weepy.

"You keep us all working," he said. "You're the captain here. I'm just barely showing up to row. Well, yeah, haven't showed up much lately. Just bringing in the money. But that's what I know how to do. That's where I'm solid. I work and bring in my share. And my career is going so well. I have to focus to keep that money coming in. If I let up now, the whole company's success could come crashing down. Without you running things around here, well, I just can't imagine it." Amy tightened her grip around him and sighed.

"I thought you didn't care. Had moved on without us. Were just going through the motions out of duty," she whispered into the top of his head. She gave him a forceful squeeze. He looked up at her.

"I still love you, Aim. Always have. Never stopped. Maybe buried it lately and I'm sorry too. I know I haven't been there for you through all of this. But I've been so afraid of losing you. I couldn't accept that you're sick. I can't see you as weak." He leaned in to her and they kissed. A loving gesture. Affection that neither had offered the other in a long time. Amy gave in to him and offered a full hug but still felt forsaken. It was too late.

Abruptly, she pulled herself out of the cushiony chair and moved back to her own. She leaned over and tipped his droopy chin up with her fingers. Made him look into her eyes.

"Tom," she said. Any softness now gone. All business. There was no time to waste. "I just will not have Maddy becoming the mom and wife and household leader. Tom, she's seventeen. She needs to be a kid and have fun and worry about normal teenage stuff. Not how to raise her brothers or keep her dad from falling apart. You need to be the adult. Not just bring in money. Not just think about the company. You've got to take an interest in the kids. Look at the boys. God, they need a father right now. They're about to turn fourteen. They need to talk to you about girls, and sex, and staying away from drugs and all that crap. I'm serious. A mom only goes so far on that stuff. Soon they'll be driving. Oh, God...they're going to high school and I'm gonna miss it."

Tom got all wobbly and looked like he might cry again. Amy swallowed hard to push back a throat lump. Just cannot be weak now. How can I get him to see we need him, more than that damn business?

"I don't know if I can manage the family and the workload I've got right now. And the travel," he said. "It wasn't supposed to be like this. This is not how I pictured my life going. Cancer was not in my life plan."

"Yeah, no shit. Your life plan? What about mine? Mine is at a premature end, you self-absorbed ass. Don't know how to manage it all? Well, figure it out. I did. It took me a long time. I made mistakes but don't you repeat them. You have no choice now but to be a dad. Grow up. Stop feeling sorry for yourself. Fuck. I'm the one who's going to die here. Not you. And let's be real. These kids are the only real legacy we're going to have. We can fool ourselves about how important we are. How invaluable we are at work. But no one is indispensable. The world will go on when I'm gone. I knew that intellectually but now I think I really feel it. I'm facing it. My presence is shrinking. Don't you feel that? You gotta be the one to move in to that void, that expanding emptiness. 'Cause when I'm gone, that's it. No matter how much you wish and pine and dream for it to be different. It'll be permanent. Gone. Get it?"

Amy was exhausted from the effort to get through to him. Tom crinkled his brow, shook his head, pushed himself out of the chair and stomped out of the room. She heard the garage door open below and the car accelerate down the driveway. He didn't answer his cell phone when she and Maddy called. He won't answer his own daughter's call? What the hell? The boys asked where he'd driven off to. Amy was furious with him but pleaded with the kids to leave him alone. Just tonight. He was upset. Tomorrow morning we'll find him, comfort him, bring him in.

"He's scared, kids. I'm not. But he is," and with that she sat the three of them down, by herself. No Tom by her side as she had envisioned. She told them that she didn't expect to live to attend their graduation ceremonies.

At work the next morning, she met with her boss and gave

notice. She realized she'd stayed too long, also out of denial. Maybe not so different than Tom, she mused as she cleaned out her office. She couldn't produce like she had before she got sick. She used to be the one they all looked up to. But no one wanted to work with her anymore. Like they think they'll catch it or something she thought. She was no longer able to do the client check-ins and up sales that had been her specialty before. The company wanted her to stay in the office, behind the scenes, not a seller or dealmaker anymore.

Her boss seemed relieved she was leaving, even though he was heartbroken. They had worked together for fifteen years. His wife called her immediately. Colleagues dropped by but stood awkwardly, arms dangling, swinging uncomfortably, gave a quick hug and exited. They didn't know what to say. She made them feel bad. The president of the board called. Congratulated her on her great work, how she'd helped the company grow, how they were so lucky to have worked with her. He wished her the best for a speedy recovery.

"Good idea to take some time with the family," he said hollowly.

Amy felt like she was suffocating. Her assistant said she'd get the boxes delivered to her house. Why didn't she go home and rest? She fled, grateful for an extra push out the door. Driving home, she felt numb. She'd miss the office, her colleagues, the purpose, the energy and quick pace. But they'll be just fine without me. It will all go on as usual next week. And she felt even more deserted.

Tom was in their bedroom packing a roller suitcase when she got home. He looked like a ghost of himself. He told her he was going to stay in a hotel while he cleared his head. Figured out next steps. He said he needed to be alone while he pondered the new reality they were in. Amy wasn't sure what that meant but taking time to ponder anything seemed extravagant at this point.

"What the hell? I'm dying and you're running off like I had an affair. Are you kidding?" She was screaming. "The kids need you.

I need you. Tom, you've got to get beyond yourself right now."

"I can't do it, Aim," he said. "I'm so scared. I feel lost. This was not the life we had planned. I'm drowning in my responsibilities at work. The kids are big now. They'll be fine. I'll call you in a few days." He pulled up the handle of the wheeled luggage and rolled right out of the house. Just like that Tom was a crater in their lives. He was just a void. She lied to the kids that he was on another business trip. She tried to convince herself that they believed her but they weren't little anymore. They could feel the stress and the weight of Tom's absence at such a time.

Amy just kept going. What other option did she have? She went to doctor appointments and infusion sessions. The new medicine wasn't improving her numbers. She started coughing more and her bones began to ache constantly. Blood in the sink was a regular occurrence. She could no longer climb the stairs. She could not eat solid food without vomiting. Dr. Chaudhary prescribed stronger pain medication. Tom returned home briefly to help install a hospital bed in the family room next to the kitchen and to arrange for a nurse to check in daily. He stopped by several times a week with take out for the kids.

"Pollo Loco again, Dad?" the twins groaned while Maddy rolled her eyes and hid behind her laptop screen.

"How are the Hep C drug trials going, Tom?" Amy forced herself to ask one afternoon when she was sitting up reading. It was one of her good days. She had a book of poems she liked to pick up when her eyes were clear. Dickinson and Tennyson were her favorites. No bitterness. Just sadness filled her voice. And disappointment. How could he abandon her these past three years of off and on illness while she worked and they had young teenagers? She had lost all respect for him. No love remaining either. It mostly broke her heart because he was the kids' dad. That would never change and they really needed him. She felt like the cancer had propelled her, unknowingly, into being a better parent. He didn't seem to get it.

"Oh, they're going well. Thanks for asking," he responded heartily. "Yeah, I'm traveling to Chile and Ecuador a lot now too. And still to Taiwan for the association and then to Vietnam for another trial. We've got a lot going on. I'll stop by when I'm around and check in on the kids. Oh, and on you too. Got everything you need?"

Amy just nodded and pushed the corners of her lips into a slight smile. He sapped her energy even further, making her feel as if she'd just completed a marathon and couldn't stay standing at the finish line. It was better if she just didn't see him at all, making her nostalgic for something that she now suspected had never actually existed. What a waste. And what a God awful model for our children she thought.

Soon the nurse put Amy on feeding tubes, and eventually inserted a morphine drip into her pik line. The bag hung on the medical stand like a sentry, informing all who entered the home hospital of her diminished status. I've become a drug addict, she thought in a daze at her lowest moments. But the pain quickly pushed aside judgment and Amy's disciplined approach to her surroundings. She was so weak. She had lost the ability to manage and direct. The dangling morphine bag was a loving companion in her demise.

When she had a bit of energy and felt reasonably lucid, Amy summoned each one of her children for a private meeting. She encouraged her daughter to be a teen, a young adult. To go to college. To not stay around too long caring for the crumbling family. She reminded each of her sons how lucky they'd been to all have each other for fourteen years. Told them to stick by their twin and their sister. To be gentle and forgiving with their dad.

A few nights later, the kids were draped over the steel frame and chairs stationed on either side of the hospital bed, doing homework, reading on iPads, listening to music. A suburban household, cancer style. She told them to sit up, stash the electronics and listen. Amy told them not to worry. She was in control, at ease. Not anxious. She explained that she pictured death like calm, strong waves of the ocean coming in and flowing over her.

"I'm ready. I need you all to be ready because I am," she said. "I'm sorry for all my mistakes. For leaving you in daycare way too long. For not being there for enough of your activities and homework sessions. For being a bit obsessed with success outside, like at work, and neglecting the family sometimes. Including Daddy. Remember to stick together. That I love you beyond words can express. And support your father. You must forgive him so you can all move on."

They returned her gaze but then dropped their eyes to the hospital bed now dominating the living room. She stretched her thin arms out. The family clasped hands. Amy closed her eyes. Her breath was more gentle than it had been for days. The four of them stayed like that, all together around Amy for some time, in a quiet, meditative manner. She fell into a light sleep.

The kids left to do homework before bed. Maddy returned after midnight and held Amy's hand, dozing by her side for the rest of the night. Amy died as the early morning light was rising. Maddy was still holding her hand. She recognized the transition and felt her mother's peace. The pain now vaporized. She picked up her mother's poetry book, opened to the bookmarked page and read aloud the first stanza of Amy's favorite Tennyson poem.

Sunset and evening star,
And one clear call for me!
And may there be no moaning of the bar,
When I put out to sea.

She gently touched Amy's forehead, as if to brush back long gone bangs. She rose to go tell her brothers and call her father with the news.

Dr. Chaudhary walked into the Thursday Group, somberly.

"We have a new member. This is Brenda. Please welcome her.

She can tell you about her diagnosis today or next time. When she is ready." He paused. They waited, sensing he wasn't done.

"I want to let everyone know that Amy passed away on Tuesday night. Her children were with her. Her daughter called me and said she was at peace. She wanted me to pass on how much all of you and this group meant to her. Please, let us hold hands and have a moment of silence for Amy Anderson. She was a strong, important member of this group for almost three years. We will miss her terribly." There was an uneasy, heavy quiet. Brenda squirmed in the hard chair during the silence, the tears.

"I'm so sorry for your loss. Was this Amy Anderson from the south side?" Brenda blurted. "I know her. I was her kids' preschool teacher years ago. A girl and then adorable twin boys. Right? I hadn't heard she had cancer. Oh, those poor children, nice kids. They must be in high school now? I'm so sad for the family. How are they doing?" and she trailed off and stopped asking questions. The silence hung, thick.

Doctor Chaudhary cleared his throat, purposefully, perhaps a little more deeply than usual.

"Let's begin," he said.

∽⚮∾

Innovation Quintet:

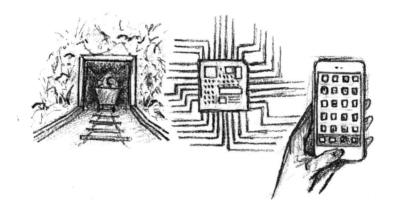

Cinnabar to Software

Land Grant

WHERE AM I? He lifted his knuckle to scrub crusted sleep from his half-opened eyes. Oh yeah, in the little apartment at the back of the hacienda, he remembered. Light skinned for a Mexican boy, with an auburn tint to his dark hair, hazel eyes traversing the unfamiliar garret, Joaquín recognized that his status had changed dramatically. Anxiety and loss churned in his stomach. Just a week ago, his mother had ordered him to pack his belongings and vacate his childhood rooms. Juanita had moved them from the master suite and wing of family bedrooms into the servants' quarters before El Capitan arrived. In disbelief, he had gazed past the wooden shutters toward the Coast Range, relishing his favorite view one last time. As far as his eye could see, tilting down the valley covered with green pastures and ancient oak trees and up the distant gentle slope on the far side, every hill, field and tree visible had been his grandfather's, and thus, his—the Castro de la Cruz Rancho.

Upon arrival just days ago, the rancho's new owner, Captain Brennan, his wife and their five teenaged children immediately colonized the bedrooms and living space built around the open-air patio. They spilled into the kitchen and dining area, smoking room and library circling the tiled courtyard with the trickling fountain and magenta bougainvillea arbor. Sisters giggled along the upstairs balcony outside their bedrooms. Boys hung on the wrought iron railings, gazing downward to the flowered atrium and eavesdropping on the business of the estate. The large family, rumored to have abandoned a dreary homestead on the plains of Ohio, seemed to revel in the spacious elegance.

Joaquín and Juanita's new quarters were miniscule. Such a contrast to the luxury of inhabiting an important land grantee's entire rancho. With only one bedroom, a narrow kitchen with an alcove for a table, and a closet, Juanita was forced to convert the storage area into a bedroom for Joaquín. He was too old to sleep with his mother. They had to use the outhouse behind the stables. No silver barreled bathtub in his own suite of rooms anymore. No hot soapy bubbles carried upstairs in buckets by a servant. Now, in order to bathe in the cramped apartment, he had to sponge off in the kitchen with a bucket of water he had hauled up from the well himself.

"But, Mama, why do we have to move?" he had demanded, pestering her with teenage indignation. "And in our own home? Abuelo would be furious if he were alive. How did this happen? Why does that horrible, loud family get to take over our house?"

Juanita glared at him with a pained grimace. "You know why, Joaquín," she shrugged. She eventually just stopped answering him. He finally ceased tormenting her and retreated to the stables where he could pretend to be a Mexican prince. An important landowner respected far and wide. The stable hand, Pablo, had the compassion to allow him to live in a fantasy world, at least with the horses.

Joaquín had spent all his thirteen years on the rancho, a Mexican land grant property with thousands of acres of rolling grassland and sprawling oaks. Perfect for cattle. His grandfather had received concession from the Spanish crown at the turn of the century and then had title fully granted to him by the new Mexican government in the 1820s. He was expected to raise quality cattle and send tallow and leather south along the El Camino Real and even back to old Mexico. He was to sell milk, butter, cheese and beef locally to Missions San Juan Bautísta, San José and Santa Clara and to government officials in Monterey, San José and even San Francisco. Don Pedro took his position seriously and kept his promise to cultivate superior cows. He prospered, built a large adobe mansion for his family and was respected by the California governors and their henchmen. He did not cheat or steal, priding himself on being a respected cattle rancher and Mexican patriot, settling the northernmost lands for the young country. He held lavish parties and exciting rodeos for the Alta California governors and diplomats from the Mexican capital. He respected the friars and tithed generously to the neighboring missions.

Juanita, café con leche skin with thick eyebrows and black hair, full lips and a voluptuous figure, was raised as a Mexican hacendado's princess, with every luxury possible. She learned to read and write from a mission priest who came to teach Don Pedro's daughters the Bible and Spanish literature. While her sisters departed lessons as quickly as possible to sew with their mother, Juanita pestered the priest to teach her English. She also begged to learn as much science as a Catholic mission priest was permitted to discuss. She acquired math skills from her father as he scoured his account books by candlelight each night, grumbling about the expensive tastes of his wife and daughters. He allowed her to put her feet up under her knees in the velvety chairs circling his grand library while he tracked income and expenses, talking to himself as he calculated. She absorbed it all as if her father were a mathematics scholar at the illustrious

University of Granada in España.

Don Pedro adored his feisty daughter and spoiled her with gifts of elegant dresses, fine horses and visits to neighboring ranchos for parties. He gave her leather-bound Cervantes classics to add to the library shelves. She was as adept a horsewoman as she was a student. Don Pedro trusted her instincts as she grew into a woman. He cursed that God had not given him a son, but at least God had the courtesy to send along Juanita. She was much better than a consolation prize. Her mother and sisters kept to the kitchen and sewing rooms, but Juanita liked to know the latest news from Mexico City or Washington. She loved the gossip from Monterey and surrounding ranchos. She questioned visitors about the changes in the East and in Central Mexico. She discussed Mexican politics, Spanish literature and veterinary practices for birthing calves equally passionately with any passersby who would engage in conversation. When the whites from the U.S. started calling on Don Pedro, he introduced her like his second in command.

According to her father, Juanita's only sin was getting pregnant out of wedlock, a serious infraction in the deeply Catholic family. Don Pedro and his wife sent Juanita to board with the mission priests hundreds of miles south in Santa Barbara, claiming she was heartsick at the death of her husband from measles, an assistant to the Governor of Alta California they fabricated. They packed her off with strict instructions to the Father in charge to treat her like a servant, forcing her to mop floors and wash pots late into her pregnancy. She was to work as if she were one of the Indians. No one was to know her true status and she was to be treated as if she were a beggar girl, not land grant royalty. She was to feel the pain of her erroneous ways as she went through her pregnancy, gave birth and recovered. The Fathers in Santa Barbara felt Mexico's pressure to end the mission era and understood the supreme power of the California Dons. They followed Don Pedro's instructions precisely and showed no mercy to his pregnant daughter.

When she returned, almost a year later, with a baby on her hip, Juanita was under a clear dictate to never stray again. There would not be a second rescue. Her duty was to help her father manage the estate and raise her son to take over once Don Pedro could no longer oversee the enormous operation. Juanita, grateful for their forgiveness and their deception concerning her son's paternity, was secretly happy to have no husband to manage. She never told anyone the truth about Joaquín's father, though Don Pedro hinted that he had his suspicions. She vowed to stay loyal to the family's life work—the Castro de la Cruz Rancho. A quiet life of celibacy and personal loneliness, within a luxurious setting no less, was a small price to pay for being able to run a land grant and return to the good graces of her family. She accepted their requirements, focusing on raising a strong son and serving as first lady of their reputed stop on the El Camino Real between Monterey and San Francisco.

Prophetic in her vision of Americans gaining importance in the future, Juanita made sure that Joaquín learned English from infancy. She sent him to study with nearby mission priests and forced him to practice at home. She trotted him out like a circus performer to practice with English-speaking travelers. Joaquín grew up in the decision-making salons of the rancho, watching his mother and grandfather manage the complications of a sprawling estate. Increasingly, English moved in as a stalwart companion to Spanish in the mouths of the Californios.

Over the years, businessmen and cattlemen from the Eastern United States stopped at the rancho and offered Don Pedro great sums to buy his land. He turned them down, arguing that the land grant system did not allow him to sell or transfer authority. This was Mexican land after all. He was not making any deals with the white men from the East, except to sell his hides, tallow or beef. He graciously welcomed all visitors and even allowed some of them to stay for weeks at a time as they rode out on the range, spying on his acres of wealth.

Then one winter, as war fever with the U.S. was percolating, hundreds of Don Pedro's cows got sick. The disease spread quickly. He had to slaughter sick cattle and quarantine the visibly healthy. His production of tallow, hides, milk and beef dropped dramatically and he had to borrow to keep the rancho operating. Wars and other distractions had left the Alta California rancheros isolated from the Mexican governors. The Mexican banks were in disarray. He had no choice but to visit the American bankers establishing operations in Monterey and San Francisco. As war with the United States escalated, Don Pedro was forced to bury his pride and beg the enemy for financial assistance.

Just as news of the U.S. invasion reached Alta California, Don Pedro collapsed on his horse while out riding to inspect the new calves. The distressed peones brought him in, bouncing on his saddle, but he was dead by the time they returned to the rancho. Juanita, her mother and sisters laid him out on the giant redwood dining table, sent for their favorite priest from the mission and prayed. What to do now? Juanita was the only one who knew anything about the family business, and at thirty-three, was the oldest. Even though she had a young son and no husband, there was no question she was in charge. Her mother was distraught and her sisters were useless, picking up their mother's helplessness and needlepoint skills as their primary talents. Juanita called in an attorney and banker from San Francisco to analyze the will and the land grant accounting records. There was no money.

Don Pedro had amassed huge debts to finance buying healthy replacement cattle. He had even borrowed on some of the land and gotten himself indebted to two captains in the Mexican Army. They had offered cash just as they were preparing for war with the United States. They had expected to win the war quickly and started buying up more land in Alta California. It would be a good location for trading with the ever-expanding United

States next door. But the war was not going well for Mexico. The Americans appeared likely to scoop up an enormous swath of Mexico. There was talk of a treaty that would move their land under American governance. Juanita suspected that the stress of his debts and the fact that his beloved land would soon belong to the United States caused her father's heart to quit. She gave her family the bad news.

"We are going to have to sell the rancho, Mama," she told her mother and sisters as they gathered at the grand redwood table in the great salon, after they had buried Don Pedro in the family cemetery behind the garden. "Papa had debts and we owe large sums to many people and banks, even to capitanes in the Mexican Army. We are facing a new front of enemies if we don't begin paying off his loans. I have gone through everything with our attorney. We have no choice."

Juanita sent word out through the bankers and attorneys, the two militaries and the land holding networks that her rancho of forty-eight thousand acres was for sale. She steeled herself and her thirteen-year-old son for the inevitable. Joaquín, an excellent horseman and rancher already, was befuddled by the news and didn't understand the changes afoot. When American cattlemen and businessmen came to call, he would hide in the heavy drapes at the back of the library to listen in as his mother met the land suitors. Young men in U.S. Army uniforms came through. Older men with swaggers and crusty language, dapper ranchers with fine horses paid their respects to Juanita. But she discovered, and Joaquín heard while spying, that most potential buyers did not have enough to buy the whole land grant. Juanita refused to accept small payments for pieces of the property. She had to have significant cash to pay off her father's debts. All the land had to go.

One day, a man about ten years Juanita's senior came to the front gate on an expensive stallion, wearing a stylish hat. He had an Irish lilt to his speech, a cocky grin and a hearty laugh. Cap-

itan Malachy Brennan of the U.S. Army spoke enough Spanish
to charm the few remaining ranch hands to let him speak to the
mistress of the house.

"Doña Juanita, I want this land and I have the money to pay
for all of it. Though I am just a humble soldier, I am fortunate
that my family has benefited from the popularity of dipping
snuff. You know I have always loved this property. I want you
to stay and work here, with your son, sisters and mother. I will
make sure your basic needs are covered. You will not have to
leave. No one else is offering you that deal. I know, Juanita. I
have checked. Where else will you go? Your son is not old enough
yet to be the man of the family."

Joaquín, hidden in the velvet curtains, was surprised at his
mother's coldness to this charming man. She did not offer him
a cordial or cigar, as she often did with potential buyers. She
seemed to want to dismiss him from the library as quickly as
possible. Joaquín saw her hesitate. He could see the anguish
and frustration in her face. But he knew she had no other buyers
with substantial enough resources to relieve their predicament.
Why didn't she leap at his offer? He watched as they shook hands.
There was a brief quiet interaction, which he could not overhear.
Then the Capitan boomed,

"I will be moving Mrs. Brennan and our five children out here
immediately from Ohio." Joaquín heard him add softly, rather fa-
miliarly, "You have made the right decision, Juanita." His mother's countenance was somber. She had found a buyer. But then
Joaquín almost fell out of the curtain hideaway as he watched the
captain raise his hand, gently caress her cheek and lean gracefully down to give his mother a tender kiss on the lips. His other
hand pressed her shoulder for a moment. Then, just as quickly,
the visiting gentleman's bravado returned, he stood his full
height, back ramrod straight, swept his hand through his thick
mane of tangled auburn and strode confidently out of the room.

Captain Brennan was true to his word, and within a few weeks moved his family into the land grant's adobe. Joaquín and Juanita's new, cramped quarters provided little sanctuary from the completely altered life the boy faced each morning. He had to watch his mother start the fire, wash clothes in huge tubs, chop vegetables and salt meat for the midday feast. His aunts and grandmother cleaned linens, swept floors, tidied bedrooms and set the redwood table. Capitan Brennan, his wife and five children seemed to adapt to their new environment quite easily. They threw clothes on the heavy wooden furniture, dusted food crumbs off the white tablecloths onto the terra cotta tiles and then insisted on cleanliness at every moment. Joaquín's whole family was kept busy attending to the most minute needs of the Brennan children and parents. He worked in the stables and at least got to interact with exquisite horses. But he too was at the constant call of El Capitán's head stableman when an extra horse needed to be saddled up or watered after long rides.

The captain poured money into the estate, ordering fine furniture, clothes, artwork and carpets from the East to please his wife. He barked orders at Joaquín's family and every staff member to assert his authority and impress Mrs. Brennan while she focused on transforming the land grant into the family estate. Captain Brennan relegated Juanita to the painful position of estate manager over a home and ranch that no longer belonged to her. It was cruel and practical. Understanding the inner workings of the rancho intimately, Juanita was a logical choice. She could curse him all she wanted but she didn't really blame the captain. She realized she would have made the same decision in his position.

She did the work but avoided him and his wife, presenting them with written instructions or sending Joaquín on her behalf. They tolerated the arrangement since Juanita was an efficient manager and the estate began to regain its former glory. Now called the Brennan Seven Hills Ranch, the cattle empire was a launching pad. From the former Spanish land grant, the

Brennans, and their sons and daughters, were staking a claim among the new elite, California landowners in the expanded U.S. territory.

As he matured, Joaquín noted his mother's deep pain at their altered status. Juanita's sadness permeated her being and molded her into a new form, as if she had been struck by a debilitating disease and never recovered. She was no longer a vivacious beauty, with mischievous energy and playful combativeness, as she had been, sparkling at her father's side in the great salons of Rancho Castro de la Cruz. Her saucy manner and smart observations, famous with Don Pedro's visitors, were only a memory. She'd aged so. Her luxuriant black hair grew thinner and streaked with gray. The furrows in her forehead became permanent as she worried over their situation and pondered every decision to develop the ranch. She never complained but neither did she smile or laugh anymore.

While Mrs. Brennan stuffed the once elegantly sparse adobe with gaudy furniture, European artwork and garish mirrors, Juanita hid among the account books in a small office behind the library where she had spent countless hours with her father. Fiercely protective of her sisters, mother and son, she also took on any chores she deemed excessive for them. But she rarely talked except to give quiet guidance on survival skills to her family or orders to key staff members.

Joaquín felt acutely the loss of his mother's dominant personality and vibrancy. He was not aware of her past secrets but could see evidence of the mission Fathers' training on how to behave like a servant. Now she was quiet efficiency. She moved like a cat with a soft touch and darting disappearance. She was so much smaller now. She fit in, did her work and almost evaporated, as if she were the iconic redwood table itself, so familiar, so constant, so expected a mainstay that it was almost forgotten. Almost invisible. The intimate moment Joaquín had observed between his mother and El Capitan was so alien to his current reality that it got very fuzzy and confused in his mind. It must not have happened that way.

For Juanita, the only thing worse than returning to her punishing mission nightmare was having her aging mother, her sisters and son join her as harshly treated servants. She did what she could to protect them, particularly her mother. Joaquín was young and loved horses anyway, so she had little sympathy for him as his work was in the stables. Her sisters sewed and crocheted but mostly became personal maids to El Capitán's wife and daughters. But her mother was assigned kitchen duty, constantly chopping vegetables, preparing fires, scrubbing enormous pots and iron skillets. Juanita took as many of her tasks as she could but had her own assignments ordering supplies, managing vendors, organizing parties and supervising the vaqueros and stable hands. For her, the new life was about survival. She made sure everyone was fed and cared for and then she had to manage the ranch back to success. Her only goal was to provide for and protect her family. She could not have them thrown off the ranch for any reason, any slight, any perceived disloyalty or faltering work ethic. Where would they all go? How would they survive in the new country that had subsumed them? They had not chosen the new U.S. landlord but now had to survive under an unfamiliar flag.

After almost two years on the Brennan Seven Hills Ranch, Juanita heard whispers in the kitchen. That Joaquín was getting so tall. And his skin was so light. Didn't he look a bit like El Capitán? Hearing the kitchen gossip, anxiety crept into her bones and flooded her with fear. She had to send Joaquín away or there would be trouble. El Capitán's wife was a possessive woman focused on the success of her husband and children. She would not tolerate rumors threatening a claim to her new estate. Juanita had to act before the new mistress heard the same talk or grew more observant of her employees. Although it broke her heart, she looked for opportunities and then devised a plan. She would have to reveal the truth or he would never accept her direction.

Early in 1849, when Joaquín was just fifteen and had been serving as a stable boy for two years, Juanita woke him in his closet bed in the middle of the night. He was startled by the tears he saw on her cheeks in the candlelight.

"It is time, my son," she whispered, gently caressing the bangs from his forehead. She touched his cheek, just once. Any softness he thought he'd heard in her tone then disappeared.

"You have to leave tonight." Joaquín was confused. What was she talking about? He didn't want to leave his home, family, the horses he loved.

"They've found gold in the foothills by the Sierra. I want you to go up there before the news spreads further. People will pour into Alta California from the East, from México, from Chile and Peru, from Europe even, for this gold. They say there is lots of it, and you can pull nuggets as big as acorns out of the streams. You must go tonight. And Joaquín, you must change."

"But Mama, what are you talking about? I want to stay here with you and Abuela and mis tias. We're here together. We're still on our land. Don't you think we could get it back some day? A lot of things are changing." Juanita sighed at his naïve optimism. What was she doing throwing him out now?

"Listen to me. You must become Joe," she continued. "Speak only English and you will pass for American. Your accent is perfect. You are so light skinned. You must do it. There's no future here for Mexicans. We lost the war and the Americans will take over everything. Look at what happened here at our family home. Don't let anyone know you speak Spanish unless absolutely necessary. Go Joaquín, become American, go find gold and make your own fortune. You are a man now."

Joaquín's head began to throb. He felt dizzy. What was his mother saying? He grabbed her hand hard. Juanita didn't stop for fear that she would never go through with her plan. She yanked her hand away, roughly.

"I am so sorry you never had a father to teach you how to be a man. And that Abuelo was just getting started when he died. But you are strong and smart. You are good with horses and people. You know how to work. You'll be fine."

"But Mama, I can't leave you. My job is to take care of you and the family. I don't want to leave you. It's still my home here. I'm not going, " he said. Exasperated with his naiveté and bravado, she coldly said,

"Joaquín, you must. There is no other way. I'm sorry to tell you in this manner but, Joaquín, El Capitán is your father. He came here many years ago to visit Abuelo and the rancho. I didn't think I would ever see him again. When we had to sell, he was the only one with enough to buy everything so I could pay off the debts. I realized there could be problems for you but I had no choice. You must leave tonight. Pablo has a horse and bag ready. Here's all the money I can spare. Hide it in your clothes."

Joaquín was speechless, breathless with a searing pain in his gut, as if a horse had kicked him. When he was a boy, he'd been kicked in the stomach by a foal. He'd never forgotten the pain. Now it felt as if an adult horse had delivered the blow.

"Joaquín, you are a good boy but you must start your own life. This gold is an opportunity. Go up to Mission San José and head toward the Eastern hills until daylight. There will be trouble for all of us if you stay here."

Joaquín saw the hard line of her jaw and the depth of the blackness in her eyes. Her pupils had disappeared. She was famous for her determination and stubbornness. He had to follow her orders. He always did. They went out to the dark, hushed stables where one of his favorite horses was saddled. There was no sign of anyone. It was very quiet. And very black. No moon to betray his departure. He realized she had picked a moonless night to protect him further. Juanita kissed her son quickly and pushed him up onto the horse.

"Now go. Be Joe. Be an American man, and don't look back."

She turned and ran into the rear entrance of the servants' quarters. Joaquín shook his head and sucked in the cool night air to clear his mind of his mother's mysterious words. It felt as if an icy wind had blown through his intestines, creating an emptiness inside and a numbness through his limbs. He did as instructed, secured his belongings, clicked the horse into trotting quietly and rode north.

Joaquín followed his mother's directions, and after several days' ride arrived at the Coloma gold strike. He settled in an encampment of foreigners and transplants. It was a rough, lawless place. He kept his belongings close and trusted no one. He protected his horse like she was made from pure gold. He spoke only English and told anyone who asked that he was Joe Brennan from Ohio, an orphan. Come out to California, like everyone else, to make his fortune. It was easy to go unnoticed.

With his mother's money, he bought his own pan and pick and tramped through the creeks with the other would-be miners. He sifted the river sand for months but never found much beyond a few flakes and enough dust to fit in the hollow of his callused palm. He cashed in his gold dust and then searched again for untouched sites along the streams. It was hard to find forks that weren't filled with rough miners who didn't like newcomers. Pristine streambeds were disappearing. Prices were so high in the camp that he didn't think he could hold out much longer. He shared an outhouse with hundreds and a thick canvas tent with twenty other gold seekers. Fresh food and tasty cooking were scarce. The tiny servants' quarters and stable hand position back at the rancho were luxurious compared to the gold fields.

He was desperately homesick. The Sierra foothills were hot and so dry. He pined for the cooler climate, the soft gray mist of sea fog floating over the coastal mountains like a comforting blanket. He longed for the smell of the stables and his authority with the horses. For his camaraderie with Pablo and the stable hands he had known since boyhood. For his mother's sad eyes and caring voice. For his grandmother's stories of the glorious era of the Dons. He even missed the most irritating of his aunts and the taunts of the Brennan teens who lorded their superior status over Joaquín's entire family. He wrote letters to his mother every fortnight.

One night after drinking too much homemade whiskey, the cheap alcohol gave him the courage to ask for details of her relationship with Captain Brennan in his letter home. Although relieved to have the mystery of his parentage solved, Joaquín was troubled by the persistent questions and the captain's behavior. Had he abandoned his mother when she was pregnant? Did he even know Joaquín was his son? How could he possibly treat Juanita so harshly? The image from the drapery hideout was seared into his memory but he couldn't reconcile the many contradictions. The captain appeared to have some lingering affection for his mother, but once moved in also seemed completely controlled by the domineering Mrs. Brennan. Maybe he really loved her but couldn't be with her because she was Mexican? But the captain had made Juanita into a servant by taking her land. Clearly there wasn't much love in that. Several of the annoying teenagers appeared older than Joaquín. Mrs. Brennan probably had two or three babies back in Ohio when the captain had visited Don Pedro.

A more mature Joaquín now realized that his mother and the captain could not have stayed together, even if they had wanted to, but he tortured himself with endless speculation about the many possibilities, the answers he was unlikely to ever get. He was confused, angry, lonely. He spiraled down into despair over the misfortune, the misplaced ideals and bad luck. And the very worst was that despite his undying loyalty to his mother, deep beneath his anger at the captain, he was furious with her. How could she have kept this secret from him? Why couldn't she have eased him into this understanding of his father? He was part

American after all and that made things very complicated. The longing for the simpler days of Don Pedro, master of land grant Alta California, consumed Joaquín.

Anytime anyone arrived into the miner camp from Monterey or Mission San José, Joaquín would pester them for information on the Brennan Seven Hills Ranch. He never got details about his family, mere servants, but he did learn that Capitan Brennan had expanded beef and dairy operations while adding sheep, horse breeding and hay production. The Seven Hills Ranch apparently had developed a reputation for the highest quality of goods among the former land grant ranchos prospering with Gold Rush population growth. Joaquín was both angry and proud. He was enraged thinking of his mother and aunts working to make the captain even richer. He knew his grandfather and mother had built the foundation that Captain Brenann was taking advantage of. Outrageous. He had to think about his next steps. He hungered for a legitimate role back on the rancho but found he had little energy to figure out what to do about it. Day to day survival in the gold fields overwhelmed most forty-niners. He grew despondent and so scratched deeper into the creeks slogging for his fortune. Maybe a gold strike would help him sort it all out. He never received a response to his letters.

After many lean months, he noticed a flyer recruiting workers to dig at the rock in the mountains. Placer mining they called it. Anxious for stable employment, Joaquín left his gold pan behind to man a sluice box. He saved every penny possible but he could see that the gold fields were no longer the opportunity they had been. Very few miners made a fortune. Mine owners were the ones getting rich. Businesses that supported the constant influx of dreamers were the ones that survived. Saloons and Chinese kitchens, laundries and barbers and moneylenders. Those were the ones that seemed to have a little extra in their pockets. Joaquín saved more quickly than most because he limited his visits to the saloon and brothel to once or twice a month. Still, his

earnings were paltry and the living hard. Placer mining quickly scooped out the next layer of loose gold flakes dusting the
mountains. The majority of the remaining ore now was embed-
ded in quartz rock and had to be extracted in a process involving
mercury.

One day, Joaquín noticed a bulletin in the dry goods store
advertising jobs at The New Almaden Quicksilver Mine. The
majority of the world's cinnabar, the raw ingredient required
to make mercury, was thousands of miles away in Almaden,
Spain. But a large deposit of cinnabar existed near San José,
175 miles southwest of the gold fields. He had heard that quartz
extraction was the new lucrative mining method and quicksilver from San José was a windfall for the California gold miners.
They didn't have to wait for months to get mercury from Spain.

"Wait!" he shouted to the shopkeeper at the counter. "That's
close to the ranch! Maybe I can move back home. Go see my
mother, grandmother and aunts. Maybe I could live with them
and work at the mine." He danced a little jig right there in front
of the sacks of flour and sugar. The shopkeeper shook his head at
yet another miner with starry visions. At the same time, Joaquín was determined to remain independent. He would support
himself until he had steady work and a home. Since he had never
heard from his mother, he didn't know if she was still at the
rancho or even alive. He continued sluicing, and saved and saved
until he finally had raised sufficient funds to leave gold country.

At nineteen, Joaquín Joe Brennan Castro De La Cruz got back
on the horse he had ridden into the gold fields and joined the
thousands heading southwest toward the quicksilver mines. He
moved into a camp near San José and immediately sought work.
Despite four years in the gold country rivers and mines, he was
hired on as an entry-level worker, climbing into the depths of
the earth to chisel out chunks of cinnabar. Six days a week he
labored, seven in the morning to five in the afternoon. It was hot

and dark and ugly. He made just enough to rent a one-person heavy canvas tent, pleased to have some privacy at last. He kept his tent clean and continued to save his money.

He told himself that he would not contact his mother until he had significant savings and could get a small cottage where she could come live with him and finally leave the Brennan Ranch. Once he had a home and resources it would be time to push aside his bitterness toward the captain and the loss of his home, his questions about his mother's betrayal and take his place as head of his family. He continued to seek news of his mother but only heard about the success of the Seven Hills Ranch. Nothing of its servants. He realized he would have to reveal his identity and find Mexican workers who delivered to the estate to get more information. But he was hesitant to do so. In the gold fields he had passed for a white American. He observed how Mexicans were separated into different tent villages and given lower paying, more dangerous jobs. He kept quiet and remained Joe Brennan, orphan from Ohio.

Determined to accumulate cash reserves, Joaquín took on extra shifts and ascended to a supervisor role, farther away from cinnabar veins. He heard about acreage nearby for sale and bought a lot, thinking that maybe more cinnabar could be found there. Each time he had some extra cash he bought another piece and added to the investment. He made plans to build a small cabin on the land to reunite his family.

Joaquín observed that in New Almaden, just as up in Gold Country, the most successful were the entrepreneurs selling food, clothes, tools and services to the miners. Back in the gold foothills, a saloon owner he knew bought the biggest house in town as his business flourished. A Chinese mine worker moved from Joaquín's side on the sluice box to become a grocery store proprietor, and then expanded to a second grocery. Chileans brought in fresh vegetables. Australians provided security to mine owners. A madam fled desolate Texas cowboy country and

flourished in Sacramento. The bank owners, the men who craft-
ed picks and shovels, that guy who made solid work boots that
could withstand water, mud and rocky soil. Those were the ones
who prospered. One day a fellow supervisor approached him.

"I'm thinking of goin' out on my own, Joe. What ya think? Ya interested? I'd like to buy the tools, the boxes and equipment needed
for quicksilver and sell 'em to the mine owners. I see it growin' and
they can't keep up. We could keep 'em supplied and repair tools
that break. What ya think? Ya want to be in this mine forever?"

Joaquín quickly signed on. He used savings to purchase tools,
and metal and woods to make more tools. Over time, they set
up a workshop on his land and manufactured the cone crush-
ers, water-cooled condensers and hot furnaces the quicksilver
miners needed to operate. They provided cinnabar roasters with
the kilns and shipping flasks necessary to transport mercury at a
cheaper rate for the quartz miners extracting gold outside Sacramento. He and his new partner began traveling to San Francisco
and Sacramento, Monterey, Nevada and Colorado. When a mini-
gold rush occurred in the very northern part of the state, they
were ready to supply the Eureka fields.

Joaquín was so preoccupied with this business that he did
not get south to the ranch to see his family. He was hesitant because of the send-off his mother had given him. Now, full grown,
he was tall and thin, auburn-haired and square-jawed like the
man he knew to be his father, Captain Brennan. He anticipated
trouble if he just rode up to the hacienda gates.

As their business flourished, Joaquín and his partner invested in buildings to house their inventory and bigger equipment
to make more complex tools. Joaquín quietly bought more land
each time he had an influx of cash. He did some boring on the
land but he never hit cinnabar on his lots. Bad luck, he thought.
But it was so beautiful with rolling hills, wide oak trees and
a creek through the middle that he didn't actually mind the
absence of cinnabar. He hiked through the dry brush often and

looked for his next piece. Land made him feel whole again. A bit less solitary. Like he was filling in the empty space with nourishment. I will never sell this land he told himself. No one will take this from me, like what happened to my mother, to my grandfather's land. I will die first. And he kept buying adjacent parcels.

Out riding with a customer after a few years in business, Joaquín met the daughter of a mine owner and fell for her immediately. Elizabeth was funny and clever. A good horsewoman. He took her riding on his property and proposed to her in the shade of his favorite oak tree. They got married soon after in the small chapel nestled in the quiet strip of New Almaden businesses. He felt guilty about not having a proper Catholic wedding or promising to raise his children Catholic, but he did not want to jeopardize his new relationship with complications. Repeating his story, he told her family he was an orphan and didn't know much about his family's background. That he wasn't raised religious. He'd grown up in Ohio and come to the gold fields at a young age. Such stories were common among the forty-niners. His wife's relatives just nodded in embarrassed understanding, relieved that he had made himself into a successful businessman. Humble beginnings and a desire to improve one's standard of living were common in Gold Rush California. Opportunity flowered but could be fleeting, like the poppies that painted the hills bright orange for a short time each spring.

By twenty-five, established with a small but comfortable home, a thriving mining equipment business, land, a wife and baby, Joaquín decided it was time to return to the rancho. Joaquín told his wife he had to travel south to Monterey to buy mining equipment. He stopped near the elaborate gate to Seven Hills Ranch and asked for the stable foreman.

"I have the best saddles and bridles in the area. Is Pablo still running your stables? I know he likes quality gear. Can you send him to meet me here? I have to be on my way but I know he needs what I have," he lied to the ranchhand near the entrance.

When Pablo rode up looking curious, Joaquín dismounted his horse to reveal his true identity.

"Pablo, it's me, Joaquín, although now I go by Joe," he said quietly, removing his hat. "Is my mother here? Can you tell her I've come to see her?" Shocked, Pablo began to stammer and look pained. In Spanish he said,

"Oh, Don Joaquín, I am so sorry to tell you this but your Abuela died a few years back and your mother and her sisters decided to leave. The señora is very mean and she never liked your mother for some reason. Even though Juanita is the one who built this place back up to richness. She is cold and hard to everyone but she was especially tough on your mother." He stopped suddenly. He too got off his horse, taking his hat off in a gesture of respect. He approached Joaquín and peered at him through aging eyes. Pablo stopped and then almost fell backward.

"Oh, but you look so much like the jefe, el capitán. I don't remember you being so tall...and your hair and your face...oh my. Oh, oh, maybe now I understand more. Ayyy, dios mío. You're his son, right? Is that why your mother suddenly sent you away? We were all shocked and so sad. You were a good boy, Joaquín. I can see you have become a good man too."

"But where is my mother, Don Pablo? Do you know where they went? What would they do? Where would they go? She lived her entire life here at the rancho."

"Oh, Joaquín, I'm so sorry but I don't know. You could try over at the mission. Maybe the fathers there will know. I heard that maybe they went to Old Mexico. Very far from here. Your mother is a tough one. But she was so hardened and sad. She missed you very much. I think it was like a permanent pain in her insides after you left." He sighed and mused, "I think being here just made her sadder and lonelier. After her mother died, I think she felt like she could finally leave. Even though it was the only home she had ever known."

"Do you know of any cousins or friends she might have gone to in Mexico? Where would she go there?"

"I'm so sorry. I don't know. I don't know anything. I wish I could help you more. I have to go now, Joaquín. You have to get out of here. There could be trouble. Do not come back to the rancho. Vaya con dios," he said and quickly rode away from the ranch's grand entrance gate.

Joaquín traveled south to the ranchos now occupying former mission lands. He spoke with workers and landowners, and former mission priests in their new church headquarters. No one had seen or heard of Juanita or her sisters. He rode on toward Los Angeles and asked at other former mission sites and ranchos and at the small towns along the El Camino. He sent word to his wife and business partner that he would be gone for some time and he continued to ride. But sadly, Joaquín never found a hint of his mother at any of his stops.

After months, he returned home, dejected. He felt he could not give up. He set aside a secret bank account to fund a continuous search for Juanita. He paid scouts to pursue the trail and lawyers to look into banking and business records. If Elizabeth was ever suspicious of his activities, she never revealed it. Dutifully, she ran the family home efficiently, managed the land acquisitions and kept the records for the quicksilver equipment business. She reminded him of his mother as he remembered her in the luxurious salons of the rancho happily working alongside his grandfather.

Joaquín's search was fruitless. It was as if Juanita and her sisters had evaporated. As if they had become ghosts, or only a distant memory. For years, Joaquín refused to give up hope, but he gradually reduced his investigative trips and bags of coins to fund search efforts. He took one long trip to Mexico, partly on the train and part on horseback. He rode through scrub brush territory and mountainous passes covered in pines. He visited cities and small towns, spreading the word of his search and even offering a reward for information leading to a reunion. But to no avail. Juanita was gone.

He eventually accepted that it was as if she had died, and indeed she might have, so he finally mourned her passing. After almost twenty years, he ceased the searches and accepted his fate. Truly an orphan now. El Capitán might be his father by blood but he was no relation as far as Joaquín was concerned. Joaquín had only ever had one parent. One set of grandparents.

To mask the heartbreak at never reuniting with his mother, Joaquín spent most of his energy on his equipment business and on acquiring land. Over the years, he amassed three hundred acres in the hills surrounding New Almaden. He and his beloved wife had three more children. Joaquín taught them all to ride, to hike and camp on the land. They never built anything more than a tent frame and deer and boar hunting shacks on the hilly parcel.

"This land is to stay this way always. To stay in this family, forever, " he lectured his children until they grew tired of the refrain. Joaquín found that riding with his offspring through the ravines and over the ridges lessened his sadness. He temporarily could forget that he had lost his mother, that he had not done his duty to care for her into old age and that he missed her passionate love for ranching. He could not help but feel that he had disappointed her by never returning, by not finding her out in the world beyond the Castro De La Cruz Rancho, by not figuring out a way to get their land back. She would be so pleased with his acquisitions, a new tract of terra firma for the family.

When Joaquín's first grandchild was on its way he took action. He decided to tell his wife his plans after the birth, the beginning of a new generation. Joaquín and his wife walked home arm in arm, glowing, after visiting their baby grandson at their daughter's little house just down the road. They felt so fortunate to have healthy, hard working children and now a grandchild. Joaquín's pride and his love for his family brimmed over.

"Darling, come sit with me by the fire. Tonight, let's not read or sew or play chess. Let's rejoice in this blessing for our family. And I must tell you a story," he said to her, arm tightly around her shoulder, as he escorted her in to their modest living room. He gently sat her in the softest chair, stoking the fire in the stove with two new oak logs. He gave them a jab with the poker and began.

Joaquín and his wife never went to bed that night of their grandson's birth. They were still talking and crying when the sun slid up over the eastern hills, casting a pale pink light on the colinas surrounding their house, their acreage.

"But I don't understand, Joe. Why didn't you tell me this earlier?" Elizabeth asked. "All these years you've carried this burden? This secret. Alone? And this searching you've been doing? I never could decide if you were looking for new mining equipment or a new woman. I'm sorry I ever doubted you. Oh, Joe, I'm so sorry about your mother," she said. And Elizabeth cried and cried for his loss, for Joaquín's real story.

"But you must go to this Captain Brennan," she said. "I heard about his huge cattle ranch and I did wonder if we were a distant relation because of the ranch's name. But I had no idea." And they laughed together at that. "And, you will always be Joe to me. I can't call you Joaquín," she said and smiled at him through her tears. "You must go to him and explain that you are his son, as your mother told you. And it sounds like it may be obvious when he sees you. And that you own a share of that land. The rancho which really was your family's in the first place."

"No," he told her, "I can never do that. He owes me nothing. He did buy the land from my mother. And he gave me nothing. He made my mother into a servant. I have no use for him. He is not family to me. I have another plan. A plan to help make some of this right for my ancestors. For our children. For our grandchildren."

Joaquín outlined his intention to establish a trust which would hold all the land he had acquired into perpetuity. He explained that when they both died he wanted each of their children to have twenty-five acres to use with their families, to pass on as they saw fit. But the other two hundred acres would go to all the children and grandchildren and their descendants, forever.

"We can set guidelines so that it can never be sold, never be mined or farmed, never developed or used to pay off debts," he told her. "It will just go on and on for the family and their friends to use. For hiking and fishing, hunting and camping. For family reunions and horseback riding. We can establish a governing board structure because over the generations, I sure hope, there will be too many people to manage it individually. Once it gets to our great grandchildren's generation, there will be an elected board to ensure it is cleared and maintained. That no one is squatting on it or mining illegally or cutting the timber. The trust and a governing board of family members will oversee the use, to preserve it forever."

He told her that he'd already had a lawyer complete the paperwork to protect two hundred acres in the Brennan Castro de La Cruz Trust initiated by Joaquín (Joe) Brennan Castro de la Cruz. He had established the trust in the memory of his mother, Juanita Castro de la Cruz and his grandparents, Pedro Castro and Juana De La Cruz.

"My darling, the bottom line is that our land can never be sold or taken away from this family," he said. "That is how I will honor my dear mother and make things right for her, to settle the score. Not to have a duel with Captain Brennan or a legal fight to get some of the hacienda back. No. I want to make sure the land we have worked so hard for, have bought legally and honorably, never, ever leaves this family. And I want my mother's name on this trust and on this land. Protecting it forever, in her name, is my gift to her. A legacy she and I can both be proud of." He squeezed her hand and smiled, a measure of calm settling over his Castro de la Cruz restlessness.

⌒⌒⌒

Blackberry Creek

"LET'S PICK BLACKBERRIES! I found a sweet one last week," Becca
called to her friends, interrupting high-pitched laughter and the
piercing screams of eleven-year-old girls. The children chased
her through the apricot orchard, lush with pinkish blossoms and
fluttering green, down the hill toward a creek, hollering contin-
uously. A billow of gray rose up from their Converse footsteps. It
floated down to layer a dusty film on the neon mustard carpet beneath the trees. Overhead, the sky spread like a protective com-
forter, not one white wisp breaking the expanse of blue blanket.

With striped t-shirts, flying blond ponytails, grass stained
and scabbed knees, scratchy throats and clear liquid dripping
from noses inflamed by spring pollen, the neighborhood friends
sprinted past the farmhouse, into the rows of gnarled tree
trunks. The children ran by graying work tables forlornly wait-

ing for the old Italian ladies who came down from North Beach each summer to deftly slice and pit apricots. They sniffed a sulphur odor as they rounded the stacked wooden trays waiting to present halved apricots to shrivel in the June sun. A gentle breeze lifted branches, cascading feathery petals to the ground, mimicking snow. Bees hummed and darted between pistils and stamens. As they reached the stream's bank, the children crashed their lithe bodies into one another and collapsed in a heap. Their breathing slowed, they giggled and sighed, languidly untwining themselves, tossing off shoes and rolling up pants. Time to go wading.

The eight wandered up the ancient stream bequeathed to Becca's family by a Gold Rush ancestor. Clustered in twos and threes as they searched for juicy treasures, they splashed the burbling water, giggling and yelling. Becca and her friends didn't care that 120 years before, after complete failure in the gold fields, a twenty-year-old adventurer in her family tree found work at Almaden Quicksilver Mine and gradually accumulated a huge swath of this land. They didn't understand that a trust with a complicated governance structure oversaw two hundred acres for use by the widespread descendants. That Becca's branch of the family had, for generations, held on to twenty acres with a farmhouse set between apricot and cherry trees. The kids just knew that Becca had the best section of creek and the juiciest fruit. She had the mysterious, cozy redwood grove and clear swimming holes on her family's land. They always ended up in her orchards.

Becca and her friends were left to themselves most of the time. They rode their bikes endlessly through the country lanes, along the dikes, into town to ice cream shops, over to parks for water balloon fights. They prowled the alleys behind their homes, played kick the can and baseball and ran through the sprinklers. Hour after hour. Until dark. Until Mom called them in for dinner. Until they heard Dad's Buick turn the corner into the neighborhood. Or until they realized they couldn't see the handlebars anymore so they'd better pedal back and wash up before Dad took his place at the head of the table.

Tuna casseroles, mushroom pilaf and boiled spinach wrung of its vitamins sustained them. Kool Aid and Tang fueled them while Mom and Dad strived myopically for that post-war prosperity. Parents were busy trying to forget European wars, immigration tragedies or family strife. The war was a fresh memory. Depression era poverty was less than a generation behind them. The GI bill, TV's glamour, advertising agencies and their leaders told them they could have it all. If they worked hard and educated themselves, they could ascend into a decent-paying profession. They could become sophisticated cosmopolitans with large appliances and glamorous secretaries. Professionals with no grime, manual labor, destitution, war. If they saved and borrowed, they could leap into debt for a mortgage and a little house. They could accumulate enough cash to buy a car. Oh and, there should be babies. Lots of them. An expectation that was included with the little house. And then the bigger house. The children, wash loads of them in most families, were almost an absent-minded afterthought. A haphazard requirement, sort of like the rabbit-eared TV on its credenza.

Just as the parents had no idea what their children were up to—as long as they got home for dinner—the kids had no window into their parents' world. They just lived for the next kickball at the corner, the next bike ride to the candy store, the next orchard tree climb.

And Jack, one of the kids flying through the orchard dust, just knew that he was undeservedly lucky his immigrant parents rented a cottage behind his classmate's home, down the road from Becca's farmhouse. Jack could play tag in the orchards, ride bikes through the hilly neighborhood and explore the creek with this group. He knew that if he didn't live behind Tim, a favorite of Becca's, they would never invite him over to join the adventures.

These graceful, athletic kids spent their summers diving deeply into the creek's pools, running in the shade of the orchards and riding horses. Jack was terrified of horses. Ever since he'd slid off one on a bareback ride, he made excuses on horse riding days. He was most comfortable taking apart phones, bikes, toasters, his dad's 1951 Mercedes-Benz, and reassembling them, hidden among the pyracantha berries and camellia bushes surrounding the cottage. Their cramped home didn't have its own garage for the car or building projects. In fact, the cottage probably had been the garage at one time. Jack pretended not to care about such facts. He just tried to keep up with Becca and her glorious friends whenever Tim invited him along.

On that first blackberry foraging of the season, Jack splashed ahead of the berry seekers, feigning confidence. He moved with a short-lived smoothness, as this was before he obtained the lifelong limp that would characterize his gait. He climbed high up logs splayed along the banks, reaching deep into the prickly brush, straining for the ripest blackberries. He ignored the itchy scratches covering his skinny arms, daydreaming as he searched. He was desperate for the best berries. To be invited again. He forced himself deeper into the thorny tendrils toward a purple clump. This summer he was determined to be included in every golden children adventure. Maybe, just maybe, if he supplied the group with juicy treats, he would become a regular.

Suddenly, up the twists of berry-adorned creek at the deepest swimming hole, far from the farmhouse base camp, Jack slipped on a barkless log, crashed through the stickered branches and spun around a dead tree trunk. He fell, crack, on the log, bounce, splash into the deep water littered with fallen tree trunks. Debris from a thrashing storm that winter. No, this can't be happening to me, he thought. Oh God, how embarrassing. They'll never let me go creek wading again. He submerged into the cold pool and his mind stopped screaming, momentarily. Dread filled his stomach while inside his head he heard a scratchy tearing sound. And then a pop. It seemed to originate somewhere down his leg. Or maybe it was his foot. Why is this happening to me? He swirled in the water and around the log. He was stuck.

The kids nearest Jack let out distressed yells, clearly a different sound than the shrieks of delight at tag in the orchard or tromping through the stream. Those lower down the creek rushed, feet splashing hard with purpose now, toward the anguished cries. All seven children had been in the creek so many times they knew there was a deep pool that formed at the peak of spring runoff after a wet winter. Spring was well along but it had just stopped raining; the water level was unusually high. As the stragglers arrived at the swimming hole, they could see their neighbor had fallen and was lodged under a partially submerged tree.

Jack was thrashing about, almost rotating on the trunk like it was a playground bar the girls spun around on top of their puffy down jackets at recess. But one of his feet was trapped below a branch so he couldn't fully revolve out of the pool. Frantically, spastically, he'd spin up, catch a breath, yell, then fall back and submerge into the deep water. Splash, splash, crash and he was up again but then falling forward. The newly arrived children started yelling, running toward the others who had not been able to dislodge him. Confusion ensued. Everyone talked at once.

"His foot's stuck."

"We gotta move the tree trunk."

"No, you'll push him under more."

"Oh, man, he was wading in his shoes. His shoe's caught under the branch."

"How we goin' ta get him out? Can more of you jump in and push him up so he can stay out and breathe?"

"We gotta calm him down. He's making it worse."

Several kids pulled the trunk on one side, others hurried to yank on the branch trapping Jack's foot. There was a lot of yelling, scrambling, splashing, nervous energy. At first everyone was working at odds. But then the natural order of the group fell into place. Becca, who felt responsible because this was her creek after all, and bossy Chrissy, who always took charge, barked orders the loudest. They directed swim team member Rick, shiny greenish-blond hair flopping, into the pool with several of the girls to each take a different side of Jack on his log perch. While trying to hold him up so he could stay out of the water, Becca worked on getting his shoe off. A couple kids got organized on one side of the sunken tree and began to pull the trunk out of the stream, while creative Tim led others to work on the branch.

Carefully, so they didn't snap his leg, they were able to move the tree closer to the bank. Rick got Jack's free foot and slid it off the trunk. He forced the boy's waterlogged shoe onto the muddy bottom and held it there while Becca pulled his other leg over the trunk. The seven of them crowded in to grab his arms, pants, shoulders and haul him onto the muddy bank, now slick from the splashing. By the time they had maneuvered the tree and dragged him ashore, Jack was exhausted, collapsing.

Pale and floppy, he tried to stand on his own, assuring them he was fine. But as he put weight on both legs, he grimaced. Pain overcame his embarrassment and fear of being the outsider, of being the weakling among the physically adept. He yelled a squawky scream, fell to the ground and slid over the slippery surface back toward the creek.

"Awwwww, my leg." Even though mortified at being the center of attention and in excruciating pain Jack despaired that they'd never invite him creek wading again. He really wanted to cry but bit his lip. The throbbing in his leg didn't quell his Polish father's accented voice in his head, admonishing him to be tough, to be a man. Boys don't cry. You have it so easy here in America, you kids. What it was like when I grew up in the war, you have no idea. You kids. No idea. You've got it so good here. The refrain continued unabated.

Jack bit his lip harder to quell another scream. Blood streamed down his chin. The seven friends rushed to stop his slide down the slick mud back into the creek and looked down to see his ankle turned unnaturally inward. His leg and foot were perfectly perpendicular. It was so unusual it gave several chills. Some felt nauseated. They all averted their eyes, even as they leaned in to grab him.

"Ohhhhh, God. His foot," someone said. "It's bad. Look at how it's pointed funny."

"Ugh, I don't feel so good," another moaned.

"Shut up everyone. Don't freak him out," Becca said. "We gotta get him back to the house. My mom's there with the station wagon."

"We gotta splint his foot first," said Laine, whose dad was a surgeon at nearby Stanford Hospital, as they had all heard a hundred times. "That's what my dad would do," she said authoritatively. The gravity of the situation suppressed their usual groans of disgust when Laine bragged about her father. She enlisted Rick and Chrissy and the others to gather sticks for a splint. They did what she said.

"Rick and Tim, you'll have to take your shirts off so we can make ropes to tie around the splint." She worked expertly to slide flatter branches on each side of Jack's ankle. She directed the others to use their teeth to start a rip in the boys' shirts, creating cotton strips for ties. Jack shivered. His teeth clicked together with cold. He was so very, very tired.

"I think he's going into shock," said Rick. My dad told me about this when we were hiking in the Sierras. We gotta cover him. I'm gonna make a blanket."

Rick's dad was an inventor so he was always coming up with crazy things the curious kids snuck into his garage to examine. Rick was usually building his own version of his dad's inventions.

"But we don't have anything else and we've ripped your shirts up for the splint," Laine said.

"You girls could give me your shirts and I'll make a blanket," said Rick. Matter of fact. No hesitation. All five girls stared at him, hard. No way. They were almost in sixth grade now and things had changed since their most carefree days as five-year-olds when they barely noticed gender differences.

"You guys, this is serious," Rick said. "Look at him. He's shivering. We gotta get him warm before we move him. It's gonna take a long time to get him back to Becca's house." Laine ignored him and worked on the splint. Jack groaned and tried not to cry. Rick was disgusted with the girl's reluctance to give him their t-shirts.

"Okay. I'll make something. I'll figure out something with branches. My dad's an inventor," he muttered to himself. "What would he do?" As he started up the bank to reach for softer bushes than blackberry vines, Chrissy pulled off her shirt, revealing a training bra. The girls raised their eyebrows in surprise but then realized it was Chrissy, a tomboy in all things. Of course she'd offer up her shirt. But a training bra? Really? No one else had one of those yet.

"I'll do it. Here's my shirt," she said. Rick grabbed it, spread it over Jack's torso. He scrambled farther up the bank, pulled at branches and came back with leafy foliage. He tied the brush to the shirts' sleeves to complete a mini-quilt which he draped across Jack, tucking it in around his neck. The other kids helped junior doctor Laine by holding the branches in place while she prepared to tie the cloth strips to secure the splint.

"Jack, it's going to hurt. I have to move your ankle to put on the splint. Hold Becca's hand and squeeze hard. Tim, hold his shoulders down so he doesn't move. OK, here goes."

Reluctantly, Jack screamed. He tossed as they pushed him down and then he was silent. He had passed out. Laine saw the opportunity and fully twisted the ankle back to a more regular position. She pulled the t-shirt strips tightly and tied knots. Despite usually being annoyed by Laine's obnoxiousness around her father's preeminence, in this situation, her friends welcomed her over confidence and apparent competence.

My dad works at Lockheed building bombers but we're supposed to act like we don't know, Tim absently thought. How would I know what to do for Jack? For once, Laine's dad being a famous doctor was a good thing.

"Now we gotta move him. How we gonna carry him and keep him flat? We need a carrier," Chrissy said. "Go find two sticks we can sit him on. We'll hold the sides." The kids ran off while Laine tried to wake Jack up and Rick monitored his blanket. Tim led the pack on the return.

"I think we can make, like, a chair to carry him so his foot won't hit the ground," he said as he tied two thin tree trunks together with the remaining cotton strips. His dad built stuff. So could he. "Let's see if this works."

As he came to, Jack observed, detachedly, the children arranging the carrier under him and hauling him up into the air. His muscles were flaccid and loose, so they struggled to keep him on the stretcher. Jack had no control over his body. Groggy, he felt like he was at the bottom of a swimming pool, looking up to see vague colors and shapes and hearing muffled sound at the surface. He was having trouble staying awake, understanding what was happening to him. Pain and fear were his only clear sensations. A refrain repeated in his head. I can't be weak. I can't be weak. And he couldn't shut off his dad's voice—boys don't cry, boys don't cry.

Two at a time, the children carried Jack with each of his arms over a friends' shoulder. Two others held the makeshift chair to support his legs, careful to keep the injured foot from striking the ground. When their thin muscles ached and their breathing got shallow, they switched to a new combination of human stretchers. Slowly, in concert, they moved him through the creek, up the hill, across the mustard field to the orchard. They stopped at a cluster of wooden picnic tables shaded by an oak tree.

The farmhouse was not far off but they stopped at the Orchard

Tables, as they were called in Becca's family parlance and, subsequently, by all the children. Groupthink operating at full throttle, unspoken agreement led them to rest briefly and assess the situation. Jack lay splayed across one of the tables, while the rest, still panting, circled him, peering down, examining his status.

"Jack, are you okay?," asked Rick.

"Hey Jack, we made it to the Orchard Tables. It's gonna be okay now," his neighbor Tim said.

"Yeah. You're gonna be fine," Chrissy said. "You got stuck but we got ya out. You just need to rest."

No one mentioned the ankle. Its strange position, the disturbing image of his lower leg in opposing configuration to how everyone knew ankles and feet are supposed to fit together. Jack grunted, rolled a little and lay there. He was very pale. His breathing was imperceptible. He did not appear to be fully conscious or aware of them.

"He doesn't look so good. I'm gonna get my mom to drive the station wagon over so we can put him in the back," Becca said. "She'll take him to the doctor," She raced off. She was very fast and it was perfect that it was her house. She'd get to the farmhouse faster than any of the others, including the boys.

"Tell your mom to call his mom," yelled Chrissy after her. Jack mumbled and turned at that. Laine, practicing her best bedside care, held his hand, leaned in and put her ear near his mouth.

"Jack. Jack. We can't hear you. We're gonna call your mom and get you in Becca's car." He tossed his head back and forth, writhing in pain and concern.

"Doesn't speak English," he managed to whisper. "Dad does. He's at work. In his lab. Never home."

"Don't worry. Becca's mom will get you to the hospital. She'll pick up your mom on the way. Be quiet now. You're gonna be okay." Laine held his hand tightly.

"Hey you guys. We're not supposed to go up that far by ourselves, to the swimming hole, right?" Someone asked what they were all thinking.

"Aren't we gonna get into trouble?" someone else said. Nods. Hmmms. Silence. They pondered the likely consequences. They shifted their weight on tired limbs and stared at the fine gray dust under their shoes. At the crunch of driveway gravel as Becca's mother backed the wood-paneled station wagon next to the tables, the kids raised their eyes, returning to the present. Becca and her mom threw open the heavy doors and rushed over to scoop up Jack. Someone pulled open the tailgate and the group slid him into the car. Becca's mother covered him with a threadbare woolen blanket she kept in the car for picnics. Her experienced eyes quickly scanned Jack, the kids and the picnic tables. She noted the splint on his foot, the t-shirt and branches blanket covering him and the makeshift stretcher lying on the tables. Becca's mom closed the back doors gently, turned, and surveyed the anxious group.

Freckled and sun drenched, with wet hair and dripping clothes, the children appeared as if they had just had a carefree afternoon creek wading. But their eyes told a different story. Concerned, frightened, the young faces were dark. She had been angry when her daughter ran into the house aflutter, yelling about an accident while wading. Why hadn't they sent one child down the creek to summon adult help? Why had they gone all the way up to the deep swimming hole when they knew the rules? But seeing the results of the rescue operation, she was amazed at the kids' ingenuity. Her frustration subsided. These eleven-year-olds actually had provided solid first aid care. Where'd they learn how to do that floated through her mind as she sought to ease their concern. She used her most steady, calm, motherly voice.

"You kids did a good job taking care of Jack and getting him back to the house," she said. "I'll pick up his mom and drive him to the hospital. I'm sure he'll be fine." She hopped in the driver's side and ambled the creaky station wagon off through the orchard. Dust spit up behind the worn tires.

Knowing the playground rules to his core, Jack lay half conscious in the back of the station wagon, wincing at each road bump, dreading his Polish-speaking mother in the car and hospital. He'd have to translate, if he could stay alert. He couldn't let down, even now that no kids were around. Determined not to show the pain, his sternum ached with desire, to run swiftly, skillfully, effortlessly, as his friends did. Confident and fearless. The dreamy image he carried of fitting seamlessly into the orchard crowd had collapsed when his body crashed into the water logged tree trunk. His pain-filled stupor was not numbing enough to prevent his stomach overflowing with dread. He felt nauseated. The upcoming summer months would be interminable.

Seven sun bleached children, five girls and two boys, so used to each other's company they were like siblings, regrouped around the picnic tables. Widened pupils, larger than usual, gaped at each other. The usually boisterous were shocked into an uncharacteristic silence.

"I'm sure he'll be okay," Chrissy broke the quiet, repeating the adult refrain. "Laine, that was good you made that splint. Maybe his ankle'll get back to normal 'cause of it." Laine nodded slightly. Drained, she didn't have the energy to speak.

"Wow, Jack was really brave," Tim said. "I didn't know he was so tough. I don't know what I'd do if that was my ankle."

"Yeah, he's kinda skinny. Maybe that's why his ankle turned like that. You ever notice he never comes horseback riding?" added Chrissy.

"But he didn't cry or anything. That was bad, that foot. Did you guys see how it was all turned the wrong way? Gross. It was sick. I think it's totally broken. He's gonna get a cast I bet. Probably crutches too," mused Tim. Nods. A recognition that he'd be the star of fifth grade's remaining days upon his return to school swelled. A slight ambivalence at the prospect crept into a few young chests.

"You know," Becca recalled to her colleagues in creek wading and orchard tag, "he always gets the juiciest berries. I think he fell 'cause he was reaching high up the bushes for the best ones."

"Yeah, well, someone else will have to get the juiciest berries. He won't be able to go wading, for like, forever. He's gonna have a cast all summer. That stinks."

"Guess he'll be stuck in his junkyard. You seen behind the cottage? He's got all kinds of pieces and parts and junk back there. He takes stuff apart and builds things. Kinda weird. I think he and his dad are building an airplane or something."

"Let's go horseback riding tomorrow."

And the seven whooped at the idea and were off for a game of orchard tag, gazelle-like in their fluidity and speed. Jack's accident quickly dimmed to the place of memories, collected like a scrapbook photo for a good story later.

Orchards

"MOM, WHY'S THERE A FOR SALE SIGN in front of our house?" one of the kids pestered. From behind her in the back seat of the car, all three of them punched her arm and shook the headrest to wake her up.

"What? What are you talking about?" she asked sleepily. Her husband Dennis nodded somberly as he turned the car into their gravel driveway. There was indeed a sign plunked between the mailbox and fruit stand at the entrance to their property. Becca sat up, pushed her hair out of her eyes, yawned and forced herself alert after the long drive down from Tahoe and the mountains. She was sore from the bad fall yesterday and rubbed her shoulder. She'd broken a brand new ski in a whiteout and was still mad about it. Lucky it hadn't been her leg. Slowly waking, she shushed the kids.

"Time to go right to bed when we pull in, okay, everyone? Right to bed," she said. Then, as they parked in the usual spot alongside the old farmhouse nestled between cherry and apricot orchards, she muttered, "Where's Dad's car?" Sensing something was out of place, Becca jumped out immediately, grabbed the sleeping bags, and hustled the kids inside. They all argued. One wanted milk, one was hungry, one wasn't tired. But Dennis got the message and moved them upstairs and into their beds efficiently.

Becca, calling for her father, went into his little apartment attached to the back of the farmhouse. A half-full glass of scotch was on the table with a nearly empty bottle next to it. The bathroom floor mat was damp like he had recently showered. Clean dishes in the drying rack on the kitchen counter. But no sign of Dad.

Becca returned to her family's section of the house and peered out the window looking for his car. She headed to the garage. She smelled it before she got even fifty yards in front of the wooden double doors. Exhaust. And then she heard the engine. She ran to the doors, pulled them open and saw Daddy slumped in the driver's seat, head against the window. Carbon monoxide fumes spewed out of the garage and she coughed heavily.

"Dennnnnnnniiiiiiiiiisssss," she screamed with such force that it felt as if capillaries burst in her cheeks, along her jaw. He'd been on his way and was already running out from the house, the kitchen screen door banging hard as he flew out. "Oh no, no, no, no," he was saying, over and over. Becca collapsed on the ground at the garage's entrance. Dennis ran to the driver's door, leaned in to shut off the ignition and took his father-in-law into his arms.

"Call 911," he barked at her, although he knew instantly that it was too late. He wanted to get her out of there. Away from the scene. Becca sprinted to the house, dialed 911, then called the next-door neighbors and then her best friend, Tim.

"I think Daddy's dead," she told each of them. "I don't know what's going on. There's a For Sale sign out front at the fruit stand. We just got home from skiing." She couldn't get any other words to come out of her mouth.

The kids were at the top of the stairs peering down at her on the phone. She shushed them with that severe mother means business look and then thinking quickly, she said,

"Why don't you all sleep in Nate's room tonight. Take your sleeping bags in there and stay together," she ordered. "I'll be up to check on you soon." They scampered into big brother Nate's room, with him leading the way. No arguments this time.

A commotion of people, mostly strangers, consumed the house that night. They stayed for hours, filling it, taking over every corner as if it were a public venue. A blue light from a police car flashed oddly, off and on, through the large living room windows. Police scanners rattled too loudly. Uniformed paramedics strode up and down the driveway, in and out of the house, carrying equipment, consulting one another, talking into radios. Strange noises and people overflowed through the farmhouse. It was all so unnatural.

Once the last of the outsiders had driven off, Dennis took Becca's hand, guiding her upstairs. He had explained the situation to the kids hours earlier and was hoping they were finally asleep. They went into Nate's room, pulled pillows and blankets from his bed and lay down on the floor, bordering the pajamaed clump of their children. It was not a night for anyone to sleep alone.

Becca maneuvered through the chaos, that night and in the following days, as if she were a deep sea diver, moving slowly, gracefully, but not hearing anything, not understanding the complexity of the full ocean around her. Just quietly swimming through an incomprehensible reality. She had transitioned, suddenly, without any warning, into a foreign world. For her, the shock was so great, and the need to keep moving forward so powerful, that the blister burns of grief and the sad questions at her father's death quickly formed into a callus. Not the soft whitish type that you can rub off with moist fingers, but the hard yellowish, crusty kind. A callus so hard and all encompassing

it formed a protective coating around Becca's heart, completely encapsulating her emotions. She was numb. She found this
tranquilizing cover to be a good thing so that she could function.
There was never a chance to scrape the callus off and expose the
searing rawness lying beneath.

Becca called her mother who, a few years before, had fled to
Hollister to be a dental hygienist and to garden in peace. She
might have moved to Florida for the amount of contact they had
with her. Dad's card games and days at the horse races had taken
its toll. Once Becca and her siblings had grown up and established their own jobs and marriages, Becca's mother fled the family home. She had negotiated for Becca and Dennis to move into
the house to care for Dad and the orchards and live rent free.

"I must say I'm not surprised. I always feared something like
this," Mom said to Becca over the phone. "Growing up in the Depression really messed him up. He never had a proper relationship with money." Becca was furious at her mother's coldness.

"Of course I am terribly sad, honey. It's just that I'm not that
surprised is all I'm saying," she explained.

"Mom, he's done with gambling. He's been working hard
pruning the orchards, helping us with the kids, gardening. He's
been going to his meetings. It's been a good transition," she said
defensively, still speaking in the present tense.

"Hmmmm, maybe. But look what happened. I'll come up
and help you honey, right away," Mom said, rather distantly, and
accusingly, Becca thought. Although Mom didn't say it explicitly,
her implied blame was probably right. They should have seen
some signs. Why hadn't they recognized the level of his depression? Had he been drinking a bit more than usual? Yeah, maybe.
He'd shut himself up in his apartment quite a bit these last few
weeks, she sort of remembered through the cottony film obscur-
ing her memories. Now she reflected that maybe he hadn't been
as upbeat and jovial as usual with the kids lately. Why hadn't she
noticed? She should have never left him alone while they went

skiing for the weekend.

Despite her mother's absence and feeling as if she were float-ing in a slow motion fog, Becca realized she was lucky to have solid support. Dennis was great, thank god.

"You just deal with the service, all the arrangements and his estate," Dennis said, giving her a quick hug and waving off her appreciation. "Figure out with the lawyer if his will was in order. I'll deal with the kids, and Tim and Matt are helping out a ton. Thank goodness. Wasn't your mother coming up?"

Tim, her childhood friend who had grown up in the big orchard house next door, came that first night and then didn't seem to leave. The calendar was foggy in Becca's mind, but, later, remembering that time, she realized that he and his partner, Matt, probably stayed with them for two weeks. They cooked and weeded the garden. They cleaned the house and babysat the kids. They distracted the children after school and on weekends, trying to keep things as normal for them as possible, especially when Dennis had to return to work only a few days after her father's death.

In addition to the numbness she experienced, Becca felt as if she had been given a swift, hard kick from a horse, knocking her off her usual feisty, self-confident balance. She had never really worried before, but now, suddenly, she knew that the world could change in an instant. Dramatically, permanently. Forever. She froze in the grocery store line one day. Look at all these people around, they're just going along like usual. Everyday life con-tinues. But mine is completely tossed upside down while every-thing else goes on like normal she thought. They have no idea my world is now topsy turvy. It's so weird, so frightening, that change can happen that quickly. Any moment, and your predict-able life was in a shambles. She worried about the kids, about Dennis driving to work, about Tim taking so much time off from his job at Pixar across the Bay. She rubbed her hands until they were chapped white.

As she made arrangements with the funeral home and prepared for a service, Becca searched through her father's apartment for his estate files and lawyer's contact information. Did Dad have a will? She wasn't even sure. She knew he had inherited the house and twenty acres of orchards and gardens and that it had been in the family for generations, since the late 1800s. It now occurred to her how foolish she and Dennis had been to move in without any information about Dad's finances or the house. She found a lawyer's number. While looking for paper to scribble it down, she stumbled upon a pile of bank envelopes with stamps marked urgent on the front. She opened one. What? It looked like Dad owed the bank? A mortgage on the house? But it had been owned free and clear for more than a hundred years. She searched through more of his papers and dusty files and then got on the phone.

As she became an investigator into her own father's finances, Becca uncovered that he had taken out several loans on the farmhouse and the orchards. There were high payments and he was behind by several months. The bank was so sorry for her loss, they said, but also insisted on a meeting as soon as possible to establish a revised payment plan.

At the lawyer's office she discovered that his will was in terrible shape. His estate attorney assured her that Dad had been saying he would make an appointment and put the house into a trust. Well, clearly you didn't get him to do that, Becca silently cursed the lawyer. Now there was a probate disaster to manage as well. But quickly she realized it wasn't the lawyer's fault. She, Dennis and her mother should have gotten the house paperwork in order years before when they moved in. She was so exhausted from the pain, the shock, the new revelations that she didn't even take that guilt on. She already had a full serving.

Each evening, she revealed the latest findings to Dennis, Tim and Matt over dinner at the large farm table with the side benches.

"I don't get it. What did he do with all that money he took out of the house," Dennis asked.

"Well, I couldn't figure it out either until I found more files hidden in Dad's apartment. He invested it in tech stocks. It looks like Worldcom, Webvan and Cisco were his favorites. Of course some of the biggest losers as the dot coms are crashing right now. And then, just when you didn't think it could get worse, today I found a late notice from an Internet poker company asking for their money on a loan. Did you know you can now gamble on the Internet? Well, of course, it is pretty new but Dad discovered it before anyone. I am so fucking naïve. Here I thought we had helped cure him and he was actually happy pruning cherry trees and planting zucchini. He always loved the summer fruit stand season and chatting with all the regulars who come to get their boxes of cherries and apricots. But you know what? He was goddamned playing poker on the Internet each night and investing in tech stocks. The broker told me he kept saying that these tech stocks just couldn't go down and wasn't that great." She put her head down on the table, arms splayed out and whimpered.

"I can't believe it. What are we going to do? He owes all this money. We don't have a way to pay it. That's why he put the For Sale sign out. He finally must have accepted he couldn't pay it all back. I was so sad and devastated when he died, what a week ago? Now I am so angry at him I can't see straight. It's really fucked up." Dennis, Tim and Matt looked at each other, then nodded over her head in silent agreement.

"Okay, Becca, we're gonna figure this out," Tim said. "Let's focus on planning the service right now and then we'll deal with all the other stuff."

"How could we have not known?" Dennis mumbled. Then realizing he had to be encouraging, added, "Well, at least I have a job at Compaq. Maybe you could go back to work, but not yet. Don't worry right now, honey. We'll figure something out."

After the memorial, Becca's childhood friends left the back lawn and drifted down the hill to the Orchard Tables, alone or in twos and threes. It was a lovely service they commented to each other. And it really had been, as they had looked out through cherry trees, to the distant apricot orchard with a skirt of yellow-topped mustard greens, seated on white wooden folding chairs on the expanse of green behind the big house. It was a bright, early spring day. Sunny, with a cloudless blue sky, but a little crispness still in the air. The colors were brilliant, clean. Becca's dad would have loved the beautiful day.

The old friends gathered at the three worn picnic tables Becca's mother had built by hand thirty-five years before. She had set them up under the apricot trees, intentionally at an independent distance from the old farmhouse. The tables were an orchard version of a tree house, a place just for kids, far from the indoor adult world. Becca's mom had wanted to get kids outside for picnics, messy art projects and sticky birthday parties. She gave Becca and her friends permission to paint them, carve their initials, glue things, whatever they wanted as long as they still worked as tables.

The only rule was, if you did something big like paint the whole table, or sand it down to re-stain it, you could only do one table, leaving the others as they were from past projects. So the tables and benches changed, but slowly, preserving the past at the same time. Becca thought this was a stroke of genius on her mother's part. She had been the most vigorous opponent of the policy when her mother announced it, but as she got older she could see the layers of neighborhood history displayed in full view on these tables. The spot had been the focal point of their schooldays, of their shared innocence.

The girls, for they still considered themselves young, particularly in these surroundings, draped their middle-aged bodies adorned in spring dresses across the benches, feeling as if they were moving into an old skin. As if they were snakes that were able to put that familiar, shedded prior life back on for a few moments, a casing that felt warm and comfortable but was loose and wrinkled and didn't quite fit anymore.

Laine caressed her fingers across the initials she and Chrissy had carved of the boys they were infatuated with in seventh grade. Rose smiled at the shells and sand shellacked into one of the tables from a Girl Scout sand candle project. Beth sat at a faded one, formerly the color of highlighter green stamped with white flowers, painted during a sixth grade sleepover. Becca picked a corner etched with a beautiful tree protected by varnish. Tim had carved it during some wild ninth grade party when he was supposedly in love and trying to impress her.

Tim now sat at the corner with the school newspaper staff photo, which many of them were in, glued down, varnished and re-varnished. It had aged in the years of rain and sun since. But if you looked really closely, you could make out familiar faces. Rick and Jack sat awkwardly on a low branch of the enormous oak situated between the tables, the orchard and the farmhouse. A slight breeze rustled the neon yellow mustard flowers and a few white blossoms spiraled to the ground from the apricot branches. They were quiet together for a while. Sobs and sniffles punctuated the stillness. Branches rustled but no one spoke. Finally, Becca stood up.

"Thank you all for being here—it means the world to me to have us together again. I asked you here because besides the fact I just lost my dad at too young an age, I seemed to have inherited a huge problem." She started to cry and choke on her words. She stopped talking to calm herself and then continued.

"If we can't figure something out quickly, because of the huge debts my father racked up taking cash out of the house and putting it into tech bubble stocks and Internet poker, we're going to have to sell everything. Move to Texas or something, somewhere cheaper. We don't even know. But through the craziness of this shock, this sudden discovery, I thought of all of you. You keep me sane. Tim and Matt have been amazing, basically running our household, while I sit and cry, or work on the logistical shit that comes when someone dies. It is quite overwhelming and something you aren't prepared for." She had to pause again.

As they looked at her, at the orchard, each one of them had memories percolating in their minds. They remembered her father, his booming voice, his jokes and deep laugh when he teased them. Although he was off at work most of their childhood, they pictured him as funny and youthful, the type who loved to throw a ball with the kids across the wide lawn. They had heard about the gambling. Everyone thought he had stopped when Becca's mother left. That Gambler's Anonymous had really helped him. That Becca, Dennis and her dad and found a successful family arrangement in the old orchard house. The tragedy was unfathomable. Becca went on with her plea,

"Your calls and offers of help have been great. Maybe there is something you can do. What if all eight of us bought the orchard, and the house too, of course? We could all put money in, pay off the bank loans and own the place together. Dennis and I can pay you rent so we can stay. I know you love this place as much as I do. Could you help me save it? I know eight is a lot of people but I am sure Jack with his business expertise or our own lawyer Christine could help figure out how to structure it. Please think about it. I'm completely at a loss." She paused, took a shallow breath, then whispered, "This land has been in my family forever."

Tears streamed down her cheeks, dripped off her chin. She sat down heavily, blew her nose. A breeze fluttered the branches. No one said anything. They looked at Becca and one another. Beth and Rose, lifelong friends and business partners, whispered to each other. Jack shifted his weight on the tree branch. Rick moved to a table and put his head in his hands.

"There aren't a lot of orchards left, Becca," Rick said, very gently. "Developers, even now with the stock and dot com crash, know housing prices keep going up. They'll want to build new homes and I bet will still pay quite a lot." Sympathy and sadness colored his voice.

"I don't know, Becs. What's it worth? I don't know how many of us have enough to put in to make it work. And some could put in a lot more than others, I'm quite sure," Laine the doctor said, looking directly at Jack Duda, cell phone company founder and CEO, balancing on a tree branch with a nervous tick in his leg.

"I know it's a crazy idea. But it just popped into my head, which is not in a great state right now, so I'm sure it makes no sense. This whole thing has kicked my butt, you guys. I'm at a loss. Can you please think about it? For me, for our memories here? I don't know what job I can get now that would even help with Dennis's salary. I haven't worked in twelve years since Nate was born, outside of the fruit stand every summer." She looked smaller than usual to the rest of them, as if she had shrunk in her grief.

"Have you talked to the bank about restructuring the loans?" Christine asked quietly, putting a hand on Becca's shoulder. "They should be open after a tragedy and such a dramatic change of circumstances. I can help. And maybe with the crazy probate situation you told me about too. I'll get in touch next week." Each one mumbled promises to think it over. To ponder solutions. They hugged and talked quietly in pairs, and then slowly, very slowly, ambled back to the other guests, rejoining families lingering over sweating glasses of lemonade and appetizer plates.

The old friends returned to their regular lives, while Becca's continued in its surreal, unimaginably altered state. Each morning, she woke up and had to recite a new set of instructions to herself. Oh, yes, Dad is gone. It's just me and Dennis here now with the kids. Time to get up and figure out how to make the bank payments. Then, as if sleepwalking, she got out of bed, showered and dressed and sat at the same spot at her kitchen table, working through her to do lists, making calls, sifting through papers, straining for new ideas. She shoved her former routine of children's school and activities, and managing the garden and fruit orchards to the background. She did the bare minimum. She wasn't sure how it all got done. Tim and Matt had returned to their home and jobs across the Bay. Dennis was back at work and had to take a business trip to Texas the first week after the service. The friends called as promised.

"I could give a few thousand dollars," said Laine, the HIV doctor and researcher.

"I could maybe round up twenty grand," offered Rick, owner of Offshore Wear, a beach clothing company. Rose and Beth, the two whose names adorned the Rosebeth Naturals organic baby products company, said they too could put in about twenty-five thousand dollars, but they figured the land was worth well more than a million, so that wasn't much help. Christine pled poverty as a Sacramento politician.

"I have some savings from my law firm work. I could put in, maybe ten thousand dollars? Would that help, Becca?" Christine asked.

Jack told Becca he couldn't get involved in shared real estate. He was so sorry about her dad and the liens on the property. But he couldn't help. It just didn't make sense. It was way too complicated for eight non-family members to own a place, even though they were childhood friends.

"But we don't really know each other as adults, do we Becca? I haven't seen most of you in years."

"Well, if you'd showed up for reunions and weddings and big events, and made an effort, maybe you would know us better," she retorted angrily and hung up. She immediately felt embarrassed by her harshness. But it was kind of true. Jack, who had grown up in a cottage right next door, had distanced himself from his old friends. She could see the plan was going nowhere.

Tim, decidedly more connected, still her best friend since adolescence, suggested that his dad, a next-door neighbor for more than forty-five years, could buy the land. Becca and Dennis could rent from him. Becca went over to the house after dinner one evening to present the idea. But Tim's dad said no, he was getting older and just his five acres was too much. He was going to sell. He should have sold before the dot com bubble burst but there were still developers building more housing he said.

"Cisco might have tanked but it's not goin' anywhere, neither is HP, Intel or Google," he said. "Plenty wanting to chop up the old orchards for more fancy houses," he said gruffly to Becca. "Of course, when we sell, Jack's parents will have to move out of the back cottage but I'll give them plenty of notice. Did you know his mom's very sick?" he added. Becca called Tim right away. Apologizing for his father's lack of interest, Tim tried another tack.

"What about your mom? Couldn't she help? Doesn't she care?" he asked Becca.

"No, my mom doesn't have any money. She's been a dental hygienist since she stopped being a hippie. And besides, whatever she did have, Dad lost in his horse racing and card shark days. That's why she left. To get away from his problems. To start over. She's done with this place. She checked out a long time ago." Clearly, none of her ideas, nor Tim's, were going to work. Becca had to devise a new plan.

The bank loan officer called for an appointment to renegotiate the loan yet again. Dennis and Becca had missed last month's payment. The bank didn't want to foreclose on Becca and her family farm, but they had to work together, he told her. She made an excuse and set an appointment for a week away. Dennis was in Texas again. The kids were cranky after school. She was listless, feeling hopeless. Worrying constantly. Desperation set in and so she forced herself to re-examine all possibilities. The only person she really knew with a lot of money was Jack. Yes, they'd growled at each on the phone, but he was one of her oldest friends. She would go see him in person. Alone. Really lay out her case. She knew that deep down he adored the orchards and creek. She would remind him.

At first, she tried to navigate the DudaTech bureaucracy to get an appointment with him, telling each assistant they put on the phone,

"Look, I'm a childhood friend. Can you please tell him it's urgent?" She felt as if the multiple layers of assistants were armed guards, keeping the lowly, and possibly dangerous, public at a distance. He had started the cell phone giant in the cottage behind Tim's house in the next orchard over. Sure, it was impressive how far he had traveled, but she was dismayed at his distant, cold affect. One of the assistants gave her an appointment more than three weeks away.

Then one night, Tim called.

"Did you hear? Jack bought my dad's place so his parents can stay in the cottage. He's already put four of the five acres up for sale, just keeping the land around the houses. No one has to leave. He must have wanted to prevent his mom from having to move when she's so sick. I think she has emphysema or something. Not sure."

That's it. Can't wait any longer Becca thought. I'm not waiting for any damn appointment. Frantically, she drove up to San Francisco and walked into the DudaTech office building, insisting on seeing Jack Duda, CEO. The security guards called the assistants, who called the personal assistant, who called the Executive Assistant, who called Jack. As Becca sat in the waiting area, feeling underdressed, she nervously pressed her sensible loafers hard into the entryway's shiny marble floor. The guard called her over to his station. He handed her the phone.

"Jack, it's Becca. Can I come up? They won't let me past the front entrance. I need to talk to you. It's important." The security guard buzzed her into the elevator lobby.

"You're lucky they let you in without an appointment," the guard told her. "He's a busy man keeping us all up to date with the latest cell phones." And he chuckled and flipped open his DudaFone and looked at it admiringly. "They give me a free one for working here. Nice, huh? Good luck, lady."

Becca entered the elegant office with the floor-to-ceiling windows and stared out at the Bay Bridge and Port of Oakland's cranes beyond. She gave Jack a quick hug, then they sat facing each other in the leather chairs in front of the view. She took a deep breath, swallowed the generations of family pride and presented her petition.

"Jack. It's serious. The only option I have left to pay off all these debts is for you to buy the land. Twenty acres. It's got a producing cherry and apricot orchard still on it. The summer fruit stand is famous in the area and brings in some income. It's gorgeous, as you know. The farmhouse is in decent shape for being over a hundred years old. It's a historic property, Jack. Your parents live next door. Dennis and I would like to stay, care for it and rent it from you. You'd never get better tenants. If it can't stay in my family any longer, then I'd like you to take it over. Almost as good," she said. A slight smile. She fought the tears back. She was resolved not to cry in front of Jack, in this high-powered office and formal setting.

He listened to her with a pained gaze, a frown on his face and his leg jiggling nervously. He pushed it down with his hand, as was his habit. He had to apply more pressure than usual.

"No, Becs, I won't do it. I'm sorry. Orchards are the past. The dried apricots come from Turkey now. The Valley of Hearts' Delight is gone and you need to sell to a developer, move out and move on. Isn't your mother in Hollister? Maybe you can get a place with a bit of land. It's cheaper out there. It's not an investment for me. I would just flip it so that doesn't make any sense."

"But you bought Tim's place," she said, more forcefully now.

"Yes, I did, but for my parents. That's why I did it. Not for an investment. I'm selling the orchard part and just keeping the houses."

"Why would you do that for them but not for me? For all those years we ran through the orchards together. I want my kids to have that freedom, that independence...those adventures...." She was sobbing now. Incoherently. So frustrated at her inability to change the present. He had so much money, no kids of his own, a bunch of houses, why couldn't he buy the orchards?

"Becca," Jack said impatiently, angrily. "My mother is dying. She is now in hospice in that cottage. My father will have nothing when she's gone but his home of forty years. That's why I did it."

"Well, then you'll know what it's like to lose a parent," she said abruptly, without thinking.

"It is time for you to leave now," he said. He was furious. His brows folded into each other and his face flushed reddish. He got up to move her out and his limp was deeper, more pronounced than ever.

"Oh, Jack, I'm sorry. I shouldn't have said that. I'm so sorry your mom is..." She could see it was too late. He was now even angrier than she was. She put up her hand to indicate she was leaving and walked out without another word.

She fumed the entire drive from San Francisco to the farmhouse. Jack had all this money and power and fame and he couldn't just help out his old friends. Once home, she was at a loss. She wandered through her house, looking at old photos and remembering the early years, the running through the orchard years, the tag and horseback riding and, oh, that creek. So carefree, those days. She had hoped her own children, and even grandchildren, would experience that treasure, that natural schoolhouse, forever. That's why she had to hang on at all cost.

The more Becca dreamily dove into her past, the more she reflected on what she had learned in those years exploring the orchards. Wow, Jack was ungrateful, she told herself. I remember the time we rescued him after he broke his ankle. That memory helped her realize why it was so important. What it was that she wanted her kids to learn. You figured it out. You rolled up your sleeves and just made things happen. No matter how bad it got. No matter how tricky or difficult, you just worked on a solution.

Well, it was as bad as she could ever imagine right now. She missed her dad's happy smile, his whistle while he pruned the trees, grumbling when he cooked fresh vegetables from the garden and his grandkids didn't want to eat them. How could she have been so deluded, so oblivious, of what was really going on inside him? How was she going to figure something out this time?

Becca walked into the bank she had been going to since she was a child. She had her first account here at about six or seven. She had picked her own bushel of cherries, boxed them and then sold them at the family fruit stand. Mom said that if she did all the stages of the process she could keep the money. She did and then Dad took her to open a savings account. Did Mom know about his gambling problem back then she wondered, her mind wandering to the myriad questions surrounding her father's death. She'd have to ask Mom if she ever got a chance. The banker talked through loan plans and ways to restructure so they could make the payments. One more chance. In a daze, Becca nodded and pretended to acquiesce and assure the gentleman they could meet the commitments this time.

"Oh, I heard that your next door neighbor is selling," the banker said. "Looks like the head of DudaFone bought that orchard property. Didn't he grow up around here? You really should think about selling, Becca. That would be your very best option. We look forward to seeing your full payment next month. But do think about selling. Bye, bye."

Becca got in her car, seething. She drove home erratically. Lucky she didn't get a ticket, she thought as she crunched in on the familiar driveway. She sat in her car for a long time before going in. Okay, she had to admit that it really wasn't Jack's responsibility to save her and her family from her father's misdeeds. That wasn't his fault. And just because he was rich didn't mean he had to take care of everyone else who came along. Maybe she had been unfair in expecting him, now so successful, to solve her problems.

She hadn't worked in years, beyond the annual six weeks operating the summer fruit stand. She had focused on raising the kids. Her skills were out of date, she feared. What have I been doing besides mothering, but gardening, managing the orchard and selling the fruit, making preserves? What do I know?

Wait, maybe that's it. I garden, I prune and pick. I pickle and preserve, she thought. She was a regular beehive of farming activity. Why not sell vegetables, jams, pickled veggies and canned fruit to the loyal fruit stand customers all year? Maybe she could bring in a little more to supplement Dennis's salary and keep the bank from hassling them. The fruit stand had been popular for generations. There could be customers who would like fresh, natural produce other times of the year.

Becca climbed out of her car, rushed into her farmhouse kitchen, sat at the big table and developed a plan. She researched online and discovered the Community Supported Agriculture movement, which had multiple models of ownership and sales approaches. After exploring other farm produce businesses, she decided to build on the fruit sales her family had maintained for at least four generations. They had a reputation with locals and even those who lived miles away. She had customers who came down, year after year, from San Francisco, up from Monterey and over from Concord and Walnut Creek to buy her orchard's produce.

Why not sell baskets of vegetables all year long on a weekly or monthly schedule? She would transform the seasonal Orchard to Kitchen, the longtime name of the family's fruit stand, into adding a monthly produce basket, delivered to your door. Becca wasn't sure how she'd do that but her old 1990 Ford F150 could hold a lot in the back. She'd be the delivery person as well as the farmer, she decided.

So Becca, some of her feistiness returning out of a stubbornness to defeat the bank and prove Jack Duda wrong, got on the phone and called every single fruit stand customer who's number she'd ever had. She developed a master email list and began sending promotional pictures of her produce. She offered them vegetables and fruit preserves while they waited for cherry season. She expanded her garden and boxed up the veggies, adding a jar of pickles and delicious apricot jam into each Orchard to Kitchen Produce Basket. Then she pulled out of the driveway in the pickup and got on the road.

She enlisted the kids to help by placing printed flyers on every doorstep in surrounding neighborhoods. She called her friends and relatives, and their friends and relatives. She called Dennis's work buddies and the kids' friends from school. And slowly, very slowly, she sold some vegetable baskets. And then, eventually, the phone started to ring with people she didn't know. Email orders started to fill her inbox. She spent all day packing baskets and delivering and all night making jam and packing more baskets. She drafted the kids to put stickers on the pickle jars, harvest lettuce, beets, carrots and onions, and stir giant pots of blackberry jam. Her family thought she'd gone nuts. She was in a Becca frenzy of activity, a buzzing of movements and to do lists, with vegetables, jam jars, and the cheapest baskets she could find at Marshall's, stacked in every corner of the house.

Produce Basket grew slowly and Becca and Dennis managed to keep up with the renegotiated, smaller bank payments. But they could see that they would never really pay off the full mortgages at the current rate.

"We have to sell, Becs," Dennis said. "You're going to wipe yourself out, or drive us crazy, with all this fruit basket shit. You can't keep this pace up and we still owe hundreds of thousands of dollars. Let's sell fifteen acres and keep five and the house. You can pay off the debts and still have gardens for vegetable boxes and some trees for the fruit stand. What do you think?"

As she watched houses going up on Tim's former property next door, she realized Dennis was right. To get free and clear, they would have to sell. It broke her heart to cut off the back acreage, like it was a limb that was adored, familiar and so useful. The consolation was that she was not completely deserting family history. They would retain some of the trees and she could keep her Produce Basket business going on the remaining five acres. After more than a year of one failed idea after another, Becca saw no other option.

Her anger at her father had lessened with time, but she was resigned to the fact that he had hopelessly left her his problems. She had to persevere on her new course and not allow Dad's tragedy, his despair, to consume her. The callus, doing its job, masked the depth of her pain but also, mercifully, allowed her to continue on. She agreed to sell the back fifteen acres of apricot and cherry orchards to a developer who was buying the final lots in the surrounding hills.

After the paperwork was processed at the title company office, Becca and Dennis went down to the bank. They assured the banker he would get the full amount of the mortgages wired as soon as escrow closed. It made her sad but she was relieved to finally be clear of debts and the persistent clamor of creditors.

Becca barely had time to process the results, to celebrate, or to mourn. She had to fill baskets and get ready for morning deliveries. She had to plant and weed and can more cherries before they were overripe. She dragged the kids even further in to the business, attempting to distract them by encouraging them to spend as much time in the shrunken orchard as possible. Maybe they don't have a creek anymore but they've got us, and our little family business, which they've helped build. That's something, she told herself. I sure hope it's enough.

One morning, on one of those teachers' workdays when everyone was at home on a weekday, all three kids were in the garden, watering, weeding, transplanting seedlings from black plastic packets into little trenches. Suddenly, they heard a loud rumble. Becca and the kids looked at each other, jumped up and ran to the fence at the back of the property, still newly damp, with fresh splinters and a pinkish tint. They peered over the top and through the knotholes to watch giant earthmovers and tractors lumber in to their former play area, growling and squeaking as they rolled down the hill toward the stream, slicing up the apricot trees in their path. The kids froze, transfixed. Becca shook her head. Thirteen-year-old Nate refused to speak, pounding his fist on the fence. The little one started to cry.

After coaxing them away from the scene, and distracting them somewhat in the kitchen with snacks, Becca went out the back door and into the garage, a place she avoided if at all possible. But she didn't want the children to see or hear her. She sat on an old sawhorse and sobbed. This new shock at seeing the destruction of her beloved orchards, her very foundation, overwhelmed her. The tears released some of the pent-up grief, frustration and disbelief that she had suppressed for so long. She missed her dad and she still felt a confusing mix of guilt over his death and disappointment in what he'd left behind. But losing the orchards, that was a culminating assault, like the last act of a play that solidifies the tragedy. The final kick in the gut.

After a long cry, she looked up and took in the garage she hadn't really seen in more than a year. Her broken skis, dulled with a layer of grime, were still leaning against the back wall where they'd been ever since that night they returned from the mountains. How she longed for that time before the ski accident, when feeling relieved that she had not broken a leg in the ski run wipeout was her strongest sentiment. Not going to be getting those skis fixed anytime soon. Don't think we'll be up for a ski trip for a long time, she thought. She couldn't even imagine returning to that state of wholeness, and freedom from worry, before the broken skis. And indeed, they remained in that exact spot against the garage wall, untouched, gathering dust, for many years.

Wine Country

"CHRISSY. IT'S JACK DUDA from the old neighborhood. Are you still in Santa Cruz? Oh, up in Sacramento again? Wow. I hadn't heard that. Sorry, I would've donated to your campaign if I'd known! Look, Chrissy, this is huge for me to call you out of the blue. I really need to talk to you. I wouldn't bother you if it wasn't important. Will you come up to my winery outside Calistoga next weekend? Say one o'clock on Saturday? We can walk through the vineyards and bike the back roads. I was petrified to reach out but I'm so glad to hear your voice, Chrissy. I'll email you the directions. It'll be great to catch up. What's that? Oh, sure. Christine it is."

Christine pushed the button on her DudaFone and wondered what the heck that was about. She hadn't seen him since Tim's memorial service more than five years ago and only a few times during college. She wondered if he had been in touch with any of the others. Chrissy? She hadn't been called that in thirty years. It made her feel muddled. Christine prided herself on never getting flustered. Jack had caught her unawares, disrupting her usual unflappability. Her signature calm. And because of that, of course, she would go. Such a mystery. She had not taken even thirty-six hours off of work in years. A Napa weekend would be a lovely treat.

Why's he inviting me to his wine country house she wondered. Here's a childhood friend re-surfacing unexpectedly, one who's been distant for years, but also is so familiar. Jack was in the purse and pocket of millions, his surname on every cell phone in America. Well, unless you had that new iPhone, which did seem to be quickly replacing DudaTech's DudaFone. It's probably a lobbying trip, using his old friend connections, she guessed. Which Senate subcommittee am I on that a telecommunications giant would want access to my vote?

Her chief of staff came in, interrupting her thoughts, and she immediately turned her attention to state business. No more than two and a half minutes on any one topic in this job. A recipe for ADD, if you didn't already have it coming into the California State Senate chambers.

Once home in her elegant Midtown condo by 10:30 that night, Christine replayed the phone call in her mind, intrigued. What was up with Jack? A winery? Really? It seemed so un-Jack-like. The tech titan was always traveling, meeting with important CEOs, providing fodder for Tech Insider gossip, flying off on private jets to world meetings. Seemed an odd fit for tiny Calistoga. But then she remembered that Silicon Valley's elite were buying up souvenir wineries, as if adding an obligatory silver charm on the current trendy bracelet. She had read that he was divorced from that San Francisco socialite. Maybe he's lonely? Any hot young thing would go up there with such an affluent, well-known businessman. Why me? Hmmm, must be politics. Well, I'll take the free weekend in Calistoga, she told herself. She sent emails to her staff and other senators to clear her weekend calendar of work commitments. Nothing personal to reschedule. No one to disappoint.

Jack waited in a wooden rocking chair on the stone porch of his winery home, nervously jiggling his right quadricep with the rapid up and down of his ankle. The damaged one. The one that gave him a unique stride. The gait that made him distinctive among the handsome, well-groomed business leaders of his era. Jack didn't know if Christine would actually show up. He had prepared a resort quality retreat if she decided to leave the world of politics for a day and a half. Unfamiliar anxiety filled his chest. The old high school nervous nausea returned as if he had been struck suddenly with an illness. He shook his head at how ridiculous that was.

Waiting for Christine, as he looked out over acres of his own Cabernet vines, he was transported to the yard behind his child-hood cottage, sitting at the workbench strewn with tools. Motor parts, bicycle pieces, dismembered appliances had littered the yard. Bushes hid his whereabouts and his tinkering passions. But every time he was out there, many days until dusk robbed his light, absorbed in building and experimenting, he always had a tiny itch, just waiting to be relieved by his mother's Polski call that one of the kids was at the cottage door. She would describe the current requestor in Polish—the one with the freckles, the one with the blond ponytail, the tall one that looked like a horse, the swimming boy with shiny green hair, the bossy girl. Even Tim, the most frequent suitor, had a descriptor—the landlord's son. She never knew their names. His pulse would gear up, he'd drop the latest invention, reluctantly, but not enough to stay, race around the side of the former garage and greet his sun-kissed neighbors with enthusiasm. What adventure did they have in mind this time? He was in, whatever it was.

Through high school, he had just felt lucky they were still

kind to him, thrilled if he was ever invited to a party or dance. He knew he was the last pick, but a safe one. So he took comfort in that and found satisfaction in the computer lab, TA-ing for the Physics teacher and continuing to take apart and rearrange radios, phones, engines and kitchen appliances. Once in college, Jack studied engineering and then established a cellular technology and network company, creating some of the first small cell phones. Henry Ford was his role model—a phone in every pocket his motto.

Jack Duda's company met that goal and for more than fifteen years DudaTech made the DudaFone, the most common label on phones in North America and Europe. In the early days, his phones even had a presence in the Japanese market. Apple Computer, his favorite tech company back in college, had resurrected itself with the iPod and iPhone to bring him the most serious competition he'd ever had. Perfect timing. He was bored with phones.

He resigned as CEO but not before his partner of twenty years sued him for neglecting his fiduciary responsibility, accusing Jack of leaving the company unattended while pursuing his new obsession, battery technology. Jack countersued. The lawyers were making a fortune and every legal meeting felt like a tooth extraction. He had hoped to use the ubiquitous DudaTech brand for his battery company. But he would have to start all over. The breakup was as excruciating as a divorce. ÔIn fact, he almost had felt married to his business partner, more than to his wife. No surprise, she felt the same way and was divorcing him too.

What a disaster. His life was exhausting just when he wanted to make it simpler. I might have been a good tech businessman all these years but not so adept at engineering quality relationships, he reflected. Jack had recently broadened his tunnel vision view of his frenetic pace, his house-airplane-office-clothes-travel rich life and saw emptiness. A blank white space. He was desperately lonely. The day he went from his Atherton renovated historic mansion, featured in Architectural Digest, to his stylish San Francisco flat to his recently acquired Calistoga winery and was alone in each stunning location, he despaired. Each house ostensibly a sanctuary but nothing reassuring, certainly no loving partner or family member in residence, in any of them. Just months ago, Jack had sat at his walnut desk at the winery main house, divorce proceeding transcripts and DudaTech lawsuit claims covering the knotty wood. That's it. No more. I'm done. I have to make a change. Where do I even begin? He'd hit a workaholic's rock bottom.

Christine's car wound in from Highway 29, the Silverado Trail, along the vine-bordered driveway. Jack greeted her on the porch steps with a shy grin and a formal handshake. Flustered, he talked too fast.

"I am so glad you came, Chrissy. Here, let me get that. Thanks for making the trip. I promise you'll have a relaxing weekend. For once, probably. Right? Do you get away from Sacramento much? You look great by the way. Strong and pretty, just like 'Chrissy, the Tomboy' but all grown up! Do you remember that's what we called you? Forever."

Jack stopped himself, realizing he was rambling, embarrassing both of them. He hauled her bag up the stairs and led her into the manor house, his limp more pronounced than Christine remembered. His black hair still thick on top, but graying slightly at the temples. A fashionable dark scruff covering his cheeks. Years of expensive haircuts, custom suits and first class living had softened his teenage awkwardness, tailoring him into a smoothly elegant man. He seemed less self-satisfied than what she remembered of him at Tim's service. Maybe it's not a political visit after all, but why?

Once nestled into a cozy corner room with a view of the valley, Christine followed Jack on a tour through the property. She had expected opulence but appreciated the tasteful restraint in the building's design. The winery's house exuded California Mission with beige adobe walls and wrought iron finishes. Maybe it really is old and he just fixed it up, or maybe it's so expensive it's made to look old, she judged. Fresh baked bread smells wafted through the halls from the kitchen. Of course, a cook, she thought. How extravagant.

"I know, I know. It's kinda trite to buy a vineyard," he admitted, talking nervously as he led the tour. "But I love it here. I just didn't realize it the first few years I owned it! Half the tech guys I know invested in backyard grapevines and sold to wineries, putting sensors out to get a reading for every single plant. At first it was just a trend I succumbed to. But then, I found I really liked the science of the grapes and how to make them into good wine. At the beginning, I didn't pay any attention, like to most things. But this old Italian guy my winemaker hired to watch the wine in the barrels and monitor the harvest was like a bulldog. He pestered me to actually observe every step of the process until I couldn't say no. He took me out to the vines, to taste the barrels, to pay attention to the timing, the chemistry of the fruit, the flavors. He had me picking the grapes at two in the morning with the farmworkers and watching every detail of the crush. So I started to learn and fell for the process."

Christine nodded as he swooshed a test glass into a fermenting barrel and handed it to her. "That guy saved me, now that I think about it," he muttered. Christine looked up sharply and stared at him. Jack ignored her and continued.

"This is at one of the last stages. A Pinot experiment we're doing in very small batches at first. Try it." Jack said and continued talking throughout the tour. "So I rebuilt the main house and added more stainless and oak barrels. I put in a larger production warehouse and even a tasting room, although I haven't opened it yet. Not really sure I want to actually do that. It's very public to be open all the time."

Christine murmured politely in typical politician mode.

"Well, Jack, this seems to be a nice new hobby for you," and took another sip of the glass from the barrel.

"Chrissy. Sorry, Christine. I know you think you know me from what you read online. In the tech gossip blogs. But I've been making a lot of changes. I sold my Atherton house and the San Francisco flat I've had for twenty years. Both just before the crash and this recession, thank God. And I moved here. This is my home now. It's so quiet. So real. I feel like I can hear the grapes growing out there. Every cell producing more sugar and flavor, acids and tannins. I've always been a scientist at heart. This is a chemistry project for me, a more peaceful endeavor than all my others, that's for sure."

Christine was surprised at the revelations. She smiled at him, finished her sample glass, and told him what a gorgeous home and winery he had.

"Thanks for inviting me here. Why did you invite me, by the way?"

"Let's go eat," he said, taking her elbow and escorting her out of the cool, damp cellar into the Saturday afternoon glow.

Jack served a delicious meal on the terrace as melon-colored ambient light struck the vineyard, turning the valley orangey pink. Christine felt like she was on a blind date. Where everyone is awkward and trying too hard and uncomfortable, all jumbled together. After dinner, he led her into the living room with gleaming Mexican tile floors, thick carpets and inviting chairs. A fire in the stone fireplace, iron sconces and tapestried walls lent an old world atmosphere to the great room. Unsure about safe topics and at his urging, Christine updated him on the neighborhood kids.

"Despite all of us resolving at Tim's memorial service to be better friends to each other, I don't really think that's happened for anyone," she surprised herself by admitting to him. "I stay in touch with Rick. And somehow I always know what everyone is up to. Student body and class president roles never really leave you, do they?" Jack laughed quietly at that but was silent for the

233

first time since she had arrived.

"But am I really friends with the kids we grew up with, went to school with? No, Jack, I'm not. But you still want to know about them, right? Laine's still a doctor and researcher at UCSF. They just profiled her for *The New York Times*. Still doing AIDS drug research, looking for a vaccine. Still trying to get the drug companies not to gouge the poor in Africa. Her kids are teenagers. She got divorced. She works all the time. Becca still has her fruit stand and produce business but I heard they had to sell more of the old orchards. Her kids are teenagers too, one in college. The girls, Beth and Rose, remember they went to New York right after high school and both had kids early? Those kids are all grown up, working now. They expanded Rosebeth Naturals beyond baby food to organic cotton clothes, natural baby carriers, non-plastic toys. They have a popular blog. Some big company will buy them, I'm sure. Super busy," she said.

"Rick too," she went on. "Not sure you knew, but even in high school he sewed shorts and rash guards in his van at beach parking lots, selling to the surfers who change under their towels behind the car doors. He gave them free shorts for feedback and then started driving up and down the coast selling to surf shops. Now he has a factory in downtown LA. Offshore Wear is popular all over the world. He even sponsors pro surfers. He installed the '72 VW van with his mom's original Singer sewing machine perched inside into the corner of his headquarters." Jack laughed at the image and clapped his knees appreciatively.

"And you probably don't know this either," she continued, "but when Tim was diagnosed as HIV positive in the '80s, Rick was so angry he wanted to do something. Our activist doctor friend, Laine, told him to promote condom use in the surfing community. So you know what he did? He put a condom in every t-shirt and board short pocket. He made t-shirt designs promoting what we now call 'safe sex.' He encouraged surf shop owners to sell condoms from baskets at the check-out counters, calling the

whole promotion Condoms for the Lineup. Anyone who resisted, he told them straight up, 'I have a childhood friend who has
AIDS and he's really sick and might die. This is serious and it's
not going away. We have to use condoms—all the time.'"

"Wow, very cool," Jack said. "I had no idea. I was kind of in my
own world, I'm ashamed to admit. But it's true. Good for Rick."

"Yeah, it was so successful he got hooked on the idea of promoting a cause through business. At the time, I was on the Coastal Commission and we'd talk about ocean pollution, the dangers
of development. After the safe sex promotions were less needed,
he joined the Surfrider Foundation. Now the surf and sports
apparel business is also really big. He was there at the forefront.

"Sorry to bore you with so much about Rick," she said. "But
ever since we spent junior year smoking weed in the back of that
van and hanging at the beach, skateboarding and surfing, we've
been close. He's sort of like a brother who I know is always there
for me. It's very comforting." She did not add out loud, because I
don't have much of a personal life. She paused. "Kind of amazing
the success of the kids we grew up with, isn't it?"

Jack nodded. He appreciated getting the update. He confessed he had made no efforts to stay in touch with anyone,
despite seeing the old friends at Tim's memorial. The shock of
losing Tim so young should have motivated him to be a better
friend, he admitted. She nodded in agreement, but said they
were all so busy with their careers and families and even their
aging parents. It wasn't really an excuse but it was something
people always said, as if it were a justification for ignoring
friendship. They were quiet together for a moment.

Then he unloaded on her about his latest business trials and
his divorce. He told her about selling off his iconic cell phone
business and moving into batteries.

"I got bored of the day-to-day of the business. Plus, you may
have read, unfortunately titillating gossip for Tech Insider, that
my partner accused me of leaving the rudder as the captain of

the ship. He's sued me. I've countersued. It's ugly. I mean, this guy and I were friends from college. We kind of started the industry together. We built our first prototypes in my backyard. You know, behind Tim's parents' house? My parents never left there, if you can believe it. My dad is ninety and still lives in that tiny cottage. My mom died a long time ago, a year or so after Becca's dad died. Of emphysema." He continued without letting her say a word. He had been rehearsing this moment like it was the principal monologue in a school play. And he was just as nervous. Jack felt this was like sending a Hail Mary.

"So, Chrissy. Christine. Sorry. I'm looking to make significant changes. I got myself into this terrible predicament. My wife filed for divorce after six months of therapy where I thought we were making progress. I had no clue how bad our relationship was. In couple's therapy, I found out my wife secretly had been taking the pill when I thought we were trying for a baby, years back. It was devastating. She said I worked too much and wasn't really interested in her or a family. Probably true, but it was very painful to realize I screwed it up. I mean, it does take two, but it basically was my lack of attention and idiocy that sank it. I was a self-absorbed jerk. I could hardly blame her by the end. We were ill suited but I did love her." Christine gave him a sympathetic look with a quizzical frown at the confession.

"No kids, no family left, no wife and few friends. I've just worked. So I gotta face the fact I've isolated myself in my company. And now I don't have that either. A company doesn't keep you warm at night and it isn't a companion on trips to the Galapagos. I want to get out, explore, do the things I never did as a young adult." He took a breath. "I'm trying to make significant changes, not just plow forward without stopping to think, like I've done my whole life."

Christine listened with increasing interest. Wow, he really is trying to tone things down. Show a little humility. Even at Tim's funeral he had been standoffish, haughty, she remembered. Who

236

can act superior at the funeral of someone who died of complications from HIV at only forty-three? And a childhood friend? Jack grew up in that little cottage behind Tim's house. Tim was the one who always brought him along on the creek wades and bike rides, to join the tag and hide and seek games. How could he be cavalier toward his childhood companions at another friends' funeral? But he had been. Maybe Jack could sense the memory. He switched topics and asked her to provide the Christine update.

Influenced by the confessional tone, Christine admitted that she too worked all the time. She had never married and really only had a sister, a niece and nephew and Rick as her close relationships. Everything else in her world was about being a politician. Working, striving.

"I'm sure people gossip that I'm gay. You know, like Oprah or Anderson Cooper, everyone is quite sure but they still won't come out or took forever. But I'm not. So now we're late forties. I've accepted I won't have kids. I have a great niece and nephew who I dote on but that's it. I've dated and even pretty seriously but just never found the right fit. Plus, being the partner to a politician is pretty grueling. I've kinda let the Senate take over my life. Hmmm, seems to be the theme of the night," she mused, smiling.

Christine suddenly flashed back to when Jack was a skinny little kid with bushy hair that stood straight up and looked like a daily bed-head mess.

"Didn't the boys call you Spike? 'Cause your hair stood straight up?"

"Yeah." He smiled, remembering, a bit painfully. "Yeah, they did. Any improvements are the benefits of an expensive stylist." His smile was warm, and his tone was self- mocking, not imperious like she'd remembered.

Abruptly, he thanked her for coming, saying the maid would make sure she had everything she needed in her room.

"Let's continue in the morning," he said. "I'm tired and pretty nervous. I didn't know if you would actually show up." They walked upstairs but stopped in front of her room. He surprised her by continuing, leaning against the bannister.

"I know it's been thirty years since high school and probably thirty-five since we actually were close friends in elementary school running around the orchards. I always felt so lucky you let me in the little orchard gang. I was a nerdy kid who liked to take stuff apart and construct weird inventions. You all were athletic and graceful. You rode horses. Horses terrified me. And then when Rick started surfing and you started hanging with him—well, I just felt ever so lucky my parents rented that cottage behind Tim's house. I knew I'd been blessed to grow up with you. That you and Rick, Becca and Laine even knew who I was. Most of the time you all were kind to me and I really appreci- ated that through the end of high school. Tim was always great, always a friend, always checking in on me and sending me crazy drawings, those personalized cartoons he did for each of us. But the rest of you...I just felt like I didn't belong any more. Like, in reality, I never did belong."

"Oh Jack, you were..." Then she stopped herself. She didn't need to be a politician here. He'd exposed raw nerve endings. She had to respect that and be honest. She took a different ap- proach, almost confrontational.

"Is that why you stopped communicating during college?" she asked. "Why you got aloof, egotistical appearing? Why you never came to parties or high school reunions? Even once you were famous and successful? I mean, we all used your phones when cell phones came out. We all knew who made them and who was making all the money." Her tone was accusing. He didn't respond, just frowned a pained grimace. He twisted and turned the lame ankle, shuffling nervously.

"But I guess I can't say much," she admitted, softening her tone and volume, "because I did the same thing—just with law and politics. I thought preserving the coastline was a critical cause, more important than what everyone else was doing. I've been a lawyer my whole adult life. I was a paralegal while I was in college. I was involved in big coastline cases before I finished law school. So I was pretty self-righteous. Then I got so busy with Santa Cruz and Sacramento politics. I'd been on the Coastal Commission and then in Sacramento for years but after Tim's death. I decided to focus locally so I ran for mayor of Santa Cruz. I went back to Sacramento two years ago to the State Senate. Always moving up, you know?" she said. A sad, sardonic grin.

"No more confessions tonight. Go to bed, Chrissy. Christine. We'll talk more at breakfast. I have bikes ready for a ride through my vineyards and up the hill." He gave her a quick hug and a little kiss on the forehead. Like he was her dad or something.

In her cozy room, under the satiny, high thread count sheets, Christine slept more deeply than she had in months. It was so quiet. No city noise. It was dark black with no moon and no streetlights. A night punctuated only by throaty bullfrogs declaring their presence on a unanimously appointed schedule. She woke late at 8.30, surprised and a little embarrassed. She hadn't slept in for years. It was delicious. She took her time showering and dressing, wondering what to expect next. What was he after?

Once out on the patio, she felt refreshed, a little younger maybe. She was curious but felt a calmness inside. Unusual for her. The breakfast table was laid out on the porch with a view overlooking the sloping expanse of grapevines. No one was around so she sat down and sipped the pulpy orange juice, taking in the scene. Jack appeared with coffee. He smiled warmly as he walked to the table. She noticed his limping gait was much slower than she remembered it from the funeral. She wondered if he had a lot of pain.

"There's no maid today. It's Sunday. I made you coffee and breakfast. It's coming right up."

"Why didn't you wake me?" she asked.

"I figured you needed to rest. I hope you were comfortable."

"Yes, amazing. Better than any B and B. I'm glad I came, Jack. Very relaxing. It's a beautiful setting. You're spoiling me."

"Don't they treat you that way as chair of the Environmental Quality Committee?" he jokingly asked.

"Uh, no. The opposite. Well, you get a nicer office, but remember it's all relative. Mostly they all hate me or brownnose in order to get something. So I have no idea how people really feel."

"Why do you do it? Politics is so ugly. It's so polarized now. Even in California with Democrats pretty much in charge of the legislature, and now Obama as President. But it's still so partisan. Who makes deals anymore?"

"Yeah, but if I leave, then it's the crazies who take over," she said. "I've seen some of them up close and there are seriously some wackos in office. So I feel the need to keep the balance with some sanity in the system. The northern coast needs an advocate in Sacramento. I'm pretty committed. I've been at it a long time."

"You're an idealist, Christine. A dreamer. One of the good guys, but maybe a bit deluded."

She was offended, taken aback by his honesty, but then she remembered she'd called him egotistical last night. Touché. He brought more coffee and a breakfast burrito. Delicious. They talked about competing wineries, oil rigs off the coast, Sacramento legislature gossip, the latest from Silicon Valley tech companies. Safer topics.

"Let's go biking," Jack said. He took her to a shed with two mountain bikes and helmets ready to go. He shouted for her to follow as he hopped on, heading out toward the winery entrance. And he was off on vineyard service roads, down dry creek beds and gullies, up hills and through the vines themselves where deep purple grapes coated with a misty hue hung low off the green leaves, some yellowing and reddening. She had to pedal hard to not lose him. Gear up, gear down, twist and turn over the roots and bumps. Stay on the path. Change gears again. Keep up but don't fall she told herself.

They reached the ridge's pinnacle and gazed down the Napa Valley. Gorgeous. She didn't say anything but felt the energy of physical exhaustion, shared confessions and hidden ponderings. And he was off again, twisting into action off jump-like bumps, down the ridge, pedaling through the trees and eventually back to the valley floor, home of the grapes. He was athletic and skilled on the trail ride. On a mountain bike, he moved fluidly and with a little grace. It was a perfect way to flee the limp. Jack didn't stop until they arrived at his large stone porch with the wide overhang. Ceiling fans slowly circling to create a welcome-home breeze.

"Come have lunch. Let's talk." The table was reset and beautifully laid out with lemonade and salad, decorated with a casual bouquet of wildflowers. Surprised, she gave him a questioning look and he grinned sheepishly. Shy and sly.

"Well, I did have her come for the afternoon today. She's a great cook." They'd been gone for hours. Exhausted and sweaty, Christine begged for a shower and change first. Then they ate lunch easily, joking about the ride, discussing the view, more politics and wine sales.

"Okay Chrissy, here's why I invited you here. It's been fun, and rejuvenating, to spend time with you. Remembering who we are, that we do have a past but also, maybe, a few values in common? You and I, we breathe Silicon Valley at our core. We work. We are ambitious and creative. Take risks in our fields. That's what we're good at. But I think you and I both know there is something more we've been neglecting. At least I have and it appears to me that you have too. And that's human interaction, personal relationships, plain old friends." He gazed directly into her face, leaning forward and pushing his knee down with one elbow to quiet his leg tremor.

"I now realize I've ignored the importance of friendship for too long," he said. "I'm determined to do a reset with my personal life. When I pared everything down, stripped away all the bullshit, I didn't have much left. No family—except my dad who is very elderly now. No companions except business ones. No friends. I know a lot of people. People who think they are especially important. I know tech leaders, New York and Hollywood people. Business guys all over the world. But are any of them truly friends? No. Not really. I've faced loneliness head on and decided to rectify it. I'm changing."

He sounded sincere. She could feel that he was speaking from a place of deep pain and pared down simplicity. His tone reminded her of a skinny, wild-haired Jack sprinting down the hill through the orchards to the creek, just one in a gaggle of childhood friends. Jack paused for a long time before continuing. His voice was scratchy.

"The only place I really have to start is with all of you from the neighborhood. I could sense at Tim's memorial service that friendship still might be possible. My idea is to form sort of an AA for Workaholics, but just for us, our old friends. Starting with me. And you. I want to convene the old gang here at the winery. I have a surprise I want to show everyone. I want them to see I'm committed to all of them, to Tim's memory, to our friendship even though our old orchards are gone. I'm inspired by what amazing, authentic people you all are. I'm in awe of everyone's accomplishments out in the world, of their entrepreneurial spirit and drive." He paused. Took a deep breath and went on. He put a hand on his lame leg to steady the fidgety bounce.

"So, Christine. Chrissy. I want you to help me get them here. I'll invite everyone and then you do your politician charm job and help me get them to show up. That's why I asked you here."

"So you want to fabricate friends?" she asked, a condescending tone and questioning tilt of the head conveyed her skepticism.

"We are friends, Chrissy. You could see the connection at Tim's service in Becca's orchard." He took his hand off his leg, pushed his chin forward and gestured toward her, "Don't you feel anything now?"

"Jack, that was five years ago. You told me yesterday you didn't connect with anyone after that. You were haughty and aloof. Be real." she said.

"I admit I was not at my best at the service. I was so shocked about Tim. I felt terrible I hadn't been a good friend to him. He was always so giving to everyone. I treated him like shit and I felt sick about it. I always felt I was holding my breath with all of you. You always intimidated me. Like any false move and I'd be out. Like someone would finally figure out that I'd never really belonged. I have no idea why you let me in that group, but it set a foundation for the rest of my life." He stopped and looked at her with a hard, questioning look. She returned his gaze, steady, but didn't say anything. Not blinking, just listening. His voice got very soft, his tone revealing.

"Chrissy, my parents were smart, hardworking immigrants who taught me to value education and American opportunities. They let me do all the tinkering and engineering I wanted in the backyard. But you all, you showed me adventure, camaraderie, a different kind of innovation. That cheerful, never-give-up spirit of being an American. Optimism. My parents had experienced horrors they wouldn't ever tell me about in Europe. Dark, horrific times. Duty kept them going." He gulped hard and went on. "They were the hardest working people I've ever known. Survivors. Survivors, like you and I can't even begin to imagine.

"They had another son, back in Poland, before me," he said softly. Christine had to lean forward to hear him. She was shocked at this revelation but listened intently, sympathetically.

"He was a teenager and was killed in protests against the Soviet run government in '56. I don't think my mother ever recovered. Sometimes she would call me by his name. They were so determined to create a middle class life for me. But they were broken people, Chrissy. My father retreated into his lab, always a scientist. My mother was like a shadow. Duty-bound but so very sad. They were older parents, didn't speak much English. They couldn't give me a lot." Christine sank back deeply into the chair with a deep but quiet exhale. She and the other kids had no idea what Jack's home life had been like. They never played at his house.

"But you all, the days in the orchard," Jack went on. "You taught me about freedom and the lighter side. Not just how to survive, but how to stretch unnaturally upward, beyond my comfort zone. How to thrive. Every afternoon I hoped desperately that one of you would knock on the door for me to join tree climbing, apricot picking, or playing yet another round of kick-the-can. When we were up the creek and I fell, what you all did to figure out how to splint my foot, keep me from going into hypothermia and carry me miles back to Becca's house...that was amazing."

Emotion clearly overcoming his steady speech, he just looked at her and swallowed. And swallowed again. He had almost never revealed so much about himself to anyone. The fans twisted above with a slight creak and brush of wind. Otherwise, silence.

Jack closed his eyes a moment. He could see the creek, hear the splashes and feel the intensity of focus, the determined creativity to solve the problem his eleven-year-old friends displayed that day when he broke his ankle under the log and got stuck in the creek. The ingenuity, the teamwork had always awed him. Despite gaining a lifelong limp, losing a summer of exploration with his golden neighbors, with his foot in a cast, and feeling his status drop after the incident, Jack had never regretted being there. It felt like he had participated in a defining afternoon. He would just wish, over and over again, for years, that he had not been the victim, but had been a member of the rescue squad.

Christine gazed toward the vineyards, away from Jack, to hide the tears rising in her eyes. She was so touched by his honesty, his vulnerability. A measure of sadness lay beneath the façade of carefree wandering they'd all participated in as children. She saw it resurface in Jack's story. Here was yet another revelation of family secrets that weighed heavily.

She and Jack had grown up in an era when many parents were escaping troubled blue-collar upbringings, cold, conservative East Coast backgrounds, Depression era economics, or even the Holocaust, to aspire to the middle class. Their parents were driven to become the new American professionals with a modern home, shiny car and a kitchen cluttered with appliances. Dad was so overwhelmed with work forging what would become Silicon Valley and moms anxiously juggled three, four and five children while cooking and cleaning to spotlessness, that the kids ran free, unfettered, through alleys and orchards, schoolyards and parks. They learned to rely on each other and not expect much nurturing back at the stress-filled house. Christine realized as an adult that this might have created independent, self-motivated kids, innovative even, but not ones with close relationships with their parents. She and her friends had no idea of their parents' reality, what they were working to overcome, until they became adults themselves.

Christine was astonished to find out about an older brother who died in Poland well before Jack's birth. They all knew Janusz (Jack) Duda was Polish. Several other kids' parents didn't speak perfect English either. But who knew what horrors their parents and friends' parents were hiding. She thought back to Becca's dad, who had suffered with a secret gambling problem and committed suicide when he'd lost the money he'd borrowed on their family orchard and farmhouse. It made her feel sad and so alone. Her parents were both gone and there was so much she didn't know. Could never ask. And Jack's parents. How difficult for them. They must have been ecstatic when their second son found technological and financial success in America. Like maybe it was all worth it?

"And Chrissy." He leaned toward her, covered her hand with his, and as he looked directly at her he was clearly startled to see her emotion. He hesitated. He coughed back a lump forming. He had to tell her strongly, resolutely what he wanted. He cleared his throat again.

"It's five years since Tim died. A lot has happened. The crash has realigned a lot of people's priorities. We're all facing fifty now. I think we can see that Tim was right. He placed a priority on interacting, on being a good friend. Human connection is what it's all about. If you don't have that, you have nothing." He paused, then continued softly. "Chrissy, I want you to be my AA for Workaholics sponsor, and I'll be yours. Let's stay in touch. I'll come take you to dinner in Sacramento. Or we can go mountain biking outside of the city. You can come out here whenever you want, even if I'm not in town. You can use it as a personal retreat. Just no political events here." He laughed at that and she smiled, her tears suppressed back where they belonged.

Wow, she mouthed but did not actually say a word. She was surprised that she liked his hand on hers and did not want him to remove it. An energy she had not felt in a long time warmed her torso. She yoga-breathed herself back to calm but she didn't know how to respond. She decided to change the subject.

"Jack, what's the surprise?" she asked.

He shook his head to submerge memories and confessions. He cleared his throat. He did not move his hand but took a breath and moved closer to her face.

"I've redone the winery. I'm rebranding it. I'm calling it Blackberry Creek like where we played. I had an artist do a drawing of the old creek and the blackberries, mimicking Tim's drawing style, for the logo and wine labels. All the proceeds beyond costs will go to support AIDS/HIV research, seventy-five percent of it in the U.S. and twenty-five percent in South Africa, where I have vineyards that are part of the label. And the one you tasted yesterday, the new Pinot. That will be a special bottling in honor of Tim. It's called Life Artist. That's how I remember him. He was an artist, but he was also good at living. At being kind. At appreciating the unique value of each person. I want to honor that, and maybe, remind us all to be more that way too." He seemed to study her eyes, then said,

"Well, I'm starting with myself. That's all I can control right now. I'm working hard, Chrissy, to reign myself in. What do you think? Will you help me get the kids from the neighborhood here? To sort of start anew? Will you be my AA sponsor so I don't overwork but actually live a balanced life which includes fun and people?" He almost sounded like he was pleading but clearly that was not a tone he was familiar with. He was offering her a challenge. Christine was speechless. She didn't respond for some minutes. Jack's hand had not left hers.

"You've completely surprised me, Jack Duda," she said with a light tone. "And not much shocks me anymore. Of course, I'll do whatever I can. I don't know if any of them will listen to me. I think it's all admirable. So are you saying I should work less? Of course if you come to Sacramento I will go biking with you or out to dinner. I don't know what you mean by an AA-type sponsor. Does that mean you'll call me in the middle of the night if you're tempted to work on batteries?" She smiled, and almost giggled, but was sincere. Her voice was gentle.

She realized she was finally forgiving him for the years of no connection, of superiority and aloofness. She was trying to realign her mental picture that Jack had gotten so wealthy, so sucked into a world none of them could imagine, even with their own successes, that he'd forgotten the kids from the orchard. It wasn't that way at all, she realized. Christine was unsure how to respond to all of this emotion, to the challenge Jack proposed. It would take some getting used to.

Then abruptly, she said, "I need to get going," and quickly fled the table to pack. She needed time to process this. She felt guilty she'd assumed he was going to advocate for a political agenda and lobby for some pet cause. A crass assumption but that was her world, and his too she knew. They both operated in locales and industries where "networking," meaning getting what you could out of somebody, was the norm. She packed her bag, tidied the guest room and returned to the porch.

"Thank you, Jack, for a wonderful, surprising and strenuous weekend. I'll be sore from mountain biking for a few days I'm sure." They laughed awkwardly. "You have given me a lot to think about. I appreciate the sincere conversation. It was refreshing. Thanks again, Jack," and she grabbed her bag and skipped down the steps. He followed. He stopped her in front of the car.

"Thanks for taking the risk and coming out here. I appreciate it. Please think over what I've proposed. I'll be in touch." He paused. Then feeling that this was his opportunity for a fresh start, a moment that might not present itself ever again, he took a deep breath but still somehow breathless, he said,

"Chrissy, I invited you here as an old friend to help with my personal makeover. But now, after this weekend, now I think we might just be two lonely people who've found each other." He moved toward her, cupped her shoulder tenderly with his hand, and kissed her sweetly. A lingering longing that she did not turn away from. She leaned in to him, engaging fully in the kiss. Then suddenly, she pulled away, blushing, jumped in her car, gave an awkward little wave and drove alongside the green and orange vines, laden with dewy fruit, toward the highway.

The Mission

"I AM NOT SELLING. You can tell that rich young man over and over again I'm not selling. The house isn't even on the market. Why does he think it's for sale?" Irene's voice rattled lightly but the emphasis was clear. She gripped the black receiver of the dial phone with one gnarled hand and whipped at the air in exasperation with the other, the spiraled cord swinging. As the lawyer's voice droned on at the other end of the line, she rolled her eyes and sighed. Irene hated being treated like an old person, like a child again. After so many years of adulthood in between, it was excruciatingly annoying.

She might be over ninety but she was not dead yet. She had control of all her faculties but repeatedly had to remind others of that fact. She proudly played Sudoku and did Luminosity online to keep her mind sharp. Most of the ladies in her pool aerobics class were afraid of technology. Rubbish, she told them. Nothing to fear. Computers are a great tool for us old people. Irene could almost feel the lawyer, through the phone line, just waiting for her to give up. Probably for her to die so he could cross her off his list.

"Just have your boss, Christine, call me back. No assistants. I need her to help me protect my house and myself. I can't have my son declaring me incompetent." She slammed the receiver down into the cradle. A very satisfying slam. You can't do that with a cell phone, she noted. Slowly, a bit shakily, with a slight lean to the right and an up and down rise in her step, she crossed the wooden floor to the Persian carpet and sat in her favorite armchair. She took a sip of tea from the delicately painted china cup on the side table covered with a lace doily and gazed out at her view.

Irene Sinclair was determined that her historic house, built before the 1906 earthquake, would stay in the family. She had resisted her son and grandson's pleas to take advantage of the hot market and sell now. She could see the green dancing in their eyes over the house's skyrocketing value. Disgusting. Although San Francisco's renewed housing boom could lead to a lucrative sale, she also wanted to protect her fourteen tenants spaced through the five apartments below her top floor flat. Who the hell did her son and grandson think they were, trying to control her? Plus, she was not leaving her home of sixty years to move to some awful old people's home filled with, well….old people. Those plac- es were so completely depressing. Irene thought they made you sick so you would want to die. She had plenty to live for still.

"Great Gram, you all right?" Her great granddaughter glided in from the kitchen through a swinging door. "What was that all about? You sounded mad. How about some lunch? And then you can lie down for your nap."

"I'm fine, dear. Just peeved. Some hotshot young Internet millionaire, or billionaire, wants to buy the house but it's not for sale." When had all the numbers gone from millions to billions she wondered. It's as if they started adding extra zeros because it wasn't exciting enough.

"Well, Great Gram, that might be perfect," said Nicole with an enthusiastic smile. She gently touched Irene's shoulder to make sure she was solidly in her regular spot, while presenting a plate with a ham and cheese on rye, no crusts, mustard only. Nicole's movements were gracefully fluid as if she were a ballerina twirling to calm nerves and serve sandwiches.

"You could buy a smaller place and not worry about all the tenants, the bills, the old plumbing. And you'd have plenty to pay someone to come help you at your new apartment. I bet you could get a lot for it. The neighborhood's hot now. I can't even afford rent here," she said, perhaps a bit too quickly. She didn't want Great Gram to get suspicious.

"That's not the point, dear. You know I just care about my home and my renters." She almost snorted in disgust. "Do you really think some rich, single guy needs all this space?"

Sensing an opportunity to keep her talking about the house, Nicole asked quietly about its history. "Wasn't your father the one who divided it into apartments?"

"That's right. The Bordens have been here ever since. They're almost as old as me. Where would they go? And what about the Sanchezes with their little twins? They live on his garbage man salary while she works at Mission-Valencia Grocers down the block. How would they afford anything around here if I sell and they have to leave?" Irene raised her faint eyebrows, now colored in with brownish pencil, at her great-granddaughter. Nicole knew it wasn't her turn to talk and shrugged.

"Hector, my favorite hair stylist," Irene went on, "told me he lives in fear of a rent increase or getting evicted because he can't afford to move. He doesn't want to leave the neighborhood. He's lived here his entire life. Nope. I'm not budging. Your dad and grandpa can carry me out of here when they're pallbearers!"

Irene's determination took Nicole's breath as if a cold wind had pushed the glass open and sailed in through the apartment windows. Indeed, she admired it. Wished she could conjure up that much passion about anything. Unsure what to do after college graduation, Nicole had agreed to be Irene's "personal assistant" for a year. "Caregiver" and "nurse" were strictly off limits, banned from the family vocabulary to dampen Irene's prickliness about independence. Dad and Grandpa were paying her a decent wage but the exchange was clear. The historic home was too much for a ninety-one-year-old. Manage Great Gram's basic needs and convince her to sell so we can move her out to a care facility. Now's the time to sell before a crash. You have one year, they said. Then better get a real job, her father lectured. Maybe you'll be over that save-the-world ridiculousness by then, he'd been sure to add.

Nicole ignored Dad's cynicism and grabbed the offer. Great Gram was old, but she was cool. A year taking care of her would be perfect. Kind of a nice break from the expectations. After graduation, she had refused to use her engineering degree to build yet another app. All she ever heard about were phone applications for shortening your dinner wait or getting take-out delivered faster. If the veggie lasagna with locally sourced Caesar salad and artisan garlic bread arrived tossed upside down in a heap anyway, did it really matter if you got it three minutes quicker?

She loved the innovation and go-for-it attitude of the Valley. Practically every street conversation you overheard was talk of a new startup, an idea for an app. But where were the businesses solving real problems? The drive to make the world a better place? Must have been a previous generation, Nicole surmised. Or maybe just not this particular Silicon Valley boom. To her it all seemed superficial, so clearly about making piles of money. She was disgusted with the consumption and excess, the traffic, the social pressure to achieve, the fixation on the next big app.

Nicole decided it was time to step off the achievement hamster wheel she'd been sprinting on since age twelve and figure out who she was beyond her resume. The "personal assistant" gig allowed her to continue renting a room in a rambling, decrepit Berkeley house crawling with grad students. She could BART to Great Gram's and avoid buying a car. Perfect. While she babysat Great Gram she would clarify her intentions and find a company that fit her philosophy, not the standard one the current Valley seemed to promote.

"Don't worry, Dad," she had told him. "Great Gram thinks I'm a cool girl engineer. I'll get her to do what you and Grandpa want."

Nicole said nothing to her great-grandmother about the arrangement and attacked the job with gusto. She escorted Irene to her favorite salon and navigated Medicare appointments. They walked to the pharmacy and bakery, cooing at the strapped-in babies on every corner, ogling the fashionistas patrolling the vintage clothing stores and giggling at the marijuana smell wafting from the park. Freed from constant schoolwork, Nicole discovered joy in cooking and experimented with new recipes. They attended a symphony or theatre event once a month. On Thursday afternoons, Nicole joined Irene in tutoring local teens at the writing center a few blocks away. She escorted her to pool aerobics and listened to the eighty-plus-year-old ladies gossip about neighborhood changes. She quickly discovered that Irene did not lead a sedentary life.

Nicole also met many of the building's tenants, tagging along to a baby shower and an anniversary dinner. Irene was like a benevolent queen in her castle home, treated gingerly with respectful distance and begrudging appreciation. The rent hadn't been raised in four years. The plumbing worked. She had put in a new elevator when Mrs. Sanchez was pregnant with twins. Nicole could sense that they were afraid to make waves for fear of losing one of the best deals in the neighborhood. Friends and relatives were moving to Oakland and even farther east to dull places like Fairfield and Stockton, forced out by rising rents and sales of the historic buildings. Below Great Gram's top floor suite, the building felt as if it were holding its breath, as if it were hoping no one noticed it in a ferocious, bustling game of hide and seek, hiding in plain sight.

The phone rang. A tinny bell from a forgotten era. Irene got up slowly, inching toward her double-layered desk. Bill envelopes, eye glasses, calendars, stamps, a dusty stapler, a checkbook and scotch tape stuck out of the mini-cubicles lining the bottom level of the antique. She turned back to Nicole before answering.

"And, by the way, it's not right that you can't afford rent here. The Mission used to be the affordable neighborhood. If any of my renters were to move out, I'd offer you the apartment at a fair rate. That's what a family property should be for."

She picked up the receiver. "Oh, Christine. Finally." Irene's voice warbled a bit at first. She cleared her throat, once, and again.

"Look, I know you're busy up there in Sacramento being Senate President or whatever it is you do. But you're still my lawyer." She turned toward Nicole and tapped her fingers to her thumb, repeatedly, up and down, gesturing that the voice on the line was talking without saying a meaningful word. Nicole grinned, and giggled, as she cleared the plate and teacup.

"Okay, look," Irene said into the heavy black phone. "I don't care how important this kid thinks he is or how much money he has, I refuse to kick my tenants out. They're just working people trying to make ends meet. The house is not for sale. And I am not going to some old people's home." She paused, coughed and sat roughly at the wooden desk chair. Nicole came over with a concerned look. Irene waved a hand and gave a don't hover, don't over protect, I know what I'm doing glare. Cowed, Nicole returned to the kitchen.

"I want you to make sure my son doesn't try to declare me incompetent. I am completely lucid. And I want you to help me protect my tenants for as long as possible. Didn't you keep the California coastline away from developers or something? Well, you ought be able to protect a historic Victorian that survived the 1906 quake. This house is going to last way longer than this current bubble we're in. I've seen it before. Soon these million-aires, billionaires, whatever, will be drowning in bank payments."

She listened to her lawyer a moment, who now had something to say.

"He'll pay cash? And how much? Oh my," she said loudly into the receiver. "My grandfather paid less than five thousand dol-lars to have this house built in the 1890s." Nicole returned to the room at her great-grandmother's raised voice. Irene looked at her, questioning, pushing the mouthpiece aside.

"He wants to meet me. Should I do it even though I'm not sell-ing?" Nicole raised her eyebrows and cocked her head to one side. Why not? she mouthed as she shrugged.

"Could be interesting, Great Gram. You're always saying you like young people," she whispered.

"Okay, that's fine," Irene said back into the phone. She in-structed her lawyer to send the potential buyer over on Tuesday at 3:30 for afternoon tea. Whether that fit in his schedule or not, that was when he was invited. And she insisted that he come alone. No entourage. She then told Christine to devise a plan to make the house a higher level of historic landmark or something creative to allow her tenants to stay as long as they wanted. Was that possible? She just knew her son and grandson would sell immediately upon inheriting the house. Could she prevent that?

"You know how my great-grandfather preserved that land for the family. That was brilliant. Can't we do that with a house? Figure something out, Christine. Good-bye." Grasping the desk with bony hands dotted with age freckles, she steadied herself to stand up. She cradled the receiver on the phone perched on the upper layer of the desk. Nicole slipped a hand under her great grandmother's elbow and guided her to the armchair.

"Oh Great Gram. What have you gotten yourself into this time?" She sighed with knowing amusement.

"Oh, this will be loads of fun," Irene said. She clapped her hands quickly, pressing them to her collarbone with glee like a small child. "You must come and serve. We'll have traditional high tea with little sandwiches and mini-scones and clotted cream," she said. "It will be like that Silicon Valley TV show." A mischievous gleam snuck out from her eyes, shrunken by drooping eyelids, diminished after ninety-one years of hard use. But still observant. Still bright.

"Of course, I'll be here. Wouldn't miss it. Who did you say it was?" Nicole asked casually, pretending not to care, as she cleared the lunch plates and hipped open the swinging door into the kitchen.

On Tuesday afternoon, Zach Turner stood on the landing outside the top floor flat of the 1891 Victorian-Edwardian he coveted. Always prepared, efficiently maximizing every minute, he had brought along his lawyer with the purchase paperwork. He planned to get Mrs. Sinclair to agree to sell the house right on the spot. He'd been told she wanted a solo meeting but he figured a lawyer didn't count. He could sit in a chair in the back. Zach was fidgety, still annoyed that he had to change a New York investment trip for his new startup to meet with this old lady. He balanced a phone on a shoulder. His usually floppy hair was combed to one side. He sported pressed khakis and a buttoned down shirt tucked in with a leather belt. He shifted from one foot to the other, uncomfortable. He was never this dressed up, except for New York meetings.

"Yeah, I'm here now," he said into the cell phone. "I know, this is so crazy, isn't it. I mean, who would turn down cash. And she's old. She can probably use the money. Okay, I gotta go. I'll text you after," and he tapped the phone off. Zach straightened his shoulders, took a deep breath and knocked on the door. He glanced back at the lawyer and grinned.

A startlingly lovely young woman in a short skirt and red top, with long brunette hair, brown eyes and a charming dimple,

opened the door. Mrs. Sinclair appeared at her side, much shorter, hunched a bit to her right, but clearly dressed for the occasion
in a flowered skirt and cashmere sweater. Her thin gray hair was
coiffed perfectly around pearl earrings, hinting that she had just
been to the salon.

"This is my great-granddaughter, Nicole. Isn't she lovely? She
just graduated from Cal. Didn't you go there?" she blurted at him,
as she waved at Nicole and reached for his hand to shake it. Zach,
caught off guard by the pretty young woman and the direct older
one, gulped a reply while shaking her slight hand, which had a
surprisingly firm grip.

"Uhhh, yeah, yes, of course she is. I mean, yes I did go to Cal,"
he said. His hair flopped off the combed perch and back to its
natural state across his forehead and right eye. "Uh, it's nice to
meet you, Mrs. Sinclair," he managed to get out. He combed his
bangs back with his fingers.

"Oh, no. He stays outside," she said, pointing at the lawyer
behind Zach. "Can you wait in the car, young man? I was very
clear no one else was invited. Didn't they give you the message?
Oh, and, let me have all your electronics. Phones, iPads, whatever you got. Hand them over." Zach looked at her quizzically. All
right, this old lady was going to be interesting, he thought. He
gave her the phone still in his hand.

"Is that it? Nothing more in there," she said in the manner of a
barkeep collecting guns at the saloon door in the Old West. Zach
shook his head. He leaned over and pulled up his trouser leg a
little to show her nothing at his ankle, as if he had been handing
over pistols. Nicole giggled. Irene did not smile but raised an
eyebrow and made a silent note. Got some spunk this one. Okay,
good. Something to work with here, she told herself.

After they escorted him in, Nicole went straight to the kitch-
en. Irene ushered Zach through the entry hall into the living
room. He inhaled deeply as he came around the corner and
faced a stunning view that included green from Dolores Park,

257

Mission Dolores's historic bell tower, the Mission Bay docks and hospitals and the Bay Bridge. Downtown's tall buildings overseeing all from the distance. Construction cranes accented each neighborhood between the windows and the Bay. Wow, his real estate agent was right. This was a gem. I gotta close this deal before anyone else gets in here.

"Mr. Turner, please sit down at the table next to the window. We are having tea," Irene said. "Have you ever had high tea?" she continued, not giving him any space to answer.

"With quality English tea and delicious treats? I think it is a very civilized tradition so we will enjoy it now. Tell me about yourself and why on earth you want my house. It's not for sale but I figured at least I could offer you afternoon tea and learn a little about you. I've always enjoyed talking with young people and it seems you may have a good story to tell me." She looked directly in his eyes and gave him her most charming smile.

Nicole entered through the swinging door with a tiered stand of crust-less cucumber sandwiches at the base, mini currant scones in the middle, and tiny glass dishes holding strawberry jam and clotted English cream at the top. She returned with a teapot, steam escaping from the spout, lingering a little too long, hoping to overhear the conversation. Irene was delighted to see that Zach had taken notice of Nicole and was sneaking appreciative looks every time she entered the room. She was hard to miss. Perfect, she thought. Exactly as I had hoped.

"Well...." Zach started and hesitated. For the first time, in maybe years, he felt unnerved. A bit shaky. Off his usual charm, bluster and smarts approach. He had presented to top VCs in the valley, to bankers in New York. What's up with this little old lady, he asked himself.

"Look, Mrs. Sinclair," he decided to just tell it straight. "I want to buy your house. I think it's beautiful. And in such an awesome location. It could really be fixed up great. I mean, it's lovely the way you have it now, but it could return to its former glory as a single family home. I'll pay cash and I want to beat the market. I don't want to wait and have to be in some bidding war..."

"You mean when I die?" she interrupted him with her perfectly sketched eyebrow raised dramatically. "Well, young man, that is quite audacious of you. I have no plans to die soon or to sell. Not sure why you thought it was for sale." She took a mini scone and put cream and jam on it. She gave him a piercing look and he quickly put a sandwich and scone on his plate. He cleared his throat and took a sip of tea.

"Aren't you from New York? Tell me why you want a house here," she said.

"Yes, Mrs. Sinclair. I am from New York." He paused. "Look I didn't mean to be offensive. I am not saying that. About you dying or anything. I just want to buy the house now. I'm ready. I have the money. I want to fix it up. The neighborhood is a happening place and I'd like to be here," he explained, quite logically and succinctly, he thought, congratulating himself.

His eyes wandered past the large windows and the view to the furniture, the living areas. He took in the aura of the room. Black and white family pictures, books in the built-in bookshelf, watercolors of familiar California scenes and old maps lined the walls. His eye stopped at a portrait of a young woman with long arched eyebrows, dark hair rolled under, in a military uniform and hat. He gazed at the picture. The woman's high cheekbones, fine nose, and eyes filled with adventure were hard to wander past. She was quite beautiful.

"I was a WAC. I enlisted at nineteen. That's my enlistment photo. Something else, huh? It was another era."

"You were a soldier in WWII?" Zach asked. "Wow, no kidding. Where were you stationed? Women weren't in combat then. What did they have you do?" Questions tumbled out.

"What do you care? Aren't you some tech guy who made a bunch of money on some ridiculous software no one needs? And now wants to buy up San Francisco from all the regular people?"

Her irritation with his rudeness and arrogance was no longer in check. He's just a kid, she thought. It's absurd that he has so much money he could really offer to buy a multi-million-dollar house for cash.

"No, ma'am. I love history. I came to Cal from New York to study history, to live in California and try the West Coast. Some of my family came from here a long time ago. My parents brought us here a few times and I loved it." He hesitated, thinking maybe he was talking too much. She was clearly in charge. But she looked deeply into his face asking for more. She was silent for once, so he continued.

"They had some family land and we hiked around. It was beautiful. I always wanted to come back. Then at Cal, it just seemed like the Bay Area was all about technology. So I got into computer science. Then a friend and I started playing around with apps when the iPhone came out. It changed everything, you know."

She interrupted him. "And what does your app do? Is it another dating site or a way you hope girls will send you naked pictures? I follow what's going on. Remember, I may be old but I had my day. I know how it goes" He blushed at her descriptions and smiled. He shook his head emphatically.

"Well, no, our app is about making public transportation easier with good maps and access to system routes on phones. I don't think that's frivolous, do you? Public transportation is a good thing. Maps are great, don't you think?" he asked, gesturing toward the framed maps in her hallway.

"Yes." She toned down her anger and spoke more gently. "But worth that much? They told me how much you sold your company for. It's outlandish that so much money would be spent on that, don't you think? Wait, and it's for public transportation? But don't you and all your employees take the corporate buses out of The City down the Peninsula?"

"No, ma'am. We started our company here. We located here because we know our employees want to be in San Francisco.

And then they can use public transit," he said victoriously, feeling a bit as if he were back in debate club.

"Sure. But didn't you sell to one of those companies with the buses? Now a bunch of them will get on those buses, clogging up my Muni stop and making me late for my hair and doctor appointments. And when you want to live here you drive up rents and push out regular people. Like my tenants—garbage men, mechanics, grocery clerks. Where will they go when you techies buy up the big old houses because it's fashionable?"

"Yes," he admitted. "We did sell to a company with corporate buses. You're right about that." He sounded sheepish and almost apologetic. He quietly crunched a cucumber sandwich. Nicole came in to refresh the tea. Irene gave her a disgusted look, as if she were a teenager scoffing at a rival's ridiculousness.

"Well, young man, I sure hope you do something worthwhile with all that money." She shook her head at him and there was an implied need for quiet. He waited a bit.

"Yes, well, I had hoped to buy your house with some of it," he finally said with a warm smile. "I will preserve it in its original state. The good thing about all that money is that I have the resources to do that. Wouldn't that be great for this house to be like when your grandfather built it? I told you I love history," he said, with enthusiasm mixed with the tone of a debater.

"Hmmmm," Irene said. And she left more silence in the conversation. Changing the subject, she continued. "Yes, maps are indeed wonderful. I love them. I have some old ones here. Let me show you." As she rose, Zach got up, rushed to her side, held her elbow gently and pushed back her chair. With a light touch, he escorted her to the hallway and adjoining dining room where she gave him a tour of her photos and map collection.

"Look, here's a few more pictures of me during the war. Here's a map of France in 1940 under German occupation. And this map is of Alta California when it was part of Mexico. Fascinating, isn't it?" She did not give him a chance to answer. He nodded slightly as he escorted her down the hallway. She continued.

"You know, I have an ancestor who bought land during the Gold Rush and it is still in our family. Here's a map of the two hundred acres he set aside for the family to use, but to be left in its natural state, forever, into perpetuity. About 160 years ago. Wasn't that a lot of foresight for that miner? A poor kid with nothing, to raise himself up, open a mine equipment business and start buying land? I've always admired the man. In fact, your interest in my house made me realize I want to do something like the Brennan Trust for this house. You know what, Mr. Turner, I hope you do something really smart and thoughtful for others with all that money. Something like what my relative did."

She stopped and appeared tired. It had been a long and heartfelt speech. "I need to sit down," she said quietly. And moved slowly, haltingly down the hallway to the living room.

"What? What are you talking about?" Zach sputtered. He quickly followed her to help her into her favorite chair. "The Brennan New Almaden Trust? But that's the land my parents took us to when I was a kid. There's a waterfall and creek and some of it is so steep you can't even hike up it? And if you want to camp or bring a lot of people you have to get permission from some board? Wait! What? Are you saying that's your family's land?"

He made sure she was seated and then sat across from her on the velvety sofa with curled wooden frame and knobbed armrests. Leaning forward, arms on his knees, he looked directly at her. His voice, with quiet intensity, probed.

"Mrs. Sinclair. That land, it's my family's too. That's why I wanted to come here. I always loved that place. That's why I wanted to leave New York and study in California. Are you saying that we are related?"

Silence expanded into every corner of the living room with the question. Dishes clattered in the kitchen on the other side of the swinging door as Nicole cleaned up the teacups and plates. She poked her face through and Irene shook her head at her. Not now. The door swung closed but not a sound came from the other side. You could almost hear her breathing behind the door. Irene raised a perfectly penciled eyebrow even higher at his statement.

"Well, now. Isn't that something?" she drawled. Neither of them said anything for a long moment, pondering the implications.

"So you must be from the side of the family that fled east generations ago. Never knew much about them. I knew I liked you for some reason. You are quite arrogant. And your manners could use some polishing. But I suppose it can be pretty heady to get billions for a college dorm project." She paused and seemed to consider the whole situation. Zach was completely speechless.

Unexpectedly she asked, "Was it clean, your sale? None of that complication with some roommate who said he really invented the whole thing? No lawsuits? I read the stories. I saw the movie. I like the TV show," she added absently. But she looked truly curious.

"Mrs. Sinclair, do you understand what I'm saying?" He stopped and stared at her. The sunlight in the room brightened as a cloud passed over and the old furniture's colors were suddenly more vibrant. He saw the tough young WAC volunteer and the descendant of proud Mission pioneers. He pictured her after Army duty hiking in the New Almaden hills. Images of a whole life appeared before him like puzzle pieces just poured from the box. A jumble he found intriguing. He suddenly regretted not doing in-depth research, as was his usual practice, after the real estate agent called saying she had a hot tip on a pre-market property. He should have known the situation, he scolded himself. He could have prepared a more palatable offer if he had known the connection. He could have used the surprise and the history to his advantage.

"No. No scorned partners," he responded quietly. "My one partner and I were very lucky. It was a clean deal." Then he moved to the subject hanging like ripe fruit about to drop. He continued, his voice barely audible.

"Look. I'm sorry I was rude. I just wanted your house without thinking about who lived in it or what the history was. You're right." Then he spoke almost in a whisper. "I've been getting my way for most of my life," he surprised himself by revealing.

"Well, yes, I can see that. Clearly. But not here young man. Not here. Now you have a stubborn ninety-one-year-old lady as a cousin and I am not going away. And I am still not selling you my house. Don't you think this relative thing has made me soft." And she snorted and coughed at the same time. She turned and looked out the window at her neighborhood as it folded into the San Francisco skyline. She was getting an idea. Zach's attention shifted to join her gaze. Neither one said anything for several minutes. Kitchen cupboards sounded again softly as Nicole put the dishes away. Irene cleared her throat to get his attention. To change the sentiment in the room.

"How about you and me go out to that land?" she suggested to him, suddenly. "This weekend. I assume you are busy during the week doing something with all your fame and money. Starting some new business now, is it? Are you on the Tech Conference circuit with all your success?" She coughed. "This Saturday," she continued. "We'll go out there and walk and talk and look at that land."

Quietly, she was scheming with her own plans. Maybe this kid's interest and money could be useful somehow. Protect the house from her greedy son. But the main thing was to get him to hire Nicole at his new company. She needed a real job. And she'd probably like what they do, Irene thought.

"You show up here at ten o'clock and bring one of your henchmen or whatever they are. One that can drive us, in a comfortable car, preferably. I'll bring my great-granddaughter too."

He turned to her with a raised eyebrow questioning the proposal. Well, if that's what it would take then so be it, he thought. This is too good a place to lose. That view, the location. A little extra effort might pay off. He never had gone out to the family's land all his years in California. He remembered it as pretty and peaceful. It would be nice to see it again, he told himself. It would make his mom happy to hear he'd visited the property.

"Nicole, come on in and say goodbye to Mr. Turner. He's leaving now," Irene called toward the kitchen. Nicole entered, drying her hands on a kitchen towel. She smiled at the two of them as her great-grandmother continued.

"Land is a great thing, Zachary Turner. So is family history. And it's all going to last way longer than that app you sold or the money you made. Mr. Turner here says he likes history," she said looking at Nicole. She turned back to him.

"I'll tell you some stories. Heck, I even found out you and I share Mexican blood. Digging through the attic and my grandfather's records, I found the original Brennan Trust document. And you know what? Your great-great-great-great-grandmother was one hundred percent Mexican—Juanita Castro De La Cruz. You'll have to put that on your next press release about the sale. A Mexican made billions on improving maps." She laughed again and gave him a smile of satisfaction. "Seems fitting, doesn't it?"

With Nicole as her assistant, she pulled herself up, laughing heartily. She took Zach's arm and escorted him to the front entrance where she handed him his cell phone and pushed him out onto the landing. Befuddled at the sudden dismissal, the revelations and the new item on his calendar, he clumsily turned to thank them. Irene waved her hands at him as if to say get along now. Done for the day. And leaning over the shoulder of her stooped great-grandmother, Nicole winked at him.

"See you Saturday," she said, and closed the door.

He picked them up at the front of the building in a black Suburban, with a matching one, perfectly synced, pulling in behind.

"I feel like we're in the presidential motorcade or with the mafia," Nicole joked. "No tinted windows?" she teased. She climbed into the far back seat. Zach blushed and mumbled about his lawyer and an assistant and the real estate agent, who had to bring an assistant....

"I just thought it'd be more comfortable for you two if we had our own car," he finally said. "A lot of other people wanted to come along."

Nicole nodded, "Sure."

Irene dismissed the comments. Having been raised in a very different era, she found an air of formality refreshing and, actually, appropriate. She nodded at the driver and climbed in next to Zach and handed him a thick manila envelope.

"My proposal is in there. Read it and talk it over with your lawyers later. I don't want to discuss it until we get to the property. Then I'll give you the rundown. Now, tell me more about yourself, your upbringing, your parents. I've been trying to get this family tree straight in my head. Nicole, take some notes in case I forget things." Nicole and Zach stumbled over each other's words trying to respond but she kept right on talking, appearing not to hear them at all.

"And then, Nicole can tell you about herself. She's a very talented engineer. Don't your companies need female engineers? But she wants to do something important, world changing. No video games or restaurant review apps for Nicole. She's uppity that way. I told her to go work for that Ironman guy making the rockets—I think that's pretty cool. She scoffs and says Mars is for dreamers. Says she wants to do good right here on Earth. My son and grandson are paying her to babysit me right now—which is completely unnecessary. But we are having a terrific time. I feel like I'm back in my twenties so I just pretend that I'm infirm and need her help. We're like post-college roommates. I just don't go out to the bars at night or have one of those dating apps on my phone," she said with a grin and wink to Nicole."

"Great Gram!" Nicole said, embarrassed. Zach and Nicole shared a look and started laughing. Irene joined in and the nervous air inside the Suburban relaxed.

The shiny black cars sailed down 280 past green hills and Crystal Springs reservoir, alongside Stanford's satellite dish and linear accelerator, whipping by one suburban exit sign after another. Once in south San Jose, they wound through a cement wasteland of strip malls and box stores out to where the craggy slope touched the valley floor. The roads narrowed and the car maneuvered, more slowly now, past tract neighborhoods, custom homes with backyard corrals and grazing horses, finally reaching a spot where the landscape looked exactly as it had more than 150 years before in gold miner Joe Brennan's time. Irene pointed out directions to a hidden dirt road, instructing the driver where to park.

The mini convoy came to a stop. Everyone, in both cars, straightened their clothes, gathered belongings, took deep breaths and exited the leather interiors to a dusty, arid patch shaded by enormous oak trees, a creek burbling down the hill. Irene took Zach's arm.

"Let's walk," she said.

Nicole was left with the lawyers and realtors, awkwardly showing them what she knew of the property, trying to explain the history and why they were all there. No one even pretended to be interested. They stood politely near her but all had folded their heads down over their phones, thumbs whirling. After an awkward silence, one of the realtors pulled her aside.

"Look, I know it's confidential but thanks for the tip on your grandmother's house. We really appreciate it because what with all the competition out there, all these tech gazillionaires right now, Zach might have missed out. I guess people knew he wanted in the neighborhood but everyone else does too. I mean, did you see on TechCrunch that just this morning another startup sold for almost five hundred million? Those guys are gonna want in too once the dust settles. It is a gold rush right now, no question. Not sure what the hell we're doing out here in the boonies but Zach said we had to do this if we're gonna make the sale. So here ve are," and she folded herself back into a hunch over her phone, laughing and shaking her head. These crazy old people. Gotta humor them, her entire body messaged. Nicole started to respond,

"She's my great-grandmother, actually, but...." Clearly no one was listening so she shut her mouth and looked away.

Strolling down the slope toward the creek, shaded by the wide branches, Irene Sinclair put out her plan to tech whiz kid and billionaire Zachary Turner.

"Isn't it beautiful here? I like to think of Joe Brennan walking this very path, or maybe riding his horse, planning how he'd save and then buy it. To protect it for us. So his descendants could experience a connection to the land, hold a piece of something that lasts, a legacy that is bigger than our day-to-day. That is some long-term thinking, Mr. Turner. I respect that," she smiled at him. "You said this place influenced you to come back here?" He nodded but figured he was there to listen unless instructed otherwise.

"Look, young man. My lawyer and I have a plan. In those papers is how you can pay for my house so my family gets the money, which is all some of them care about, and my tenants are protected. The house would be governed by a trust but you would own it. We've put in an application for the National Registry of Historic Places, which could provide some tax benefits down the road. My tenants are protected until the last one of their family members leaves, and then, only then, after no one is left, you get the house—and only since, it turns out, you are family."

"What? But, Mrs. Sinclair, that might not happen for years," Zach said. "It could be decades until I could really take ownership of the house."

"Yes, exactly. That could very well be. In fact, I hope so. But then, you will have done something right with your bravado and desire to acquire things with your millions."

Irene's eyes twinkled. She was quite proud of how she pictured the outcome of her maneuverings. He had so much money this was like an extra toy or something. She hadn't wanted to sell, but once her lawyer named the interested buyer, she'd Googled his status, read his Wikipedia profile and figured he'd be perfect to hire Nicole for his new company. Then she and her lawyer had conjured up a way to protect the house a bit longer using Zach's interest in buying. In her plan, she'd protect her house from random predatory buyers, her son would still benefit from the sale, she'd have enough money to hire a new "assistant," get to stay in her apartment, and Nicole could finally be an engineer. How perfect. But she had to move things along quickly. No time to waste at her age.

"See here," she continued. "I wasn't going to sell at all. I was just going to die in that place and let my son and grandson have to deal with it. Pay all the taxes. Ha! Would serve them right. But since you are really in our family tree, I reexamined and figured maybe your money could help me achieve my goal. I want my tiny part of the Mission to remain as is. I've been fighting off immorality and greed associated with progress my whole life— remember I was in WWII. Dying is a lousy excuse to lose a fight. Our ancestor Mr. Brennan taught me that."

Zach was speechless. What was it about this feisty, stooping nonagenarian who kept leaving him without a voice? He surveyed the dry brush, the grasses swaying, the fluttering leaves casting shadows, the felled branches across the water. Rounded stones littered the streambed. A pile of sticks and pebbles had collected in one spot creating a mini dam. He had to resist the urge to jump into the creek and clear the debris, setting all the pooling water to flowing freely. Why would I buy a house I can't use, possibly for years? Maybe the whole idea is frivolous anyway. Do I really need a big house to remodel? I've got a lot going on with the new company. What was I thinking? But I do need to invest and diversify too. Zach stared at the creek while debating silently.

"Mrs. Sinclair, with all due respect. This doesn't make any sense. Why would I buy a house I can't live in or control for years?" Irene poked a finger into his side.

"Consider it an investment. I'm quite sure you could afford another house to live in while you wait this out. Do the right thing, Mr. Turner. Don't be a cliché," and she punched his chest with a craggy finger.

"Long term, thinking, Mr. Turner. Long term thinking," she said. Startled, he stepped back, stumbling on the downward slope and rocky ground.

"And do consider hiring my granddaughter. I bet your water company could use her help. You can interview her right now," she said, pointing up at Nicole leaning against the parked car.

Irene didn't wait for a response. She turned and ambled slowly, carefully placing each foot, up the rise toward the gleaming Suburban. She reached the car, whispered to the driver who escorted her around to the other side and into the front seat. She stared out at the tree-dotted hills, the dryness starting already in the browning grasses. The broad oaks sending branches low and stretching outward over the dusty ground. A cool shade covered the clearing. And in the foreground were the hangers on. Each cradling a cell phone in one hand, shoulders curved forward, heads bent with intense focus on their screens. Thumbs jerking madly. The internationally recognizable cell phone hunch. Irene sighed. These fools were missing the scenery, the beauty of the place. They'd driven all that way just to zip through their newsfeeds, emails, apps, texts, photos, tweets, pins, and potential hookups yet again. It all changes, and yet it never does. Youth can miss the most basic of things.

Zach plopped on the ground next to the creek. Well, this didn't turn out exactly as I had planned, he mused. What am I? The preservation society? She wants me to do her favors? The girl wanted me to buy a place that wasn't for sale. Now granny's got some cockamamie idea to make her house a museum? What the hell? He groaned and threw some pebbles into the stream. He liked being in control. Nothing was going his way here and these two women each wanted to manipulate him. He shook his head angrily and continued to throw rocks into the water. How had he gotten himself involved with this dysfunctional family? Nicole stepped carefully down the slope in her city shoes and sat next to him.

"Well, will she sell you the house? Did you get what you want?" she asked him with a smile. "Cousin," she said laughing. Zach frowned. He didn't see anything funny in any of this. He was furious.

"Nicole? Right? Why'd you do it? Why'd you sell out your great-grandmother? Why'd you call and tell my real estate agent it was for sale when it really wasn't?" His face was flushed. His throws got stronger and longer. The splashes bigger. One of the stones hit a boulder in the creek and there was a loud crack. Nicole startled at the sound. She looked down, embarrassed. She was mortified at getting caught. She had grown to adore her great-grandmother and now regretted that call. But he'd probably never believe that.

"She won't really sell," he continued. "She just wants my money to keep the renters until each one leaves of their own accord. And protect some historic designation or whatever. What kind of a house purchase is that? It could take years before I could get control of it." He was angry but took off his shoes, looked over at her and growled. "Wanna go creek wading?"

She nodded, removed her shoes, rolled up her pant legs and followed him up the stream. Neither spoke for some time. After pushing aside big branches and splashing through the rocky creek, finally Nicole felt she had to confess. She had to get him to keep quiet. She feared Great Gram learning what she'd done.

"Okay, I get it that you're mad. My dad and grandpa hired me to take care of her but I had to get her to sell or move into an old people's home. I didn't like my job options. Great Gram is ninety-one. I figured my dad and grandpa knew what was best for her. But now, I've lived with her for months and see she's fine. Amazing, actually. She loves it there and has friends and routines. It'd be cruel to move her out. If someone helps with cooking, cleaning and taking her to appointments, she can stay forever. But when I first got there I was trying to get a quick sale so I researched all the young company founders with big buyouts. Everyone wants to live in the city now. While I was researching I found your family history and the Brennan Trust connection." He turned to look at her, brow scrunched with questioning, his scowl only slightly diminished.

"*The Daily Cal* interviewed you way back as an out-of-state undergrad and you described the land. It came up in my search-es. I figured it'd be a win-win all the way around. Didn't quite work out that way. And now, I can't let her go to an old people's home. But I gotta get a real job and she needs the money to pay someone to replace me. Please don't tell her what I did, okay?"

"Hmmmm," Zach nodded. He appreciated her honesty but was appalled at her naiveté and her manipulations. He changed the subject so he could think.

"Let's keep walking up the creek a bit. Those guys will be fine awhile longer. Look at that big rock up at the bend. It's so pretty here. I haven't been here since I was a kid. I never did come down when I was at school. And starting the company...it's been busy. I've been pretty mono-focused..."

He drifted off and left the rest unsaid. Maybe he could get away for a weekend and come camping here with some of his friends. It was so tranquil, so removed from the noise of a Sili-con Valley boom, the ubiquity of the frenzy. His mind wandered, and then focused, as he moved into the Zen of creek wading, stepping over submerged logs, pushing aside branches and tossing damn creator stones onto sandy peninsulas and muddy tributaries. Zach moved to the stick rock blockage and cleared it. Mud and leaves sailed downstream. Then a gush of clear water returned between the banks. He watched the stream flow freely again with great satisfaction. He had to let it go with Nicole. Everyone was out for his or her own best interests in true Silicon

Valley style. He probably would have done the same thing if he'd been in her position.

"What is it that you want to do, Nicole? Why'd you agree to take care of Mrs. Sinclair instead of getting a job? Are you the clichéd lost soul trying to find yourself?" Zach couldn't resist a little cutting remark. After all, she had betrayed her great grandmother and used him. She explained that she hadn't liked any of the companies when applying. She liked solving real problems for real people. He listened. He wandered farther up the creek and sat on a big boulder protruding from the bank, water swirling around the disrupted path. He tucked his feet under his knees on the rock and stared at the mini rapid it formed. She thought he was ignoring her but then she could see he was thinking. Sunlight peered through the thick cover of trees overhead, dotting the creek with light and shadows.

"What is it that your new company really does? I saw online something about working with government entities?" she asked before he could give her a judgmental response to her self-absorption or betrayal of an old lady, a family member no less.

"Water," he said. "This is what we do," splashing his feet around the rock. "We're just getting started but we map ground water, the aquifer, wells, runoff, reservoir capacities. We've developed water-mapping technology and systems we're convinced can help the farmers and the water governance bodies in this drought. We already have a water agency customer. And we're working with some Central Valley farmers too."

"That's real," she said, with wide-eyed appreciation. He saw that she finally was impressed. Her forehead furrows lightened and a smile started on her lips. He had noticed since the first moment at the tea that she always appeared to be judging him. She had a cynical view of Silicon Valley success. He found it refreshing and infuriating at the same time. After all, that's how he'd achieved his status—building something unique and selling it for enormous sums. But she had not appeared dazzled one bit.

Now her face softened, her smile widened with sincerity and the endearing dimple re-emerged.

"Mapping water, hmmmmm," she said and got very quiet. She tucked her knees up under her on a rock and stared down into the creek. "I think we should go back," she said, after neither of them had said anything for a long stretch. She began wading. He followed. They traipsed and stumbled, forging up and down through the stream. Zach looked at the water, at the surrounding scenery, at the parched beauty, at the girl. They walked in silence. The oak trees and playful brook, hilly banks, rounded rock outcroppings and drying chaparral spied on them as yet another set of explorers ambled past.

"You can apply for a job at our company if you want. You'll have to go through the application process. But we do always need engineers. You never know," he said. She looked at him in surprise, then waited for something more, a willingness to help move her resume along, or something. He was silent. She realized he wasn't going to offer anything else. They finally reached the clearing where the cars were parked and stepped gingerly up the bank in bare feet, mud sticking to their soles.

"And I'm not going to buy your great grandmother's house," he said. "I am not the historical society. She's got too many conditions. I'll find somewhere else." Zach motioned to the realtors and lawyers waiting that it was time to go. He opened the Suburban door and they climbed into the car. Irene noticed the tension between them but chose to ignore it.

"Well, Mr. Turner, did you enjoy the creek?" Irene asked, a serious expression on her face but a gentle tone in her voice. "Remind you of your childhood? Did you sense Joe Brennan's ghost out there? I hope he lectured you that nothing lasts like land, and family, Mr. Turner. And we are family now, aren't we?" She lightly touched the driver's shoulder indicating it was time to leave. They drove off in silence, uncomfortable and unbreakable. After many miles, Zach asked,

"Mrs. Sinclair, how do you get permission from that board to go there? I'd like to take a few friends and camp and do some hiking one weekend."

"I am still on that board, Mr. Turner. So you better do what I want or I'll use my influence to vote to keep you out." He turned sharply to look at her with questioning eyes and found her laughing.

"I'm just kidding. Can't an old lady have a little fun too? It would be great if you came back for a weekend," she said, chuckling. "I'll send you the details." He nodded, still surprised at her initial response. The awkward silence returned.

"What's your new company work on?" she asked in a conciliatory manner, slyly leading him to the subject she wanted discussed.

"Water," he said. "We use technology to improve mapping of water sources and coordination between water agencies. We're in the early stages, but we already have a water district and some farmers using our software. We think we can improve water protection and allocation in this drought." It was an elevator pitch he'd used many times.

"Really? Water? Hmmmm, interesting. Well now, that is something of use right here on Earth. There just might be some hope for you yet, Mr. Turner. There just might be some hope."

Nicole pursed her lips and exhaled through her nose quietly to suppress a rising giggle. She turned to look out the window to hide her smile. Irene tilted her head back on the headrest and closed her eyes. Zach stared straight ahead. They settled in for the long drive up the Peninsula back to the Mission.

"He won't buy under my conditions, Nicole," Irene told her a week later after getting off the phone with her lawyer. She brushed sandwich crumbs off her blouse onto her napkin. Seemed to get harder every day to eat neatly. She shook her head with annoyance.

"So I figured out a new plan, with Christine's help. Sit down, I have something I want to discuss with you." Nicole put down the sandwich plate and sat across from Irene at the window table. She almost never sat there. Irene liked to eat more formally with Nicole serving and cleaning efficiently, like an old-fashioned housemaid.

"Great Gram, I'm sorry the sale didn't work out with Zach Turner," she said.

"Yeah, well, I guess I just tried to get way too much out of the deal. I was hoping he looked at his money more casually than most people! Ha! Foolish of me. But maybe he'll go out to the Trust land and go hiking. That would be good for him." She smiled, remembering him wading up the creek.

"Nicole, you've got to get a job quick. Because if you do, I have a proposal. As soon as you get an engineering position, I'm going to change my will and leave this house to you. Not your dad, my son or anyone else in the family. It will be in a trust and you will be the trustee with full control over the property. But you have to promise me you'll let my tenants stay until they leave on their own. That's the condition. You'll get this apartment." She brushed the final crumbs off her lapel, folded the napkin, set it on the tablecloth and stared across at Nicole, the expanse of San Francisco clear through the window at her side.

"Well, what do you think? But you have to get a job because the rents barely even cover basic expenses. The place needs to be fixed up, retrofitted for earthquake safety and maintained properly. Mr. Turner helped me realize that was important. But it costs more than I take in. So start applying because I'm ninety-one and you never know about time when you're my age. I actually did start the paperwork. But you have to be employed for this to work."

Nicole almost fell off the chair, which she had perched on lightly, anticipating a quick command from Great Gram, not a major announcement. Her cheeks turned pink as blood rushed up, her stomach clenched. She was overwhelmed by the generosity of the offer, but at the same moment, filled with the shame of her betrayal. And a little what-will-Dad-and-Grandpa think flitted through her mind.

"Great Gram, what?" she flustered. "Give me the house?" she asked in a whisper.

"I know you are a little young to inherit such a big house but your dad and grandpa don't need anything. And I don't really trust them to do what I want. I've come to trust you. I think you'll respect my wishes when I'm gone. And that means a lot to old people. I'll control as much as I possibly can from my grave, damn sure," she said. Eyes glistening, she smiled and patted Nicole's hand.

"What do you think? Do you want it? Can you start looking for a real job?"

"Yes, Great Gram. I already started after we went to the property. I applied to Zach's company but I don't know if I would want to work for that guy. But I also found others working on water, his competitors and some in related fields. I'll keep researching. But he won't help me get a job, you know. He basically told me that."

Irene shook her head. The arrogance of some of these uber successful kids. Why wouldn't he give Nicole a little pull up? I guess I really offended him with my controlling house sale plan, she thought. Oh well, Nicole should be fine in this job market. Nicole interrupted Irene's thoughts with urgency in her voice and a squeeze of her hand.

"Great Gram, I have to tell you something. I'm really ashamed now and I am so, so sorry. But I'm the one who called Zach Turner's real estate agent. The truth is, I promised Dad and Grandpa I would try to get you to sell or move out during this year. I didn't know you very well when I first moved in. But now I do and I can't imagine you anywhere else. I am so sorry I did that behind your back. I feel terrible about it. Don't change your will for me." She leaned back in the chair and looked at her great grandmother with sadness. She figured their relationship would fracture right there. She really regretted she'd run headstrong along with someone else's plans and not waited to get to know Great Gram before acting.

"Don't be silly, Nicole. I'm not changing my will for you. I'm changing it for me. I had a feeling that might have been what happened. I was just waiting for you to be honest with me. Thank you for telling me now. When it really does matter. But you know what, I think you know you made a mistake. And I trust you, even more now, to do the right thing with my house. A little guilt can be quite motivating! And I just knew I didn't trust my son and your dad. How devious of them. Work on getting yourself a job and let's see if we can finally get this sorted out right. If you get a job in the city, then you can move into the apartment with me now and keep helping me out. That would be cheaper for everyone. What do you think?"

Speechless and trying not to be tearful, Nicole got up and kneeled down next to Irene's chair to hug her tiny great-grandmother. Fragile but wiry tough, Irene hugged her right back. But then no nonsense,

"Now go make us some tea. I could really use a cup right now." And as Nicole stood up, brushed back a tear and swung through the kitchen door, Irene called out in a scraggily voice,

"Oh, and Nicole, by the way. I have a confession too. I mostly invited that Zachary Turner guy out to the Brennan Trust land because I found out he had a water mapping company. I figured you would think that was valuable work and maybe he could get you a job. One that you would be willing to take." She laughed, resettled in her chair and smoothed her skirt. Confessions all the way around this afternoon it seemed. She took another bite of the ham and cheese sandwich, chewing carefully so as not to dribble crumbs, and looked out her window, admiring the view below of her neighborhood and her city. Beautiful.

⚘

Acknowledgments

I have always thought it odd that the Acknowledgments in most books start with the sort of lesser contributors and end up, at the very last breath, recognizing those who are closest to the author. I want to start out thanking those who helped me the most—umpteen times—patiently asking questions, explaining serious concerns, suggesting alternatives, well beyond their family duty.

My husband, David Payne, and my children, Sarah Payne and Dwight Payne, each spent hours reading and re-reading story versions, typing up questions or sitting with me in "intervention" style face-to-face meetings giving me feedback, and sometimes hard to hear, tough love. I am so thankful and indebted for their commitment to my project and to understanding my change of career and focus. And most of all, for encouraging me when all the self-doubts a first-time fiction writer faces, multiple times a day, became overwhelming. Their patience and never-ending belief in me, and my goals, has been some of the best love I've ever received. I will be forever grateful.

I want to thank the few other early readers who gave honest feedback and heartfelt suggestions. My dear friend, Carolyn Prowse Fainmel, read many stories early on and gave me detailed notes. I am so thankful for her touching support. A gifted, accomplished glass artist, Carolyn has inspired me as I make this life change to become a fiction writer. I loved our "Studio/Study Hall Time" where we worked together, each on our own projects, in her studio or at my dining room table. Once I finally figured out that she needed to do her art alone, I realized how great a gift it was that she granted me the shared Studio Time weekly, for almost a year. Plus, Carolyn fell in love with Sal, the principal, and kept asking me what happened to him. How can you not adore a friend who falls for your characters? And it was such a good question. I finally figured out an answer but might not have if she hadn't kept asking. I am forever indebted, dear friend.

Thanks to my other very early readers, all long-time friends, who put up with raw manuscripts and uncooked stories—Barb Takahashi, Tracie White and Jane Grossman each read the first story. Eric Roos, bless his heart, read a whole pile of an incomplete mess of stories. Just that they read way back in the process, said it needed some work but told me to keep going, was so helpful. They are each true friends and I hope to return the favor some day.

I want to thank my excellent professional editors who were both so good at being encouraging, while also giving pointed, detailed, practical advice. Rachel Howard was an insightful and thorough content editor. She gave me craft articles to read and instructive homework assignments even before she read my manuscript. And then, her feedback was spot on. Her deepening questions, detailed guidance and sensitive insight forced me out of my comfort zone to explore my true intent. She gave me her honest opinion and pushed me to move past the conventional or mundane, all while being encouraging. I loved that—just what you want in an editor! She is a gifted writing teacher and editor and I feel so fortunate she took on my project.

Larry Habegger did a great job as copy editor on this book. Extremely detail oriented, Larry is a highly experienced editor and small press publisher. His edits and suggestions were professional and insightful. He also gave me useful advice on publishing issues. He was timely, thoughtful and always very encouraging. I really enjoyed working with Larry and know he'll be honest but supportive whenever I need his professional guidance.

I'd like to recognize two San Francisco organizations that really kicked me into fiction writing mode when I was tentatively making the move into the writing world. In November, 2013, each week I attended the Shut Up and Write Meet Up at Borderlands Books in The Mission neighborhood of San Francisco, California. This was a huge breakthrough for me as I finally delved in to my fictional characters and put my energy into developing them. I loved the productivity I experienced in three hours of communal work time. I commend the Meet Up community, particularly the Shut Up and Write folks, as excellent practitioners of the shared work/everything shared economy and workspaces.

In the same time frame, I attended a Connie Hale workshop at the San Francisco Writer's Grotto on writing methods illustrated in her book *Sin and Syntax*. The workshop, and her book, were crucial in motivating me to keep going. Connie is a true inspiration because not only is she a great writer and advocate for writers, but she also is a superb teacher. As a career educator, and always a teacher at heart, I value good instruction and appreciate the effort it takes to not just know something about writing, but to be able to communicate that knowledge in an enticing and entertaining manner. Connie also graciously recommended both Rachel Howard and Larry Habegger to me. I couldn't be more appreciative. She was completely right and her editing group, The Prose Doctors (of which Larry is a member), is worth checking out.

Jess van der Westhuizen is a gifted artist and graphic designer starting out her career. I am so fortunate to have been friends with her parents for years and to have seen her gorgeous large paintings in their home. I always knew I wanted to present my stories with elegant illustrations to activate reading minds. When I contacted Jess with my vision she was gracious, enthusiastic and open. She cared about each detail and she met her deadlines! I can't imagine a better collaborator. And then her patience, guidance and detail-oriented approach to putting the book into a workable e-book and print format have been invaluable, as has her work on the cover. I am so grateful to have her on my team. Jess is a talent I am sure others will find a treasure to work with as well.

Finally, thanks to all my friends and family members who

have asked about this project and shown interest in its progress. I know that is a tough thing to do when it is buried in my computer, invisible. A visual artist might have a half-completed painting on an easel. A sculptor might have a body springing from the stone, still partially encased in it but clearly on its way out, for the average observer to see. But a writer has little to show in terms of "progress" to her friends, family or colleagues. It takes a great deal of faith to demonstrate engaging support and encouragement to a writer. I am so very grateful to all of you who have done that for me over the past few years. Your belief that there was indeed something real behind my dream is a gift. You all inspire me every day and that inspiration is partly where these stories come from. I hope you will find them worth the wait.

About the Author

After a full career in education and business, Mary Smathers shifted her focus to creativity, particularly writing and photography. In her new vocation, Mary reports for *La Voz de Guanacaste*, a bilingual, regional Costa Rican newspaper, and produces travel blogs and personalized cookbooks filled with her commentary and photographs. *Fertile Soil: Stories of the California Dream* is her first work of fiction.

Smathers's interest in both the resilience of working people tackling adversity, and the historic roots and wide-reaching consequences of Silicon Valley's innovative spirit, spring directly from living and working in California her entire life. She grew up in Silicon Valley during its infancy, before it received that ubiquitous moniker. Throughout her career she served as a high school teacher, administrator and educational entrepreneur, helping to found three education companies and a public charter school. She was repeatedly inspired by the complexity, diversity and endless work ethic of Californians as she crossed the state, working with tens of thousands of students and families throughout the East Bay and Central Coast to Central Valley towns, from inner city Los Angeles, Oakland and Sacramento to the Imperial Valley border region. Smathers is now based in Costa Rica where she lives with her husband and two big dogs. She is at work on a novel and more stories.

CPSIA information can be obtained
at www.ICGtesting.com
Printed in the USA
FSOW01n0600070317
31512FS